THE BLOOD OF THREE WORLDS

John Knapp II

THE BLOOD OF THREE WORLDS

EPHEMERON PRESS

FOR 328 DAYS ALL REGULAR
ELECTRICAL POWER HAS DISAPPEARED

ALL ELECTRONIC EQUIPMENT
HAS BEEN DESTROYED

PEOPLE WERE NOT
DIRECTLY HARMED, BUT

IN THE NEW SUSQUEHANNA TERRITORY
3 OF THE 5 PERSONS BELOW

Rev. Dr. Jonas Harwell
Marvin Cample (teacher)
Michael Hammond (18)
Triana Simms (16)
"Marcus" (young space pilot)

ARE ABOUT TO
QUICKLY DISAPPEAR FOREVER

FROM THE RECORD THAT FOLLOWS

5:30 AM, Sunday, Day 328 AEMP

A thin man…pushed the old side-by-side double-barreled 12-gauge into place…Only five inches of metal protruded inside…Gently he eased the short window (just under the stained glass one) down…and with a jeweler's caution a special shell was slid into each barrel. The stock was raised and snapped back into place.

The minister would be first…the witch girl would be next.

Noiselessly, the man…disappeared into the darkness.

"Michael, son…you know I speak to you as your second father," said Rev. Harwell, "and…"

"I know that, sir," Michael interrupted.

….

"Triana Simms…Triana Simms. Is there anything I…I need to know about the two of you?"

"No sir…"

"What about her off-handedly mentioning the other night that you 'loved her'? I've no memory of her dating anyone."

Triana had said in so many words…that she might be leaving forever…How honest and naïve could someone who believed in God the way he and Jonas did possibly be? And with her eyesight, how could she go anywhere alone on any kind of mission to anywhere new… and far, far, far away? He pushed out of his mind the brilliant "space pilot" who he'd never met.

As silly as it sounded, Michael knew that as long as he lived he could never let anything happen to her. And she couldn't stop him from following her.

5

Reactions to the *prequel* of this story…

"[EARTH IS NOT ALONE] *raises intriguing questions and makes… plausible conjectures about Christianity in other worlds.*

— *Jack Maynard*
Avionics engineer

"*Reminiscent of Lewis, Tolkien, and L'Engle, EINA… swept me away —laughing at the cleverness of the heroes and crying at their joys and defeats…*"

— *Stephanie Whiticare*
Project & Family Ministries writer

"*As a Fortune 500 software engineer who grew up in what becomes… the 'Susquehanna Territory'… [EINA] is a riveting read that will keep you guessing with each twist…*"

— *Eric Wood*
(whose old home is near "Big Bend")

"*Love, romance, tragedy, and responsibility after… Earth's modern technology collapses. This tale has enough mystery to inspire readers — young and old — to discuss 'theories of truth and being'… Be prepared to travel to other worlds.*"

— *Gladys Hunt*
(critic of literature for Christian young adults)

"*The best book I ever read!*"

— *Eleanor Knapp Coates*
(declared at age 100. Thanks again, Mom)

6

Response to reading ms of *The Blood of Three Worlds...*

"As an ex-scientist, I enjoyed it as science fiction (devastation by EMP, interplanetary travel of a trans-dimensional sort). As a retired theologian, I thought it gave an interesting treatment of the gospel and extra-terrestrials. It also has a gripping plot... It contains valuable thoughts on coming of age, what life is all about, and how the truth of Christianity impacts this. An excellent read!"
— Robert C. Newman, PhD, MDiv, STM
(astrophysicist/theologian, seminary prof. of New Testament, founder of the Interdisciplinary Biblical Research Institute — IBRI.org)

"Jaw-dropping from beginning to end. TBOTW reminds me that things are rarely what they seem and that love can be the most surprising action we can choose... Will keep the reader engaged from beginning to end."
— Stephanie Whitacre
(Project & Family Ministries writer)

"If we weren't good neighbors, I probably wouldn't have given your [long] manuscript a second look. It takes me ten days to finish [such a] book. But John, I read TBOTW in four days... I couldn't put it down. At a couple of parts I had to stop and fight back tears... can't remember any other book that's had such an effect on me."
— Charlie Ellis
(A reviewer across the street who I rely on for real answers)

[Thanks, also to Amy Wood, Dr. Charles Thomas, my wife Karen, and sons Eli and Andrew for their private comments, critiquing, and proofing.]

ISBN 978-0-912290-36-2 (paper book)
ISBN 978-0-912290-37-9 (ebook)

Version 20190510

Address: Ephemeron Press, 1510 Perdido Ct., Viera, FL 32940 [ephemeronpress.com, or amazon.com, or see adozenseconds.com sidebar.]

✹

This story is a work of fiction. While it assumes certain scientific concepts and the acceptance of conservative Biblical interpretation, the author in no way insists that correct Biblical or scientific understanding must follow his reasoning that reaches beyond known science and looks into the future; instead he holds only that Scripture might allow, and be concordant with, the logical interpretation given in the story if the events described actually happened. It in no way "replaces" commonly accepted Biblical end-time scenarios. Names, characters, places, and incidents are products of the author's imagination though some Earth events are based upon modifying some actual named locations in NE PA (in the new "Susquehanna Territory"), where the author lives part-time. Other than that, any resemblance to actual events, locales, organizations, or persons living or dead, is entirely coincidental and beyond the intent of either the author or publisher.

✹

✹

The few Scriptures cited, or alluded to, are from the New International Version ©1973 by International Bible Society.

✹

I have many to thank for input and encouragement: Dr. Larry Proffitt, Tennessee pharmacist and passionate turkey hunter, for feedback on firearms; Jack Maynard for his input on electronics and EMP; Master Frank Shermerhorn for instruction in Soo Bahk Do karate in which I'm a 2nd degree black belt; Master Mark Shuey for instruction in cane defense (any misguided application of excellent training is my own fault); my wife and children for now and then advice and encouragement; and former student Dr. Dominic Catalano on whose MFA art committee I sat on as an English professor, and who has written and illustrated several picturebooks and illustrated dozens of others.

✹

Still others are mentioned on the dedication page. (Dr. Shechtman's picture, by the way, hangs on the wall of my Pennsylvania office.)

✹

Cover art, illustrations, and layout design are by Dominic Catalano.

Rarely to a piece of detailed futuristic fiction, or any modern fiction these days, does an established artist invade the inside pages to ply his trade. Ephemeron Press once again is very pleased to have Dominic Catalano (*The Bear Who Loved Puccini*, *A Tree for Christmas* among his books), teaching now in Uganda, select scenes and draw for this volume. His cover and 15 inside sketches for not one, but two, planets—the unfamiliar one only selectively detailed in print—is a monumental task.

His art can make a story come alive.

If you start paging through to see what's here, don't miss his rendering of teenaged Michael's thoughts expressed as "four white boxcars" (p. 81) and as a "disingenuous Darwin's head" (p. 114) as he works his way through Esther Crandel's "clock catechism."

To: Dr. Dan Shechtman
Israeli Chemist

Shechtman: "I was thrown out of my research group. They said I brought shame on them...I never took it personally. I knew I was right and they were wrong."

Said Dr. Linus Pauling: "There is no such thing as quasicrystals, only 'quasiscientists.'"

Winner of the Nobel Prize
In Chemistry, 2011

"for discovering quasicrystals"

To: Dr. Robert C. Newman
American astrophysicist and former seminary professor
of New Testament

Without your continual encouragement through the years, this book would never been written.

To: Ethan Knapp
Israeli businessman and teacher

Your careful, patient, skilled editing, and comments helped me more than you'll ever know.
Thank you, son.

"... take nothing ... except a ... staff ...
[and] wear sandals."
Mark 6:7-9 (NASB)

God, may we properly accept and
use the holy passions you
have put in our hearts.

The Blood of Three Worlds
– A Beginning Note –

In the past several years, astronomy has discovered – one-by-one – hundreds of planets that exist beyond our solar system. A tiny fraction of these may have "Goldilocks conditions" just right for life as we know it.

Now to go beyond (known) science.

"Emryss" and "Elphia" are two alleged, faraway exoplanets. That's where **The Blood of Three Worlds comes in.**

We have in our possession four narratives about Planet Emryss (and that planet only). Chronologically, they are

The Fourth Prince*
Inside the Hollow Spear**
Death in a Tavern
The Secret of Zareba

These four, which in many ways seem like classic folklore, with minor links between them, are complete stories in themselves.

DIAT and TSOZ (above) appeared in their entirety in the first "Emryss Chronicle" **Earth Is Not Alone** and are integral to that story which is only a prequel to this one. TFP* and ITHS**, exist on paper and were promised to be included in this second, final, and primary Emryss Chronicle, but alas, that will not happen. One reason is that their surprising content dealing with entirely separate problems in those stories would have overwhelmed this volume and would have required 600 more pages than what's here, detracting from the main story's dramatic conclusion involving people from Earth.

So?

12

*As one might use an old encyclopedia, we have clipped away nearly all of TFP and ITHS for this story and have included only small pieces from those promised stories that were needed to justify a "one-way, forever trip" to a third planet Elphia. This in no way spoils those two missing stories if you encounter them later. The parts selected from TFP and ITHS that now appear here in Parts II and IV of **The Blood of Three Worlds** are included for two reasons: (1) to show the space travelers the alleged genealogical connections between three planets and (2) to describe how the God of the Whole Universe — and the Bible — might be involved there.*

Just as one can profitably read The Odyssey before reading The Iliad — a linked story that deals with previous events — you can read TBOTW (this book) before EINA.

As to what lies ahead:

As America and the rest of Earth fall apart after EMP explosions destroy all commercial electrical power everywhere, two orphaned (and unmarried) precocious Christian teens, with a gifted unmarried pilot 10 years older, must decide whether to risk everything on an untested maiden and final, one-way flight into space from the mountains of Northeast Pennsylvania. The destination: an atheistic exoplanet inhabited by humans that seems to be asking for help. The vehicle: a supersecret "tiny" spaceship that insiders laughingly call the "Space Goose" that has never previously risen an inch from where it is hidden, pointing towards the sky.

In their supplies, if the three leave, are four Bibles — all in English.

Following this story are three somewhat detailed appendices dealing with EMP, the Sabbath, premises, science concepts, "memory clocks," passions, and narrative style which are in no way "required" reading.

Except for a few of you.

Hence, we couldn't leave them out.

The Blood of Three Worlds

Commercial electricity has suddenly disappeared...

Introduction:
The Epistle To Big Bend
[excerpts from…]

The following document, typed on an old manual, nonelectric typewriter and crudely printed on a hastily restored hand-cranked mimeograph machine — both at least 60 years old — was handed out at the Grace Missionary Alliance Church of Big Bend, Pennsylvania, on a Sunday in May on Day 12, AEMP 01.

Dr. Harwell, the pastor, while claiming no special divine authority, puts several pages of what he thinks has happened in the form of a NT epistle. In addition to his seminary training, Harwell has a PhD in astrophysics.

*   *   *   *   *   *   *   *   *   *   *   *   *   *

The Rev. Dr. Jonas Harwell, pastor by the will of God at the Grace Missionary Alliance Church at Big Bend, to all Christians and Other Fellow Citizens and Refugees on the newly formed Susquehanna Territory:
It is now the 12th day since our global catastrophe.
I say "global" deliberately, though I cannot prove it.
After days of continually scanning shortwave bands on our 1930 vacuum-tube Philco radio…in the narthex of our church, we have picked up only two signals in addition to intermittent broadcasting…of Radio USA from

Maryland.

On Day 4 we heard...[a] garbled broadcast from Radio Jerusalem. On Days 4, 5, and 7 we heard news of horror and tragedy from one of the most powerful stations in the world, HCJB in Ecuador...

....

We, and much—if not all—of the world, have been drained of our invisible life blood, regularly transmitted electricity, for 12 days, and I am convinced any transfusion to restore life as we knew it is very far off. ....The culprit, I believe, is EMP or electromagnetic pulse...

....

There is much we do not know. There is much for us to discover. Much to rediscover.

....

As Christians we have a blessed hope...But upon Earth we may be called to suffer....Be as wise as a serpent with your time and talents, but always be generous and kind, reflecting God's love.

....circulate this letter...to believers and all others living within the Susquehanna Territory.

[The complete local "letter" appears in Appendix A.]

He pushed the old side-by-side double-barreled 12 gauge into place.

CHAPTER I

The Witch And The Gun

[At various points in the story certain places, dates, times and even commentary will be included and repeated for clarity as events whipsaw back and forth.]

> Place: Left outside auditorium wall of Grace Missionary
>   Alliance Church, Big Bend, PA,
>   Susquehanna Territory, USA, Earth

> Time: Day 328. 5:30 AM, Sunday, AEMP 01,
>   328 days after EMP has destroyed nearly every
>   thing electronic
>   (A Spring in the first half of the 21st century)

SKRRAAAAK.

The crowbar eased up one inch the small movable clear-glass window immediately below the much larger stained glass one.

A thin middle-aged man, with thick unruly hair that went poorly with his neater dark tie and white shirt that very few still wore on Sunday, pushed the old side-by-side double-barreled 12-gauge into place. The weapon had been cut several inches shorter than it once was. Only five inches of metal protruded inside, hardly enough to be visible since only a single light hanging high over the auditorium would be on, powered by a small generator in the church basement. Gently, he eased the short window down pinching the twin barrels in place. He carefully put in place a small piece of wood on the windowsill outside so the barrel inside would tilt slightly downward.

Just inside the ragged arbor vitae, the man took aim and smiled. Carefully, he broke down the gunstock. Yes, the gun could easily and silently be opened to reload from the outside. With a jeweler's caution, a special shell was gently slid into each barrel. The stock was raised and snapped back into place.

The witch girl should be sitting only a dozen feet away in a pew near the front on the left. Above her and behind a lectern would stand the man in black. The minister would be first, then with attention at the front, the witch girl would be next.

Noiselessly the man in the tie disappeared into the darkness back to the stone-slab sidewalk just beyond the old hitching post.

CHAPTER 2

"The King In The Iron Cage"

Place: Rev. Dr. Jonas Harwell's office in the church parsonage

Time: **8½ hours earlier on DAY 327**, *Saturday, 9 PM,
and 8 days after a 10-hour, now resolved, parent/
student/teacher confrontation on Days 318-19*

Persons: for both Parts I and III

Marvin Cample *– atheistic English teacher and accuser, now
satisfied.*

Michael Hammond *– a senior student (almost 18)
Honor student/athlete and local orphan whose parents
were killed in the same auto crash that killed Rev. Jonas
Harwell's wife. Though living with his dying great-aunt
and being legally adopted by Harwell, Michael has a
new growing attraction to…*

Triana Simms *– a senior (though only 16), designated
valedictorian of BBHS. Triana was a sudden
mysterious arrival to Big Bend two years earlier, and
now is legally a foster child of, though not adopted by,
Rev. Harwell. With long dark blond hair, partially
masking a serious visual handicap, she is fiercely
private, independent, and rumored to be a rare
polyglot or language savant. A week earlier, after
successfully defending a highly unusual charge of*

23

cheating alongside Michael, and in the process
trusting him with sensitive information about herself,
he appears to have become "very cautiously attractive"
to her. Still, even though both are connected
with Harwell and go to the same church, the two
high-schoolers have rarely even spoken to each other.
It is she who lives at the parsonage under the
watchcare of 60-year-old Sally Ferguson, a live-in
caretaker, cook, and nurse who Triana has assisted in
giving nursing care to an unusual older man on the
second floor who died only days earlier.

Rev. Jonas Harwell - *solid, balding, and fit, mid-fifties, pastor*
of Grace Alliance. He has a PhD in astrophysics from
Cornell (which will be explained) and is seminary
trained. Further, Harwell has some connection with
the old fenced-off, unused, city watertower uphill
behind the church and parsonage in a grassy field at
the edge of Big Bend.

*   *   *   *   *   *   *   *   **

Michael, from whose viewpoint we encounter the entire story (except for Chapter 1), learned about the exchange below the day after it occurred.

●●**T**hanks for seeing me so late, Jonas." Marvin Cample slipped into the familiar leather chair that he sat in just eight days earlier. The thin teacher, in his 30's, again wearing a plaid shirt, ran his hand over his slicked-back black hair. "I...I'm coming 'around.' I apologize for the..."

"Nothing to say you're sorry for," Harwell interrupted. "In fact, if it weren't for the seriousness of the horror going on all around us,

24

I'd say it was the most fascinating—and intriguing—conversation I've ever had."

"And it included two kids and went for ten hours," Cample added.

"With a break or two here and there," said Harwell.

"And a memorable dinner here," said the teacher, "with clever drama acted out by your 'children.'"

"And your students, Marvin. Tell me, do they spend time together at school? I'm a little surprised at their sudden new connection. Am I missing something I should know about?"

"Jonas, before our confrontation a week ago I've never personally seen them speak as much as a word to each other."

"What?"

"And yet I, alongside you, have never seen two respect each other so completely and care so deeply—together as a couple—of any age, that I've ever met. I certainly wasn't expecting that. For me, that opened the door to consider what the three of you care about so deeply. Haven't you seen that at home?"

"No, Marvin, I haven't. But to be honest, I'm not surprised. You see, Michael lives with his great aunt, who he looks after—three blocks away—not here. And until the recent fight on the outdoor basketball court, he's been wrapped up with school, taking care of his aunt, and playing sports and basketball. Triana's always busy in school or here helping Sally with things, as well as helping care for our long-time boarder upstairs, a brilliant man from far away, who died just a few days ago."

"Triana's 'Igneal' from very far away? I know we've mentioned that possibility earlier, but are you really convinced of that?"

"I think so. I believe her, Marvin, but I know very few beyond the parsonage who would. And Triana's a gifted polyglot or as some say a language savant. She seems to have perfect pitch with words and how they go together, wherever they come from. And Igneal speaks, not only English, but an unknown tongue no one else seems to understand."

"And this lovely young woman's poor vision?" asked Cample.

"I'm not sure where that comes from, Marvin. Perhaps it's psychosomatic. Or something that resulted from a 'crash landing.' We just don't know. But she hardly lets her eyes get in the way of anything. And she can read very fast when she's close to print. It's almost like she has extrasensory ways of knowing—remember a week ago when Michael brought that up?—but I'm a doubter about things like that."

Harwell moved from behind his desk to the wingtip chair on the other side of where Triana had sat next to Michael a week earlier during their inquisition. He descended into it, now only a yard away from the English teacher. Now both men could see over the desk, on which lay a Bible and a dim oil lamp, to the tall narrow window behind it. By uncanny coincidence, the window just then almost exactly framed the giant vertical "black candle" water tower more than a hundred feet uphill. The full moon was directly behind the "candle" lighting its wick, in fact the whole top, with a silver-green halo of fire. In seconds, the effect would be lost.

" 'Around'…Marvin, you said you were 'coming around,' " Harwell mumbled aloud. He turned to face the teacher. "As you move around, I hope you keep going at 180 degrees, and not end up back where you started."

Cample smiled wryly. "To think my new mountain preacher is at home with math and science!"

Harwell stared absently down at the floor.

"Giving me a complete pass on science is premature, Marvin! As you may or may not know, it is commonly accepted that if any other Earth-like planets exist in other solar systems, they're so far away that we could never reach them.

"However, in our region of the universe, here on Earth, within the

26

walls of the Susquehanna Territory no less, there's said to be a device that's able to temporarily unlock curled extra dimensions that, some have said, stopped growing immediately after the Big Bang, and are in some way related to quantum theory. That's, of course, absurd. This 'curlcomb,' or 'Space Goose' as I've heard it jokingly called, is said to be able to travel at impossible speeds, erasing friction — also impossible — and aim itself outward with microgyroscopic precision and pinpoint accuracy."

"Do you understand this?" asked Cample.

"No I do not. Now I must share some special information that cannot leave this room. Can you agree to that."

"I can."

"To be blunt," continued Harwell, "some scientific details that have been whispered about by certain space technicians who were terrified of losing fascinating high-paying jobs, with lifetime annual retainers for keeping silent, has left me — a volunteer — an apprentice custodian of a hanger sheltering an unprecedented space ark, that took years to build, assemble, and save for — to put it crudely — a small crew of Noahs. Why? To provide transportation for three or four adventurers to attempt a one-way 'overspace' trip to a faraway place inhabited by an unknown, Earth-like people!"

"I can see," said Cample, "why some people wonder about you Christians!"

"Oh, I understand completely," said Harwell, "and they'd wonder more if they knew what I just told you, but some religious noise here is also my cover as far as they're concerned. These people who secretly worked in and filled up our empty water tower are deep into science, equipping their space ark with unexplainable special technology — that may or may not work. To top things off, they designed and refitted our retired water tower with an observatory roof that can mechanically open. To stay sane, and employed, they seemed to let their interest begin and end with that."

"And then," offered Cample, "many months later came EMP and our four connected stories arriving from three or four different places."

"And," continued Harwell, "the arrival of two 'special people' as well as a gifted young pilot who's stayed out of the, should I say it, 'lamplight'?"

"How do you feel about this?" asked Cample.

"Let me put it this way, Marvin. If I lived in the days of Ben Franklin and someone placed in my hand a metal object the size of a pack of chewing gum, and told me there was a library inside, and that if I pressed a certain number code I could open its door, and not only find books, but a list of books that contained certain ideas I was interested in, do you think I would hand it back and walk away?"

"I suspect," said Cample, "you would approach it as Colin did the 'lightsticks' in the Tower at Tesmond [as to whether or not they were evil magic or legitimate] in *Inside the Hollow Spear*?"

"Exactly!"

"Now," said Cample, "let me put words to the obvious. What concerns you now is what's in your Tower—a masterwork of untested great technology…or the most colossal fraud of our own time."

"That's correct, Cample. You've said it well. My problem is that I have seen what's there and have been entrusted by the last U. S. President, as strange as that sounds, with its future. Further, I've had two people land on my doorstep said to be a part of an advanced alien society that has rejected God and rejected everything from their religious past, destroying all copies of their holy book—that's said to so strongly resemble our Bible. And this is the society said to be responsible for creating the unbelievable technology hidden in our tower.

"Even more, both of those who have come here have responded with great enthusiasm to the message of our Bible. And more than that,

28

one of them, the girl we both know, had been made aware by the other, an old man, of an odd prophecy from their destroyed holy book that refused to be forgotten, 'When the blood of three worlds mingles in a child, a remnant (of their) society will once again believe.' The child, it's been said, would be an ordinary one, simply a 'marker' for new change that's expected to come. Now the man is dead and the girl has been confronted with the possibility of taking the Christian Gospel to her people."

"I don't know what to say," offered Cample. "Except that the unrest now growing so fast in the Territory as we speak could make this our last time for this kind of conversation.

"Now, Jonas, it's my turn to embarrass myself.

"As a new believer in a real Jesus, there's something I must share with you that just may fit into all this—and from what I've been hearing—it may matter immediately."

"Tell me," said Harwell.

"Harwell, last night I had a dream. And this was before I heard about the new breach in our wall, through and past the burned ground surrounding the 'oval fence' that circles our 25- by 18-mile Susquehanna Territory. As I share my dream, I can't help but think of the four stories we've recently discussed. He held up a sheet of paper. I call it

The King in the Iron Cage

Once a good king on an island in a sea of islands had three children, and all the children seemed to share many of their father's good traits.

Now the sea became filled with fierce and terrible creatures and so an iron fence was quickly built to keep the creatures from coming ashore, as well as anyone from leaving.

One day several holes appeared in the fence, and on this same day the king was walking in the meadow to once again consider the God who made every-

thing.

Suddenly, an enormous bird arose from a pile of ashes and stood before him.

"Don't be afraid, Your Majesty," said the bird. "I'll do you no harm. But I must warn you. Your iron fence has been ripped apart, and fierce creatures nearby have come ashore." The bird paused and drew his wings close together. "The world as you know it is doomed. There's nothing you can do," he continued, "but I can do one thing."

"What is that?" asked the King.

"In my talons I can carry those you call your children safely up and over the iron walls to a place where you'll never see them again...but only if you let me."

--The End--

"That's it! Can you say any more? Anything else?" Harwell asked.

"No, that's all I dreamed. That's it. Oh...there was one more odd detail, but I don't see how it possibly fits in."

"And that was?"

"At some point, the spectacles will be smashed beyond repair.

"What I can't see, Jonas, is the '3' children. It's a common motif in folklore but here I..."

"I can see it," interrupted Harwell.

Both men stood and faced the window. The moon had escaped the window frame. The water tower now reflected a vertical pencil line of silvery-green light. For a full minute there was silence.

"Jonas, could you pray something aloud before I leave? I don't think I have the right words."

"Nor do I," said the minister, "but I'll do my best."

EARTH

CHAPTER 3

Flashback:
Father, Son & "Daughter"

Place: Harwell's study

Time: Go back one week earlier! **DAY 321**. *Sunday, 8 PM*

> *Note: This occurs one week earlier than Chapters 1 and 2, only 2 days after the cheating incident that's discussed in* **Earth Is Not Alone.** *The details of that event have little bearing on what follows other than showing how Michael and Triana met and first talked with each other.*

**M**ichael, *son…"*

The boy flinched before shifting himself back into neutral in his chair across from Harwell's desk. He unzipped his leather jacket before quickly running his fingers through his dark curly hair. He would respect, though not capitulate to the unspoken authority underlined by the familiar large desk.

"Michael, you know I speak as your second father and…"

"I know that, sir," Michael interrupted.

The bond between the two had rarely been close, but it was real nonetheless. He hadn't forgotten that his pastor's beloved wife had died alongside his parents years ago in the fiery crash on I-81 just south of Binghamton, just after the pastor's arrival at the church. Together they had a shared faith, and by coincidence Michael and he had a background in the same system of karate, which prompted, or reinforced the frequent "sir" in his speaking and his ability to focus and listen, especially when clueless about what was going on.

Michael had welcomed his formal adoption by the pastor partly because, then as an eighth grader, he'd no family except for Great-aunt Steffi now in her late eighties. And now in very poor health he, though a boy, had to carefully take care of her needs in ways he never dreamed he'd have to. There was no one else. So he lived at her rambling house three blocks from the parsonage. There he'd cleaned and managed as best as he could without complaint, preparing simple food and serving it on a tray. All special medications were long gone. Such practical arrangements in AEMP era were not uncommon.

"Michael?"

"Yes sir?"

"Triana…Triana Simms…Is there anything else I need to know about the two of you?"

"No sir…If you're wondering about our big discussion two nights ago, I think it all came out right. We were both telling the whole truth… and standing up for what we believed."

"It was unrehearsed?"

"Totally. In fact, it was, I think, the first discussion of any consequence that we ever had. Really."

"Really! What about her off-handedly mentioning that you 'loved her.' I've no memory of her dating anyone. Was it just her way of saying she appreciated your listening to and standing beside her in the middle of everything? Or was it more than that?"

"Well" — Michael forced a neutral look — "I think it was just her way of saying she was grateful."

Harwell paused.

"Well…she certainly should be! You both, I might add, acquitted yourselves well…with even a certain amount of dignity. It could even be turned into a fascinating Sunday school play. Now, let me ask…is there something important here that I'm missing?"

"Well, Jonas, she did say that she could 'read my mind,' and even more, that 'reading my mind was easy.'" Michael leaned back to catch his breath.

"Can she?" asked the pastor.

Michael smiled and extended his arms expressing bewilderment.

"Okay, then, did she?

Michael stood, catching a foot in the thick throw rug and tripping. His cool demeanor slipped away. He walked to the window, nearly tripping again over a large canvas backpack almost invisible in the dim light. He stared outside at the water tower far away uphill that had already lost its silvery-green to the growing darkness. He felt his eyes moisten. Though he hadn't cried at his parents' funeral, Jonas had openly shed tears at his wife's coffin. So let Jonas see his tears now!

Triana had said in so many words…that she might be leaving—forever. Perhaps she didn't know any better, but no one else would have used such words, "Thank you, Michael, for loving me," that she had in front of Jonas and Cample. No wonder Jonas had asked what he did. How honest and naïve could someone who believed in God the way he and Jonas did possibly be? And with her eyesight, how could she go alone on any kind of "mission" to anywhere new…and far, far, far away? He pushed out of his mind Marcus the brilliant "space pilot" who he'd never met.

As silly as it sounded, Michael knew that as long as he lived he could never let anything happen to her. And she couldn't stop him from following her.

After all, she'd already openly declared that "he loved her," which didn't cause her to bat an eyelash two nights earlier in their teacher's

34

inquisition at the parsonage. And, to his credit, he'd made himself appear so emotionally neutral by holding his breath that he'd nearly choked. Then in the wee hours of morning when he had to stay at the parsonage and he was on the living room sofa that Sally had converted into a bed, Triana had suddenly reappeared in her housecoat and slippers — pressured by Sally, so she said — because "she hadn't given him enough time to kiss her goodnight," something he'd never done before.

Then without difficulty he did and she willingly accepted, and they stood there embracing until they both discovered Sally tapping them on their shoulders. Then Sally shooed her off to bed, kissed him on his forehead, and pulled the covers over him on the living room sofa to lie there and stare at the Tower out the window in the moonlight. He would go to his grave with that memory. This mysterious girl could not now just disappear — alone — from their crumbling world to go to some faraway place that neither of them knew anything about.

If she was going anywhere, he was going with her. If it's God's will, of course. It had to be.

"Come back to Earth, Michael."

He returned to his chair, wiped his face with his sleeve, and brushed back his dark curly hair.

"Michael, I want you to do three things."

"Okay, sir."

"The third is, Don't read anything definite into the first two. The first is, in three days I want you to have packed into the large canvas bag by the wall the things listed on a sheet of paper inside it. Have it back in no later than three days, preferably sooner. The second thing is that I want you to visit Esther Crandel."

"Mrs. Crandel, old Amos's wife?" interrupted Michael. "Why?"

"None other," said Harwell. "And you'll see her in church. Make some arrangement then. And 'why?' Because I'm asking you to. You need her help. Your surprises are far from over! One word of advice about Mrs. Crandel—and listen carefully. Begin by asking her questions."

"Questions? What questions?"

"You'll figure that out. And she'll understand what and why, and probably will tell you. The three of us have something in common. Can you remember all this?"

"Yes sir," said Michael, rising to his feet again. "Anything else?"

"Pray, Michael, pray. Test the spirits as I've taught you. We're in uncharted territory, a dangerous place where every choice seems wrong."

The minister's eyes moistened. Michael nodded, shaking. Once again, his life was about to head in a new direction.

— Fast-forward now to one week later —

CHAPTER 4

Snow In The Church

Place: Grace Church

*Time: Now jump ahead one week to where things
started! No more flashbacks.*

DAY 328. *Sunday, 11:20 AM (6 hrs. after Ch. 1)*

How Jonas ("Rev. Harwell" to old ladies) in his jacket
and tie, balding and ramrod straight, stood calmly behind the narrow
pulpit and slowly scanned the audience pew by pew, missing no one,
Michael couldn't fathom.

Michael's mind wandered. For some reason, his head turned left
and up to the narrow, clear horizontal window that recently had been
installed under the middle part of the large, century-old stained glass
window above it. Why would anyone place a piece of pipe, no two
pieces, under the top panes to let in just an inch of air for ventilation?

At the end of the pew, next to the center aisle, sat a bent older man,
then housekeeper Sally, then Triana, then himself. To his left was Esther Crandel with her thick leather-bound Bible who he'd managed
to squeeze in next to, while on her other side at the other end of the
pew sat her husband Amos, obviously the oldest church elder. Above
the center aisle, a single 60w halogen lightbulb attached to a long cord
dangled down from the darkness at the top of the steeply arched ceiling. The bulb and Jonas's small pulpit lantern provided nearly all the

light inside, except for the small amount of daylight that made its way through the windows here and there. Fortunately, the sun was shining.

Dimness, as few realize, is not hard to get used to; a single small light can reveal much—yet not everything. The church was at least three-fourths full, but just who sat where wasn't easy to determine. The faint hum of a generator echoed from the basement. Somehow Michael's right hand fell down upon Triana's left one. Never before had he sat anywhere near her in church, much less beside her. Slowly she inched both hands out of sight under her hymnal. Without turning she eased off her thick glasses, which she lay in her lap.

She's certain to think I'm a middle-school idiot, he thought.

Triana turned just enough to peek up and smile. Cupping her other hand, she leaned just close enough for her dark blonde hair to brush against his cheek, and whispered, "Seventh grade is just fine with me!"

"Uhh…" Michael reddened, thankful for the dimness. He started to draw his hand back.

"No!" she whispered, holding it tight. "But remember I'm new at this. And…and, by the way, I enjoyed middle school!"

"How did you…?"

"I told you, Michael, it's—"

"Alien power, again?"

"Michael…I have to act my part! But just 'remember where we are!'"

He could sense that Sally had turned and was staring. Both turned their eyes to the front. Triana had to be imitating Mira in the story they'd found and discussed with Jonas and Cample more than a week ago. Was she making fun of him, thinking of him as a dumb athlete who couldn't even keep from being kicked off a team? No matter, since that silly altercation weeks ago on the outdoor basketball court, sports were over. "In this Territory, we all hang together, or we all hang one by one," declared the Governor General on the spot, publically banishing him permanently from the sport. But what was basketball anymore anyway, played outside under cold gray daylight? Head cheerleader Stacy had never spoken to him again. No… that…was… not… the… way… Triana…was, he reminded himself matter-of-factly. To her credit and now his better sense, Triana was no Stacy Martin. And her hand was warm.

Michael drew in a deep breath. He sensed the girl was trying to keep from laughing. Triana, the girl he'd so naturally sat beside when, without even a practice run, they'd boldly responded to Cample's accusation that the two of them had cheated together. And after ten hours — moving from the school to the parsonage — of keeping on what seemed like a script that never existed, they'd been vindicated.

Triana may have never dated before — as if that would worry her! So why should it concern him? Yet she'd teased that she could read his mind. And that it was easy. So he must go easy. "Measure twice before first cutting the cloth," he'd learned at the do jang.

SKKRAAAWWWK.

Suddenly, all talking ceased. People shifted in their seats and all eyes pulled their way as if drawn by a magnet, yet not to them but above them. Michael looked up…up to the narrow clear window just below the stained glass one. Only yards away the two odd-looking pipes that kept the old upper panes up had twisted unnaturally toward the front of the church. Tiny flecks of old paint fell from the window ledge.

It was a double-barreled shotgun! And now it was aimed directly toward where the minister had moved from his expected place. Without a word Michael stood and pointed.

Taking the cue, Harwell pointed to two elders standing near the back row. Both disappeared out the back door, one with a pistol.

"**Everyone down!**" shouted Harwell. "**Get under your pew! Down and PRAY!**" The minister himself knelt in front of the first pew after deftly lifting Mandra Hemmings from her wheelchair to the floor, and shielded her as best he could with his body. How to respond to armed attack had been thoroughly discussed in an elders' meeting and explained to the church only a month earlier. There had been warnings, and those at Grace Alliance knew there'd been ridiculous talk of religion and the strange "outsider" girl and her minister somehow being behind their tragic loss of power and possibly invasion from Binghamton in the north.

Still people came to church, whether to worship, refute gossip, or just to be around others was a matter of opinion. But they came. And now their fears appeared to have some foundation. With a minimum of confusion, people scrambled to the floor to slide under the pews and protect themselves. And pray they did!

Kaa-liiick

The first of probably two triggers had been pulled, but the round didn't fire! A dud! How could a failed shot echo so loudly! Probably the hand-loading had been done poorly or the powder was bad.

SKKRAWWWK

The barrel then twisted lower toward where Triana had been sitting. The space under her pew there had filled and she was badly exposed.

"Mrs. Crandel, your Bible!" shouted Michael. He tore it from her hands and holding it high over his head, he jumped on the pew and with both hands thrust the book up into the firing line, only three yards from the weapon. If only he had something better!

He wasn't a second too soon!

KAA – BLAAAAAAMM.

The sound of the actual shot rang throughout the auditorium. Since

40

the weapon was angled downward, it caught the Bible straight on, tearing it out of his hands, sending him down backwards hard on the pew. The thin pages of the center of the book were shredded into bits so fine that, hitting the draft from the open back door, they flew up like a plume of confetti.

For several seconds the center of God's Word fell back like snow on the huddled congregation.

Thankfully, the load was just pellets! Which it didn't have to be, but the powder had been heavily packed. Esther Crandel said later that Michael reminded her of an old movie version of an angry Moses who, descending the mountain with the 10 commandments on tables of stone, saw his people dancing around the golden calf. With the stones held high, Moses had thrown them down, smashing them. With Esther's Bible, however, it had been ripped away, with pieces of the leather cover later found at the opposite wall. Michael, flat on his back, had one hand numb, the other peppered with several shallow cuts. He was otherwise unhurt. Triana was untouched.

Bits of the Bible continued to flutter down, settling on worshipers' clothing as far away as Harwell's pulpit.

The sound of a scuffle came from the church entrance in the back.

"All clear, Jonas! There's only one and we've got him!"

Harwell walked up the center aisle, his own large Bible in hand, and waited for the two elders, one a former policeman, to bring forward a middle-aged white man in a suit and tie with his hands cuffed behind him. By then almost everyone had returned to their seats, including Mandra Hemmings who was restored to her wheelchair. No one showed any signs of leaving. Other elders who'd left to search for other possible troublemakers returned empty-handed.

Harwell ordered a chair to be brought and the man was seated upon it in the aisle in the center of the church.

"Explain yourself!" ordered the minister in a voice that everyone could hear.

"It's that witch girl," the man snarled.

"Speak up so others besides God can hear you!" said Harwell.

"It's that witch girl," the man repeated, **"and you, her priest."**

"I see you're dressed up for worship today? Is that true?"

"Yes!"

"And where, I might ask?"

"The True Church of Divine Revelation," he replied, drilling his eyes straight ahead.

"I see…and they sent you here to kill me and people in my church!"

"No! It's not like that! You're putting words in my mouth!"

"Okay, put some of your own words in my ears! We're all listening. Why did you do this?"

"A lot of people, Harwell, a lot are certain there's something fishy, really wrong about that 'girl' with strange powers and that strange man from 'far away' who lives in that house over yonder." He nodded toward the parsonage. "Before they came we had electricity…and then there's you…"

"Me?" Harwell pressed his Bible up against his chest.

"Let me inform you, and everyone else here, that the 'odd man' as you called him, who was old, sick, and dying, in fact actually died two days ago. And with witnesses, in the way we have to do it now, we buried him quickly as possible behind the parsonage. For some time he'd been nursed by my housekeeper, with the help of Triana, my foster daughter. I assure you, sir, that they had nothing to do with the EMP attack — which, as far as we can tell has occurred across the country, if not the whole world.

"As for me, I've been private about my personal life, but having lived here now long enough, anyone — before AEMP, of course — could

42

have checked out my work in science and my seminary training that followed.

"And now let me ask you, Mr. .....?"

"Smith," he replied.

At that point the head elder interrupted. With his back to the congregation he approached the minister and whispered in his ear. Harwell also turned around and held an open palm close to his chest. The head elder dropped something small into it. The minister nodded, whispered back, closed his hand, and the elder scurried to the back of the auditorium.

Harwell continued:

"Mr. Smith...Mr. Smith, do you and your church believe in Jesus?"

"Of course!"

"And how far does his offer of salvation go?"

"Everywhere, of course. To anyone who believes. To the end of the world!"

"And how big is that world?"

"Everything we see anywhere."

"Even to places we see in telescopes?"

"Everywhere! He made everything. It's all his!"

Harwell turned to Triana.

"Stand please, Triana." Immediately she stood.

"Triana, do you believe in the God of the Bible and Jesus his Son?"

"Yes, Jonas, I trust in Him with all my heart." She turned to the man in the chair. "Mr. Smith, or whoever you are, I'm an orphan." Carefully she raised her glasses and put them on to actually see where the man sat. "An orphan who's been passed along. And I don't think that matters to Jesus. And though I can guess, I'm not at all sure where I came from. Do you think my ignorance about that matters to Jesus?"

"Personally, I don't think he gives a damn," huffed the man.

"Smith," said Harwell, "but God gives you the right to try to kill us?"

"The Bible, Harwell, it tells us to fight evil. Two days ago I read about a good woman, Jael, who was praised for putting a tent peg through Sisera's head. After that evil man was dead, the people of God started to move ahead. Then I dreamed a powerful dream that told me to come up here and 'do likewise' to you, the evil man who brought this electrical curse to us."

"What a coincidence, Smith! I just read that same passage in Judges 4 and 5 this past week, and you know what? I'm having that same feeling right now, and words are coming to me. 'Immediately, get rid of that evil man who tried to kill innocent people!'... But since that sounds extreme, I'd first have to confirm that feeling with those around me who believe in Jesus. Smith, did you discuss your dream and what you planned to do with anyone who believed in Jesus before you came here?"

Silence.

The minister squinted his eyes and looked toward the ceiling as if lost in deep thought.

"Damn you, Harwell!" Sweat began to bead on the man's forehead.

"Tape his mouth," ordered the minister. "This is a house of worship. Just relax, Smith, it's your turn to listen. And you're going to have to keep your mouth shut. I won't kill you if you cooperate. My people here wouldn't let me even after what you just did. In fact I'm now convinced" — he glanced down to something he held in his hand — "that your attempt to kill us was very half-hearted. And if I have to testify later, I'll say why. But now our conversation is over." Harwell glanced at the elder by his side. "Tape him to his chair. Until I say so he quietly stays right where he is."

The minister turned to his congregation.

"Let us pray." And pray he did, as if it were an ordinary Sunday in AEMP, as if ordinary days were still possible. The most noticeable difference now was that he spoke from the center aisle at Row 6 facing an attempted murderer three rows back, taped to a chair, with his mouth covered with tape.

CHAPTER 5

Harwell's Story

Place and Time: **DAY 328.** *Same as Ch. 4*

After brushing bits of Bible pages off his dark jacket, Harwell began.

"Susquehannites, now that we're reasonably sure that we're not going to get shot at again, at least in church, and you seem to be unwilling to go home, and because we have with us a special guest, though he stays only because those beside him insist upon it—perhaps some of you can relate to that, and..." Harwell paused at a ripple of light laughter. "And you seem wise enough to always wonder a bit about our young people, one of whom has been called into question"—he glanced at Triana—"and to those of you who have children, you know what I mean."

More laughter.

Michael's eyes grew large. Was this his adopted father speaking? Rarely did Jonas play the crowd, especially on a Sunday. Suddenly he felt a slight pricking. He looked down. Triana, as secretly as possible, with a fingernail had teased out a shiny b-b-sized pellet from just under the skin of his injured hand and began studying it.

Harwell continued.

"Let me remind you that when EMP struck and automobiles died, it was the bicycle brigades of our children who circulated valuable 4-H and county food preservation and health-care pamphlets over dozens and dozens of miles on mountain roads, saving lives, fending off hunger and giving care and comfort to the old, the sick, and the dying when no adults were available.

"And this occurred in my own home." He pointed in the direction of the parsonage.

"You've heard me preach nearly four years, and now in the last year we've struggled to live together without nearly every technological device, as well as without commercially generated electrical power. Many here have suffered and died in ways never expected two years ago.

"But outside the guarded walls of our Territory untold millions must have died, largely because people, especially in congested urban areas, have lost their knowledge about how to live without electricity.

"I'm telling you nothing new, but realize once again that we've survived comparatively well.

"On this morning when we've been challenged, I will once again mention children and what they can do. So I, as the Apostle Paul on occasion felt led to do, will share information that's not found in the Bible. In sweet memory of my wife who was killed just after we came here, and my two daughters and four grandchildren whose fates I still know nothing about, I will tell you a story about a lost child. I'll do it as best I can without notes."

The Lost Girl

Once upon a time years ago an 18-year-old girl with a B average graduated from high school. She did nothing memorable enough to be to be recorded in her high school yearbook.

With almost no family support, she moved out and rented a tiny apartment. Three weeks later her high school boyfriend, the former football quarterback, moved in, and there was casual talk about marriage probably later in the summer. He was athletic, though with no scholarships offered yet, his future was very uncertain; and the girl, noticeably attractive and similarly uncertain, was, though she probably wouldn't say so, the settling-down type with no special plans in place for her life. For two months their relationship was "hot," she later admitted, but work was scarce and with the warmth and beauty of summer, the former quarterback played softball three evenings a week, and arose late every morning. Since it was in the days before everyone had computers, what mornings he experienced were spent with sports magazines in front of the TV. And yes, according to him, efforts were made now and then to locate a job. But none was found.

The girl, however, found employment in a nearby supermarket, at first shelving newly arrived groceries until midnight in order to buy food for the two of them. And slowly, because she was reliable, and finally off drugs, she realized she wasn't as dumb as she first thought she was, and consequently was promoted to jobs in the supermarket with greater and greater responsibility.

And by the end of July she found out something else about herself: she was pregnant.

The next morning in tears she gave her boyfriend the news.

"How could you let this happen?" he'd howled. "Don't you have any sense at all? I don't know any other girl who would have ever let this happen! I'm not ready for this. And neither are you. I let you into my life and now you've ruined it! I…I've got to think this over."

Grabbing his light jacket, and reaching for and finding a small package in the corner of his closet, he left, slamming the door behind him.

They didn't speak to each other for two days.

When she came home from work at 1 AM on the third day, he was gone along with nearly all his things. She never spoke to him again.

But the next evening, his mother came to the supermarket while the girl was stacking merchandise in the pet supplies aisle and gave her such a loud and severe tongue-lashing that the manager appeared and asked the mother to leave.

As the mother spun on her heel and left, the manager, not many years older than the girl, but married, who had overheard almost everything, asked if she wanted to talk or needed any help.

"No," said the girl.

When she returned home later she found her front door open, and that the quarterback's mother had broken into her apartment and taken away all her son's sports trophies that he'd haphazardly left behind.

Two days later, after she'd paid the rent on her apartment – she'd always paid in full and on time – and had only five dollars to her name, the girl found herself in a booth in the back of a popular diner in the center of town.

"God help me!" she cried for the first time that she could remember. And she meant it, not having a clue of what might follow.

Her jacket slipped to the floor under the seat and she got down on her knees to retrieve it. A wave of nausea swept over her. She fought the urge to throw up. In the restroom, above some scribbling on the wall were a couple of wall mottoes. Not knowing why, she read them. The first was "The journey of a thousand miles begins with a single step." The second was "No act of kindness, no matter how small, is ever wasted."

It didn't sound like the Bible but it didn't sound bad.

Returning to her booth, her eyes were red, her coffee and toast cold. Coffee was the last thing she wanted, but a little toast she could manage.

As she retrieved her jacket from the floor a second time, she spied a small black purse the same color as the floor tile. It had to belong to the thirty-something-aged couple eating sausage and eggs just ahead of her. Even the thought of sausage and eggs made her queasy. With her foot she quietly dragged the purse back to where she could reach down and pick it up.

"I think you dropped this," she said to the woman, standing, but not quite managing her full height and extending her arm with the bag. Oh...and I *think this envelope that fell out and stuck in a crack in molding nearby must be yours, too.*

The woman, turned, inspected the envelope, and quickly studied the girl. Gratefully she thanked her.

After the girl sat, the woman herself stood and apologized for staring. "Would you like to talk?" she asked.

"No thank you," said the girl politely. Probably a preacher's wife, she thought. And she said nothing else to the woman — then.

But she did a week later.

Seven and a half months afterwards she gave birth to a baby boy. She called him "Jonas" and gave him her own last name, "Harwell," and much, much more I can assure you.

And fifty-four years later I stand before you sharing these words that she passed on to me.

And, believe it or not, I'm sharing them here for the very first time.

"If what my mother did for me was my first blessing, my second blessing was her eventual moving into a tiny apartment next to a small planetarium and observatory attached to a college. About the time I learned to read I was awestruck by the planets and stars and how much we could learn about them even though they were so far away. As a child I hung out at the building sweeping floors and cleaning chairs, even dusting and cleaning equipment — you could do things like that in those days — doing anything to stay inside the wonderful temple that allowed me to see farther and farther into the heavens. And sky-watchers and astronomers who understood me were never far away.

"My third blessing came from the husband of the woman who helped my mother so much. He was a pastor, and when I was 11, I discovered that his tiny church had needs I could take care of. So I swept, emptied wastebaskets, and cleaned for the privilege of silently, and I mean silently, doing homework and studying at a second desk that was jammed into his office. My reward was the chance to ask him any, and I mean any, serious question before we headed home in opposite directions. Sometimes he would answer then, sometimes it would be the first thing when I saw him the next time.

"His gift to me? He took me seriously. In his office one day I accepted Jesus as my Savior and soon realized that my body was a valuable temple of another kind. He also introduced me to martial arts, and I became a black belt when I was in high school. That taught me discipline. Discipline that eventually took me through my doctorate in astrophysics. But all I've said so far pales to that commitment I made to the one who made the stars, Jesus who is my Lord.

"Why am I saying all this?

"Because if you wonder about me and where I come from, this is who I am. I'm sorry, and I'm not sure why I waited so long to tell you this. But I've learned how important questions can be. Even if answers are hard to find."

A man two-thirds of the way back in the auditorium raised his hand.

"Yes, Thomas?"

"Jonas, here's my serious question. How safe are we now?"

"As to trouble from the hands of men, we are not safe."

"Why's that, Jonas?"

"No hard facts yet, but I've been told indirectly that our 25-by-18-mile 'oval,' if you can call it that, wall, or barbed fence, around us has been breached in several places by outsiders, and —"

" 'Indirect'? Dr. Harwell. Can't you be more specific?" came a loud voice from somewhere in the darkness in the back.

"I can!" said Marvin Cample, jumping to his feet. "I...I saw it clearly in a dream."

This began a loud whispering. "Isn't he that fairytale teacher at the high school?" said someone.

"Well," said someone else, "I heard that there was some unusual trouble in the south just last night."

"And at Choconut in the north," said another.

Harwell raised his hands.

"Remember, once again, that survivors from Binghamton to the north, after a face-off against survivors from Syracuse further north, may come our way. The same goes for Scranton and Wilkes-Barre in the south. You all have defense responsibilities to your mayor-colonels and the Governor-general. I will remain at the church and parsonage, doing what I can for what God sends my way. And not knowing what might be coming — we must be ready to make horrible choices probably within days.

"Since, as a nation, we were unwilling to face the weaknesses of the past — our near-total dependence on unprotected, not quickly replaceable electrical power — we now face future weaknesses that we can't escape.

"Brothers and sisters in Christ" — Harwell raised his thick Bible overhead — "nowhere in here do I see mention of the United States as a privileged country favored to be spared because of special obedience to God. Is this the end of the world, the great time of tribulation that is prophesied to come, ending metaphorically, or as some say 'literally' in 'a final knee-deep-in-blood war on horseback' in Jerusalem? Once again, I cannot say, no more than I could have said twenty years ago that we'd be now living in these circumstances. All I can say is that Christians in the Ukraine, Somalia, Sudan, Iran, and recently Hong Kong, South Korea, and southern China have all asked the same end-times question.

"This I can say: if the final end of things is not yet, and if the Ameri-

52

can 47 of what was once 50 states somehow survives, it will be in a very different form from what we all have ever known.

"Finally, let me remind you while we still all have responsibilities here, St. Paul has declared that for Christians, our most important 'citizenship' is in Heaven."

After a pause of several seconds, Harwell turned to the taller of the two elders standing nearby.

"Bring me Mr. Smith's sawed-off shotgun." To a second elder he ordered that the man be thoroughly searched for ammunition. In seconds, receiving several rounds, he broke down the barrel, turned his back, and acted as if he were loading the weapon. Snapping the—still empty—weapon closed, he carried it in ready position and approached the sitting man.

"Open his cuffs and cut him loose," he ordered. The man's eyes were huge and he was sweating profusely. The tape was pulled from the man's lips. All tape that held him to the folding chair was cut except for one leg that was still bound to a chair leg. "Don't try to run," warned Harwell, fingering the gun. Smith raised his hands in surrender.

"Duh…duh…don't…shoo…"

"I told you I wasn't going to shoot you, Smith, even though you tried to kill my foster daughter and in the attempt injured my son. Instead, the Governor-general would love to make short work of you with a hundred of our witnesses testifying about what you did."

"Nooo! No!"

"Wouldn't that be fair?"

Silence.

The elder with the pistol drew it.

"Cut him totally free. Then the four of us will walk slowly to the door. Understand?" As they walked, another elder took Harwell's place, lifted his hands, and asked everyone to stand while he led in prayer. Elder Amos Crandel swiftly moved down the side aisle and met Harwell and the others by the door.

At the bottom of the church steps, Harwell took the oldest elder aside.

Amos later told Michael what happened next.

"Wait here," said the minister. The two moved out of the others' hearing. Turning their backs so no one else could see, he held up something from his pocket. "Amos, are these what I think they are?" He dropped the contents into the elder's hands.

"Jonas!..." He raised his hand higher. "These pellets have to be... have to be silver! Remember the old stories? That's said to be the only thing that can destroy werewolves!"

"Unbelievable!" mumbled Harwell. He slipped the pellets in his pocket.

"Go home, Mr. Smith," said Harwell, "and tell your people we oppose witchcraft and all Godless evil spirits as much as you do. And we, without reservation believe in the God of the Bible. Remember what happened here. I'll urge my people not to press charges against you, though I can't guarantee it, please understand. As God has forgiven me of my sins, I forgive you. Please come back in two days—without a gun—and tell me what you've learned. We must stand together. I pray that God's Holy Spirit may be your teacher and guide...and oh, here's your gun. You may need it elsewhere in the days to come. I'm sure you've more ammunition back home."

Harwell, turned abruptly and proceeded back up the stone steps and disappeared inside.

"You got off easy, Smith," said the head elder, "I hope you're smart enough to know that. We've even got some folk wisdom that beats the crazy ideas you brought here: Good arguments wear dry pants."

"Oops!" said the second elder, glancing down at the intruder. "It clearly looks like Harwell wins again, Smith. See you in two days. Don't forget!"

CHAPTER 6

The Inquisition

Place: The study in the parsonage
*Time: **DAY 328.** Later, Sunday afternoon*

"**M**ichael, did you pack your bag packed according to the instructions?"

"Yes, Jonas. The only important thing missing is my karate cane and the flannel shirt that I'm wearing."

"And Triana, yours?"

"Yes, Jonas."

"Questions?"

Silence.

Harwell turned and moved down the hallway and opened the door to his office. Together, careful to avoid even touching, Michael and Triana followed through the door, but then stopped.

By prearrangement, they'd agreed to ask nothing about what might come next until Jonas got more specific. Would they "go somewhere," or not? And, if so, with or without his blessing?

And who else would be going along? And if Jonas was going to be mysterious about all this, and they said nothing, the minister eventually would be forced to step in and level with them.

While waiting, they would display as little emotion as possible and none to each other. They would simply act if each was preparing individually for a first trip to a new college, and just happened to be sharing a car or a bus to get there — which, of course was now impossible.

For Michael, obeying Jonas was the most natural thing in the world, even if he wasn't perfect about it. But rebelling? Possibly. Rebelling against Jonas? Never if he could help it. He suspected the same was true for the girl. Would Jonas hurt them? Never deliberately. And if Michael were headed the wrong way and was about to hurt himself, wouldn't the minister stop him, or warn him in no uncertain terms? As to the immediate possibilities of what lay ahead, he couldn't even begin to consider them. Every direction was crazy. He would hide his unease. Triana would go along with that, but how could he be so sure? To begin he leaned toward her and cupped his hand to her ear so Jonas could only hear with difficulty.

"I'm reading your mind," Michael whispered. Their game — totally unrehearsed — was back in play.

"Really!" she whispered back, "Well, you're braver than I thought. But you know…you know what I like more than bravery?"

"What?"

"Honesty."

"Even if we're facing a lion?" He poked the thumb on his other hand back in the direction of their minister and parent who'd already seated himself behind his desk watching them while they stood whispering deliberately a bit louder than they should just inside the door.

"Good point," said Triana, "but in the case of a lion I'd prefer speed."

"But lions run much faster than people," he returned. "That doesn't make good sense."

"Oh but it does. I'd pray only to run 'humanly' faster than you."

Michael laughed.

"But wait," she interrupted. "I take back all I said." Uncharacteristically, she looked away, then down at the floor as if studying his shoes. "But then I'd have only the memory of your laugh. That's too sad to think about. Too sad. Oh…wait…I shouldn't have said that, should I? Sorry!"

"Triana, what can I say to that? You win!—this time. Don't look, but I think Jonas is getting impatient."

"Questions?" Harwell repeated.

Seating themselves in chairs deliberately several feet apart, each silently examined their questioner as if he were the only other person in the room.

"What questions should we have?" offered Michael.

Harwell suddenly stood and, turning his back to them, walked to the window and stared at the water tower. Turning back, he completely circled his desk and fell back in his chair where he started. He eyed each one sternly back and forth since they purposefully sat far enough apart to divide his attention. At last he spoke, reminding Michael of a judge he'd once seen in an old movie.

"Do you recall in the Emryss story, 'The Secret of Zareba,'" asked Harwell, "when Galen's father saw smoke from the fire that was destroying the Holy City only a few miles away, and he suddenly blurted out, 'Today, my son, I declare you to be a man'? His words were a surprise that circumstances demanded."

58

"Yes, Yes," Michael and Triana declared almost on top of each other, as soon as Harwell's words ended, with neither one moving a muscle other than their lips.

"Today, Michael, I declare you to be a man.

"Today, Triana, I declare you to be a woman." Only Jonas could get away with such a silly formality.

Silence. The wait to break it this time wasn't long.

"If you're looking to receive any royal rings though, it'll be a long wait."

Michael smiled. Triana stayed expressionless.

"Tell me," the minister paused, "do you two love each other?"

"Yes, Yes." Again both replied at almost the same instant. It was obvious that the minister was surprised by their lack of hesitation.

"Now wait a minute. I'm not talking about the 'Christian love' that God expects all believers to have for each other. But the other kind. Let me ask you again, do you two love each other?"

"Yes, Yes."

"Again, let me be clear, I'm not talking about 'brother-sister love' which your special circumstances have presented you with, but the other kind. Do you two love each…"

"Lord, have mercy on us all!" came a new voice. Without so much as a knock, the door swung open, and Sally strode into the room with a tray of cups, a pot of hot sassafras tea, several slices of sourdough bread and a dish of butter.

"Jonas, you'll just have to excu…oo…ze me, if you will, 'cause though minding my own bizness, without trying, I couldn't help but hear this inquisition thing you're havin' with these kids, I mean this 'man' and this 'woman,' about love and all that. Figured something to eat and drink was called for. An' oh, if you want my say on what's going on here, Jonas, just see me later. The 'other kind of love'! Dear me, Jonas" — she paused and rolled her eyes — "Where'd that come from? Another planet?"

At that moment Michael and Triana, still not even looking at each other, jumped up, and the boy kissed one of Sally's cheeks, the girl the other. Together, they escorted the woman through the door, each hugging her on the way out, and closing the door behind them after she was gone. Returning to their chairs exactly as before, each found a full cup of tea waiting. Harwell was already chomping on a piece of buttered bread.

"While you eat, let me share a story," said Harwell as if nothing had just happened. It was told to me, just days ago by someone you know very well.

*   *   *   *   *

[Harwell then shares"The King in the Iron Cage" that he'd deliberately kept from the two until he'd learned more about them. In it as you recall, a giant bird, seemingly helpful, had offered to carry three of the King's children to safety, but only with his permission and the understanding that they'll never be able to return. Afterwards the three — the pastor, the newly-declared-to-be man, and the newly-declared-to-be-woman — discussed and pondered four questions:

1) Could the "doomed kingdom" represent the Susquehanna Territory?

2) Can, will, and should three people — without mentioning any names — forever escape the "kingdom" on a one-way trip?

3) Can, and should, a metaphoric story like this serve as a model for attempting real, irreversible action?

4) What signs, if any, could confirm or reject using this story as a model for action?]

For Michael the conversation seemed unusually polite and

60

kind, more academic and guarded than practical, especially if their limited circumstances were soon to disappear forever. It certainly explained his surprise at seeing Marvin Cample stand up and speak so boldly to the church members. As to how he felt toward Triana and she for him, there was no more questioning.

This off-and-on week-long romance fueled only with words would fail miserably as a C-grade movie, if there was such a thing, or an old Hallmark movie he would occasionally watch with Aunt Steffie before EMP.

Michael would have part of a possible answer to the fourth question waiting for him back home, when he found his Great-aunt Steffi dead in her favorite chair. A peaceful death it seemed.

Properly burying her would be his last major defined family responsibility.

At least on Earth.

*   *   *   *   *

But first, as they left Harwell's office, Triana, with her radar at work, led. She would walk him home part way. As she blindly reached back for him to take her hand in the dark hallway, which he did, she snuffled loudly.

"Sorry, Michael," she said. She turned and her eyes were filled with tears. At this point, part of the hallway jutted off at a right angle into even greater darkness. She pulled him around the corner.

"Here." Impulsively, Michael extended his arms and unbuttoned his long flannel sleeves. "Casimir is at your service." Without hesitating, she wiped her eyes and face on the soft cloth and snuffled again, her nose running. "Here, blow!" he said, feeling like an idiot for suggesting it. But needing to, without thinking

61

she did…right into his loose shirtsleeves. Surprised at herself, in a way Michael had never seen, she jerked back.

"You must think I'm the most disgusting girl in the whole world!" She fought to hold her next snuffle back and nearly choked.

Michael held her back at arm's length. Some long hair had fallen across her face. Gently he pushed it back.

"I think you're the most beautiful and most wonderful girl in the whole world."

This time her arms went forward and pushed back.

"I knew you were crazy!"

"Well, Casimir's future wife didn't think that way when he was helpful… We've got to read again that story, *The Fourth Prince,* that Cample brought us — read it together."

"I still think you're crazy."

"I heard you the first time." He held out his arms, encouraging her to move into them.

Not budging an inch, she pointed her forefinger at the ceiling.

It was that magical sign that they both knew about.

"I see," he said mechanically. "Only one time." He agreed without thinking or arguing. He inched forward and she lifted her head. Wiping her face on a dry part of his shirt, he found his fingers now in her hair. He pulled her close, and they kissed. He was amazed at her willingness and how easily she slipped into his arms. At last, he steeled himself to gently push back — and just in time. She sneezed, and had he not still been holding her, she would have fallen back to the floor. He wiped his face.

Mortified, she regained her balance, turned, and fled down the hallway.

Never, never would he let anyone hurt her and, God willing,

he'd never leave her no matter where she went. There was no one in this world — or any other — like Triana Simms.

CHAPTER 7

Esther Crandel's Attic

Place: The Hotel Crandel

*Time: **DAY 329** (the next day) Monday, 11 AM*

Great-aunt Steffi's death was a mercy. Months ago her medications had run out, and with them the last of her memories slipped away.

As Michael approached the Hotel Crandel, he recalled the bustle of all that had happened.

Secretly he'd already built a crude wooden coffin, although that was no longer expected in AEMP. And two weeks earlier he'd actually started the backyard grave. Only last night after finding her he'd finished it. In tears he'd carried her body to the old sofa, laid her out flat, and tried to clean the dirt out from under his fingernails. He'd gone to bed without supper.

Early in the morning he'd walked to the parsonage and notified Sally it was over. She would take over the preparations. A brief service with two or three people would occur later in the afternoon. Nowadays, it had to be done that way, and quickly. There were no resources to allow lingering and ceremony. With Bible-promised strength, Aunt Steffi had more than reached the "four score years" allotted to the hearty.

Only Sally knew about the death, and only Sally would know where he would be this morning. In fact, she'd encouraged him to go and not change his plans.

He could put it off no longer. Why had Jonas insisted that he must go — immediately and alone — to see Esther Crandel? Why? He hadn't a clue but this morning it was a perfect distraction. He'd made his appointment while they sat next to each other the day before on the pew before everything happened — at church and at later at home. Destroying her heavily underlined Bible was hardly the way to start off talking to an old woman he'd never had a serious conversation with.

Her notes in the margin after so many hours of study and meditation! Yes, it had stopped a gunshot, perhaps saved a life, but what would she say? Yesterday, she'd abruptly said he could come, and that 11 o'clock was fine.

At Esther Crandell's — Day 1 (Monday)

He was at her door at 11 sharp.

He would steel himself, hold in his feelings, and be kind regardless of what would happen. He'd long ago learned that when one knew as little as he did, he could fake it, and put his ears to work instead of his tongue. His martial arts experience reinforced this. The worst thing was letting his feelings get hurt and losing his pride which, according to Jonas, happens to everyone now and then. When it does, swallow it, recover quickly, and move on. "Who you are," Jonas had often said, "is not what others say, it's what you know you are" — under God's private spotlight, of course.

Be sure you immediately "start with questions," Jonas had insisted, without explanation.

Odd for an old lady it seemed, as well as for Jonas.

But stubbornness had kicked in. He could play with cards close to his chest. His few words would be distinct enough so she could hear him the first time.

He was now at the Hotel Crandel where Amos and Esther lived off to the side on the first floor. The building, in need of a facelift, had seen better days. The old street had little traffic, even before EMP. Three stories high plus an attic, with only stairways and no elevator, which wouldn't have worked anyway, the hotel still had six rentable rooms he would soon learn, three of which on the second floor were now used long-term, by people whose homes had been destroyed. He'd been directed to the small side door that served as the Crandels' personal entryway.

He reached it. He knocked. Seconds later it opened.

"Why Michael, it's you. Come on in!" Mrs. Crandel wore a flower-patterned cotton dress, attractive and suitable for her age. He noticed how perfectly it fit her straight slender frame. Her silvery-gray hair was pulled tightly into a bun on the back of her head with no escaping strands. Shiny wire-rimmed full glasses in perfect ovals covered her eyes, and make-up, if she wore any, was as invisible as her perfume. "You're just in time for morning tea."

"Ma'am, may I help you?" was the first question that came to mind.

"Certainly!" She smiled, acting as if the question caught her by surprise. She pointed to an empty vase alongside a short candle that lay next to a candlestick and a rare booklet of matches on a small round table set for two. "Follow me, please." She entered a small kitchen, neatly kept, that was an extension of a long living room, that had obviously been specially created and updated within the last two decades. A door at the far end led to what he would discover was a small nondescript courtyard at the rear of the hotel. Traces of snow and slush from recent weather, and tall clumps of yellowed grass that had survived the weather was all that was there. "Go, Michael, and bring me some flowers for the vase."

"Flowers?" He inflected his voice, creating a question.

"Yes, Michael, I need something for the vase." She handed him a pair of scissors. Immediately, she turned back to her woodstove, and pulled away a pot of boiling water.

Michael paused, for a couple of seconds. Okay, it was time to act. If the woman wasn't crazy, this was some kind of test. He would play along, not his first attempt at this sort of thing recently, especially around older people.

In the courtyard, obviously there were no flowers. And the empty vase inside — what was the purpose of that? A brick wall surrounded the courtyard. At its base, he saw that the remains of something had been planted or had accidentally grown there, grass, sedge, or golden-rod — weeds, he hadn't a clue what — that now was just a clump of yellow stems with a head of seeds or flower hulls bunched together that was reasonably intact. He carefully cut a tall bundle with the scissors, blew away the loose dead stuff on top and returned inside.

This had to be a game.

He would go along, pretending to be interested. Taking the vase from the table, he carried it to the wastebasket by the backdoor, cut some of the stems off a bit, and then, when they all wouldn't go through the opening in the vase, he carefully discarded half of them without cluttering the floor. Then he nudged the other half in, fluffing them out a bit as if it truly mattered.

It was the first time he'd put anything in a vase in his life. But he wasn't done. On the table he carefully slid the vase of weeds gently to the side where it wouldn't block vision between the two who would be sitting across from each other. That made sense. Without a second thought he stuck the candle into the candlestick and lit it. Then he moved it close, but not too close, to the weeds. He felt her eyes watching his every move. He fought not to look back and smile. Flowers? Really! Never had he felt more foolish.

Finished, he stood behind his, or what he presumed was his, chair and rested his hands on the back of it. She placed a thick round cloth pad on the table, and set the teapot on it.

"Is that acceptable, ma'am?" he asked.

"Almost perfect," she replied. "You have a good eye. And if you're wondering why all this fiddling around with cutting weeds, jamming them in a bottle, and setting it on a table beside a pot of tea makes any difference at all, just let me say this: What you've done is attractive. It acknowledges that you can see beyond what you first care about, and that you see me as an honorable woman and worthy of your respect. And it matters to me. And..."

"And?" Again he inflected the word.

"And it will matter to her."

A chill ran down Michael's back. He forced himself to hold back any emotion.

"Is there anything more here"—he extended his hands toward the table—"that I should know that you can tell me?"

"Yes, as a matter of fact there is. You want more?" Michael marveled at the very tone of her words: How soft and compelling!

"Yes ma'am."

"Okay, now I know you've been taught to use your eyes carefully. You can even train them to quickly take in 150 degrees in front of you without turning your head. Now please look at the table for ten seconds. Remember everything you see. Then turn around and count slowly to twenty. Then I'm going to take all this away and ask you to restore everything as it was. Is that okay?"

"Yes ma'am." His attempting this shouldn't be more difficult or crazy than what she'd done.

So he agreed. He carefully studied the table. After turning back around when his lips silently reached twenty, the table was empty down to the bare wood. So much for old age slowing her down! Even the tablecloth, which he hadn't really noticed, was neatly folded on the

68

"Almost perfect," she replied. "You have a good eye..."

counter.

"Now, Michael, restore the table exactly as it was before." And he did, even relighting the candle she'd snuffed out. At the last second he correctly swapped sides with the fork and the paired knife and spoon and turned the cutting edge of the knife toward the plate. The only thing he'd overlooked was replacing the pad that went under the teapot which, without a word, she corrected. Another first-time experience.

"Not bad, Michael. Now you can do that, when it's appropriate, for her without even asking...and if a proper setting involves other things, she'll let you know. Of course, table-setting varies from culture to culture, so you'll have to adjust. But wherever the two of you may be, you can remind her of where you both came from by setting the table for her the way you just did. And doing it without being told."

"Do you mean the 'Earth Way,' ma'am?"

She smiled.

"Michael, there are several different table-settings on Earth."

Michael shrugged and smiled back.

"But let's move on. Have some tea and biscuits. And, if you will, watch what I do with my tableware as I eat. Is there anything else you'd like to ask? And you may ask anything. Anything at all."

"I think that may be dangerous, ma'am. I have an active imagination."

"So do I, Michael." Her eyes twinkled.

"I think you gave yourself away, ma'am, with the '150 degree-vision' comment. Did you have a child study martial arts?"

"No, I did not."

"Your husband Amos?"

"No."

"Then...how..."

"Michael, let me put it this way: As you know, your father Jonas is

70

a black belt, fourth degree." She raised her cup and sipped her tea.

"He was my finest student."

Michael's jaw dropped.

"Then you are an…"

"An O-dan, or fifth degree. And you're a cho-dan, Michael. I have ways of knowing. Now don't let your tea get cold! I'm Amos's second wife, and of course he knows about this and, by the way, he's away on business all day at the southern wall. I am another 'outsider' come to town, but that was twenty years ago, and have been here longer than you have. Now I'm going to ask you, Michael, to let this be our, and Jonas's, secret. For very complicated reasons a veil of secrecy must cover my past that I'm not at liberty to discuss. I can say no more. Can I trust you on this, Michael?"

"You can," he replied. He stood and bowed, and she standing, returned the formality. "Teacher, may I ask you more questions?"

"As I said, you can, and I think you should, though as you can see, my answers may not be as complete as you would like. Oh, and let's stop this bowing and 'teacher' thing and karate talk at once lest we raise eyebrows elsewhere. If you like, you may call me Mrs. Crandel. In fact, I prefer that." Before sitting she refilled both cups and uncovering a loaf of sourdough bread, set it on a cutting board on the table by the biscuits. "While this bread cools a bit more will you do me a favor?"

"Certainly!"

"I've got some stuff in the attic that I need moved, but right at the top of the first set of stairs is a flat-topped trunk with leather straps. Would you bring it and the rocking chair beside it down and place the trunk in front of the sofa and the rocking chair to the side of it at a right angle?"

This took no more than four minutes.

"Open the trunk, please, Michael."

He did. There was nothing inside but a dozen or so old magazines.

"Please put these in the trash with your plant stems."

"May I have this old Life Magazine from the 1950's?"

"You may, and any other if you like," she replied. He took five of the magazines.

When he returned, he found her seeming to decide how the box might serve as a coffee table for the sofa. At last she shook her head.

"Michael, this just won't work. Please take them back upstairs where you found them." In ten minutes all was as before and Michael was back at the table where the bread lay, keeping his utter bewilderment to himself. The woman handed him a knife.

"Now let me see how you go about cutting this. The first thing we've already done is to let the bread stand and cool just a bit to firm up. Then it's ready for the knife. You draw it slowly back and forth like a saw across the top until the teeth break through the crust."

"Yes ma'am, Mrs. Crandel…I…I take it that testing me on knife defenses is not on your list?" he asked, smiling.

"You are correct, Michael…And…well…I hope that's not a mistake. Remember, Michael, because I'm trying to encourage you, I won't consider you rude to ask any questions, though I'll assume the right to say 'I don't know,' or 'I can't' or 'won't answer.'"

"Why, all of this, ma'am?"

"First, Michael, I think you need some help—a lot of it really, and very quickly. I've gotten wind that serious things lie ahead. Secondly, I think it's better if our conversation goes that way. At some point you may be asked, 'Whatever did Esther Crandel teach you or tell you about?' and I'll want you to be able to honestly say, 'She wanted help moving some furniture up and down stairs which I did, I apologized for destroying her Bible, she fixed me some things to eat and, of course, tea, and I asked her some practical questions I needed answers for.' That's all true, and that's enough to explain why you're here.

"There's a certain special girl that we both know who carries an air of mystery about her. And that's fine. There's a lot you and I don't know about her. That puts us both—especially you—at a disadvantage."

"Why?"

"Because I'm convinced she's ahead of you, but…not in every way."

"She is."

"So you realize that? Well, there's hope for you!"

"Thank you, but…"

"Well, Michael, you're letting the bread get cold! Please take a couple of bites! Why? you ask. Michael, you're a kid, a smart one, and an orphan. And your Great-aunt Steffi is old, and there's Jonas—well, he has limits in some areas, especially in expressing himself to kids. I think, however, I can take you a few important steps farther. You need some secrets of your own, but I'm not sure just what they should be—so you'll have to help me. As I said, I'll respond to whatever you ask. We all have knowledge that's private to us, and to God, of course. But I think you need some new things to think about, and perhaps unfortunately, very quickly. I can be faulted for telling you what to do, but I can't be faulted for responding to your questions."

"But why? Why the urgency?" What had he missed?

"Serious trouble lies ahead," she offered. "Jonas has shared that three people may have to quickly leave and you're one of them. Where? I'm not sure. Nor am I sure that Jonas knows either.

"Oh, and it also involves a wonderful girl that we both love."

"Love?" When no response broke the sudden silence, he continued. "Can you tell me about girls…women?"

"Oh my…yes I can. And we'll include in that a bit about the world—their world, this world—in which they and we all share. And let me say, I have absolute confidence in Sally. She can teach you as well. But remember, she's a 'first-friend' to that mysterious girl I've alluded to."

"A 'first friend'?" Michael asked. "What's that?"

73

"The term, Michael, is said to have come from the Pennacooks. The last five known men of this North American Indian tribe gave everything they had to keep a village of European colonists from starving one winter. Then the five disappeared as quickly as they'd come and were never seen again. All this was totally unexpected."

"Mrs. Crandel, since you've told me this, will you be a first-friend to me?"

"Oh my, that's totally unexpected also! Is there no man who—"

"There is none," Michael interrupted, "and I'm still not sure what I'm asking...but, regardless, I want you to be my first-friend. Will you do that?"

"You must really love this girl!"

Michael forced his face to be expressionless.

"Oh my," she repeated, "but since you're so hard up and time may be short, I will accept. "But you must trust me completely and play by my rules!"

"Agreed. I will do that. And what else does that mean?" He determined to conclude with a question.

"And you'll have to permit me to share certain confidences with Sally, and perhaps with Jonas, but I'll treasure and keep our secrets as private as possible? Is that all right?"

"You may do that."

"And you really trust me, never having met me before?"

"Yes."

"Why?"

"Because I may not have time not to."

Michael tilted his head down in a slight bow.

"Michael, that is your last formal bow. Your karate days are over. Forever. I need 'a few things brought down from the attic.' The attic—that's your and my cover if we need it. No one will need to know anything else. And, of course, God will be nearby listening. And we'll also

74

invite Him to be part of our conversation."

"Mrs. Crandel, you probably don't know" — he paused to collect the right words — "but my great-aunt Steffi died yesterday evening. We're having a burying at 4 o'clock today. I need to get back soon."

"Oh Michael, why didn't you tell me sooner?"

"Ma'am, it didn't come up and, well, our talking about everything else helped more than you realize."

"Then come back at 10 tomorrow morning."

"I'll be here ma'am, and I won't advertise our meeting except I'll tell Jonas."

CHAPTER 8

The Watch On The Wall

Place: Harwell's office
Time: **Day 330** *(the next day) Tuesday, 4 PM*

Once again, Harwell had asked his adopted son to come, not to the living room, but his office. Michael said he could make it at four, and though on time, apparently he was early for the minister. He sat silently in the familiar visitor's chair, staring outside at the strange, silo-like steel water tower farther up the hill behind the parsonage.

And while he waited, he had time to think. A lot had happened in the last 24 hours:

Great-aunt Steffi's Funeral

First, there'd been the funeral in the late afternoon on Monday.

After leaving The Hotel Crandel, he'd hurried to the house where he and Great-aunt Steffi had lived. He'd joined Sally in giving the downstairs a once-over for whoever might soon arrive.

Twenty had actually come, a few with picnic baskets of simple food for those who would linger and talk after the service. Sally had made Steffi surprisingly presentable in her best dress and since there was no one else to do it, Michael had laid her in the coffin he'd made.

His stomach had ached.

Yet since he knew that only unwanted pity was gained by acting weak, he'd made himself be kind and talk briefly with several he barely knew, and especially those who seemed deeply moved at her passing. Triana had arrived with Jonas, but had hung close to her foster father, matter-of-factly kissing Michael on the cheek at the proper time, and disappearing soon after the service. He was surprised to see both Amos and Esther Crandel. "God be with you, Michael," Amos had offered. "Esther's looking forward to tomorrow." Mrs. Crandel had played the perfect "grandmother," which she was not, and had shown no sign of her new friendship with him. Still, as one time she'd glanced his way he noticed her eyes could still twinkle with kindness behind real tears.

Harwell's words had been brief, but moving. Afterwards others present fell to covering the lowered coffin with dirt he'd so carefully piled on a tarpaulin next to the grave in the backyard.

Rejecting offers to spend the night elsewhere, he'd remained alone for the first time in his great-aunt's, now his own, house. He felt wooden, hollow, empty.

"See me at four o'clock tomorrow," Harwell whispered to him.

He'd gone to bed exhausted and slept soundly.

At Esther Crandel's – Day 2 (Tuesday)

Finally, the next day arrived. As Michael sat in his father's office and watched the late afternoon sun melt away, he recalled his second day with Esther Crandel that ended only an hour earlier. Aside from the Sunday attack, it had been his most unusual morning ever—since the visit of EMP, that is.

First, there'd been no extra duties at home for the first time he could remember. Morning had never been noisy, but the new quiet had seemed to signal a new turn in his life had come. Still, after carefully dressing behind his closed bedroom door as always, and eating nothing, he'd made his way to the Hotel Crandel.

As he now waited in Jonas's office, he could still crisply recall details of the day before.

He'd arrived at the hotel at 10 AM sharp, and Esther Crandel had begun with toast, eggs, cups of tea, and *The Watch on the Wall*. He could remember it all almost word for word, partly because of what she'd taught him there.

It had gone like this:

"Please write nothing, Michael," she'd begun. "Paper can be taken away or lost. Electronic information can be cut off as we know too well. But as long as you have the cave of your mind, you can dig into the riches that you've buried there. Imagine please, a large pocket watch with numbers circling the dial—not a digital one—hanging from a wall."

And without questioning he did.

"Now, Michael, look at '1' on the watch and think about God. There is one God over everything. Now imagine a picture and don't worry if it looks ridiculous; in fact the sillier the better as you will see. Then associate this picture, not a picture of God by the way, but with something to remind you of God, who perhaps smiles at your, and my, weak understanding of how real, omnipotent, and caring He is." She had stopped and looked at him. "I'm serious, Michael, trust me. Just let go and let your mind fly!"

Once again, it had been time to play along. So he did. He pictured a gigantic, birthday cake with a thick, tall, single lighted candle on top which rose high and lit up the whole sky so anyone looking at it was almost blinded. This would stand for one God. He felt ridiculous.

"Is it okay to imagine a…"

"Stop!" she'd said. "Your picture is private, yours alone to represent not what it is, but what it stands for. Ready?" she'd continued. He'd nodded. "Now for '2' on your watch. Create a picture to represent the two basic sources of knowledge God has given us: (1) Divine words, mainly the Bible, and (2) the natural world that we can informally observe and study by science. Now, I know we learn by thinking, talking, reading, and such, but I'm talking about basic *sources*."

His imagination had leaped ahead so much it surprised him.

Almost instantly he'd created a Roman numeral 2, or "II," with the II drawn as two pillars with an open Bible on the top of one, a framed picture of a Grand Canyon cliff with conspicuous oversized fossils showing in the rock layers on top of each other.

"What's the point here?" he'd said. "I can remember these things without pictures."

"Of course you can. These are easy but important," she'd replied. "I see you are catching on. Now the fun begins. Here is a learning I want you to picture at '3,' and be sure to include 3 of something in it: *'Everyone comes from somewhere, so expect some baggage.'*"

Before he'd realized it, an attractive girl with a blank face had flashed into his mind. She'd stood on railroad tracks that disappeared into a point straight behind her. She had two suitcases in her right hand one suitcase in the left, making 3 altogether.

"Do you have your picture?" she'd asked.

"Yes."

"Good, now hold onto it while I share my picture, but don't copy it. Pictures that represent ideas can vary greatly, and my creation will be an inferior 'hook' to your own. Here's mine: I see a long-haired girl smiling, and dragging three chests end-to-end behind her down a dirt road raising dust so they're barely visible and pretending that people can see her but not the trunks. Do you get what we're doing?"

"Yes, I get the idea, but what does that mean?"

"One thing is that beautiful girls may be thrilling, but be around them long enough and things will appear that you don't like or can't understand and will lead to difficulty. The same is true about how you appear to them. You must understand that will happen, and be open to some surprises and changes, and not let it unsettle you."

"Everyone?" he'd asked.

"I said 'everyone,' Michael. Now realize I'm trying to get you to focus on a particular issue and we may not have much time."

"But wait. Is all baggage bad?"

"A good question, Michael! No, of course not. But baggage from the past is there—from everyone. Before you make a big commitment, you must discover what you can put up with, or build upon, or not abide with at all."

In his mind, the girl on the tracks had two bags of good baggage, one of bad. He had to think more about this.

"Now let's curve down to the '4.' Attach that to something that says: *'Nobody cares for it like you.'*"

This game had been silly, but doable. And it certainly took his mind away from the day before. It was unmistakable that his new first-friend was taking this very seriously. So must he. Who knows what it might mean? All this foolishness could...could hardly have been an accident.

This picture had been harder to make. Since he liked railroad tracks, he would use them again. In his mind he'd created a locomotive pulling four boxcars along tracks. It had just pulled into a station. All four boxcars were a brilliant white, highly visible—and memorable. A large black "IT" was painted on the side of each boxcar. Also, he'd put a person standing before the train and another after the train, both looking away from the train as if the train weren't there. The picture was ridiculous—but vivid!

"Got it!" he'd declared. "But what does this mean?"

"Michael, for almost everything you personally treasure, others won't share your passion for it. They simply won't. That's the way life

All four boxcars were a brilliant white, highly visable...

is. They'll be busy caring about their own things. And, incidentally, you don't really care about their things either, so don't be too disappointed. That's normal. On a rare case this rule may be broken, but don't count on it. And if that happens, it might be part of a foundation for real love, or romance, and that's hard to explain. But don't count on that either! Real love and romance depends mainly on other things."

"An example of this, please?" he'd asked.

"Okay, take Amos. He learned that I loved quilt shows. Really loved them. Somehow on his own he would find a show, or a display, that I'd missed, or while we were together at a show he would point out certain features, or idiosyncrasies, or fabric choices that I would overlook, though he never picked up a needle in his life. How he did this I never quite figured out. Perhaps because once he was a materials engineer, a job I never really understood, by the way."

"Another—different—kind of example, please."

She'd paused and looked deeply into his eyes.

"A boy giving up everything, maybe even his good sense, to follow a new girl he hardly knows who's determined to go to a strange new place that's important to her but brand-new to him, and who's willing to die beside her if both end up having made a mistake."

"But I do know her," he'd blurted back.

"I see," she'd replied without further comment.

How foolish! He'd blown his cover. He didn't really know her. He was grateful she hadn't followed up on that.

"Number 5. Ready? Tie this down with an absurd little picture: *'Little things matter most.'*"

"Got it," he'd replied almost immediately, surprising himself. He'd quickly pictured five little pieces of white thread on a dark black carpet with a frantic woman pushing a vacuum coming up behind. When Mrs. Crandel had seemed to think he'd gone too fast, she quickly offered an example.

"An honest compliment can say 'I saw, or heard about, what you did and I thought it was great!' This can do wonders for someone and even be remembered for years. It costs nothing. Seeing and doing the little thing that matters, especially for someone you love, is freighted with meaning. And *not* doing certain little things." That was more like his not dropping white threads on the rug, or if he had, not to forget to remove them. "Of course, the little things that really matter varies from person to person in ways that are easy to overlook."

And for '6' which was *"Discover and speak the proper love language"* he'd pictured a face with a large mouth with sixxxxxx, x's or kisses, coming out of it aimed at a smiling girl. Discussion had followed about the different love languages people know and use. Mrs. Crandel had identified six: (1) *talking* using lips and ears, which involves both saying and hearing the right things; (2) *spending time together,* "elbow to elbow," as she put it; (3) *giving gifts,* small or big to the other person; (4) *performing service,* whether or not it was expected by someone; (5) *touching,* hand to hand or body to body; and (6) creating and embellishing the right *background tone.* The tone — she underlined the word in the air — a person displays really matters.

Since he'd never really thought about this sort of thing before, his picture had to be truly ridiculous. He would change it later. But erase this mental picture? It was already rooted in the "cave of his mind."

Then she'd paused.

He'd determined to keep continuous eye contact. And he did.

"Good people," Mrs. Crandel had continued, "whether you're in love with them or not, can be so different in what matters to them and sometimes can surprise you by seeming to be nearly 'monolingual.' That is, they almost always use only one love language.

"Here's a key for you: *The girl you love will most likely value one language above all the rest; however, she will probably also depend on a second language, as well as be aware of the other four. Discover her first language,*

learn it well, and speak it every day. Also, go out of your way to try out the
other languages which may have effects that surprise you both. Look after her
every day. You owe it to her, yourself, and God. Store what you learn in
one of your watches."

"Watches?" Michael had said. "There's more than one watch?"

"Many, Michael! We've just begun!"

" 'Tone,' " he had said. "You said nothing about that. Could you..."

"Michael with tone there's so much more! Much, much more. That
would take weeks...We've no time to..."

"But the different tones, ma'am, the issues? Can you at least name
them?"

Pause.

Her eyes had drilled back.

He'd not look away. His boldness seemed to have taken her by surprise. It certainly had him. He'd smiled. Her edge seemed to soften.

"I'll just mention six, of many, and I must go fast."

"I'm ready."

"First, without your making any picture at all, shape the words that
come out of your mouth. May they be finely 'turned,' honest, as few
as necessary — although sometimes they must be many, as now — and
let them all pass through your brain. Sometimes, words must be held
back. It's not a girly thing, and the girl we both love will value that.
You already seem good at this, not embarrassed at all, so that's in your
favor. And, of course, I know where some of that came from: the karate
training we share."

"But—"

"Now hang a large 6-pointed tin Star of David on the loop of the
6 on your watch," she said, ignoring him. "Use a Christmas tree orna-
ment hook. Can you accept that?"

"I can."

"Now there's a hole at each point, so with hooks you can hang pieces of paper there. And make the tin star bigger if the papers get in the way of each other."

"Done, ma'am."

"There will be 6 numbers on this circular attachment. Space them equally."

"Done, ma'am."

"Now watch me carefully. Start at 2 and go clockwise. This should help with each of your pictures."

She'd begun with **Tone 1.**

She'd stood at attention and extended her arms straight out. Then she raised and curled one arm up and with her fingers touched down to her head. She turned her head to the left looked at her extended fingers. "This is a 'P' lying down. She extended her arms again and curled the other arm down and touched her head. Again she looked at her extended fingers. This is another P. Remember this. Then she extended both hands again. Now imagine a large purple capital P standing on each palm. The standing P's are your picture. Got it, Michael?"

"Yes, ma'am."

"One P is for 'private' and the other is for 'public.' Normal, healthy people differ sharply on what they consider private and public, often with very strong feelings. You must find and carefully honor those differences between the two of you."

"But how…"

"Here's **Tone 2,**" she'd declared, ignoring him. "Hang up this paper at 4." Then she'd turned to her left and with her arms made a large C. "With a flat palm hold it up. With your other hand hold it at the top." The song "YMCA" flashed into his mind. But it was really more like she was embracing a huge ball. Then she'd turned to the other side and did the same thing, making a backwards C. With the backward C her arms had become 'wiggly' or not at rest.

"Done, ma'am. It looks like a large C at rest and another large C that's backwards and antsy. Am I right?"

She'd nodded.

"And," he'd added, "if I put these C's back to back I have sort of an X with 4 points for the Number 4."

"Very good Michael, I didn't even 'see' that. And the 'proper' C stands for 'Clean' and the 'backwards one' stands for 'cluttered.' Two people are usually not the same about this. They can argue forever over how they care for the material things around them. One may want a 'few' things 'perfectly in place' and the other may want 'many' and thrive on 'tangling things up' with each other. But if they really love each other they will face this and work out this difference. You must lead her in this, adjust if necessary, and honor her."

"I take it Mrs. Crandel" — he'd done a quick scan of the room — "you and Mr. Crandel are both 'Cleans' or 'Cleanies.'"

Mrs. Crandel had offered a thin smile. "*Things are often not what they first seem,*' Michael. This truth, by the way, merits its own number somewhere. Sometimes I think Amos is happiest when he works in a sea of paper, books, tools, and metal parts in his office downstairs. But when he comes upstairs, he often tells me how wonderful I am and he doesn't leave tracks. When I go downstairs I hold the railing to keep from tripping over things and killing myself. He has everything everywhere. In this case I led our working this out. And especially in the common areas we share. And believe me, Michael, this matters!

"Now what have we done? PP and CC..."

"Private-public and clean-cluttered," he'd muttered to himself.

"**Tone 3** — keep moving, Michael! Watch. Paper 3 hangs at 6." She'd stood at attention in front of him and suddenly wrapped her arms around herself, bowed her head and closed her eyes. "That stands for **S**AFE." Then she extended her arms and softened her stance. "This is **O**PEN. There are times when you must keep the other person safe, and times you must allow the other person to be open to risk and danger. So what? So 'SO,' Safe, Open; Safe-Open. **SO, S**afe, **O**pen. Both extremely important. But no more time to talk!"

He'd no time to draw, so he'd simply put a large SO on his imaginary paper. He'd draw a picture later.

"**Tone 4** is this": She'd dropped to her knees drawing a huge capital "**F**" in the air. Then standing and pointing towards him she'd drawn a much smaller "**f**" in the air. "These both stand for faithfulness.

"The big F is for God and the smaller f is for the one you love. Both are terribly important. And when they conflict you have to work that out." In his mind 'F' and 'f' became stick figures holding hands at 8 on his clock.

"Michael, you have to be getting bored!" she'd then said.

"Not at all," he'd replied.

She'd paused, staring. He'd smiled back.

"Now **Tone 5**." Puffing her cheeks, she'd pretended she was blowing up a balloon with lighter than air gas, which is impossible of course, which she then tied on a string. Michael had resisted smiling. She'd then held the imaginary string as she watched the balloon rise. Then she slowly with her fingers on the other hand acting as scissors, she'd cut the string and watched the balloon drift out of sight. "This one's about **H**olding on and **L**etting go. When I was young this was very hard for me. When you're together with someone special, there's a proper time to 'hold on' and 'let go' about many things. And this may bring pain or joy, sometimes a mixture of the two. But it's normal and has to happen as we get older and events affect our lives.

For his picture he'd had a woman holding a balloon in one hand and an open pair of scissors that looked like an **X**, the Roman numeral for 10 in the other.

"And here's **Tone 6**. I'm not a figure in this one. Picture yourself in a car at a **R**ail**R**oad crossing. Trains race across your path of vision. Cars can wait, go ahead, or turn around. But your job is to cross the tracks.

As you do, God wants you to be **R**eal because He's created you in his image with real desires and feelings, real abilities, real responsibilities, real hopes, and real fears. It's wrong to ignore them. But it's wrong to misuse them. He also wants us to be **R**ight. In fact he commands it."

"How do I do that?" he'd asked.

"I don't know," she'd replied. "But Michael you're now a man, like it or not. And in the back of your mind you're hoping to become a married one. Figure it out. That's what you have to do. The only thing I can say is stay on the road and deal with the danger as trains come and go. The 'tone' you display as you decidedly cross the tracks is how she will see you. This is terribly important. Sometimes you will be terrified, but rein in your fear and move ahead carefully — sometimes slowly and sometimes very quickly.."

It was interesting how in all this he'd seemed to forget himself. How easy it had seemed to review the pictures he'd quickly made and hung on the points of his Star of David! **PP, CC, SO, Ff, HoLe**, and **RR**. He'd gone over them, again and again. These letters could bring them to mind to think about later. They would be easy to add to. And what was he doing? Winding his 'watches'? No! Never! They were "clocks"! His **clocks**. He might not understand them, but forget them? Never!

"Michael, I didn't expect this," she'd confessed. "You seem such a quick learner. I'm honored that you trust me, but remember I'm just one person and I can be…"

"It's not wrong that I'm here!" he interrupted. When she raised her eyebrows, he smiled. "It was RR, ma'am, and I crossed the tracks quickly. And you're my first-friend."

"And you sense that our time together may be very short," she'd replied.

"I see that 'service' is your first language, ma'am," he'd offered.

"With 'talking' right behind it," she'd replied.

Before he'd left the Hotel Crandel, though he'd not written a word, he had four clocks on the wall in his mind—an ordinary one, and one red, one white, and one blue—that only he knew about and could see, and on them were 48 different observations or truths that he could think about or discuss with the person who gave them to him—as long as he could remember them. There'd been no mention of Triana by name and no holds barred when even private matters arose. What was a little embarrassment if God knew what was being said anyway and soon you'd never see the person again? Would he ever have another chance like this? Well, tomorrow he'd hoped. And when asked, she'd agreed to a third visit.

"After all, Michael, we've just begun!" she'd declared. "And I must show you some more things upstairs."

"The tea was great ma'am," he'd declared.

A sound at the office door where he sat ended his musing.

Harwell Finally Arrives

The doorknob turned, and Harwell entered.

"Sorry I'm late," he offered, "but these are unusual days."

"They certainly are, sir!" Michael replied.

But still no sign of Triana.

CHAPTER 9

The Space Goose

Place: Same (Harwell's office)
*Time: **Day 330** Tuesday, 5 PM. Continues immediately.*

For an hour Michael had been waiting. The solitude had been welcome, however. He, with Sally's and Jonas's help, had set up everything for a respectful burial. For the first time in more than two years, he'd no more responsibilities for his great-aunt. That was over. He'd been faithful and God had helped him with that.

And his two times at the hotel with his new secret first-friend had given him plenty to think about.

"Michael, could we bow our heads in prayer—silently?" asked Harwell.

"Of course." Squinting his eyes, Michael watched the second hand of his adopted father's wind-up Timex desk clock make a complete rotation. Closing his eyes, he waited for what had to be another minute.

Before he left the room he realized that his life was about to completely change. He just knew it. Did God give that kind of knowing to a person in quiet moments before praying aloud with someone else? Did Esther Crandel's words apply here? If something "real" arose, would he be *real* and face it the *right* way, of course, avoiding any collision with passing trains? And if change were necessary, could he *let go of the balloon he held* whatever that was, and accept the *right* thing that came next? How silly it would seem if anyone could see the pictures behind his thinking! He shivered when thoughts of Triana flashed in and out of his mind. Yes, his private thoughts were "private" and Jonas was the only one now nearby. But would he soon go "public" with his musings?

"O God," said Jonas, breaking the silence and strangely echoing his thoughts, "may we do the *right* thing, and give me—give us—confidence about it. Amen."

Michael shivered again.

At that moment, by providence or accident, Sally entered with a tray of bread and jelly in one hand and a pot of tea in the other. She left the moment she set everything down. How much tea could he drink in a day! But the bread he welcomed.

"Michael, talk to me about Triana…Is she special to you?"

"Special?...Yes."

"Can you…uh…add to that? Has there been any problem over the last couple of days? I…I'm not sure if I'm asking as a father, a minister, or what. Do you *care* for her? I think you know what I mean."

Just as Michael had finished arranging some appropriate words, the door burst open. Sally returned and stood with her hands on her hips.

"Michael, Jonas, saints p'serve us! I heard you earlier! You're both startin' up again! Would you two stop this circlin' roun' playin' games with each other!"

"Sally!" Harwell stood and glared. Michael was shocked. Never had he seen Jonas like this.

"Jonas, stop interruptin'! I'm not done!" Nor had he seen Sally like that. "Jonas, Michael loves Triana and Triana loves him, LOVES 'n' that's that. And you know what I mean! I'm sayin' it, I am, so's both of you can recognize it if your heads are so fogged, 'cause, Jonas, if what you 'n' I just heard together before you came in here is true, neither of us might be able to say anythin' by tomorrow! And if what I heard inside here is true, 'bout doin' the right thing 'n' all, then I'm God's five-minute angel to help you git movin' along. Now I'm done, I am, with three minutes to spare, so get back to your whatever. Rrrrr. Men!"

"Women!" muttered Jonas.

Slam. The two were alone again.

"I'd fire her, Michael, except for one thing."

"One thing? Help me, my 'head's fogged.' "

"She might actually leave…"

Michael buried his head in his hands and struggled not to laugh. "Five-minute angel!" he chuckled.

"I'm glad someone can laugh, Michael. But please understand, this may prove to be the hardest day of my life. Remember Smith?"

No one else, including Triana, could turn so fast without flashing a signal.

"How can I forget!"

"Well, he returned as we told him to, but with terrible news. The wall has been broken through on the northern side. He and his family and nearby friends have been run out of their homes by starving families from Binghamton. And Binghamton itself was having trouble from farther north. 'Just couldn't shoot,' he said. A bit ironic, wouldn't you say? Now Smith and his extended family have fled here, armed, but peacefully and are now under our protection, and are grateful refugees in our church basement. And others have come with them. People are beginning to set guard watches around their houses, ready to shoot anyone who invades our town without permission.

"And what terrible decisions that might call for!

"Now there's the water tower. The tower that two years ago you so carefully painted in that white suit designed to protect you from the supposed radiation that signs warned about.

92

"The time has come to tell you about what's in that former water tower. I'll be as brief as I can. And, yes, it will sound...unusual. Are you ready?" Michael nodded. "Then buckle up.

"First, I in no way sought any connection with this. None," Jonas emphasized.

"It all began soon after I came here four years ago. Out of nowhere I was suddenly and secretly approached at my front door by a direct emissary of the then President of the United States, who was an old college friend—though this wasn't common knowledge.

" 'Why this visit?' " I asked.

" 'We know about this old water tower,' " he replied. 'And the President knows about you!'

"When the emissary sensed my suspicion, he smiled and enabled me immediately to make a direct phone call to the Oval Office.

"Without that connection, nothing further would have happened.

"With hardly a personal word of greeting, the President told me that 'a troubled time' that he could not discuss had come to Washington, and with it a sudden need to do something highly unusual. He himself had to deal with a delicate matter: He had to (1) destroy a highly classified tiny, almost finished secret spaceship called the *Elphlander* that contained unparalleled technology. For 'several' years it had been secretly built in modules, partially assembled, stored, and hidden away. By whom and for whom I, and I believe even he, had no idea."

He paused.

"Are you with me, Michael?"

"I am nowhere else," said Michael. He determined to stay expressionless, though his body felt as hard as wood.

"Or (2) he could put it somewhere out of sight—at his own risk." Harwell continued. "Oh…and those housing it, namely me if I agreed, would be able, with a digital code, to destroy the tower and anything

93

"Or he could put it somewhere out of sight..."

in it completely.

"The shape and technology of this ship — except for the critical propulsion system — had spun off the small X-37 A, B, and C space vehicles developed at the turn of the millennium at Boeing's Phantom X-Works. This newly branded X-67 was so revolutionary and beyond anything remotely familiar to astrophysicists and NASA engineers, that he and others feared a panic, fueled by hysteria about a foreign invasion, or worse, an alien invasion from a code-named world called 'Elphia,' a world rumored to be scientifically superior to ours, or at least it once was, and of course 'impossibly far' from Earth to ever travel to.

"The tiny ship, with four small individual, almost claustrophobic pods, that could be loaded with special food and supplies, contained ingenious minimal-exercise equipment and an electronic library categorically unlike anything seen at Cape Kennedy or elsewhere. It was said to be capable of a nearly noiseless electromagnetic lift-off, and needed only to rise 31 miles from Earth's surface to a thinner atmosphere for its programmed electronic gyroscopes and computers to smoothly kick into play for the rest of its journey.

"Quite frankly, according to our best engineering that's an absurdity. The good news, if there is any, is that some re-entry chute can be expelled for a 'safe' return to Earth if something goes wrong. For example, it's back to Earth if the first thrust upward fails to disambiguate the final figures that send the Elphlander into the proper higher dimensional tunnel erasing friction — think of unproven teleporting — that's said to require only minimal human pilot correction at any point. The bad news is that because of distance, a one-way trip to Elphia is wired in. *Once it leaves the power of Earth's gravity it's said to be impossible to return to Earth.*

"And, yes, Michael, 'Marcus the pilot,' as we've referred to him, is a young pilot-trained avionics genius who's grown up studying about this, and is said to be better equipped than anyone in using the new electronic gyroscopes, that replaced their older bulky metal predecessors to focus any human 'steering,' or correcting that may be required.

"And though I don't know him well, and nothing negative about him, he's eager to attempt this mission. And, Michael, he's a 'certified genius,' a *human earthling* a decade older than you who obviously carries DNA from Earth."

Harwell paused to let this detail sink in.

"Perhaps this tiny transporter in our tower belongs in the hanger alongside Howard Hughes's 1947 WWII 'Spruce Goose,' that huge wooden plane, that Hughes himself was forced to fly — and eventually did for a single mile — to avoid imprisonment for misusing Federal funds during WWII. And, as you may know, the explaining of all that is another political tangle that defies belief.

"The science behind the telescoping of light-years of distance into days, or hours, of travel is beyond me, and everyone I know, though perhaps not to a growing number of secret *zocentrists* who split off from some biocentrists, the latter of which include some Christians, by the way."

Michael twisted so hard in his chair that the arm cracked.

"There's more, Michael. These are the folks who insist that the only way to *logically* reconcile the conflicting madness of small particle physics with 'ordinary' Einstein physics is to *begin with mind*, instead of with *matter* and its almost infinitely tiny particles that misbehave so badly that they hardly could — on their own — 'accidentally,' make themselves into a brain to house a mind.

"In other words, something *we* think of as 'mind' had to precede what we think of as matter. The 'Lego pieces' from which stars and planets and people are made did not just 'poof' come from nowhere and randomly and accidentally assemble themselves into much larger and more complex pieces that eventually would include us humans who can talk about them.

"They had to be made and put together by a mind that didn't come from those self-same particles. And, incidentally, nothing says this better—though in general terms only—than the first sentence in the Bible: 'In the beginning God created the Heavens and the Earth.'

"Now where am I going with this?

"Some 'suggest,' theoretically, that leads to the possibility that a 'real traveler,' *with a certain limited amount of 'real baggage' around him,* can somehow mentally 'push through time,' that is 'old-fashioned relative time,' *compressing it* and breaking through Einstein's old-fashioned wall with its 'almost absolute speed limit'—the speed of light."

Through all this Michael felt glued to the chair he was sitting on. His scientist father would never share such things casually, yet it was scary that Michael seemed so clueless about this! He would not lose eye contact. Surprisingly, he kept his composure and felt no fear.

"Of course, Michael, you can join the long line of those who call this nonsense." Harwell smiled. Michael noticed beads of sweat on his father's forehead.

"And you, Jonas, what do you think? Where does this take us?"

"It 'takes' us to, or leaves us with, what to do with the Elphlander, or 'Space Goose,' that's said to be able to do things never done before—at least near Earth.

"And that decision is in my hands.

"Michael, let me put it this way: (1) Most scientists would say what I've just told you makes no sense whatsoever. (2) Nonetheless, they also must admit that physicists are all over the place on trying to explain small-particle physics which so far, *they* say, has wiggled out of their grasp. (3) Tying together everything we've learned about the universe *into one logical package* is still as illusive as a so-called 'Theory of

Everything' that very few think is possible...or at least simple enough for humans to ever understand.

"So Michael, let me turn a bit and ask you a question. Why are we having this conversation? *And please start at the beginning. The very beginning.* But be brief."

"The 'beginning'...uh...scientists have found evidence that billions of years ago there was a big explosion and simple molecules somehow formed, then stars, our sun, and Earth and other planets. Then... then on...on Earth simple animals and plants formed, then more complicated ones, then eventually people, people that have problems and possibilities like we're having now."

"Nicely said, Michael, but I noticed you've not mentioned causes for how this came about."

"O...kay...I believe God somehow did it. You've told me he made the molecules that eventually became us. And he specially made Adam and Eve. Just how, I'm not sure."

"I agree, Michael, but I'd add—and I think you'll agree—that the Bible is not just some made-up myth, but with its obvious limited language it is still surprisingly concordant with much that was later discovered by science, and by psychology, and by the reasoning of new philosophy. And, although the Bible isn't a science textbook, it helps us understand that God, must be the 'original Mind,' that was involved in how everything was made, even suggesting that the Bible as well as the geologic record shows the sequence of many things that came to be.

"The naturalist, on the other hand, automatically dismisses God or the idea of a God having a hand in anything, believing—without proof—that a bunch of tiny particles just appeared from a big explosion of something from somewhere. This led to millions of random accidents among atoms and molecules with no overall purpose, that on their own in a series of steps changed the tiny particles into the persons saying and hearing these words right now. Of course, with a 'multiverse' — or an infinite number of, unprovable, universes — anything is possible, ruling out God, of course. That takes a lot of faith, I'd say."

"More faith…more faith, Jonas, than what's needed, to believe in the Space Goose?"

"A good question, Michael, and a logical one! Sorry, I can't answer it to most people's satisfaction."

"And doesn't that bother you, Jonas?"

"No and yes. No, it doesn't bother me that you ask — or even doubt. That's natural at times if you dare to think and be honest where there's real confusion and unprecedented possibilities…And yes, the science and the possibilities of what lies ahead does bother me."

"Such as?" Michael interrupted.

"Such as (1) the ins and outs of particle behavior; (2) the posited existence of and nature of qubits, quantum computing, and strings; (3) extra-dimensionality at work today; and (4) in the particular aiming of a cannon at something less than a speck into unempty space that is both filled and unfilled — things like that."

"Details," offered Michael.

Harwell laughed.

He continued. "The technology of this beautiful and intricately designed shuttle, headed not to a satellite but to an exoplanet beyond our solar system is as clear to me as a flashdrive containing a library of books would be considered an absurdity to Benjamin Franklin, who nonetheless, if he had the tools, wouldn't hesitate to try to unlock and open the library door to learn more. Simple tests that could be performed in the tower behind where we live have been checked over and over and are said to work flawlessly. But there've been no tests outside the tower walls.

"Whether the Space Goose will lift off out of the tower or even an inch off its pad and head anywhere else is conjecture.

"I suppose, we can be grateful to the UFOlogists whose tabloid nonsense has silenced much speculation as to what our tower might hold. That is until now.

"The thing I remember most is this: As the President who knew me lay dying, later in a brief note told me he couldn't bear to destroy what could become a thing of beauty and distinctive and unparalleled technology that fell into his hands as several, he said, had encouraged him to do. Nor could he release even knowledge of it at that time because of the panic he sensed it could cause. So 'through the back door,' it fell off his shoulders into my hands."

"Why you?" Michael asked.

"I can't say. One reason might be that the President and I share the same faith, and as surprising as it may sound, we had two of the same teachers who instilled in us a passion for science. He knew I was open to what I didn't know, and that I could be trusted. And, remember, he insisted that the tower be equipped with explosives so that, if necessary, it could be quickly destroyed by my pushing a coded set of buttons. And I have a personal, notarized, signed letter from the President, vaguely written, but thanking me for help in this matter. 'If all this gets out of hand, Jonas,' he told me, 'this may get you only 20 years instead of the chair. As for me, I'll be safely Upstairs, tuning my harp and waiting for your arrival.' " Harwell paused and strode to the window, Michael following. "*Son*, I have the ability to blow everything in that tower to bits.

"The most amazing thing I've ever witnessed, Michael, was the ingenious transfer of the *Elphlander* to our tower. First, came the preposterous claim that 'parts from a classified aircraft' from Fort Drum in New York had fallen and precisely landed on the top of our retired, built in 1920, steel water tower, smashing the roof, requiring repair or replacement by our government that caused the damage. And since the tower, close to becoming a national historic marker because it was built on a site that was part of the underground railroad, that belonged to the church, I 'happened' to be the one to be informally approached about resolving this issue.

"Of course, they had to temporarily 'seed' the ground around the tower with rods that produced tiny harmless, but measurable amounts of radiation so as to claim some minor 'radioactive damage' — a story passed around locally — so the area could be 'fenced off,' and 'repair-men' in special suits, could enter, after which they could secretly take their suits off to more easily 'clear away damage,' rebuild, and wait for that one pitch-black night when the main part of the Elphlander could arrive and be lowered by helicopter through the deconstructed roof, and carefully be set on a special launching pad on the floor of the tower. That occurred, and the craft was systematically put in finished form, and an observatory-type sliding roof was installed to replace the old one. At that time some worker referred to it as the 'Space Goose' and to insiders the name stuck.

"Then, nearly all of the radioactive rods were removed, though the barbed fence with its razor wire remained to discourage the curious.

"Now, Michael, yes, the science is bewildering here, so what else do I have to consider? Here is where I think you can begin to understand.

"First, there are the two fairytale-sounding stories, *Death in a Tavern*, carefully told to Triana by Igneal; and *The Secret of Zareba*, which independently I located years ago, and you, Michael, found in my office — and it was both of these, so similar and related, though obtained far apart from each other, that led to the alleged cheating episode with Marvin Cample. *And these suggest strongly, that some of Triana's ancestors were Emryssites from planet Emryss, and that she was actually the descendant of a royal family there.*

102

"Of course, scientifically, we've no knowledge of such a place, much less that humans like us might live there, and even more, that there might be a way to travel from there to here…or to any other planet.

"Very significant 'details,' Michael.

"And then there are the two stories, *The Fourth Prince* and *Inside the Hollow Spear*, that Marvin Cample of all people had in his possession. And he obtained them at some yard sale in the Midwest where, as far as he could tell, they might have been earlier obtained, even worked on to some extent as curiosities, by some former retired Tyndale Bible translators. These people, perhaps without heirs, or with no one interested in what non-Biblical work they'd done, abandoned them considering them trash, not realizing that these two stories — though differing sharply in style and perhaps being reworked and modified as often happens to folk stories — *are, according to Cample, uniquely connected to the two stories that arrived in my office and caused your trouble at school.*

"And while Triana certainly had doubts about whether she personally had any real connection to the first two stories I had, the second two provided by Cample had changed that.

"So now this mysterious nearly blind orphan girl, a genius, a language savant, whose memory is almost totally blank about her early years, is largely convinced that **these four stories from Emryss may have a special message for her.**

"And then Igneal, who claimed he'd been hidden away in institutions for his own safety — for who would believe the ravings of such a wild old man — is mysteriously sent to me, and soon after, Triana comes almost anonymously to me with all sorts of government classified protection. And while Sally and Triana tend to Igneal's needs, he reminds Triana, several times that though he's an Elphian — but not related to her — that she is not only a kidnapped Emryssite princess, but that *she also carries Elphian blood.*

"And then comes the bombshell: This Igneal declares that his scientifically superior planet rebelled against what they called the 'God of All Worlds,' and then systematically destroyed every copy of their 'superstitious' I-Rex Code, or Bible, that he says tells a story very similar to our Bible. It even mentions something about a God-Son I think. Now Elphia has fallen into a time of great tragedy, some of it biological, that encouraged those few who were able to escape their planet to do so. Consequently, a few are said to have come here.

"And here's the second bombshell, that lies right at our feet. Though their Bibles, if we can call them that, seem to all be destroyed, one curious prophecy has not gone away: It's common knowledge, he says, that Elphians recognize that *"When the blood of three worlds mingles in a child, a remnant of Elphia, will once again believe."* That unique child is not the God-Son who already came, taught, died, and was resurrected long ago, but an otherwise normal human. And Elphia now is experiencing great calamity, perhaps similar to what we have here, and because they believe the existence of such a child can't be possible, and many, with second thoughts about the God-of-all-Worlds, now believe they have no hope.

"Add to that our present circumstances. The wall of our Territory has been broken through. At any time we could experience the presence of desperate refugees. What they will ask, demand, or simply take remains to be seen. In hours, the preposterous possibility of a trip to Elphia could easily disappear without being attempted."

"Jonas, what does Triana think about all this?" asked Michael. "Think about it *now*? And where is she? Isn't she supposed to be here?"

"I talked with her earlier, Michael. She says she's determined to go. It doesn't help that I read about extreme missionary evangelism this morning. There was a period of time when people so loved God, and took their faith so seriously that they sailed in ships to lands where they knew the Gospel wasn't known. On the way they got sick and died, thanking God they had the privilege to die going to serve Him. When word of this got back to their families, ones that had stayed home prayed, trained, and took the places of those who died before them.

"Then there was the story of two warring Chinese families that finally became Christians, and suddenly reconciled. Overwhelmed by this turn of events, they became so concerned about loving their neighbors, and sharing their faith that they sent their willing teenaged daughters with one-way tickets to towns that had never heard the Gospel to share the faith that had become so precious to them.

"Of course, the Bible says that if people don't want to love and follow Jesus more than family or anything else, they're not worthy of the Kingdom of God.

"Michael, I'm just not sure how I think about that when it comes to practical choices that lie ahead. I think I could find good reasons to prudently postpone such youthful enthusiasm. Running off half-cocked doesn't do anyone any favors."

"Jonas, would you preach that to your congregation?"

Silence.

"Not in those words, Michael. Remember, you're…you're my son."

"Dad, if Triana is going, I'm going with her — to Elphia…or Heaven."

Silence.

"I'm of age, Jonas, and you've already declared me to be a man. *And I'm packed just as you told me to be.*"

"That was for the *possibility* of going, Michael. If…if, say, a sea of armed men came running up the driveway. But Triana is not yet of…"

"Jonas, you've already declared she's a woman…whatever that means."

"Michael, do *you* know what that means?"

Silence.

"Jonas, Triana's not going without me." Michael knew at that moment he'd make a third trip to the Hotel Crandel whether he was expected or not—just as soon as he could.

CHAPTER 10

First Friends' Farewell

Place: *Hotel Crandel*
Time: **Day 331**, *5 PM* *(the next day)*

The next day it was four-thirty before Michael could break away from the parsonage, though he'd sent a message earler.

Meeting him at the door for the third time, Esther Crandel ushered him inside, told him to sit on the sofa, and shooed her husband away. Amos, with a handful of paper, willingly disappeared to the basement. Michael wondered about how the clutter down there really spread itself out, contrasting with Esther's spare décor where he now sat. He looked down and found a steaming cup of tea already at his fingertips. Mrs. Crandel pulled up a straight-backed chair and sat erect. Michael couldn't help but notice her excellent posture.

"Mrs. Crandel, I hope you don't mind another visit. May I ask some more questions?"

"That's what first-friends are for, Michael. I'm on the hook and I'm here. Ask away."

"I've reviewed all four watches, or 'clocks.' I like to call them 'clocks,' though they still seem to hang on the wall by nails, not chains. As I wind them, I'm missing only four of the 48 connections, but I still think I can bring them back if I work at it."

"Well done, Michael. Even if you lose a few connections, there may be good reasons why. God may be protecting you from me! Still, Jerry

Lucas would be proud of you."

"Jerry Lucas?"

"Well, he was a memory expert, though I don't recall him using watches or clocks as devices. And, incidentally, he played your sport but not your position. I'm not surprised you've never heard of him though in the last century he was considered by the NBA as one of the 50 best players in history playing with pro teams you've never heard of, but ending up with the Knicks. He was perhaps the best truly outstanding scholar/athlete."

Michael swallowed hard trying not to choke. Wherever did that come from! Without moving his body he tried to take a deep breath.

"I...I'm not quite in that *league*, or even aware of..."

"Don't tell me what I already know, Michael. And you shouldn't demean yourself unnecessarily. There are thousands of important things that even intelligent people don't know. That's one reason we need to pray daily. God expects that, and He can give us answers to what we need. We can and should look *bold* and *confident*, smacking down the *arrogance* and *cockiness* that can lurk in the shadows. And she will appreciate and respect that.

"Oh...let me add: A reasonable boldness and confidence is a matter of *tone* that should go somewhere on the 6 on your first clock."
Michael smiled and glanced away at the window. In his mind he saw the 6-pointed Star of David suspended there. He would fit it in somewhere. When he looked back a plate with a thick slice of buttered bread was in his lap.

"Ma'am, please, what more can you tell me?"

"Finally a *question*! Remember that. I'll start from there. But perhaps you'll need to 'hang' another clock. A yellow one, perhaps?"

"It's green, already up, and already half full."

"Good for you! It's your wall and your 'clocks' as you prefer to call them. You're the master of them and the only one connected to them. And to keep them, you'll have to remember to regularly 'wind them.' As long as you have your mind, which is probably directly linked to your soul, your clocks are yours forever, adding to, subtracting from, and modifying what you seem to think they should store for you. And if you find something that is wrong, and it can't be corrected, get rid of it.

"Remember that, for I fear our time together is running out."

"But…"

"Let me go on, Michael…Oh my, our cups" — which had appeared earlier — "must be too small! They're already empty." She reached for the teapot and slowly filled each one resting on its saucer. "Now, what do you need to know? …But first, see that small chest by the stairs?"

"I do."

"I may suddenly ask you to move it to that small room upstairs, where we were yesterday. Okay?"

"It is," he quickly replied, again hiding his total bewilderment.

"Now, Michael, may my tone be bold and confident about some details that we ignored yesterday?"

Michael swallowed hard. He gently nodded.

"Okay then, may I invade your space," Mrs. Crandel continued, "and reserve 10, 11, and 12 on your new green clock, and create pictures there that you can later discard or rearrange to your liking? I won't do this again."

"You may."

"At '10' a large thin '1' and a large and thick '0' sit side by side on a dining room chair that you're looking at sideways. The back and the seat of the chair make an 'L' that stands for 'LOVE.' Can you picture that?"

"I can."

"The '1' stands for 'on' or 'yes' and is ordinary; and the '0' which happens to be thick and dark stands for 'off' or 'no.' "

"Got it. A 1 and 0, like in digital computer language."

"Correct." Lifting her cup, she took a sip. "Now let me divert. We've talked about 'little things,' your #5 for whatever you drew on your first clock."

"That's right!" said Michael, lifting his cup and already finding it empty. "But what if the little things I put there don't work?" Perhaps he could redirect where this might be going.

"Oh, many little things you think will work, won't, Michael, and women, good, good women value many different things. In this special case can you share with me your secret picture about this?"

"Yes. A…vacuum cleaner is attacking 5 short pieces of light thread on a black carpet, sucking them up."

"I see. You are thinking about little things that annoy, and probably some people and not others. That's good. But let's go positive and raise up the suction of your vacuum to a sofa. With a hose attachment you go under cushions and down deep in the cracks. Can you save that picture?"

"Yes I can."

"Good! Now ting, ting, ting, ting. Can you hear that?"

"I think so," Michael said.

"So you stop and examine the bag. In it you find small golden coins that had fallen out of everyone else's reach. You pocket these to carefully spend later."

"Gold coins?"

"Yes, gold and small. Don't be too logical here. Just be vivid, wild, and memorable or you'll miss the connection.

"Before the days when Starbucks finally reached us, my first husband Carl, found a blazing hot cup of coffee fixed the way he liked it in a special cupholder, in the day when cupholders were rare, waiting in his car as he raced away for his last final graduate exam at 8 AM while I was still sound asleep in bed. He never learned how I did that."

"But…"

"Now — don't distract me, Michael — God's gift of physical love is one of the silliest, and most hoped-for, and most fulfilling things ever, and…and one of the hardest things to talk about."

"Which is one reason we're talking about clocks, right?" Michael still felt his face redden.

"Partly, Michael, and partly because this is so individual to each person and beautiful that you need daily to talk openly *with* God for help with the fine print. You men can be so silly for reasons you can't begin to explain, and women are right behind you. In considering love with a particular woman — and, forgive me, I'm trying to speak from a man's viewpoint — there are times to say 'Yes,' but more times to say "No." At first, many times. Now that's what the '10' is for."

"I see — with the '**0**' in boldface." Michael felt his ears burn. There were two numbers still to go!

"Now Michael, here's how the '11' I give you will look. I'm making the 'ones' " — she raised both hands to eyelevel and began drawing in air — "snake-like and squiggly like two S's that have been pulled out long and been stretched. I draw them — picture this — in flat wet sand at the beach with a stick. It looks like a 'melty' or stretched-out eleven. Proud of that one, I make a second snaky, melty eleven under it. Why the second one? I'm not sure, but quality and responsibility are the issues here. The elevens in the sand stand for 'start slow' and 'stop smart.' Note that the 'start' and 'stop' are wired in so to speak. That's almost it for '11.' Glancing back up the beach, I almost miss a rogue wave rolling in and washing away my number and my sandals as well."

"This picture is a video then," offered Michael.

She ignored him and continued.

"I then pray to God for a wall to protect me and my number the next time I draw. And He provides such a wall. Again and again. Then one special day comes and I again pray for my wall, but only half-heartedly, and to my surprise it suddenly appears, but not in front of the water but behind me! I have no way to escape. The wave knocks me off my feet and I am soaked. 'O God, how can I run?' Then His words come to my ears, 'You can still run, just hang your clothes on my wall to dry and head out to the sea. I am with you.' Before you head for deep water, however, be sure whose voice was speaking and what is being said."

"Oh my!" said Michael.

"Sadly, most of the high school world that you may quickly be leaving won't quite get that."

"But *I* will?" said Michael.

"Oh, I think so. You're smart enough. And normal. Look how this girl has suddenly captured your attention! And you'd 'follow her' to anywhere? It's my turn to say, 'Oh my!' I'd show you some Scripture verses, but you saw to it that my Bible was blown to bits."

"Sorry," said Michael, not hiding his smile. "What if I let the '2' on my green clock be erased by the '1'? You know, '2' become '1.' "

"That's excellent! I hope the picture you create nails that down so you will never forget it! And I hope it connects in some way with the '1' on the first clock. Of course, almost all these pictures are secretly yours. I won't pry there. Oh…and go easy on videos, as you put it, for your clocks. They're harder to wind."

Mrs. Crandel had to be about 70. Still Michael braced himself for the arrival of Number 12.

Yes, his relationship with a 'particular' woman, as Mrs. Crandel put it, would involve more than two persons. It would involve the two of them becoming one in the eyes of God who made them both. He could make a picture for that. A simple picture.

112

"Now for the '12' you generously gave me," continued Mrs. Crandel. "I'll show you how *extremely* ridiculous things can make information memorable. Relax. You'll never have to be embarrassed by any examples you've made — or will make in the future."

Michael smiled. He clutched his cup with both hands.

"Almost every science book has a picture or drawing of Charles Darwin. Picture a bug-eyed 'Darwin head' looking sideways to your right as on a Lincoln-head penny. Can you do that?"

"I've got it," he chuckled.

"His head," she continued, "is capped by an Abe Lincoln-like top hat with a large '!' and a large '?' painted on the smokestack top part."

"Got it!" he replied.

"Now stretch your mind a bit and think of these symbols as an altered '1' and '2' for 12."

"Got it."

"Around the base of the chimney part of the hat is a hatband with four beautiful eyes painted on the side of the band facing you. Later you might want to modify these. Repeat this to me, Michael."

"Top hat on bug-eyed Darwin head facing on my right with '!' and '?' representing '12' painted on the side with four big eyes painted on a hatband that no hat should have."

"You will never, never forget that, Michael. And you'll be too embarrassed to share it or even write it down."

"Correct."

"Okay, now we'll let this absurdity work for us. Just remember you said you needed help. And when you do that, you can never be sure what you'll get. This is simply a framework to hold important truths offered by your first-friend. Do you understand?"

"I do."

"Mr. Darwin and his followers made a lot of interesting suggestions about how animals might have changed on their own from simple to

"You will never, never forget that, Michael. And you'll be too embarrassed to share it or even write it down."

more complex over many years. His ideas were fascinating and got many interested in science. But he knew nothing about the machinery in cells and how cells actually worked, and how such changes came about chemically.

"But more than that — and I'm jumping way ahead — he would never have been able to explain how your 'particular girl' and you will still enjoy each other three days, or three weeks, or three months, or three decades after you're married, that is if you're a good husband and have been using the information you're storing especially at '5' and '6' on your first clock."

Michael found it hard to keep looking straight ahead with a straight face.

" 'Why on Earth are that boy and girl wasting energy like that and seem to be having so much fun?' mumbles Darwin at the top of your green clock. But since he didn't have a chance to overhear what we're talking about, he probably was more surprised than just curious.

"So let the exclamation point stand for that! And let the question mark stand for his bewilderment. You see, science can talk big, but it has limits in the exact details it can explain and the language that can be used to express it.

"Let me think for a moment." Rising, she walked to the one window where in the distance a small part of the top of the water tower could be seen, and stared at it for several seconds. When she returned, she found her cup as well as his filled with tea. He could pour, too, but how much could he possibly drink? Michael wondered. Still the cups were tiny…

He suspected his face was still some shade of red. He offered a careful smile.

"We still have the four eyes, Mrs. Crandel."

"Good! So you remembered! The tall top hat was just too good to create without using it. So here goes:

115

"You wanted to know about women, and how a man thinks or should think about them. As to how a man thinks, oh my, I'm the wrong person to ask, but now you're stuck with me. Let me tell you what my first husband Carl told me not long after we were married. It's about 'eyes.' There's an old saying that 'the eyes are the window to the soul.' But let's not get into that.

"Carl was a good, smart, and passionate man. He was a serious Christian and a real man who unfortunately died far too young.

" 'Esther,' he told me, 'a woman has one of four different kinds of eyes: (1) eyes that are "still," (2) eyes with a hint of sparkle, (3) eyes with sparkle, and (4) eyes with heavy sparkle. Now a real man looking for a real woman begins with the eyes, not necessarily ending there, of course.' Now Michael, can you picture each of the four types?"

"I can start to, ma'am, but I'll need to work on that more a little later." Michael shifted in his seat.

" 'None of the four in itself is bad,' Carl told me. 'For example, still eyes can be a covering, for hiding or just keeping things safe. But some important things in every life just shouldn't be always kept hidden.' "

She paused.

Whatever was she talking about? Michael wondered. File it away and look like you're ready for more, he told himself.

"Observations and ideas behind still eyes," she continued, "may range from empty nothingness to the stuff of real genius. You, the one looking in, as I am doing to you now, Michael, may never get very far at first because still eyes can be so comforting—or more often just over-looked. And they can become a disturbing wall that prevents reaching out. For a couple to be happy *over time*, he told me 'the woman's eyes must have or gain sparkle.'

" 'And my eyes?' I asked Carl after a year of marriage. Carl had paused briefly, then smiled.

" 'A hint of sparkle,' he said, 'that slowly grew over time. But never,' he emphasized, 'did they have "heavy sparkle." Eyes like that are kind of scary.' "

"And," asked Michael, "how do women look at men's eyes? And how do you see my eyes?"

He paused.

"I think you can figure that out for yourself. I'm talking too much. And, as to women, don't be too upset if you find a good woman always keeps a few secrets tucked away."

"I'll have to work to find a place for this on one of my clocks," he said.

"You see, Michael, peculiar problems arise when a man chooses a woman to be his first-friend." She smiled back. Michael noticed her eyes sparkled. "But, as I've said, now you have to put up with me."

"That's not a problem, ma'am." Why did he say that? He wondered. Still their conversation wasn't over.

She raised her cup and looked over the top as she drank.

"Be careful if you share this, Michael. People may think you're a little crazy…possibly because they don't know what 'sparkle' means, though I think you do. But by all means, Michael, marry a girl whose eyes sparkle."

That would be no problem with Triana. But marriage! Wait a minute. What was she thinking about? Fortunately, Mrs. Crandel didn't ask him to repeat any of this to see if he remembered what she'd said.

"I suppose you were once a biology teacher?" he asked. She nodded and smiled once again without clarifying. "I'm afraid to ask, Mrs. Crandel, but if it's not too private, what were you just thinking about over at the window? If I'm following you properly, your eyes were especially sparkling when you returned to the table."

"Oh my!…Ah! A good question, and one that begs me to answer. Michael…Michael, what I'm going to tell you now I've told absolutely no one else, oh, except for one person. It's the kind of secret that one

117

and only one other—not even my beloved Amos, by the way—knows about, except for God, of course."

"But why me now?" Michael interrupted.

"Because, like the last of the Pennacooks, I'm a person who soon may vanish away."

She paused and smiled. If she was fishing for confidence, she didn't have to cast too far. Michael shook his head and smiled back, glued to his seat.

"I'm ready, ma'am," he announced. And, uncharacteristically glancing once more back to the window, she began.

"Soon after I was first married, and quite happily so I must say, to my first husband Carl, he got so deeply involved with graduate studies with his comprehensive exams coming up, that before the supper I would dutifully fix, he would study and study as if I wasn't there. For several days I pretended that I didn't care. But Michael I did." Hardly lifting her arm, she pointed to the ceiling reminding Michael of his English teacher emphasizing a point. But first, the image of Triana and his flannel shirt flashed into his mind. He covered his mouth with his hand, converting an inappropriate laugh into a cough.

"One night," she continued, "after finishing a quiet supper, I sat drinking a second tall glass of iced tea which was still almost full of ice cubes while my husband returned to his stack of notes at the desk with his back to me. Without a sound I crept up behind him, pulled back his tightly tucked-in shirt as if to rub his shoulders as I'd done several times before. He slowly relaxed without a glance or a word my way and continued reading as if I weren't there. Then I leaned over and kissed him on the back of his ear, not the first time I'd done that. He flinched for a second and reentered his private world.

"Then up went my glass and down the back of his shirt went the cubes and the rest of my tea. Later we found where his pen had flown up and landed across the room almost under the stove.

" 'Oh…oh, sorry. Things kind of slipped,' I volunteered in a perfectly normal voice as his yell wakened the baby in the apartment overhead. Then I left everything alone, said I was tired and going to bed a little early, so would he please turn out the lights and close things up that night. And turn in early he also did.

"Our Darwin in the top hat would really be puzzled by all that. 'Why on Earth are they wasting energy and acting so crazy?' he would mumble. So he's really earned his question mark because that's all he — and anyone else — is allowed to see.

"You acted boldly and confidently, I see," said Michael, almost choking on his words.

"Of course!"

"Uh…uh…What happened after that?" he asked.

"Oh, a lot of ordinary normal things I'll not bore you with, Michael, but nine months later, God gave us a beautiful little girl."

"Whoa-ho! I don't need a clock to remember that!"

"Ah, but you can so easily sketch my daughter smiling at a confused Darwin on top of number 12. Science and yes, literature too, often miss a few things. I might be wrong, but I think Darwin maybe could profit from what it's like to love and play at the same time.

"Do you know how to play, Michael? There must be time for that. Do I have to tell you, Michael, that you have to give yourself, all of yourself, to the one you marry?"

"Uh..no ma'am."

"There's nothing wrong with that. Nothing. God made us that way and it's a sin to ignore it."

"Yes ma'am."

"But it must be with the right girl at the right time in the right way. Remember the railroad tracks, Michael? The picture I helped you create?"

"Uh…" Michael forced himself to cough while he pulled himself back together. A question…he needed a question.

"Mrs. Crandel—I hope I'm not being impertinent, but…but I can't help but wonder who was the first person you told about this? You said, I think, it wasn't Amos."

"Yes, Michael, you are pushing the limit here…but I really don't mind. That, however, is still another story, and I don't want to bore you."

"Ma'am, you don't have to worry about that!"

"Well, then, when my daughter grew and was a bit older than 17, by three months, I said I had a small gift for her. Just the two of us were sitting at the dining table in the early afternoon. I handed her a large thick candle like you, when in your right mind these days, would put on a dining table, maybe like the one you put on Number 1 of your first clock.

" 'Monica,' I said, 'in less than a year, in fact in exactly nine months, you'll be 18, and legally of age. May I tell you a story?' "

" 'Of course, Mother, you may tell me anything you like. Anything, since I'm going to be an adult.' And so I proceeded to tell her just what I told you. And when I did, her jaw nearly fell to the table. 'Mother, *how could you*?' 'Oh it was easy,' I replied. 'Oh…oh…no! Mother, that was…was…was exactly 18 years ago from *today*! Arrrggh!' Jumping up from the table, she fled to her bedroom and slammed the door.

"For dinner, fearing perhaps I'd overstepped, I fixed her favorite supper, and I was relieved when she made her way to the table on time as usual. During her father's, blessing, however, she snickered. I totally ignored it. Ignoring certain things…That's something else for you to remember, Michael.

"We all have feelings, sometimes even strong ones. But they must be saved for expressing until the right time.

"After the blessing, my husband asked, 'What's going on here between you two that I don't know about?' I replied, 'Just some women things.' And then Monica added, 'Daddy, I'm a grown woman now. Thank you for your part in making me what I've become.' After she realized what she'd said, she excused herself and fled to the bathroom.

"Every year until Monica married and moved away we, just the two of us, have had a private nine-months-before-her-birthday celebration. And though my first husband never learned anything about this, he and Monica were very close until his death."

"And, why, ma'am, are you telling me all this?"

"Because, Michael, the stories and pictures we make ourselves are often the best way to put important things together. You wanted a first-friend. I had to step in quickly because you were…you were as I said a little desperate. You can build off *your* own pictures and stories for your own children someday."

"I have to ask, ma'am, are you pushing me to get married?"

"Look at me, Michael. The 'Lady Wisdom' of Proverbs 8 declares that you are too young to get married, and I think you're smart enough to understand that. And have I mentioned any girl by name since you've come here?"

"No ma'am, you've not. But you have mentioned a strange situation a 'particular' girl and I may be facing."

"I have. And I don't have any solid answers for you about that. But I will say this. The one particular girl that we both know, who you know much better than I, is a treasure waiting to be claimed. Lady Wisdom also declares that she is also too young to marry. But I'm glad you asked this question. I have a gift for you, Michael."

She held out a small velvet bag that buttoned shut. Michael took the bag and opened it.

"It's a ring!"

"Yes, Michael, it is."

"Where did…"

"It was mine, Michael. Carl gave it to me." Michael glanced at her hand. "Yes, Michael, I'm wearing one, one that Amos gave me. A woman can't, or shouldn't wear two wedding bands, you know…or don't you? When a husband dies, especially at a very young age, you must mourn his loss. He was a gift from God." Michael noticed Mrs. Crandel's eyes start to moisten. "At a husband's or wife's death, the marriage is over and memories must gather and sort themselves. You tell yourself you can never, never marry again. The thought itself is preposterous.

"A year later I found myself looking across the aisle in church at a man whose wife was killed in a car accident two years earlier. He caught me looking and so he took me aside after church and said 'You can see me much better' over lunch. Then I really stared. He slowly raised his hands and said 'I promise not to touch you.' Then he smiled.

"Then, Michael, I acted cool and calm like you pretend to be even when you're all emotional and confused."

"And then what happened? — it's another question, ma'am."

"His promise lasted for a week. Then we were together almost alone in a small theater watching a silly movie and I suddenly started quietly crying, something I almost never do, and kept it up for nearly an hour. Fortunately or unfortunately, it was a long movie, long for those days. When I stopped, I found his arm on my shoulder.

"Later at home that night I discovered I had feelings for him and felt guilty. 'Why is this happening to me?' I prayed.

" 'Because I made you that way,' God seemed to answer. 'If you love Me,' he seemed to say, 'Don't be selfish. I want Amos and now he needs you to listen to him.'

"That's enough about how I met Amos!"

"And then you married him?"

"I let go of my balloon, Michael. Remember? The one I was holding. And yes, I married him not long afterwards."

"But you just said…"

"Michael, I know what I just said. This ring is for you to give to whomever God gives you when that time comes. And for however long or short that time might be — perhaps short like it was for me — you must continually wind your clocks. Enjoy every day with small surprises that makes her certain that you're the one for her. Who knows, circumstances may change Lady Wisdom's mind…Of course I may be overstepping and even wrong…"

"But I can't…"

"But you can and will take this, Michael. I may never see you again."

"But…"

"I insist you take it. After what Amos has just learned, the Susquehanna Territory, as we know it, may be coming to its end."

"Thank you."

Just as he stuffed the velvet bag deep within his pocket, treating it like a fragile egg, there was a frantic knock at the door. Esther Crandel, despite her age, almost glided across the room. After peeking through the peephole, she whispered back clearly, "Remember, Michael, what I told you earlier!" Sliding the bolt back she opened the door.

From the growing darkness a bent figure stepped inside. She wore a large hooded jacket and held a cane in one hand, a canvas tote bag in the other. Michael gasped as he saw the notched walking stick with the pointed crook. It was his own martial arts cane. Down came the hood, and dark blonde hair fell back. It was Triana.

"Jonas sent me to get you, Michael. People are starting to roam the streets. Jonas said you might want your cane. But I got the feeling I was being followed. I got here as soon as…"

"Michael," Mrs. Crandel interrupted, "Uh...excuse me, Triana, Michael, could you quickly take that chest back upstairs where we've been working, thank you." How maternal and grandmotherly she suddenly became. And with a formal edge that was absent before. Michael sprang into action.

"Triana, check the blinds, please, and I'll find us something to eat. Amos should be up from the basement any minute and Michael knows how to finish up. He'll be right back." She put her hands on her hips and slowly rotated as if to adjust for stiffness. "He's sure been a help to me."

"Thank you, Esther," said Triana—using her first name unlike Michael, but without a trace of disrespect. "I've not seen or heard any shooting, but new faces are out on the street. How the Governor General and Mayor Colonels deal with this is anybody's guess. Guns are visible everywhere, but we—between the church and us here—have seen no open aggression. Armed people sit on their front porches or behind upstairs windows, cross-watching all sides of adjacent buildings with their neighbors, so any newcomers would be crazy to start anything."

At the sound of steps Amos Crandel emerged from the basement. "Triana! Welcome, but we're going to have to work on that wardrobe!" said the church elder, inspecting her disguise. "I don't know if you've heard about it or not, but there's another group of crazies who've been talking about 'taking care of the witch girl,' and these have nothing to do with any church. And your disguise—it may discourage thieves, but not them. This isn't a group that Harwell can talk down.

"You and Michael are going to have to stay here tonight," he added.

The next sound of steps brought Michael out in the open and down into the room. He'd overheard everything.

"Hi Triana!"

124

"Aren't you going to say I'm beautiful, Michael?" Her words sounded too light-hearted, out of place.

"I've already done that," he shot back, smiling.

The Crandels looked at each other.

"A perfect fit!" whispered Amos.

"Not yet," returned Esther.

"Room 301 on the third floor will be Triana's," said Amos. "The bed is still fine and has been made."

"The storage room on the other side of the wall will be close and within hearing range for Michael," added Esther.

Other considerations remained unspoken.

CHAPTER II

Room 301

Place: Hotel Crandel
Time: DAY 331, 8 PM

Fortunately, the lock to Rm. 301 required a large old-fashioned metal key before Day 1 of AEMP, so room security had not changed. The tiny windowless room next door, large for a supply room, however, had acquired a padlock requiring a special key.

Triana opened her door. A nearly full moon bathed the room with its only light. Without looking back she handed the key to Michael. Not expecting it, the key slipped through his fingers to the floor. Quickly he picked it up, pocketed it, and scanned the room. The wall seemed circled by a thin wainscoting of fake walnut paneling probably tacked on over plywood. The dresser, small desk and chair, and single bedside table alongside the old four-poster double bed seemed dwarfed by the thick darkness that overhung the room.

While Triana inspected her bed, Michael, just inside the door to the right, found and ran his finger over the two thin separations about 30 inches apart from each other in the wainscoting, which appeared as pictures of "wooden boards" stamped on the side facing the bedroom. When he checked the two windows, he discovered that the one parallel to the bed, close to the far wall on the left, just beyond the bedpost at the footboard, opened to a narrow, metal fire escape outside just below

126

the window. The rusty metal steps switched back and forth down to its final segment held up horizontally by a rusty spring, only a single story, or eight feet, above the sidewalk. Not a difficult way out to the sidewalk—or in to the third floor. He checked the window lock.

Taking her hand, he led the girl back out, unlocked the door to his own small room nearly filled with boxes and paint cans.

"I want to show you something," he said. Kneeling in total darkness, he ran his hand along the thin wall that separated the two rooms. Finding the backside of the panel between the two separations he'd detected earlier, he traced along the floor till he came to the two handles he'd discovered previously. With both hands he tugged at a 30-inch-wide panel that was almost as tall. He pulled it out. The semidarkness of Triana's room was by contrast a beacon, erasing the total darkness of Michael's. They both crawled back into Triana's room through the opening, showing how easy that was. Michael pulled a mop and a broom after him. He led her like a child to the bed and seated her on it. "Your weapons…but please don't kill anyone." He lay the broom and mop on the floor between the bed and the far wall.

"We'll lock your door on the inside, then no key can open it. You can call out or tap on the floor if you need me." He bent over and quickly kissed her on the forehead as Sally might do, turned abruptly, and though it was still early, went back to the opening, and disappeared into his room. Which number on which of his clocks prompted that? he wondered. He pushed the panel most of the way back in place, giving him just enough light to manage.

He removed his shoes, rolled himself into a blanket on the floor, and lay back on a pillow he'd taken from Triana's room. His mind raced: Igneal dying, Steffi dying, digging two graves, talking—but mainly listening—with Jonas about the uncertainty of the days ahead. Then there were his secret days with Esther Crandel, a typical grandmother beyond her front door, anything but while inside, who after the oddest introduction, had become his "first-friend" as she called herself. She could hold secrets, talk about love, and underline the obvious such as "they were too young to marry," but then give him a wedding ring perfect for "that day." More than that, she'd been so insistent that their days together were about to "quickly end." And, of course, the Space Goose which he'd never seen. Add to that his strange new "personal" world of clocks. Clocks and Jerry Lucas. Never would he have trouble falling asleep again! He would always be winding them.

And now strangers with guns were roaming the streets. He should think about God, Jonas would probably say, and lay out this matter before Him. And if Triana read these thoughts, she'd say, "Cliché! Michael, you can do better than that."

But since they'd started up the stairs the girl hadn't said a word. Despite his leather jacket he felt chilled. For the first time in months he felt alone—when he actually wasn't. Really alone. What else did he have but God to thread things together? "God," signaled in his mind by the tall, thick candle blazing with light, the "1" on his first clock. He would start there. Cry out, quietly, to God who welcomes children... because...it was Number 4, "Nobody cares for things, your things or 'it,' like you." God would know that. He could visualize the four ridiculous white boxcars, 'boxed in' by people who only looked the other way. And he could visualize the eyes of God upon everything.

"Michael...Michael,"

"Yes?"

"Come here. Bring your blanket and pillow." Her voice sounded weak and mechanical.

So he did, bringing his bag, blanket, pillow, and cane.

"Are you okay?" The girl, still in her clothes and even her jacket, lay on top of the worn bedspread, her head on the pillow.

"Yes."

"Yes? You sound..."

"I feel alone, Michael, alone like never before, or at least as far back as I can remember."

"Me, too, Triana…You're…you're so honest with me…you just pull words out of me before I even think about them."

"You too, Michael. Just listen to yourself. Yes, Michael, I'm honest with you — usually. And even though you scare me by being here, I still trust you."

"I…I think I'd better go back."

"No! Michael, you just scare me here, not terrify me. But if you leave…I'll be…terrified."

"Uh…"

"Sorry, Michael, I'm trying not to be complicated. Let me put it this way: Remember *The Fourth Prince* that we recently received from Cample, and read independently?"

"How could I forget!" Michael smiled. She was coming back to her old self.

"It's that book and *Inside the Hollow Spear* that came with it that has made me seriously consider going to Elphia — if it's possible."

[Note that relevant parts of TFP and ITHS will be discussed in Parts II and IV.]

"Okay, and…?"

"You be Casimir on the chest."

"Even though they were…"

"Stop! Don't read too much into my great-grandfather's story, if he's actually my great-grandfather…be like him that evening. You're a good actor. I'll be your audience — your only audience." She pointed to the floor where she'd laid another blanket next to the wall just beyond the window.

"In spite of what Mrs. Crandel might say or think?"

"Yes."

"She knows nothing about what happened to the young king!"

"But we do, Michael."

Slowly but deliberately he moved to the bed on the floor and wrapped himself in his blanket, carefully laying his cane by his side. Rolling partway to the wall, he closed his eyes against his will. Without a sound the girl was suddenly kneeling at his side. He felt a light kiss on his forehead.

"Uhh.."

"That's from Sally." In a flash she was back on her bed pretending that she'd never left it.

Michael stared back at the hole he'd crawled through. Triana had no idea what she's doing. He groaned. He still felt her soft kiss. Every friend he'd ever had would now call her foolish, childish, at least naïve. And him? Crazy! Except maybe his new first-friend. Didn't Triana know that every bone in his body wanted to throw away everything and lie next to her? But something here connected with a silly number on his silly red, no, it was his first ordinary clock. He was more than his bones. Good timing was beautiful. Bad timing was not, at least not in a lingering way. It was sin, even a curse. In his mind a tall white candle from the ordinary clock was brightly exposing his every thought. Stupid candle!

Little did he realize that his not moving to her bed, as well as his not returning to his own room, would for the time being, save her from suffering a grizzly death.

CHAPTER 12

The Removable Panel

Place: *Hotel Crandel*
Date: **Day 331,** *11 PM*

Ka-chinka-chink-tinkle-ti-tinkle-clik.
Michael instantly sat up from what seemed like a deep sleep. In the gray darkness he could see Triana's head on the pillow where she now lay under the covers.

His eyes turned to the window. A bare hand reached through what was left of the middle upper pane of glass in the lower half, and reached for the lock lever just above it. In seconds the lever was pulled, the bottom half of the window was up, and Michael was standing out of sight against the wall.

He pulled his hickory cane high over his head, cocking it back behind him. The hand now with a pistol, pushed a foot-and-a-half through the opening. A Glock or something like it moved as if centering on its target. The gunman's face must be pressed against the dirty upper half of the window. Seeing couldn't be easy. Michael knew his timing must be perfect.

Suddenly, Flot-flot-flot-flot. Four silent shots.

Too late! Stuffing flew up from the pillow, splinters of wood from the headboard.

...a pistol pushed a foot-and-a-half through
the opening.

Furiously he came over and down with his cane, striking, bending, and breaking with a loud snap the bone and artery of the arm that held the gun. A fifth silenced shot wildly tore into one of the thin bedposts, shattering it before the gun fell into the room. Without a second's hesitation, Michael spun around face-to-face with the open window, and pulling his cane back like a cue stick, he speared forward and struck hard—chest, head, or neck—he wasn't sure which. With a muffled cry, the assassin with his unnaturally bent forearm already dripping blood was thrown back. With another cry, loud this time, he fell back into the air and disappeared.

Were others below or not? He didn't care. It was so dark—both outside and in. Slamming the window down, he dreaded turning around. Why, why, why had he waited so long? He tiptoed to the bed.

"God, no! God, no!" He reached down to a strange gray mess that seemed to cover the pillow.

"Michael, Michael."

He spun around. Inside, against the wall just beyond the window, lost in almost total darkness stood the girl, holding the broom. She was still in her clothes. Immediately, she was in his arms.

"Thank God! Thank God! Thank God! You're alive! You're alive!" Still holding her, Michael turned the two of them back to where she'd lain. "But the bed…?"

"It's the mop, Michael. I heard sounds. Didn't want to bother you. I thought it was probably nothing. So I put the mop there, and…" That bullets could do so much damage to a mop head astonished him.

"Triana, gather everything and crawl into my room."

He grabbed the pillow, dropped it to the floor where some blood had fallen. Removing the mop, he replaced it with the now bloody pillow. After what had happened, and the presence of a body below, he doubted anyone else would try the ladder entry, or try to enter the

133

hotel at any point. Pains had been taken to use a silencer so as not to disturb anyone else inside, but Michael had been waiting. Retaliation had been swift and deadly. Only a fool would follow.

But he couldn't be sure. If anyone else tried the window, they could see the blood, consider the job done, and not risk more angry resistance by proceeding further.

Quickly, he wrote and left a short coded note on the bed that only Mrs. Crandel would understand, and not cause her to suspect the worst. If the noise had been enough to wake others, especially those who lived below, with just enough of the right information his secret first-friend could delay any further searching until daylight. With what he knew, anyone, even the Crandels, would not find them until morning.

Gathering all his stuff, including the pistol, he unlocked Room 301 from the inside, allowing easy entry to the hallway and followed Triana into the hole in the wall to his own room. He replaced the panel that connected the rooms.

Inside, he shuffled a few boxes, and found the ladder of slats nailed to studs that he'd discovered the day before. Michael went up first and Triana, still wearing a skirt disguise, followed. After what had happened, the climb seemed easy. At the top, Michael slid back the large piece of plywood that covered a square opening. They climbed through it. The large attic floor was mostly empty except for years of dust and grime. A large brick chimney in the center seemed to hold up the roof. A small windowed alcove nearby allowed a hint of moonlight. It was perfect!

Michael made a second trip down, brought everything else back up and eased the boxes they'd moved back into their place. On top he slid the plywood back in place recovering the hole. And since a small discarded air conditioner lay nearby, he pulled it over the plywood. Only half the floor area of the attic seemed to be covered with wood; the rest showed open insulation that couldn't be stepped on without risking falling through the ceiling.

He pulled out a small lantern and lit it. With just enough light, he laid one blanket and two pillows on a place with secure flooring near the window in the alcove.

"This is yours," he said. " 'The little room,' if you need it, is somewhere on the other side of the chimney."

With her things in place, she started to take off her skirt. Michael turned his back to her.

"Michael, I have shorts on underneath! You don't think I'd…"

"Well, so do I," Michael interrupted.

"And I *don't* need to see them!"

"Okay." Michael struggled not to laugh.

"Stop staring!" Again he turned his back to her.

"Come over here, Michael."

He came, proud of being able to resist saying a half dozen things. Tears were streaming down her cheeks.

She fell to her knees.

"We need to pray, Michael. That man may still be alive. We must pray that, if he is alive, that somehow he gets help and finds Jesus. And the others…there are so many out there… And we need to pray about tomorrow, about you…about me." Michael noticed she didn't say "us." He knelt beside her and together they prayed, easily and naturally in words few others would understand. "Don't go away, Michael."

He lay down slowly beside her, imagining a carton of fragile eggs keeping them an inch apart. Then he handed her the other blanket with which she immediately covered them both. Then, since it was chillier in the attic than down below, she pulled her long wrap-around flowered skirt that opened to a large trapezoid of denim over the blanket that covered them both. He found himself closer to her. Her body was warm and the carton of eggs slowly disappeared. He searched for some appropriate words. Then he felt her silent tears on his cheek.

"Michael, there's one more thing...Can I ask you to do something for me?"

"Of course. Anything...anything up to one-half of my kingdom." Once again words tumbled out of his mouth without passing through his brain.

"Michael"—for the first time he could remember, she looked away somewhere at the ceiling, rather than directly into his eyes while she spoke—"Michael...Michael, *for as long as I'm with you, will you protect me from myself?*"

"Is that an order from the Princess from Emryss?" he shot back, again his brain not filtering the words.

"Yes."

If ever there was an occasion to want more special words, it was now. But knowing her, it wasn't the right time. Nor did he feel it was right just then to prod. But when should he? Would that time come?

"I have the story with me, Michael. Jonas says it now belongs to me and no one else on Earth. His responsibilities to other worlds, if they exist, he said, must end. His attention now would only be on his congregation on Earth. And I may or may not be part of that."

What next? Michael wondered. It was time for a lesson, a review—anything else—to focus on...

"Then let's reread together the shorter story Cample gave us, *The Fourth Prince*, about your great-grandmother and other ancestors on Emryss. And do it now or until we run out of kerosene.

"That story," he continued, "is so different, and so differently written than the others. It discusses simple politics, dividing people into "Golds" and "Greens," and magnifies supernatural events about a flying horse and a golden sword, just like old folktales—from Earth.

"*Inside the Hollow Spear*, on the other hand, is so long and detailed that the action has to fight its way through. **Still, if you take that story**

136

seriously, it was what finally convinced you of your unusual Elphian connection, even though it says nothing about you, or what you must do later.

"These two stories, alongside *Death in a Tavern* and *The Secret of Zareba,* that also came to Jonas, but not from Cample, make it hard to argue against the probability that you in fact carry blood from not one, but two different planets—neither of which is Earth.

"And, Triana, while we have humans, with similar appearance and, most probably, nearly identical DNA from two different worlds, if we now add in Earth, we have a new application of some old math: '2 + 1.'

"God just may have created specially designed humans in His image in several places from the same blueprints! Atheistic naturalists would love to have that idea shoved under their noses!"

What was he saying out loud!

"And you still want to protect me from myself, Preacher Michael?"

"I do and I will." How could he answer so fast? He shuddered when he realized these words sounded so much like part of a wedding ceremony! He fought to keep himself collected.

Without hesitation, she extended her hand, palm down and smiled.

"For me to kiss an Emryss princess?" he asked.

She nodded.

Pushing her hand away, he kissed her lips, easing himself slowly back only seconds after they touched.

He picked up *The Fourth Prince* and opened it to the first page, adjusted the lantern and began to read.

[The Fourth Prince begins on the next page.]

EMRYSS

The Fourth Prince
(a story from PLANET EMRYSS)
was planned to be here.
But it won't be.

First, this story was one of two discovered at a yard sale in the Midwest by Marvin Cample, a folklorist who is also Triana and Michael's honors English teacher. It is Cample who brings it to his two students' and Harwell's attention.

This complete story, with its own separate purpose, has been alluded to in small ways in several places, especially in Chapter 11.

However, there is no significant connection between that story and the one here.

Here are the facts from The Fourth Prince that catch Triana's and (of course) Michael's attention. They concern her possible background. Key details:

(1) The story only takes place on (earthlike) Planet Emryss. There is no mention of Earth, Elphia, or anywhere else.

(2) A partial, fragmented genealogy is mentioned in the background.

---------- ? ----------- (unnamed ancestors are assumed)

---------- ? -----------

King Merrick (has 5 children below)

— Three naturally born sons (not named and who die early)

— **Princess Lurinda**

— and an adopted son (who becomes the "4th prince").

(3) **Triana** has received information from several different sources, one of them Igneal, that say she is a *direct descendent* of Princess Lurinda. This is one such source.

Cample suggests that this "discovered" story, may have been as a hobby translated by, if not created by, retired Tyndale Bible translators who died without heirs and who had few possessions to offer anyone.

Cample, Jonas, Michael, and Triana have read and been moved by this careful romance, though it offers few facts relevant here other than an overall look at political factions and the difficulties that people face in an authoritarian realm (on Emryss). Little scientific information is revealed about this world.

Still, it seems to link with a very different second story, *Inside the Hollow Spear,* that Cample also said he found alongside *The Fourth Prince*. This second story will be discussed in Part IV, along with a few links to *Death in a Tavern* and *The Secret of Zareba*, stories that came from Harwell's office.

The four stories about the same supposed exoplanet named "Emryss" are very different in purpose, length, and even writing style.

But their connections to one another are hard to deny.

PART III

EARTH

CHAPTER 13

"A Nasty Problem"

(Follows ending of Chapter 12)

Place: Side Door of Hotel Crandel

Time: **Day 332, 8 AM**

As she shooed them out the side door of their living quarters, Michael noticed that Mrs. Crandel once again wore the kind, familiar grandmother mask that showed just part of her amazing talents and resourcefulness. Later he "recorded," in his mind of course, on Number 1 of one his clocks, the blue one, her admonition, "Remember, Michael, don't forget, 'Important things are often not what they first seem.'"

She'd even wrapped a small still-warm loaf of bread and given it to him in a clean white kitchen towel with the letters "E. S." sewn on it. The "E" he knew, but what did the "S" stand for? Would he ever know? He stuffed it in his pocket. Triana handed him his cane. She would carry a canvas tote filled with small things Esther Crandel had given them.

"Don't dawdle!" she'd urged. He could imagine her wagging a finger at a 10-year-old. "Go directly to the parsonage. It's uphill (of course it was…) and stay together. The streets are attracting unfamiliar faces, and there's a gun showing at a window in nearly every home."

"And forget the disguises. The locals know you, and to any who may still question Triana, it's daylight, and that's to your advantage with those that live nearby," added her husband. "The plan, I've been told, was that the Mayor Colonel, who ended your basketball days, and today's militia is on its way to push any new folks away from here to God knows where. Don't stop. Get to the parsonage! Goodbye. God be with you!"

"Goodbye and thanks," said Michael. He looked at Mrs. Crandel who remained silent, a loving arm around her husband's waist.

"Amos and Esther will pray for you every day, Michael and Triana," said the man, rattling off all four names. Never could Michael remember ever talking to the oldest church elder before yesterday.

And never would he talk to him or Mrs. Crandel again.

*   *   *   *   *

During the night, reading *The Fourth Prince* aloud together had taken several hours. Just how long? He'd no memory. The kerosene lamp, turned down to just enough to read by, could last for hours. When he'd finally awoke, the lamp was out, and the first daylight was working its way through the window.

They both had lain side by side on their backs, covered by a blanket and her wrap-around skirt. Once in the night he'd thought she'd finally fallen asleep though he'd still kept reading. But when he'd come to the part about Casimir on the chest in the castle bedroom, he felt an elbow nudge him in the ribs and she whispered, "That's the part."

At once he'd begun to slide quarter-inch by quarter-inch away from the warmth of her fully clothed body. In seconds she'd turned toward him looking puzzled. It was his turn: "That's my promise — the one you asked me to make." Her next poke in the ribs had been harder, but barely so.

How much did she *identify* with her great grandmother in the bedroom scene in that story? "Resonate" was the way Harwell probably

143

would have put it, in the same way as when he'd described how our Biblical Gospel would, or should, sound against the memory of a lost similar Gospel on another planet.

Fortunately, he'd been holding the book so he kept reading. Words, words, words that God had given him for more than one reason. It had helped him tunnel into the possibility of the impossible mission that might lie ahead. Safety lay staying inside the words they were sharing.

God couldn't have missed his quick promise last night. He could never break it now if he expected God's help in whatever decisions may be only hours away. Why since she was so intelligent, did she trust him so much? It had to be naiveté. On his first clock, at 3, his first-friend had declared that everyone comes from somewhere with baggage. If this was part of hers, though it puzzled him, he could carry it. And would. And he would have read until noon even if he had to go back and start all over.

But that hadn't been necessary, and storytime had ended.

And with it their time in the attic.

To his surprise, an accounting of how they'd spent the night hadn't occurred. If it were an issue, it wasn't mentioned. It was an extraordinary time. He knew the Crandels had the highest moral standards, but somehow they'd trusted them. Perhaps their minds were otherwise occupied. And, right or wrong, Harwell had declared to them: he was now a "man" and she a "woman" — meaning 'adults,' whatever that meant. But that certainly wasn't the same as "husband and wife," or permission to do what husbands and wives do.

When they'd awakened to the sounds of the Crandels' footsteps and voices in the bedroom below, they'd simply called down telling where they were; then they'd descended into the storeroom. Together they'd crawled through the wall. Mrs. Crandel had stood expressionless as she held the bloody pillow that was intended to bewilder and confuse—as well as reassure. Michael's note had explained just enough. Triana had entered wearing her skirt and carrying an armful of blankets. Michael had handed his new Glock to Amos.

And Triana had handed Michael his cane.

Then they'd shared highpoints of what happened, and after a bite of breakfast, and a word of prayer, their morning adventure outside had quickly begun.

*   *   *   *   *

Now they walked side by side in the middle of the street, eyes straight ahead. Five or six strange men and a couple of women with several children were moving the same way up the street, empty of course of the cars that had died months earlier in the EMP blast and had been pushed away. They kept to the streets as was preferred in AEMP since sidewalks, close to doorways, windows, and alleys with armed defenders nearby seemed more risky.

"Triana, if we're seriously encountered, give me several feet of space, and if you have to, throw yourself flat on the ground." She said nothing but he knew she heard.

After two blocks, with houses and shops still on both sides, that moment came. Two men in grimy baseball caps, in their 20's or 30's, one unusually stout—unusual in AEMP—wearing filthy camo pants and a canvas hunting jacket, the other lean and slightly taller than Michael, in jeans and a hooded mud-stained sweatshirt, but no jacket, came from opposite sides of the street and converged slightly behind them.

Michael, effecting a slight limp, slowly turned and faced them.

"What do you want?" he demanded.

"Just a trade, cripple boy," said the lean one, offering a quick wink to his companion. "We just may have something to give you that you really need. Let me see that leather jacket."

145

"And what do you have to offer me? I see no tote bag."

"Oh, I've a lot I can give." Smiling, he patted a bulge in his pocket. "I can give you the rest of your life! Now let's see that jacket!"

"I beg you to leave us alone!"

"Beg?" He laughed. "Now! And I mean now!" he growled under his breath. "We don't want to make a scene, do we?"

"Again, I beg you!" Michael answered, raising his hands in surrender. He backed up several feet, Triana stepped to the side, matching the distance he had taken. Those carefully watching from the darkness of their homes could now clearly see who was attacking whom.

It was then the stout one made his move toward Triana. "Sweetie, you've no idea what you've been missin'!" Reaching inside her open coat he grabbed at the tie holding the wrap-around skirt together. It opened to the shorts she wore beneath it. She let herself fall backwards, then slowly rose to her knees on the pavement as if to plead with her grinning attacker.

At the same time Michael collapsed to the ground, thrusting behind him the hickory cane. His attacker pulled back his foot to kick his face, which couldn't have been more perfect. With a mighty swing parallel to the ground, Michael caught the support leg of his attacker just at the ankle, upending him. Sound of the cracking bone preceded a scream behind him. Michael dangerously turned his head.

Triana's attacker was bent over, eyes shut, holding his groin. Triana, down on one knee and leaning back, swung up again, this time the top of her fist hammering the bottom of his jaw. His eyes snapped open in a fury as blood dribbled from the side of his mouth.

"Run, Triana!"

The man tried to follow but his legs were rubbery. Michael's cane blow to the head finally took the man down.

Michael spun around to his attacker who was unable to stand, and stared into the face of a pistol.

BLAM.

146

Smoke rose not from the pistol, which danced into the air, but from a rifle sticking out of a store window across from where he stood. The lean man's body lurched upward, fell, and lay still.

"Come, Michael." The girl took his hand and pulled him away. The rifleman had saved his life. Outsiders who were walking the street drifted away. A rifleman from each side of the street emerged from nowhere and without a word escorted them three more blocks to the edge of town.

"Thanks, kids, for taking care of a nasty problem." Just as the speaker for the two riflemen ended, a second shot rang out. "Here, this is yours. You earned it." He handed Michael his attacker's small pistol which he shoved into his pocket. The barrel was warm.

Without looking back Michael knew that Triana's attacker was also dead. In Year 1 of AEMP there were no jails for deliberate criminals, no places for proper surgical repair, and certainly no coddling rehab. The judge and jury had acted fast. There had been witnesses. They would not be challenged.

CHAPTER 14

"No!"

Place: The Parsonage Study
Time: DAY 332, 10:30 AM

Triana had quietly cried all the way back to the parsonage. Michael hated killing, but not the way she did. She hadn't pulled the trigger, but she'd set the stage for it by her unexpected self-defense that later, he discovered, Harwell had insisted she learn and made her practice. "Sometimes," he'd said, "we have to fiercely defend our own lives to keep those around us from getting hurt." That was his argument and the end of his discussion of it.

They held hands but said nothing on the way. Before they realized it, they found themselves in chairs waiting for their minister and father to arrive. How odd to have two of Smith's extended family meet them at the door cradling rifles and being rushed like visiting royalty to the pastor's office.

"Jonas 'as been waitin'," one of them said. As soon as they'd entered the office, the men disappeared. Then, as if scripted, Sally appeared with some sort of steaming tasty gruel—yes, "some things really aren't what they first seem"—and bread still warm and left over from breakfast. She disappeared so quietly that a shiver went down Michael's back.

When Harwell finally arrived, he stared down at the small pistol

Michael had put where his Bible usually lay. After a quick glance he sat and slid the weapon to the side like a memo that he didn't care to consider right then. If he'd been startled he didn't show it.

"Talk to me," Harwell asked.

For a whole minute neither spoke.

"I assume it's very bad out there," said Michael, breaking the silence.

"It is," Harwell returned. "One of Smith's sons returned this morning from militia duty near the north 'wall' and was scared out of his wits. The wall's been breached and at least two Minutemen guards have been killed. In a couple of hours I expect an unwelcome visit here. Our men have been briefed over and over: Shoot only if fired upon and after everything else fails. But how they all react is anybody's guess."

Triana pulled her hand away from Michael.

"I'm going, Jonas," she said, turning the conversation. She nodded toward the window.

"You're sure?" Harwell's eyes glistened with tears. "I just…I just don't know about this —"

"The Space Goose, Jonas," she interrupted. "We can't let it be destroyed. It's not an accident. Too many impossible things have brought it here. And Marcus. And the four stories, especially *Inside the Hollow Spear*. I just can't forget what we all learned in that long tedious tale from Emryss, about Colin's incredible patience with a real witch girl, the awful battle at the tower, the underwater attempt to escape, the unexpected ending, as well as what kept Colin from finishing when —"

"Jonas, I'm going, too," Michael interrupted.

"Michael!" said Triana, "This is a 'forever' trip."

"Yes, Triana, one-way for years, for a lifetime, or maybe just a few seconds. I get the picture. I made you a promise and I plan to keep it. That's the way it is!"

"Michael, I release you from your promise," she whispered, but

149

loud enough for Harwell to hear. "Besides, it was just between us."

"I can't accept that," he replied.

"Why not?"

"Simple, Triana. Just think about it. I wouldn't be keeping my promise *now* if I let you change this. Think about what you asked — the *logic* of it, if you will! You're not going away alone, do you understand?" Let Marcus what's-his-name come to terms with that!

"I knew you were crazy, Michael."

"I am the one being crazy here?" he replied, arching his eyebrows. That's something else for you to think about!"

"Okay, okay," interrupted Harwell, "let's cut the play-acting that you two enjoy. You're right, we have no time. But, for the record, I'm really the crazy one here. Make no mistake about it."

"Perhaps craziness runs in our 'family,' sir," offered Michael.

Harwell offered his first smile. His eyes drilling straight ahead met four eyes staring back. Slowly, the two simultaneously worked their chairs sideways increasing the distance between them, forcing the minister to focus on just one of them at a time but not both at once. Harwell smiled for the second time.

"Isn't this better?" offered Triana.

"Now the two of us have a chance!" added Michael.

"How do you do things like that? Did you plan this? Have you really thought about it? You both remind me of Greek thinkers with time on their hands…willing to hear and talk about anything because they could handle it…like those St. Paul was preaching to on the beach in Athens. Paul's words seemed to be going well, until he mentioned 'Jesus rising from the dead,' information that was beyond their science and their common sense, and everyone left, rolling their eyes and laughing."

"Except two people stayed," offered Triana.

"And here we are!" added Michael. "But we're not staying for long.

150

We've read everything and discussed it. You've taught us well!"

At that moment came a knock on the door. Before Jonas could respond, Marcus stuck his head in. "All is ready, sir."

"Come in, Marcus," said the minister. He quickly did, glancing to the side and pulling up a chair on the other side of Triana. "You still agree to all this, Marcus?"

"Absolutely, sir."

"Then get back to the Elphlander and wait for my signal."

"Yes sir." With that he disappeared as quickly as he'd arrived. The door closed so quietly Michael wondered if he'd just dreamed what had happened.

"Jonas, last night I asked God for a sign that we'd *see more clearly* that we're on the right track in what we're doing," Michael said. "Is that okay?"

"And I agree," said Triana. *"I prayed for 'a sign that we could **see** more clearly.' "*

"A good question I'd say," said Harwell. "Triana, I've already told Michael, that the only thing that could persuade me to let a son and daughter do something so different, so untested, and so unexpected like this is to see an armed group of outsiders coming up the driveway planning to kill us. That was the sign I asked for. You've no idea how torn apart I am!"

He stood, stretching his legs.

"You know," said Jonas, "the best of the first missionaries died for doing their jobs."

"But," said Michael, "in Jesus' stories, didn't he like most those who took risks and did the right thing for the right reasons?" The clock with the Star of David on it and the car and the railroad tracks flashed into his mind.

Silence.

"Let's talk to God," said the minister.

151

Harwell dropped on his knees in the center of the room. "Thank you, Jonas," said Triana kneeling beside her foster father followed by Michael the son on his other side. Their heads together, they wrapped their arms around each other's shoulders. Harwell began: "O Father, may we do the right thing the right way at the right time and for the right reasons. And may we do nothing that will dishonor your name..."

Blam...Blam, Blam..........Blam

Michael sprang to the window.

"And?" asked Harwell.

" 'An armed group of outsiders is coming up the driveway trying to kill us,' " said Michael. "Maybe thirty. Several more are heading for the water tower. We're cut off. We've waited too long! We'll never get there now!"

Baaa...lam. The office window shattered, the slug ending in a book on the top of the bookcase across the room. It leaned forward and fell unceremoniously to the floor.

"You have everything you need?" said Harwell, asking a ridiculous question.

"It's already been packed according to your specs," said Michael, "except for my cane and what we've brought from the Hotel Crandel."

"Your things are stored in Pod 3," said the minister. "And you, Triana?"

"Yes, I'm ready."

"Yours are in Pod 2."

"And Pod 4?" asked Michael.

"No one," said Harwell.

Michael knew he didn't have to ask about Pod 1.

"And just how are we getting to the tower?" asked Michael.

"Think of Mt. Zareba, Michael."

"Whaaat?"

"The special place at the top…the best part of that story! Now give me a little help."

Together they rose to their feet and pushed back the ancient desk that Harwell spent so many hours behind. Finally it was off the occasional carpet underneath it. They rolled back the heavily worn fabric. Exactly under where the desk had been was a trapdoor with recessed hinges and handle.

"Don't looked so surprised!" said Harwell. "Some folks like saving old things like the hitching post down by the road, and the tunnel that was built for the underground railroad that begins right here"—he pointed to the floor—"and runs uphill to where an old underground hiding place that—"

"To the flat part of the hill that the water tower was built on!" interrupted Michael.

Jonas pulled the door open and Michael was first down the ladder. He caught Triana's and his bags they'd just brought in, along with his cane.

Triana followed and then Harwell, flicking on a small pocket solar light. The tunnel was cool, damp, and a bit larger than one might expect, tapering slightly to a roof of especially large flat stones. In some cases there was evidence of modern repair, perhaps done at the time of the arrival of the Elphlander. They walked on, slightly uphill and in relative silence for several minutes before they came to the end. A metal ladder of seven rungs led to an overhead door. Harwell pulled out his pocket phone and talked into it.

"Marcus is waiting. He'll take things from here. Unlike Earth spaceships, Elphian ones, at least this one, have tiny private pods completely equipped with personal necessities with access to a tiny communal area that can be reached by crawling through connecting windows and tunnels where some food can be obtained and wastes recycled. It's ingenious, and the pods are equipped with directions for everything. You're about to have at your fingertips a lot of practical information — and you've both proved that you can read and understand things."

Michael and Triana glanced at each other.

"So get ready for anything!" continued Jonas. "I want to say three things:

"First: All your knowledge of what's going to happen in the Susquehanna Territory and the rest of Earth disappears in minutes as you successfully leave this planet. Or die in the attempt. You will never know what caused the EMP explosions. I suspect it somehow is tied in with end times as we've often discussed. One thing that seems certain, however, is that the United States as a nation will not be a significant factor in what takes place. We've forfeited that opportunity. Now we may have to learn to endure severe suffering like much of the world already has for years.

"Second: Remember God's great summary commandments. (1) Love Him with all your heart, mind, soul, and strength and then wherever you end up (2) love your neighbors as *yourselves*. And you have to love yourselves to obey that. But don't let that love" — he glanced at each of them — "don't let that get in the way of the first one. I don't know what else to say."

"You said there were *three* things, Jonas," said Michael. "And the third one?"

Harwell paused.

"I'm glad only you two and God can hear what I'm going to ask. Everything normal and natural has disappeared. These will be the last words you ever hear from me. I have to be blunt."

"And?" asked Michael.

"With God's blessing, I would like to marry you two. Under the circumstances I know about, I think this should be done. I know you both. It's the proper thing to do and I have the authority to do it. Do

154

you object, Michael?"

"*Marry?*...No...no I...I don't object." Again his words worked their way out without thinking. He felt sweat cover his forehead.

"Triana, will you marry Michael?"

"No," she answered softly but firmly without explanation.

Immediately, Harwell pressed into Michael's hand a tiny flash-drive. "It has the words," he said, "if you need them."

How he could ever get to them was overlooked.

Michael was first to climb through the door in the steel floor of the tower. Triana was right behind him.

CHAPTER 15

Unexpected Visitors

Place: The Elphlander

*Time: **Day 332** (immediately follows)*

The gap between the launching platform and the small middle of the otherwise tapered tail of the Elphlander was only two feet.

But there was no time to even glance around inside the tower.

Michael quickly entered the open doorway at the center of the spaceship's tail, and found himself in a cramped triangular tunnel in the middle of three standing cylinders tapered at their tops, that looked as if the three were stuffed beside each other into a larger "mailing tube" cylinder where they exactly fit. Each cylinder contained a pod, over which Michael suspected rested the perimeter of the base of Pod #1, an inverted cone welded to the tapered noses of the three lower pods.

He began climbing straight up an incredibly narrow ladder, his tote bag and cane awkwardly squeezing their way up in front of him. He came to a round door on the side of a cylinder marked with a well-lit 3. Slightly behind him to his left and right were similar doors marked "2" and "4."

Pushing his door open, the entry door to the entrance to the interior of the circular pod was a scant three inches thick. The pod itself was

156

barely 6 feet in diameter across most of its length, and was 11 or 12 feet deep from the narrowed nearly pointed top to a circular floor no more than 18-inches across at the bottom. Barely keeping his bag from emptying, he dropped it safely to the pod floor. Then he climbed through and down onto a stiffly padded chair that at first glance seemed to "float" in the exact middle of the pod. At first it reminded him of an old leather-covered barber chair positioned higher than it should be from the tiny floor.

As he sat in the chair, he faced a wall straight ahead labeled "FRONT." Part of the curved surface there was flattened, and for want of a better common description, the flat panel in front of him resembled an old-time post office with various-sized boxes, some with clear plastic doors, some covered with knobs and sliding switches seeming to be filled with various foods, materials and services. To his right was the round door he'd just come through marked "RIGHT." Opposite to RIGHT, and marked "LEFT," was a thick glass window no bigger than a salad plate. There were two other larger round portholes, big enough to climb through if necessary. One was just to the left of RIGHT and above it was written "TO POD 2," where Triana should be, and the other just to the right of RIGHT announced possible entry "TO POD 4," said to be empty except for extra supplies.

From the chair in pod #3, however, all the remains of Michael's world seemed to be in reach, since by metal hand- and footholds on the wall, he could climb down, or pull himself down to the floor if there was no gravity and actually stand on it.

With a low hum a plastic-visored helmet slowly descended from the top point of the pod and dangled from a long tube.

"Put it over your head and fasten about the neck," said a recorded voice, "and tighten snugly by adjusting the knob at your right ear to inflate the neck collar. Unscrew to admit air, screw down to expel," added Marcus through a speaker Michael couldn't locate. "This isn't the air you'll breathe, just air that makes comfortable the fit of your helmet. This is temporary to help with pressure changes in lift-off. The air you breathe will come from the tube, though just for the beginning. Also, make sure the body straps around your legs and chest on your chair are secure."

Click.

Michael did as he was told. He could just touch the window to his left by leaning that way. In addition to the directions mentioned, he noticed "UP" painted just where the ceiling began to taper in to almost a point, and "DOWN" he discovered was mostly under where his bag had landed.

"Why these words?" asked Michael, certain that he would be heard.

"Your chair can turn 360 degrees," came a quick reply from overhead. "It's easier than you think to get confused. An Earth compass will soon be useless. I'm overhead at UP, and if we later land properly, DOWN will be down on Elphia in the way as down is on Earth. In space, we'll probably float more or less, and the magnets — just fastened to the side near DOWN, if turned on, can help you anchor yourself. Remember, the laser pointer on your chair arm can 'fix' on any of the 'mailboxes,' as we call them, and give you access to information, as well as things you may need. Later, you'll have time to orient and educate yourselves." *Selves* — That must include Triana who'd successfully boarded and was listening. Michael had been told to climb first and she had to follow though he'd not seen that happen. "More later. Prepare for 'lift-off.' "

Why did he feel a little lightheaded when they hadn't even moved? Was the air different in the spaceship?

"Triana?" Michael called.

"Later," said Marcus.

158

Orient me? wondered Michael. *"Mailboxes"*? Really! But it was hard to find a better word. Row after row of various-sized rectangular boxes were straight ahead and each box was lit with a tiny light. The first-time encounter with the inside of the pod was breathtaking, surreal. What was the outside of the Space Goose like? He still had no idea. Nothing he saw anywhere looked like anything he'd seen years ago at Cape Kennedy. Was he dreaming?

Oddly, a defect jolted Michael back to reality. Halfway to 'Left,' like a sliced, curled-in piece of onion, one top-to-bottom section of the wall in front of him was dark! Totally unlit.

A connection somehow must have broken. This wouldn't happen in a dream. But would this be critical?

But critical to what?

The darkened panel was the trigger. The projected trip, long or short, was real. A real attempt to pass through the impossible. A hundred things could stop them, kill them. Maybe a thousand. Yet Triana, examining everything so carefully, had the faith and determination to enter this unknown. She had to go. Go to people where stories strongly suggested that she could help. The princess from Emryss had dual citizenship, but on Earth, where she quietly and invisibly fit in, she had only some sort of visitor's visa. Earth DNA could come from either of two nearby sources if the ancient Elphian prophecy was to be literally fulfilled. So he had to come. But he refused to take that further.

And him? His heart was hardly as pure as hers. God knew that. Yet he'd also promised to follow God even if he'd mistakenly made a fool of himself. And he'd made a promise to a girl he hardly knew! Yet if ever there was anyone he would do that for, it was she. And, in the longest, and most wonderful, night of his life he had lain pleasantly, tensely, but innocently by her side, feeling her hair fall as silk on his shoulder, as he'd read to her. He sensed she'd welcomed every word, even identifying with distant royalty — a possible ancestor — at one part in the story. Her heart was calm, her body warm, even after just barely escaping being murdered. His heart, on the other hand, well...

And Jonas — who they'd never see again — had agonized over all this. Yet he hadn't stopped them.

The darkened panel. If they made it to Elphia at all, would be because of God. But that didn't mean it would be easy. He thought back again to "*The Fourth Prince*," still fresh in his mind. The magnificent horse, without which all would've been lost, had brought the young princess in that story and her husband to the final battle that had to be fought. But the special horse could not see, and in the heat of battle was brought down by an unattended spear wound.

A poem — not in the story — came to mind. Where had he heard it? It fit perfectly.

> "Your prayer has been answered,
> And not without cost;
> The battle you'll win,
> But the horse will be lost."

With wins, even unexpected promised ones, come losses. They'd knelt before God, feeling both scared and privileged to undertake such a risk. A questionable trip with a guaranteed no-return. Though he wasn't sure why, he felt God somehow would look after her...and him. At least for a time. But what would be the cost...what horse would he lose?

"All straps and helmets tight! We're lifting off," came the overhead voice.

Suddenly, Michael became aware of an extremely bright light coming from the window. Rather than a typical blast-off, there was a loud hum that grew louder and louder. He felt the Elphlander slowly begin to rise. Whatever was its power source? Why was he so clueless about that? They'd entered through the center of the very end of the ship where a rocket engine would be expected. But no engine was there. It had to be somewhere beneath the three pods, perhaps directly under his feet. Loosening his chest straps, he leaned toward the window as close as he could.

"Back in your seat!" came an order from above. Michael ignored it.

Down below, at the wire fence, a mob had broken through and surrounded the tower, staring upward. Obviously, the sliding observatory-type roof door had opened and the Elphlander had nearly passed through it. The people below became smaller. Most puzzling, however, was the intense bright light that seemed to come from somewhere out of sight behind him. People below began covering their eyes and falling backwards. Then he spied what had to be Jonas, his back to the ship, giving orders of some kind to men around him, who suddenly rushed to the fallen people and began gathering weapons before running as fast as they could back to the parsonage. A couple of hundred people farther down the driveway, staring their way, stopped in their tracks and became as trees, one by one toppling backwards until all were down.

Within seconds the ship began gathering speed and more sound with it. The people down below slowly shrank to the size of ants.

Then came a powerful explosion that brought small bits of debris almost as high as the spaceship.

At that point the lights inside briefly winked out, then all continued as before. Michael pressed his head against the window.

The tower they had come from was no more.

The humming of the ship grew louder. Whatever was driving them was hard at work. The ride so far was smooth. How fast they were going he could not determine. Though he hadn't been given permission, he removed his headpiece.

Michael recalled the strange explosion in the sky in the story, "*Death in a Tavern*" that they'd first discussed with Jonas and Cample only days ago. On impulse he aimed his laser pointer toward the mailbox labeled *Index*. A large keyboard appeared above the top row of boxes. With a bit of fumbling with the button on the end of the pointer he typed in "DISTANCE TRAVELED." Immediately 3.24 km flashed in one of the boxes in front of him. Then it jumped to 4.78 and began rapidly moving higher.

Next he entered "*Death in a Tavern*" in the Index. Immediately appeared "No entries found." Of course, that was expecting too much on such short notice. He loosened his straps, reached down to the floor and pulled out the loaf of bread wrapped in the towel with E. S. sewn on it. How good it felt to hold the familiar loaf! When he unwrapped it a folded piece of paper caught his eye. He opened it. On it was a note.

> M & T,
>
> > I do not trust your pilot. He may get
> > you there, but be very cautious after
> > that. Be aware that if you leave Earth,
> > Jonas is determined to keep details of
> > all this as private as possible. Our
> > concerns in Big Bend must take priority.
> > But a select few will quietly pray for you
> > daily. E. is in tears as I write this. May
> > God be with you two.
> > > —A. C.

Michael shivered. He must find a way to adjust the temperature.

But first to connect—privately—with Triana. Carefully, he tore the loaf of Mrs. Crandel's bread into two parts, putting one back into the bag. On the back of Amos's note, he scribbled, "We might be bugged. Enjoy the bread lest it be confiscated as 'unapproved.' Read and destroy this note. We're off. Thanks for the ticket to run away! Did you see the light? What did you think it was?" Carefully opening the windowless round door to Pod #2, he discovered a connecting tube big enough to crawl through to a similar door six inches away. He set the bag in the tube, tapped on her door and quickly closed his own. No sense of alerting Pod #1 of this exchange.

Five minutes later came a knock on his door. He let out a deep breath. She had to be there and be okay. He opened the door to find the bag carefully wrapped in several turns of denim cloth. It was her long skirt, and inside it a thick binder holding together many pages. It was "Inside the Hollow Spear," which never had a chance to be converted into electronic form. A penciled note was on the title page.

> Michael, I did what you asked. Here's the story,
> the final "evidence," right or wrong, that brought
> us here. Know it well! I certainly do. Since you're
> cold, here's our quilt—temporary, of course. Stay
> warm! The great light? I saw it at the edge. It was
> something like what happened in the beginning of
> "Death in a Tavern." Outside protection of some
> kind. Unexpected but reassuring. Your note's in
> the bag. The bread is delicious and welcome.
> 'Sanitation' is an important mailbox. Anyway, that's
> what it's called. I'm glad you're here.   —T

He pointed his laser to a large box at the lower left. It slid out. What promised to be some kind of toilet appeared. Michael shivered. And sending her skirt! Was he out of his mind — with her reading it as she claimed she could? How would he face her? His note. He searched the bag. Tiny bits of paper were at the bottom. How could she tear paper so small? Immediately, Michael scribbled a return note on a blank sheet he tore from the back of the manuscript. He felt like he was back in the fifth grade.

> Triana, but aren't you cold? Study the boxes. Take
> care of yourself. More later. — Michael

"Sanitation" was welcome. Pushing the indicated button, the box closed and disappeared. But there was no further sound. He noticed the box was next to the dark left panel.

In no more than three minutes…or three minutes it seemed, a second note came back.

> M, I'm a little scared, but fine. Plently warm
> because of something you — sort of — gave me.
> So don't worry. — T

Bluntly declaring she was "a little scared"… That was so Triana. But whatever had he given her? Michael noticed the humming rise at least a half octave higher. He would make himself relax. He gave himself to God and the chair, snuggly strapping himself down, leaving himself enough flexibility to read. He found and turned on a reading light. Just before he began, he decided to check the distance traveled once more.

Oddly, the digital light fluttered so fast he couldn't make out any numbers. No matter. On ordinary journeys to Mars, it took ten months in a regular spaceship. But he was going much farther than that — and in anything but a regular spaceship. He'd done all he could do. It was to Elphia or Heaven.

And he wasn't going alone.

He took several bites of the delicious bread from the Hotel Crandel. His mind modestly journeyed from the dining table on the first floor to the bed they had made in the attic. He began to read. He would study the mailboxes later.

PART IV

EMRYSS

Inside the Hollow Spear
(a story on and about Planet Emryss)
was planned to be here.
But, as with *The Fourth Prince,*
it will not be.

Michael and Triana have recently encountered four written adventures that have occurred on Planet Emryss, and that exoplanet only:

> *The Fourth Prince* (already mentioned in Part II)
> *Inside the Hollow Spear* (to be discussed here)
> *Death in a Tavern*
> *The Secret of Zareba*

None of these accounts concern Earth or Elphia.

Yet Earth and Elphia, are briefly mentioned once — and that was in a *prophetic vision* (which we will include here). One other mention of Elphia occurs, but it's marginal even to the story where it's mentioned. To record here all these stories would more than double the size of this book.

So why even mention them?

First, though they don't include Michael or Triana in any way, they have strongly suggested to Triana, not Michael, that she may have blood "connections" with Planet Emryss and Planet Elphia. Both teens, however, share a common physical and spiritual humanity designed by God.

Ephemeron Press suggests to deal with these four stories this way:

"In Part IV," we should provide only four kinds of relevant information from these accounts — and do it briefly. Consequently:

(1) We will extract any genealogical data that may concern Triana. (We've already done this for *The Fourth Prince* in Part II.)

(2) We will share part of a universal prophetic vision that appears in *Death in a Tavern*.

(3) We will present an overview of each of the four Emryss accounts that face entirely different problems and issues.

(4) We will introduce calendar and time similarities and differences on the three planets. (These will be further discussed when necessary.)

*　　*　　*　　*　　*

As to *Inside the Hollow Spear*

Important ancestors are assumed but not mentioned. Said to go back to the Mother of the God-Son on Emryss.

--------?---------

("many" generations and gaps implied)

King Agnon the Great

King Hendrick *(son of KA)*

King Merrick *(son of KH; had 4 sons and 1 daughter)*

Princess Lurinda *(daughter of KM; who had 4 sons including* **Crown Prince Gavin, Prince Fairold, Prince Crispin** *(dies after birth) and* **Prince Colin** *and a daughter)*

Prince Colin is the main character in this impossible quest.

In this story he must warn people in three locations ("cities") near the palace to flee their peninsular kingdom that's about to be destroyed for forsaking the God of Heaven.

Colin, with his "message," is joined by an irascible and unexpected menagerie of questionable true believers, only to face grave robbing, witchcraft, other forms of the macabre, an illiterate priest, fighting to stay alive, personal imprisonment, natural disasters, and a questionable romance.

In the account that he reports, but is unable to finish, Prince Colin unexpectedly learns that *one of his near ancestors came from a world called Elphia* — a place far away and unknown to Emryssites.

This is the first of the two places in the Emryss stories that Elphia is mentioned.

*　　*　　*　　*　　*

-------?--------

(Again, many generations and gaps are implied.)

King Agnon the Great

--------?--------

The "Queen" *(name omitted, but said to be granddaughter of KA; most probably **Queen Lurinda; who had 4 sons including Crown Prince Gavin, Prince Fairold, Prince Crispin, Prince Colin,** and one daughter)*

The Queen and her first- and second-born sons land on a beach in a small boat, escaping the destruction of their small kingdom. The three are awakened in the middle of their first night ashore by a profound shared vision.

The content of this vision, goes far beyond the story that immediately follows it, and is significant to understanding the world of worlds that includes Planet Emryss and two other faraway places.

So we include a portion of it here.

In the supernatural vision, three men in shining white robes appear on the other side of a dying fire where the Queen and her sons were sleeping. The fire springs to life. On the left is **Prince Crispin** (in "adult form" from home planet Emryss); in the center is **Abel** (from unknown Planet Earth); and on the right is **Vandor** (from unknown Elphia); they face the startled royal family.

We break into the middle of the vision.

..."Crispin, I'm puzzled," said the Queen. "According to the Holy Book there is one God-Maker, who is one with the God-Son; and there is one death — that of the God-Son — and one coming back to life for the forgiveness of sins, yet the cross that Abel wears on his robe, and the [target-like] circles that Vandor wears on his robe are unfamiliar. Why do they not wear the stakes? Are there many God-Sons in the flesh and many holy deaths?"

"ONE GOD...ONE SON IN FLESH...ONE WORLD OF MANY

169

WORLDS... ONE DEATH FOR SIN ONE TIME FOR ALL... PRAISE
THE LORD... PRAISE THE LORD... PRAISE THE LORD!"

From behind them [a line of others also in white at the shoreline] the words echoed. Their arms were lifted. Above them the stars seemed to dance. The music was joyful, pleasant, daring imitation, contradiction.

It was Vandor's time to speak. His voice was gentle, but strong enough so not a syllable was lost.

"My gracious Queen, there are many worlds which look the same, feel the same underfoot, and have similar plants and creatures on the ground and in the air. However, there are differences: In my world [Elphia] there are two moons — one the size of yours here, and one smaller, like the moon in Abel's world. Our three suns, though, are mirror images of each other and our minutes, hours, days, and weeks — which are a special gift from God — are exactly the same. 'Teach us to number these our days, O God, that we might serve you.'

"Now as to Emryss, the God of Heaven and his Son have come as the Holy Book bears witness.

"In Abel's world, the God-the-Father as they call him and the God-Son have come and left a book that is very similar.

"And in my world, called Elphia [Vandor continued], God and his Son have also come in the same manner; but years ago in a great act of evil, then called 'wisdom,' my people destroyed every copy of the I-Rex Code, the special Holy Word that God had given us. Almost everything from that book has been lost; nevertheless, one curious prophecy refused to die: 'Thus says the God of all worlds, in the days to come many will fall away, but a remnant will be spared. And after the BLOOD OF THREE WORLDS mingles in a child, my people will once again believe.'

"My gracious Queen, from your children will come a child who is also from my world, who will return to my people with the lost mes-

sage of the Son-of-the-Highest-God's great act of salvation which is for everyone who will believe."

[End of Quotation]

It was the prophecy about revival that deeply caught Triana's attention. But not, apparently, the Queen in the story. For her, it was a second prophecy that immediately followed the one just mentioned.

"…[Your] old kingdom is only hours from its promised destruction…Dry your tears for your youngest son [Colin who was missing] and go with your two remaining sons immediately and rapidly far west for a great King on Emryss needs help from a remnant of your tiny kingdom. The reputation of your royal family has traveled far."

[End of special prophecy]

Though it may seem surprising, it is at this point where the action of *Death in a Tavern* actually begins (at Chapter 2 of 10)

*   *   *   *   *

As to The Secret of Zareba

The timeline here begins about 15 years after *DIAT*. It assumes the previous genealogy with the following additions:

Prince *(called "Lord") Fairold*
Prince Galen *(son of PF)*
Princess Triana *(daughter & firstborn of PG; mentioned only as a detail at the very end of the account)*

In this story, after Emryss's holy city Zareba falls miles away, a confederacy of kings from the "south" who openly reject the God of Heaven, with an army of a thousand soldiers, arrives to conquer the small unwalled Zareba Village, home of Emryss's famous weavers. Earlier, the village was quickly evacuated by Lord Fairold, leaving much behind. Teenaged Prince Galen and eight others—joined by a young defector from the south—remain in an attempt to spare losing a hard-to-reach unoccupied walled fortress atop Mt. Zareba (a 3rd "Zareba"). This unusually shaped "mountain" is an easy walk from the village. In their months on the mountain the defenders learn important secrets—and several give up their lives.

At the end of this written account, a strange note was penciled in:

"*Emris grohw smaal lik pohnt. Girrrll now leffft oft criing.*
Hav al books in haanfd. Saffe liftoff once agin.

It was this ending that specially held Triana's attention. To her, it seemed that someone new to Earth language must have scrawled this in to suggest that the girl Triana was real along with the story of her past.

*   *   *   *   *

Calendars and time on the three planets are alike in some ways and different in others. The following foreshadows what will be developed—as needed—later, as action in a new world suddenly races ahead in several directions.

Planet	Days in Year
Earth	365
Emryss	420
Elphia	420

All three planets revolve around suns. In all the seconds, minutes, hours, days, and weeks are identical. However, the 12 months in Emryss and Elphia all have five 7-day weeks. Earth is the oddball here.

What are practical consequences of this? Here are two:

(1) A comparison of ages in "years lived" on each of the two exo-planets will be slightly less than years on Earth if one considers "days lived." For example, a year "there" would equal 1.15 years "here." Hence a 7-year-old on Elphia would have lived about as many days as an 8-year-old on Earth.

(2) *The Sabbath* (as the 7th day of the week) is assumed — and later established.

The reader is now ready for Part V.

ELPHIA

CHAPTER 16

The Journey Ends

(Immediately follows the end of PART III)

Place: An unknown ocean shoreline
Time: Day 1 ALOE (early evening, warm)

A new reckoning of time begins…

When Michael came to, he smelled smoke. Where was he? He struggled to remember. Then a wave crashed down, mocking and spraying him with a shower of water.

What!

He smiled, suddenly recalling what must have been Prince Fairold's reaction at the first part of the story that he, Triana, Jonas, and Mr. Cample had discussed — was it only "days" earlier?

His eyes opened wider. But this was hardly a story! He heard a squawk of approaching birds, some kind of gulls, but why were they dropping down from the sky?

And why could he see them!

A wave smacked the outside of the Elphlander and more water slopped over the ragged edge where the top once was attached and sprayed his face. The air was warm, the water salty. Immediately, he loosened his chest and leg seatbelts, grabbed the printed story still in his lap, so far barely wet. He reached down to the floor, pulled up his canvas bag, and jammed the binder inside. He grabbed the skirt/blanket caught on his chair arm and also stuffed it in. He zipped the bag shut, praying it was waterproof.

Overhead he saw what seemed like a sunny late afternoon sky. But it contrasted badly with a horrible rotten odor. Several squawking gulls landed on the part of the overhead wall that was still left.

He stood on his seat and grabbed the built-in ladder rungs that let him climb at least three feet higher. At least half of Pod #1 had to be ripped away. Through the torn-open side Michael saw about eight feet below what seemed to be inviting sandy beach receiving a strong incoming tide.

Whatever was left of the overhead pod? He dreaded turning around. At least half of what had to have been instrumentation had been ripped away. Drops of blood and excrement seemed to cover every square foot of the remaining inside wall. A tied boot was pinned between a ladder rung and the wall. A gull dropped and landed on a detached lower leg bone that projected from the boot. There was no other trace of the pilot. Somehow a pressure seal must have ruptured in Pod #1, and everything above his ceiling had exploded into the vacuum of space, probably only seconds before landing. Death must have been instantaneous. Michael barely swung around in time. He vomited into the sea.

Each pod was a self-contained unit, he'd been told, and his had been obviously spared until the landing. But what about Triana's?

He scrambled down the rungs, moved to the round door where he'd exchanged bread and notes, opened it, stretched out his arm, and pounded on Triana's porthole door six inches away.

Nothing.

He pounded again and began screaming. Just as a tidal wave rocked the ship, the door slowly opened. He sensed what was left of the Elphlander had sunk further. Triana stood facing him, groggy and

177

glassy-eyed, wearing his flannel shirt that he'd looked for everywhere while packing and couldn't find. He slapped her cheeks.

"Triana, your bags, everything! Hand it to me quickly!" Automatically, she did. Michael stacked things in his seat, praying they wouldn't slide out. Then as she crawled through the door into his pod, he shook her to make her wake up, and helped her attach to the hand- and footholds along the wall. Fortunately, she and all she had was surprisingly intact.

"Go up the ladder. GO!" He pointed to the opening overhead. "I'll hand you everything. Throw it out, don't lose sight of it! The tide looks pretty rough here. I'll be right behind you."

"And Ma...Marrrr...cus?" she said slurring his name.

"He's gone, Triana. Gone."

She climbed the rungs and sat on the floor of Pod #1, dangling her legs down in Michael's face.

"Look down, Triana, down, outside and in. BUT DON'T TURN AROUND! Do you hear me, Triana?" He discovered his ears were ringing. "Down, down, but don't look up or back! You hear me?"

"Yes, Michael! Yes! You don't have to shout!"

Good! She was coming around. He handed up everything, one bag at a time, his cane last.

"Jump!"

Oh God, let it be deep enough! he prayed.

SPLASH.

At the last second he wondered if she could swim. After a last glance down in his pod, he followed her.

SPLASH.

When they both surfaced, and found they could just barely touch bottom, a large wave immediately took them both off their feet and back underwater, only to dump them abruptly in a heap at the shoreline twenty feet away. All of their belongings, had been pushed ahead of them another ten feet or so. He grabbed his cane as the water started to pull it back. They raced to take everything farther up the beach to dry sand. Triana was now wide awake. It was Michael who did most of the coughing to clear his lungs.

At last they stood in a clear spot, maybe fifty feet from the water, and the same distance from a seventy-foot vertical cliff that ran in a straight line both ways along the beach as far as they could see.

Triana immediately unzipped her bag. Michael watched her quickly inspect and repack all she'd brought. Something was very different about her but what? Surprisingly, almost nothing packed was seriously wet. Michael, seeing a small row of scrubby bushes nearby, eventually found an armload of enough burnable wood he could later use to build a small fire that he hoped would last when the sun disappeared. Matches? He had a thousand of them if they were still dry, as well as a solar lighter.

Strangely through all this, neither spoke. She smiled at the puzzling look that he tried to hide.

"The girls' room is behind there," he said, pointing back to the bushes. When she looked bewildered, he added, "That hiding space behind the brick chimney in the Hotel Crandel is very far behind."

"How far, Michael?"

He smiled and turned away before he had to say more.

"I'll never forget the Hotel Crandel, Michael."

"And the gun in the window?"

"The gun in the window? Oh, I'd almost forgotten." She grit her teeth and offered a faint smile. Then she leaned down, picked up her bag, and just as she'd started toward where Michael had pointed, she stopped and reached in her bag.

"Here, Michael." She underhanded him a bar of soap. "The *bathroom* with a bath is that way."

She'd packed soap, at least a bar of it—not something in a bottle!

179

Well, that was Triana. He was glad. He wondered what else was tucked away in that big canvas bag.

He tossed her his cane and moved to the shoreline. Fortunately, the distance was enough so that with her limited vision he could strip to his shorts, which he could wash along with himself without offending. He plunged into the waves and soon emerged scrubbed clean and in good spirits.

As he approached the water's edge, a glint of fading sunlight came from a small piece of metal sticking up from the sand. He looked down and gasped. It was her glasses. But more than that, the rims were bent and both lenses were smashed. He picked up the pieces. How could he show her this? That's why she seemed different! As long as he'd known her at least a half-dozen times or so an hour, with a slight of hand, she'd put on and take off the thickest glasses he'd ever seen. Without them she was truly beautiful. Yet vanity seemed so foreign to her. That just wasn't how she presented herself. Without glasses he knew she could happily disappear into her own thoughts and switch on the disarming "radar" wired into her.

Halfway back he pulled on his jeans—clean now but still wet. She would expect him to do that.

She was smiling when he met her.

"Here—I'm so, so sorry." He handed her the remains of her glasses. She received them without seeming at all upset. Then with a huge, un-characteristic smile, she looked at him, trying not to laugh, it seemed.

"Will you promise me something and not try to get even?" were her first words.

"Whaaat? What's wrong with you?"

"Just say 'yes.'"

"Why?"

"Because, Michael, I'm asking you to." For an instant she looked helpless. He shivered.

"Yes."

Pause.

"Help me, Michael. You were out there washing your shorts and I was watching you."

"Uh…watching?" he interrupted. He let his jaw fall and, crossing his hands over his chest, he made himself look shocked. Slowly he inched backwards.

"Stop, Michael, you're making fun of me! Our prayer for a sign has been answered. I'm sorry!"

"Sorry?"

"But Michael, I watched and watched you!"

"Triana, it's okay, okay. You're a…a little bit scary…and…I'm a bit shy too, but don't worry."

"Michael, stop! I'm the one that's shy and I can't help it! But Michael… Michael, I can *see*! I can *see* without glasses! And…and the first thing I saw was you!"

He was totally without words…words properly passed through his brain as Esther Crandel would expect.

He reached out and put his hands on her cheeks. Red face to red face, he pulled her toward him and touched his lips to hers. Then he pushed back. It wasn't the right time for anything more. "Thank you, God," he prayed aloud.

"Thank you, Michael," she whispered as if she were hearing his deepest thoughts and others were standing within earshot.

It was Michael's turn.

"Triana, life has called both of us to do some very unexpected things. I did nursing care for Aunt Steffi, simply because there was no one else. And I suppose you did the same for Igneal. Why? We had to. Circumstances changed everything. Now everything has changed again."

"Michael, I don't want anything to stand in the way of what we're

181

supposed to do. I don't want God to turn his back on us!"

"Don't worry, Triana, everything's okay."

"Okay, then, please turn your back on me. Okay?"

"Uh..."

"I need to wash and I need you close by because—and you probably don't know—I can't swim. But, of course, I made it to shore and right now I need you looking the other way."

"As long as you keep splashing louder than the waves, I will."

He sat in the sand. With his back to the water, he studied the tall cliff that rose almost vertically several dozen feet away. He hardly noticed his old flannel shirt fall in the sand next to him. In many places trees came to the very edge at the top. In others it was tall grass. At one place stood an unusual row of six posts or burned-off trees—two one-third shorter than the other four.

It was then that his eyes rose to the sky.

Where in the world were they? This was too much like the Earth they left. But never had he seen cliffs so suddenly steep and tall. Maybe he was in shock of some kind. Yet they'd skillfully, or providentially, saved themselves and what they'd brought with them. The sky began to slowly darken. Automatically, he found himself thinking about where to set up a camp for the night. That was the only logical thing to do.

Several dozen yards away and further down the beach, to their left as they faced the cliff, the remains of a spaceship that they'd never really seen intact were about to sink out of sight. Had they fallen back somewhere on their own planet? Or had they done something no other earthling, which at least one of them was, had ever done: enter another Earth-like world without a spacesuit? And how could they be alive anywhere if part of their spaceship had blown apart?

He glanced higher in the ever darkening sky and gasped. Suddenly, he had one of his answers. There were footsteps behind him.

...an unusual row of six posts... two one-third shorter than the other four.

Suddenly, he had one of his answers.

"Michael, give me a few seconds, please."

From the corner of his eye he saw his flannel shirt rise from the sand. When he was allowed to turn, she had the large, oversized shirt on. The rest of her clothes she carried.

"Sorry about my short hemline."

How was he supposed to respond to that? She was—well, he couldn't say that, either. On one of his "clocks"—one of them—was that thing about "timing."

"It's just fine," he offered. It was time, however, to turn the conversation.

"How did you get my shirt? I looked for it everywhere when packing!"

"At Aunt Steffi's funeral, I sneaked it away. I had to wash it for you, remember why? No, please don't!"

"Can I have—"

"Sorry, I still need it."

"Triana, it's yours…for as long as you want."

184

They moved to where their belongings were.

The sky became darker. Hand in hand, they walked to the water's edge, then carefully into the shallow waves, back and forth along the beach, careful to not take their eyes off what they'd left behind. They hardly spoke. It wasn't time for any more words. The beach seemed to go forever in either direction with little change. They returned to where they started.

"It's getting a little chilly," he said. "I have our skirt blanket. I need to fix our bed."

"Our bed! No, Michael. Fix my bed. If you get cold and uncomfortable, you may lie beside me…and your flannel shirt."
He forced himself not to laugh, even smile. She was a "word girl" and he didn't want her to hold back or change a syllable of what she said.

Darkness fell.

After some bread, cheese, and hardtack that Triana produced from somewhere, she lay down and Michael, suddenly shivering, and not hiding it, breathed a short prayer, and lay next to her, his knife and cane on his other side. Without a word, she lay her head on his shoulder. Michael slowly tucked his arm around her, which she allowed, and stared overhead to try and find the brightest star in the unfamiliar sky. It was a perfect time to start winding his clocks. Immediately, she was fast asleep. How could she do that so quickly?

Not so with Michael.

The fire burned down to glowing ash. Unknown to Michael at the time, the six dark fence posts on top of the cliff had disappeared.

The First Morning

Time: Day 2 ALOE (after landing on Elphia) 7AM, it seems

Facing the ocean on their left, an early sun announced the first day of the rest of their lives.

Would they live together and die together in a new world? If so, for how long? The answer, Michael suspected, wouldn't be simple. But never would he have suspected the path that lay ahead.

But he was with Triana, and both had survived unhurt and with perfect vision. That was enough for now.

"Okay, let's go over everything," he declared. "We're not on Earth, because —"

She pointed to the sky. The double moons Michael had just noticed earlier were still visible and had squeezed even closer together during the night, seeming to start to join, though obviously one was behind the other, probably moving at a different speed. It was as if someone in need of glasses was seeing double. But "glasses" now? None were needed as only Triana could appreciate.

Michael wondered how that affected the "fine-tuning" argument that, according to Harwell, demanded a Creator. The two moons were an obvious difference from the perfectly made world he had left. If gravity, air, and animals here were similar, the oceans with their for-midable, and highly irregular, tides probably caused by independently moving moons—now close to each other and combining their effect on ocean water—was not. As if to punctuate Michael's thoughts, the tide had now pulled away the edge of the shoreline nearly a hundred yards. Left behind was fresh sand with shallow puddles, probably containing trapped marine life that might be edible.

"Gravity and the air seem the same," added Triana. "And the birds—"

"The ones at the ruined top of the Elphlander," interrupted Michael, "were like our herring gulls, though a little larger and striped differently." He looked back to the water. The ruined spaceship, fragile like a broken eggshell, had somehow tipped over on its side during the night, and had been rolled and torn and carried farther to their right, as they faced the sea. He suspected all sizable traces of it would soon be gone.

"Then," he continued, "there's the radiation from the sun, growing warmer by the minute, and the water itself and what's in it, chemicals, animals, plants, bacteria—we've no idea what—or how it will affect us. We've got to be careful. Our bodies must have to adjust at least a little. Perhaps a lot. Whatever we eat here will—"

It was Triana's turn to interrupt.

"Yes, Michael, don't forget me, an alien on Earth! If things were fine-tuned enough on Earth for me to exist there, then maybe wherever there are humans created in the image of God, the blueprints for a humans' world also must be similarly and carefully crafted. And, *yes, of course it's impossible to get to such a world, yet here we are.* And we got here in almost no time at all…at least time that we're aware of. Uh… Michael, why are you looking at me like that."

"I was thinking about…the fact that…I slept with an alien last night."

"MICHAEL! You were sleeping *beside* me, not with me! And, by the way, *you* are the total alien here. I'm just one-half—or probably a much smaller percentage!"

187

"Triana, yes, the 'one-half' is a bit off, if your grandfather, or great-grandfather, was Elphian. But…but can we kiss and make up?"

He was surprised how quickly, though mechanically, she moved toward him, with her forefinger raised.

"Okay, just once," he said, initiating their private Earth tradition into a new world. "Sally would be proud." And so they did, without anyone within sight or earshot, or so they thought. Now they must move on to mundane things like survival, protecting themselves from whomever might be watching — as they would soon learn was actually happening.

Back to business: Food… he'd never felt so hungry! Theirs was gone.

But Triana's stomach was first to grumble. "Sorry, Michael."

How unexpected an apology for something like that!

"Now, Triana, as dumb as this sounds, while we are *fasting*, we need to kneel right here in the sand and bring to God — and each other — every little thing that pops into our minds, and thank Him for success so far. We've got a thousand things to think about, but first we need to pray."

A blessing perhaps, for some kind of meal. How ridiculous it sounded, but he was with her and *talking her language*. And it seemed appropriate to do. Didn't God love little children? Without even suggesting it, both removed their shoes and dropped to the sand side by side. Michael took her hand. They bowed their heads. He began:

"Dear Lord, thank you for bringing us safely here in spite of almost every reason that this couldn't happen. Thank you for restoring Triana's eyesight, even though…" — he felt her fingernails press into his palm — "…even though, it might have been presumptuous to ask for a sign after all the signs You'd already given." He heard her expel a quick breath, and the next thing he felt — right in the middle of his praying — was his hand being lifted and receiving the split-second touch of her lips. Automatically, he continued praying what he hoped were the right words—though he couldn't recall them later. He paused several times to let her interject words of her own. How unbelievably easy it was to kneel beside her and ask God honest questions like "Where should we go?" and "What should we do?" in ordinary words.

He'd never learned that in Sunday school.

When they'd finished, without even discussing direction, they, barefoot and wearing quick-dry cargo shorts, headed "left" (as they faced the ocean) along the beach, working their way closer to the incoming water, as if wanting to put what remained of the Elphlander, now covered with scavenging gulls, as far behind them as possible.

Their bags of belongings were manageable.

High above them on the cliff, though unnoticed just then, the six "blackened fence posts" also moved in the same direction. In just minutes, Michael's attention was captured by a shallow pool that the retreating tide had left behind. In it were several trapped fish, five to seven inches long—one kind, long and narrow, dark gray with a light blue underside, that resembled perch, the other, flatter and more football-shaped like croppie, though mixed orange and pink in color.

Using his shirt as a crude net, he waded into the shallow water and in almost no time had thrown three of each kind out of their watery world. But he would not eat raw fish. In minutes he'd gutted two of each kind, as Triana located some dry twigs and larger dead branches from shrubs at the base of the cliff. And she'd started a fire with wood shavings using a solar magnifier as they'd once practiced in school. From his bag he took a small tarp, large enough to sleep on, and a favorite tin skillet with a fold-over handle. Though he'd no grease, two of each kind were carefully fried—*separately*—stopping to scour the skillet with sand in between.

"Why, Michael?" Triana asked.

"We have to eat something," he replied. Triana's stomach grumbled

In minutes he'd gutted two of each kind...

again. "These fish could help us or kill us, Triana."

"How about an 'in-between'?" she offered.

"Triana, each of us is not going to eat both kinds. You pick one and I'll take the other. If one of us dies, the other could do the burying…"

Without responding, she knelt and inspected them, as if they were a piece of jewelry.

"I'll take the long skinny ones, please, unless…"

"The long skinny ones are yours." Together they sat on the tarp and with their fingers slowly began eating, one small bite at a time until one of each of the fishes disappeared.

"Delicious, Michael! I didn't know you could…" She watched Michael struggle to his feet. "Michael, are you all right?"

"Ahh…uh…uh…I…I…I…" He stood, staggered, and stumbled toward the water's edge. When a wave reached his ankles, with a loud retching sound he vomited. When more wanted to come up, he vomited again and stumbled facedown into the next wave. Triana ran to him and pulled him up. But that wasn't all. He felt fire all the way down to his stomach. His body begged to let go. "Oh, oh, ohno!" He felt his bowels relax. Fluids pored from several parts of his body. He was waist deep in water. "Oh no! This can't be happening!" At least he still possessed his voice.

"Well, it is, Michael. Come where it's shallower. You need to have your clothes off and we don't want to lose them." It was then that he fainted, or halfway so, and he imagined himself to be Aunt Steffi, and standing over her, his ghost began attending to very personal needs. With Steffi he'd faced such scenarios like this.

Because there was no one else.

But this time it was he on the ground with Triana kneeling beside him.

He became fully conscious on the tarp with one side of it folded over his bare body. In the distance Triana, with her bar of soap, was

191

washing out everything he had worn. She returned to where he lay.

"Here are just your cargo shorts. They're damp, but put them on. The other things need to dry a bit. That's all you're getting for now. I'll turn around." And she did, struggling, Michael suspected, not to laugh.

Though still a bit dizzy, he quickly did what she ordered.

"You're convinced I'm okay now?" he asked.

"Healthy enough. That's the quickest turn-around of a case of bad food I've ever seen. I don't think it had time to do any real damage. I had a similar scare a couple of times with Igneal, so I learned on the job."

"Weren't you scared just then?" he asked.

"No, not scared, but I'm thoroughly soaked. Michael, your making us test our food was wise. Fortunately though, my choosing was wiser!" How could she say such a thing? "Michael, I know what you're thinking. I know we can fail in what we've come to do, but we used our heads as best as we could, so we just couldn't fail *that* way."

Michael stood. He only had on his cargo shorts. He could smell soap on his arms and chest. He leaned forward and felt the breeze push several strands of her damp disheveled hair brush against his cheek. He searched her eyes.

"And you can still stand to be with me? And…and still like me?"

" 'Stand to be with you'? Yes, Michael. I don't have much choice here, do I?" She extended her arms and offered a patronizing smile. "And 'like' you, Michael? I much more than like you, and have ever since the day Cample accused us of cheating. Here, Michael, if you're up to it, here's my other fish. It's delicious, by the way."

Only Triana could say something like that and immediately change the subject. Little did Michael know their day's adventure had just begun.

CHAPTER 18

The Deadly Falls

Time: Day 2 ALOE (8 AM)

"Yak a do don gamboline, Shirra, Gurdon, no! NO!"

The yelling came from the cliff not quite 200 feet away, or counting in the height—midway up the cliff—60 feet further.

Triana put down what she was packing and Michael reached in his bag for a dry shirt. "Keep your eyes on *them*," she said, before darting behind him to open her bag, pull out a dry pullover top and her familiar long wrap-around skirt. As they studied the cliff face, she started pulling a comb through her hair. Ahead, like flies on a wall, six men with long staffs, or spears, and what looked like folded-up nets were running along some path that zig-zagged down the edge of the cliff.

Soon it was clearer. Two smaller men—no, it was children—were in front.

"Shirra, Gurdon, ondey yen! No!" shouted a large man with a deep voice several feet behind them.

"Ginga lay ee!" exclaimed the man behind him, stopping for a second, pointing toward Michael with his spear.

Michael attached his sheathed knife to his belt and automatically took a short coil of rope—a favorite outdoor accessory—from his bag

193

to carry on his shoulder. Just as Michael picked up his cane the first child slipped. Michael gasped. Now the child was over the edge, hanging by his fingers. The second child behind was down on his knees. He reached for the first one's arm, but was too far away, as were the men running toward them.

Then came the horrifying falls, first one then the other. They began with short slides, each reaching back for the occasional clump of grass or a shrub. But it was too steep. The last thirty feet or so was a free fall to the sand.

Immediately, Triana and Michael were beside them, kneeling. Seconds later four men in black hooded jackets stood before them with raised spears. All appeared to have thick dark hair and wore short beards that seemed unnaturally groomed.

"**Arvarham! Farno! NO!**" screamed Triana. She pushed the palms of her hands straight ahead as if daring them to come further. She dropped her eyes to the children without waiting for their response.

The spears were lowered.

The men, with hoods still covering most of their faces, fell to their knees on the other side of the two who lay motionless. It wasn't two boys, but a boy and a girl, maybe 9- or 10-years old. (They would learn more about their ages later.) The boy was motionless, not breathing — clearly dead. The girl was screaming. A bone pierced the skin of her lower leg and stuck out about three inches. One of the men turned to the side and vomited.

"Calm her, Michael," said Triana as she turned to the boy. His motionless head was bleeding. Michael handed her his shirt. She pressed it over the bleeding. She kissed the boy's forehead and held his head tight in her arms. She whispered a prayer, "For your Name's sake, O God."

Suddenly, the boy took a deep breath.

But the girl continued screaming and began to shake. Michael held her firmly against his chest and ran his fingers through her long dark hair as she began to go into shock. "You're going to be okay, you're going to be okay," he said in his perfect English as she continued to sob.

Triana pointed to the smallest man to step forward and waving her hand urged him to take her place with the boy. She turned to the girl and checked her breathing. She nodded to the large man to kneel beside her.

"Michael, your cane and your —"

"Got 'em right here." He began uncoiling his rope.

"We've got to get this bone back in place."

"But Triana —"

"We must do it, Michael. The tibia, the bigger bone, may be cracked, but the bone sticking out is the smaller fibula. While I push the bone back in place, you and our new friend, pull the leg out — hard, but slowly." She nodded to the man who had vomited to hold the girl's head — tight, she emphasized with her hands — and pointing to a spear, asked him to take it. Then Triana stuck her hand in her mouth, and biting down indicated that the large man should do the same with the spear shaft in the girl's mouth. This was going to hurt...

The girl screamed as Triana slowly pushed inch by inch, and the bone somehow made its way back inside the skin. Instinctively, Michael wrapped the leg with a favorite T-shirt and tied a knot to hold the bandage in place. He lay the cane beside the leg, and with others slowly lifting the girl as she continued to wail, he wound the rope around and around her leg from the middle of her thigh to the end of her toe. As Triana had done to the boy, Michael kissed the girl's forehead and cradled her head in his arms. Triana knelt beside her, and when the men looked puzzled about what they were doing, she bade them kneel as well.

195

They did.

"Klaven deto Grott a Harven!" she declared. "Nardo Grott dimren laude. *["Pray to God of Heaven...Give God praise."]*

"Garvatten cano det?" asked one of the men. *["Where you from?]*

"Cai munlolo, det **Elphia**." *["My great-grandfather, from Elphia."]* Triana made a circle like a basketball with her hands, pointed to the ground, and smacked the sand beside her with her palm. "Cai mun, rexati det **Emryss**." *["My father, a prince from Emryss."]* Making another circle she pointed to the sky. "Cai hanred det **Earth**."*["My man, from Earth."]* Making still another circle she pointed up at the sky to another spot. "Grott farnon caium det Earth deto Elphia" *["God brought us from Earth to Elphia."]* She pointed up to her Earth in the sky, then to Michael and herself.

"Cai Grott!" exclaimed the man. *["My God!"]*

"Caifutu vagoon-oofa!" said the large man. *["We saw the airship!"]*

"Pragattan prando!" ordered Triana. *["Talk later!"]*

"Michael," said Triana, "we must pray against infection. I've no idea what dangers they have here, and we have nothing we can give her. Pray for everything you can think of."

"Got it," he replied. But before he started, he spied a man pulling out a bottle. Michael motioned for it and he received it. After sniffing it, he took a swallow and almost choked. "This will kill any germ on any planet!" He poured some on the wound where the skin was pulled together. The girl screamed. The spear handle was pressed between her teeth. He handed the bottle back to the man. "Triana, tell him to give her a little to drink if she screams."

Without even glancing at the men, Michael and Triana raised their hands to Heaven, and the men—after the large man, apparently their leader, nodded—also stayed on their knees and raised their hands as well. The two prayed to the God of Heaven, the God of all worlds, the

God who had made everything and had safely brought them from a distant planet that none of their companions knew anything about.

While they prayed, and for a short time afterward, a cloud, very much like Earth clouds moved directly in front of the sun, blocking the direct sunlight, but causing the whole cloud to glow without shape like melted butter. Seeing this, the men one by one lowered their strange hoods. Their skin was lighter than one would expect for fisherman. Were they especially sensitive to sunlight?

Triana returned to the boy and checked for breathing. He was. She kissed him again on the forehead, then on each cheek. His eyes opened. He moved each arm. Slowly he stood. There was no mark on his head from where he'd been bleeding. The men's jaws fell. Michael tried to hide his surprise.

The girl, her leg now secure in the rope-and-cane splint, finally closed her eyes and lay quietly in the net, soon to be converted into a litter with the insertion of a spear into each side. While they packed to leave for wherever the fishermen's destination might be, Michael again and again checked her breathing. It was regular and when he kissed the back of her palm, her hand was warm.

*   *   *   *   *

When Triana rubbed her stomach and pointed to her mouth, the men returned to where she and Michael had eaten breakfast, and provided bread and a kind of corn on cobs only half as long as cobs on Earth. It was chewy, but surprisingly tasty. "Kerm," they called it. This was followed by dried fruit of some kind. Most welcome, however, was pure, salt-free water.

There was no testing, no selecting this time.

When the men saw the remains of the flat, orange-pink fish, they were horrified. "Proxin!" they declared. Michael learned later that the

197

fish was deadly poisonous—in fact, the name of the fish was the same as poison itself—and since Michael had eaten nearly a whole fish and had survived, the men stared at him in unbelief. "Parlaten," the long slender fish chosen by Triana was not only rare but quite edible, and actually considered a delicacy by many.

On they proceeded along the beach, away from the remains of the Space Goose, taking advantage of the cloud canopy that masked the sun. Soon after midday when it melted away, the men raised their hoods and everyone sought shelter in a brushy area near the base of the cliff. It seemed hardly time for a daytime nap, but Michael and Triana made no objection when others stopped and laid down some outer weather covering for them to lie on. Even though it was quite early, they immediately fell asleep.

CHAPTER 19

"Eyefor, Eyefor, Eyefor"

Time: still later, Day 2 ALOE (2 PM)

When Michael awoke, the sun was lower in the sky. When he rolled from his side to his back, his arm and ribs struck something hard. He sat up. His hand fell upon his cane.

"Socomay," said a young girl who knelt unashamedly by his side, smiling.

"That means 'sorry,' " came a familiar Earth voice behind him. As he glanced up and turned, he caught sight of the four men sitting in the sand several yards away and staring without shame. They were talking quietly, their hands animated, punctuating what was said. As Michael sat up, the talking ceased, and all eyes stared intensely at him and the girl.

"Sah lee," repeated Shirra. She pointed to the coil of rope she'd placed by his side. She slowly came to her feet and the boy, who was called Gurdon, dropped to his knees and carefully pulled out the girl's leg from under her and touched the thin but noticeable four-inch scar, now covered with sand, on her lower leg. Michael leaned forward and touched the smooth scar that had been an open tear only hours earlier and smiled, trying to hide his astonishment.

"We thank...Grott...or as we say, 'God'—your God and our God who is one and the same," said Michael, not sure exactly how his Earth

199

words would be understood.

Triana tried to clarify what he said for the girl, who showed no sign of injury besides the obvious scar. Gurdon leaped to his feet and clapped his hands up and down, up and down, which was the way they seemed to applaud in Elphia. The men stood and slowly moved forward in a line.

"Oh…Sarken nomany *eyefor, eyefor, eyefor!*" said Shirra, jumping and finally throwing herself upon Michael, knocking him backwards, hugging his neck, and covering his face with happy tears. He struggled to sit back up and hold in his own tears. Gurdon, his eyes sparkling, began to laugh.

"Help me, Triana. What did she — "

"She said, 'Now I am yours forever, forever, forever.' Now you have two women in your life to contend with. And believe me, I'm thankful. It takes away the pressure."

"Eyefor, eyefor, eyefor…for…ay…ver, for…ay…ver, for…ay…ver," the girl repeated, jumping to her feet and retreating back into her own world. When Shirra saw this pleased, Triana pushed further: Looking at the girl, she pointed to her own open mouth.

"Food, Shirra, food. Food…food for Michael."

The moment the girl left, the men, still in a line, seemed as a single person to press closer. Michael hid his fear and stood. When they were a couple of arms' lengths away, together they dropped to their knees, and put their faces to the sand.

"Caine Grottim argen andeloose vanu kem!" they declared.

"Help, Triana!" he said softly.

"It's something like 'gods and angels…have…come' I think."

"NO! NO! NO! Up! Up! Up!" Michael said waving his hands up and down. He was grateful that "No" and "Oh" seemed the same in both languages. Immediately, they stood. He pointed to his chest and shook his head. "NO GROTT! NO ANDELOOSE! Grott is up, up, up." He pointed to the sky. He wasn't sure where to point for angels. "Me, 'man,' 'man,' 'man.' " He stepped forward and tapped each of the men on his chest. "Man, man, man, man." He glanced to the side and noticed Gurdon's and Shirra's mouths silently moving, trying to shape the words.

When the largest one, Klingor, who happened to be father to the children touched his son, Michael said, "man…little man…little man." He stopped and scratched his head, "Or, 'boy'…'boy'…'boy' "

Then when he realized that he'd neglected Triana, he turned to her. "Woo…man…woman."

By then Shirra had returned. He pointed to her. "Woman…little woman…little woman."

"Or girl," interjected Triana.

The girl without a trace of fear—which melted away anyone's remaining caution—turned to Michael and without touching him, she pointed to his mouth. "Fooood? Fooood?"

"Yes," he replied.

She handed him her own plate, which, after she'd wiped it clean, now held some kerm and a large piece of bread. And though she didn't know it then, a similar plate would play an unusual role in her future.

"Yesss, fooood," she announced, nodding her head up and down. "Proxin, NO!" she added, shaking her head from side to side. Unlike the way of clapping, "no" truly was clearly the same in both worlds. Language study had begun.

And laughter was the same—which followed loudly. Perhaps humor between planets was also similar.

Gurdon, without asking, had also sprung into action. Without Michael even seeing him move away, he'd quickly prepared another plate for Triana.

"God has given us healthy children," Michael whispered.

"And good translators." Triana reponded.

"If they'll hear what we say," said Michael.

"And God gives us the right words," added Triana.

Klingor was leader of the four fishermen who were returning home from three days of fishing, salting, preserving, and caching their catch each day before moving on. On this trip, however, they were to stop at a special outpost far above the shoreline for supplies before returning home.

And would it be "home" for them, Michael wondered, and if so, for how long?

It was time for several more miles of travel along the beach before nightfall.

*   *   *   *   *

As they would soon learn, Klingor's son Gurdon was 7½ in the longer 420-day Elphian years, which figured to about 8½ in Earth years, and his daughter was about 8½ or a bit less than 10 in Earth years and was a bit smaller than one would expect considering her father's size.

As mentioned earlier, the hours, minutes, and days, however, are exactly the same as on Emryss and Earth. Whenever a "year" is mentioned from here on, it will be considered an Elphian year without further explanation.

Certain details about the Elphian calendar will appear later.

CHAPTER 20

The Outpost

Time: Day 3 ALOE (7 AM)

By camping on the beach at night, the men seemed willing to forgo the more comfortable hours for traveling. Everyone arose at dawn, and prepared for what seemed like another long hot trek on the beach.

But as Michael soon learned, how the tide rose and fell was a large part of what determined travel along the sandy shoreline—day and night.

If Gurdon immediately became a shadow to Triana, which she seemed not to mind, Shirra, showing no sign of injury except for the hardly noticeable scar, kept within sight of Michael. That is, except when she would dash off to pick a berry or leaf to show him or Triana.

Her questions were endless, and Michael would puzzle over nearly everything she said, which she didn't seem to mind. He had to smile. She was so much like a miniature first grade teacher, except in this case she would also ask him questions in return and give him a chance to provide answers. She would watch him carefully as he did this, and would imitate his sounds and mannerisms. He was amazed at how much both of them seemed to be learning. Triana, much quieter, was amused. Was God behind this? When that moment came when Shirra sensed he'd finally had enough, she would stop and smile until he returned it.

"For…ay…ver" she would say accenting each syllable, "For…ev… ver," he would correct, until he realized his mistake, and saw that she was playing a game. He soon learned that while her delightful accent showed through, she could say almost every new English word perfectly when she wanted to. Another language genius like Triana. The sort of thing not restricted by age. In fact, he'd learned in school that young children, unknowingly, often could outstrip older people in understanding and speaking a new language. He knew, too, that he wasn't bad with words either, but he had to work at it.

Complicating this was that he soon learned Klingor was a widower, and that's one reason why his children had come on this trip. And now, whatever else Michael meant to Klingor, the man probably welcomed a newfound peace, as brief as it might be. "Forever?" Ha! God help her future mate! And what had the Elphians learned on these first two days? Along with the clear miracles of healing, his surviving eating the poisonous Proxin, their special kindness to the children should show that whoever Triana and he really were, they weren't evil. But if they were looking for gods or angels, they'd soon see that for such exalted personages they didn't qualify.

Here and there they'd go partway up a narrow trail, picking berries to eat, and *metka* leaves from short bushes to chew on and suck out their pleasant sweetness, later spitting out the waxy skins. "Met…ka" Shirra would say, insisting that he voice both the "t" and "k" sounds. Fortunately, the new food proved agreeable.

Then it was back down to the sand.

Whenever they ventured up a trail, everyone shared the load. If the trip was to the top, the fish were carefully cached below, waiting for their return.

For clothing, the fishermen wore strong sandals, a durable brown woolen wrap-around garment called a "karpon" that usually fell from the shoulders to just below the knees. It tied at the waist with a strong belt that could holster a serious knife or working tool. Underneath, the men wore thinner undershorts called "dinays," or "dinnies" which they would learn was the same word that women used for their undergarments.

The dinays were much shorter than Michael's cargo shorts and usually were out of sight. With men, especially fishermen, the garment sometimes had a clever double-sewn side pocket so if even wearing them alone they could conceal a narrow, safely sheathed small knife, perfect for gutting small fish or, if necessary, for self-defense. And when women, or strangers, were comfortably far away, and if overexposure to the sun wasn't an issue, it was acceptable for the men to strip down and work in these light-weight shorts, as long as a karpon was handy to cover-up with. In their karpons however, he could picture most of them in a Christmas manger scene.

That is, without wearing the last standard piece of clothing, a middle-weight multi-pocketed hooded jacket for outdoor wear. When worn, it fell to the middle of the thigh, and could cover the head with a hood if it rained or the sun was too severe.

Of the six, Klingor and his children were noticeably darker, about the color of Michael's skin, and were not troubled as much by sunlight.

"Ogthorp! [outpost]" declared Klingor walking briskly ahead. He pointed up to the crest of the cliff. Everyone stopped and immediately examined what he was carrying, fastening a strap or tying a cord here and there. Klingor called to his children, and Shirra retied her karpona, similar to what men wore, but as he would soon learn, the female karpona usually included distinctive inch-wide borders at every fabric edge. And often included were small hand-stitched designs, probably to dispel the monotony of the dark fabric of work clothes. Inside them also, as with men's clothes, were ingeniously hidden pockets that hardly showed from the outside. No purse or handbag needed! Small children's clothes for both boys and girls, he would also discover, were similar but usually plain, coming to the top of the knee.

The borders of Shirra's karpona showed what had to be carefully stitched block letters in black, hardly noticeable from a distance. Was this the Elphian alphabet he would be confronting?

Most surprising was the ease with which the men deftly removed their fierce metal spear points, which were slipped into inner jacket pockets, converting the weapons into walking sticks for the trek uphill.

It was afternoon. The trail zigzagged up the cliff wall and was a serious climb, requiring careful navigation—as already shockingly demonstrated.

At the top, the main building of the Outpost had a corrugated metal roof that reminded Michael of a Pennsylvania indoor flea market. In several ways it was more modern than an Amish one on Earth from a century-and-a-half ago. So much for Elphia—or at least the part they were on—of being an advanced scientific world!

A third of the items for sale seemed familiar—bags of what looked like flour, or its equivalent, saws, hammers, hoes and rakes with steel cutting blades and prongs, other gardening tools, long rows of bins of several kinds of nails. Also there were bins of different seeds, and shelves with bolts of what seemed like handmade as well as machine-made cloth, alongside what had to be some sort of silk, and even some nylon-like or synthetic material!

But how could all this exist together? How could a planet that could send a spaceship to at least two exoplanets leave behind such a primitive-appearing society? Still, the Earth Michael and Triana had left behind with its EMP history would be hard to explain to a visitor from space.

One thing was certain: They were here—in Elphia. The twin moons, unlike anything he'd ever observed in the night sky, confirmed it.

Time to observe and learn everything one could while the fisher-men went about seeking the small items they'd come for.

Michael found himself standing at the end of a long aisle of bar-rels, three-tiered display tables, and bins: one with loose buttons and clothing fasteners of all kinds, another with spools of thread. Metal me-chanical parts he couldn't identify dominated the next aisle. And at the end were what had to be five foot-pedaled sewing machines of some kind.

Another third of the enclosure held obviously used pieces of un-familiar modern things that were judged somehow useful, and had to have "belonged" somewhere else that was quite different. And what many things were…he hadn't a clue since the labels and descriptions were to him — as of today — unreadable.

From a stack of what had to be plastic plates of some kind he impul-sively picked up two salad-plate-sized ones exactly alike that caught his eye. These he would try to buy and examine later.

That set his mind in motion.

Then off in the corner he couldn't believe his eyes. There, standing about four feet tall was a roll of butcher paper, or perhaps newsprint paper that was badly stained on the outside, though how far deep the stains went he had no idea. So maybe they had, or once had, newpa-pers, or pamphlets. He recalled Ben Franklin's important tiny press that he'd seen on a trip to Philadelphia. He wasn't sure why, but he had to obtain this roll, and when Triana had seen his eagerness, she began talking with the men as best she could about how to purchase it. Not just some of the paper, but all of it. And to go with it, some graphite-appearing round sticks nearby that had to be pencils of some kind.

The final third of the Outpost seemed like an indoor recycling yard that spilled out into an acre of open air. There were dozens of care-fully stacked piles of previously used boards and flat sheets of wood and metal, even sheets or table-tops of what looked like plastic, and coil after coil of insulated wire. Everything was used, roughly cut, and obviously taken from somewhere — somewhere different and more advanced than anything he'd seen here so far. Most likely many of these things couldn't be made, or easily made, here — at least nearby. Perhaps strangest of all were mounds of reclaimed plastic piping, alongside small-bore water pipes made of cement.

Outside Michael spied a piece of smooth slate about 18 inches square. He handed this to Triana, and Shirra, finding an identical piece of slate, handed hers to Triana as well. After rummaging through several boxes of what had to have once been some sort of office or business supplies, he spied several boxes of chalk and more pencils. He sent these to Triana by way of Shirra.

And, not to be overlooked, for the first time on Elphia he saw electricity in use, mainly in overhead ceiling lights. But only four, where more would have been helpful. The electric lightbulbs and fixtures didn't look that unfamiliar.

So there was electricity. And somehow, somewhere, the ability to make and send power. But no telephones were present, at least nearby. When Klingor saw Michael staring at the lights, he took him to a window and pointed to four thick black poles that looked like enormously fat smokestacks that standing isolated near the top of the of the cliffs behind the Outpost, deliberately it seemed, to be out of sight from the sea.

"Solendrico stellars," he declared, pointing to the poles and then to the electric lights. These "sun pillars," could somehow efficiently "take energy" from sunlight Michael would learn.

Suppose, Michael wondered, this were a planet mainly of isolated rocky islands separated by wild seas. Igneal, Triana said, had once told her this. And suppose, great technological advancement had occurred in secured places far away. But not here. If great tragedy occurred in those highly modernized places, perhaps simpler peoples on "fringe" islands nearby might take advantage of it.

Perhaps, the "best" of Elphia had destroyed itself—by EMP, nuclear radiation, other forms of poisoning, disease, genetic research gone bad, war, murder, or famine. Perhaps such disaster was what propelled Elphians who were able to flee to places like Emryss and Earth.

Perhaps, as Jonas once told him, they, like some wealthy on Earth who'd sought "Scientific Furtivity," tried to relocate and disappear anonymously in clandestine places that would call little attention to themselves. SFers, for a fee, he said, could obtain "a set of numbers" that would identify safe out-of-the-way places for certain preferred services and opportunities.

But disaster had come anyway. When such rich places of personal invisibility on Earth had become exposed, they became targets for the uninvited and organized crime. Scientific Furtivity fell apart, the effort a disaster.

But perhaps backwater islands like Elphia (the island that was named for "ELPHIA," the planet, which will now be written in caps to avoid confusion) was protected just enough by extreme tidal effects. And it was just far enough away from a destroyed modern land, maybe also an island, so as not to attract serious outside attention. And suppose on Elphia (Island) there were entrepreneurial master sailors who would risk sailing the high seas to gather and bring back discarded, or partially destroyed manufactured materials considered trash where they were found, but still could improve Elphian (Island) life without attracting outside attention.

It was something to think about.

There was so much to learn.

The toilets, he discovered, were flushable, crude, but durable, and surprisingly clean. When "checking out," he found the cash register was mechanical, receiving both brass and silver coins and some paper, which Michael could make no sense of. To pay, Klingor had added to his coins a bag of salted fish that was weighed and exchanged as barter. All expenses for their small purchases, including what was requested by the Space Goose survivors, were then covered.

Surprisingly, Triana (who'd worn her skirt) and Michael (his jeans) hadn't attracted too much attention to themselves by the few Elphians already there. The ogthorp, perhaps, was an out-of-the-way place for unusual, special shopping and exchange without unnecessary questions asked. It was obvious that Klingor, his men, and the two children had been there before. The two new arrivals from Earth blended in well enough not to be a distraction. Their business done, they gathered their purchases and headed for the path back down.

Soon after starting, the spear points were quickly refastened to the walking sticks, and Michael and Triana changed back into their cargo shorts. As Michael picked up the pieces of slate, Shirra insisted she carry the one that was hers along with her share of the load. And, smiling at Triana, she openly helped herself to two large pieces of chalk from the box they came in, and nested them like eggs in a pocket inside her karpona. Two men, without complaint, took turns carrying the large roll of paper in addition to their other things. Quietly, everyone found their way down to the beach and the hidden fish.

Now there was more to carry and stops came more often, but nobody complained.

After three more hours of travel, they stopped to make camp. Gurden and all the men except Klingor, moved a hundred feet further ahead, stripped to their dinays, a seemingly accepted behavior, and refreshed themselves swimming in the oncoming tide. When Shirra wanted to join them, her father said no, she could wade in the water nearby and must keep her karpona on. Reluctantly, she obeyed and removing the chalk from her pocket, she took her new slate to the water's edge and scrubbed it clean with sand. When she returned soaking wet from head to toe, Klingor shook his head, Michael smiled, and Triana took her aside and opened her bag.

When Michael turned around he did a double take. Shirra was wearing his "missing" flannel shirt.

*   *   *   *   *

Day 4

After a light breakfast of something like hardtack and smoked fish—which Michael at first slowly swallowed—they were off. With the sun rising to what seemed like ten in the morning, up came the raising of the hoods. Klingor was the last to do so, perhaps more for the sake of his men, humbled by their seeming weakness to the strong sunlight. What a strange problem!

As three men and Gurdon took the lead with all of their possessions, an animated discussion began that Michael couldn't understand. Even Triana seemed bewildered. Klingor, with touches of gray in his thick beard, walked last, carrying over his shoulder a huge net full of smoked fish, and seemed to pay no attention. He said nothing. And Shirra, back in her karpona, soldiered on next to Michael and Triana with a large bag of her own as well as her precious slate. Michael could hear the slide and scrunch of everyone's feet in the sand and the smell of smoked fish was everywhere. He discovered if he closed his eyes he could tell where everyone was by just the sound.

In the silence he noticed something else. Shirra had hardly said a word. He smiled. Perhaps she had used them all up. What did she do when she wasn't talking? Carefully smiling, he glanced at her hoping not to break the spell. Catching his look, she jerked her head away and looked up at the sky over the ocean. Suddenly, she tightened up her load and almost skipped over to her father. She pointed up to the sun.

Klingor stopped. The clouds were turning black and heavy darkness was moving toward the sun. The two talked rapidly back and

211

forth. Klingor dropped what he was carrying and raised his hands to his face and shouted so loud that Michael jumped.

"Noli, grandalo! Grandalo onkay!"

"I think Noli is one of them," whispered Triana. "I think he's telling him to go, and go now. But where and why, I've no idea."

At once Noli, the smallest of the three and with the thinnest beard, was out of his karpon, which he tightly rolled up to carry. From inside his hooded jacket he slipped a short slender knife into the special side holster-pocket of his dinays. His jacket, sandals, spear, everything he'd been carrying or wearing except his knife and rolled-up karpon fell into the sand at his feet. As the dark cloud had not quite yet reached the sun, he sprinted into the water to moisten his skin for some protection.

Then he was off. How fast he seemed to travel! By the time the clouds began to darken the sunlight, he was almost out of sight. Catching up with the two men who were ahead, the seven divided the runner's load among themselves, making the back-breaking journey even more difficult.

Heavy rain came and went. Everyone was soaked. For the entire day the sandy beach was forever before them, the ocean to the right. To their left was the gentle sandy uphill slope that ended abruptly at the nearly vertical wall of stone, now varying in height from 60 to 100 feet, with occasional fringes of greenery at the top. This was Elphia so far, except for the empty grassy land on the other side of the Outpost that suggested the cliff was a "rim" to something larger, rather than the beginning of a plateau. But how far did the cliff and sand go? What was beyond the cliff? An answer would soon come.

At one point, Klingor urged everyone to move faster. He was shouting now. With one hand pointing to the sea and the other to the cliffs, he moved his palms closer and closer together until they nearly touched. Then he indicated with his finger they must travel through a tiny area that seemed to end in a point straight ahead, almost out of sight. And they must go quickly! Each wave series that aimed toward the cliff seemed to dare them to go further.

When they reached it, waves were already licking the base of the cliff.

The men in front, who'd waited to see sand after a retreating wave, at last finding it, sprinted across and several yards up to higher ground. Dropping what they carried, they sprinted back to help the others.

"Karrando! Karrando!" Klingor shouted, indicating the danger. With such rapid rising of the tide the trick then became to enter the water when the retreating wave was still knee deep.

At last, all belongings and the canvas-wrapped fish were on the other side — dry. However, the carriers were not. At one point, Gurdon, after dropping his load, slipped and was pulled back to the sea, only to be rescued by one of the fisherman.

But at last they made it.

The cliff and its sandy path then bent to the left.

Five minutes later they arrived.

A nearly vertical crack in the base of the cliff ran straight up about fifty feet getting narrower and narrower until the "point" of the upside-down V disappeared at the top. At the bottom an eight-foot-wide iron-hinged pair of wooden doors, that was almost twice as high, opened from the middle to the sea.

At the bottom of the doors a long stone step ran the length of the opening, and kept the tides from forcing the open doors inward. Nine more similar stone steps ran up to a cement and stone and pebble floor that appeared to end at some dimly lit wide area inside. But in only minutes the incoming waves would forbid the closing of the door!

A dozen people clad in colorful karpons and karponas lined each side of the stone steps to meet the seven drenched travelers. At their head was Noli, who was nicely dressed. Several of his companions halfway up, rushed to relieve the returnees of their heavy loads. With

213

At the bottom of the doors a long stone step
ran the length of the opening...

eyes mainly on Triana, Klingor signaled to several women he knew to come forward. Immediately, they whisked her away for dry clothes, Shirra following.

With a loud thunk, the doors were shut back in place. They would be impossible to open for several hours.

Just beyond the long top step, to the far right was a large auditorium-shaped cavity, a giant cave, partly natural, partly hewn out of stone. Here, the ground was dry and nearly flat with crushed stone or pebbles and cement as hard as stone filling any cracks. It crudely resembled the hub of a mid-sized mall, a place to gather with benches, chairs and tables, and room for portable chairs or blankets that people could bring for sitting — and to buy and eat readily prepared food.

But that wasn't all.

A hundred feet to the right of the top step the cave dead-ended into a natural wall that met a sloping stone ceiling that curved down to the floor. Here a long wooden platform a foot-and-a-half high had been built where a speaker, actors, or a musical group could benefit from an outstanding acoustical effect with or without an electrical sound system. Overhead hung a few crude electric lights that barely expelled darkness until a person's eyes adjusted to the inner dimness.

To Michael it would become what he would call "the Auditorium." The term, if he and Triana were accepted, could eventually be transliterated into Elphian, spelled with their own letters to make it sound exactly as it does in English. Whatever was he thinking! He was an outsider with no right to suggest or make plans for anything. If one could know less than nothing, it was he. God forgive me! God, I put myself in your hands! he muttered aloud.

If he was to do anything, it was to follow through on his promise. He must quickly observe everything as best he could.

From the platform, and a speaker's point of view, straight ahead to

..."the Auditorium."

the rear, a bit more than a hundred feet, beyond the steps to the left that led back down to the sea, was the other side of the cave floor. A dozen feet further past the steps was a wooden stairway with a railing running up about four feet higher to a second stone "floor." On this floor stood a modest, but solid outdoor-style one-story house with, oddly, a pitched roof built back against, or perhaps into, the cave wall behind it. Two small attic gables protruded from the front of the roof, pointing directly back about 120 feet to the platformed stage and up to a large crevasse, which was one of several, that opened to the darkening sky.

Because of its location, the house had to be a building of some prominence, perhaps home to some official, or dignitary. This "Gatehouse," as he would soon learn, was the first of three very similar houses, the other two slightly smaller, that ran in nearly a straight line, all within sight of the platform. Never had Michael ever seen "outdoor-styled" houses inside what was essentially a large cave, except for several large gaps in the stone ceiling that opened to daylight, the stars, or occasional rain.

Directly ahead from the top of the stone steps was a long tunnel that led to other occupied parts far inside the mountain and other entrances into another large area that he would learn about later.

Michael and the others were immediately led to the platform at the front of the Auditorium. The space in front of him began to fill. For whatever would now happen, there would be no delay, no food or rest. He was offered a fresh karpon and, as the fishermen circled him for a moment of privacy, he gratefully slipped it on. Probably not an unusual behavior in such circumstances. When he next looked up, at least a hundred people had arrived, with more coming by the minute, carrying chairs and blankets.

On the platform he was seated in the third chair facing the crowd. Then Triana, carefully climbing the three steps that led there, joined him, wearing a beautifully colored karpona and sat next to him in the second chair. With her presence a hush fell over everyone. Michael's mind flashed back to his first impressions of her in high school before he knew her. Though fiercely private, still by the way she handled herself in a group, he could easily see her ruling as a young queen, as her great-grandmother Lurinda briefly had once on Emryss when circumstances demanded it.

And there in Emryss the royal family had learned an important lesson: When you're in charge and know nothing, keep your ignorance from showing as you race to learn more. Quietly observe everything and, when appropriate, be ready to ask rather than tell, as you gather facts. Her eyes were busy. And it was those eyes that seemed to hold everyone else's gaze. She was missing nothing. He must do the same. Shirra, also in fresh clothing and enjoying being in the center of everything, found herself sitting by Triana's side, watching and imitating her every move. Or so it seemed.

Klingor sat next to Michael on a stool he carried, and Gurdon sat on the floor at his father's feet, his own feet dangling over the platform edge. Five mugs of a steaming beverage suddenly appeared and were handed to each, and since Michael and Triana set theirs nearby at their feet, the others did the same.

By then perhaps 150 Elphians had arrived.

For some reason five large older women sitting in the back caught Michael's eye. They seemed, strangely, to be laughing and loudly arguing at the same time, indifferent to turning heads in front of them.

It was time to begin.

But to begin what?

That was answered by a sudden start of a humming sound.

It was as if a plane were flying overhead, coming closer and closer. But how could they hear it closed off in what was essentially a cave?

The effect on the people was strange. Some seemed to hear it, others did not. The humming grew louder.

CHAPTER 21

The First Night

Time: Day 4 ALOE (evening)

[Comments on language will appear near the end of this chapter.]

The humming increased.

Wind seemed to blow though the air was still.

Darkness, strange as it sounds, suddenly disappeared.

A bright light filled the room.

Michael looked out at the people before him. Some had suddenly vanished, but just which ones he couldn't remember later. The ones who remained, perhaps half of them, were immovable white statues, but each with a spot of light on his or her forehead, brighter than the new light surrounding them, and each seemed unaware, or indifferent, of how anyone else appeared. But then they were motionless statues! Klingor, Gurdon, and Shirra had the lights, as did Triana who was, as he, the only other one whose head and body could turn and observe. He was sure his own head also wore a spot of light. Surprisingly, the five strange women in the back who stood out earlier—spots of light were actually on each of their heads except for the one in the center who'd actually disappeared with the others.

The reason for her absence would become clear. Whatever was going on was out of his hands.

During this, Michael and Triana became painfully thirsty. He tried to speak but his tongue felt tied in a knot. Reaching down each took long drinks from the mugs brought to them. Then, not knowing why, both fell to their knees in front of where they sat. They closed their eyes and raised their hands. The people before them remained frozen in place. Together the two whispered private prayers to the God of Heaven, begging for wisdom, asking for His hand to fall upon them, even though they were children facing adults in a world they knew nothing about, that they would do the right things in the right way at the right time so that those before them would come to know the true God who made the universe and his Son, that somehow they might...

Suddenly everything white returned to its muted color and the regular dimness provided by the small electric lights overhead. Everyone who'd "disappeared" earlier was back in place. It was business as usual, if you could call it that.

The humming stopped and all was quiet except for waves occasionally slapping against the great outside doors now closed against the tide.

It was Klingor, now holding his mug along with the others who were now drinking from theirs, who suddenly rose to speak. He pointed to the woman who sat at the left end of the five. How could these five shapeless old women who seemed barely able to move without a cane figure in to what was happening? Klingor's eyes were riveted on them.

"Galandra, who brought these drinks that we hold?" he demanded in a loud voice that couldn't be missed.

He was answered by a hideous cackle amplified by the stone ceiling from the woman in the center who didn't have the spot of light on her forehead.

"The brewer is waiting to be served by those who thirst," screamed the voice, cackling again. *The words shouted in Elphian were received by Michael's ears in English.* He knew also that his knotted tongue had be-

222

come free. Some of Jonas's puzzling words from long ago flashed into his mind: "In direct spirit warfare, God always wins."

They had to be witches of some kind. Everyone turned their way. With both hands, the woman in the center stood and thrust up a large jug. Her eyes were as large as eggs and even from a distance her hideous grin was terrifying. Could she actually see? How could she even manage to hold such a heavy jug? Galandra, the woman sitting at the end pointed to her. **"Roxandra—she made it and brought it."**

"May the evil in these cups consume you!" Klingor shouted, taking his cup and smashing it on the floor.

"Arrrugggggh!" The farthermost bench suddenly fell backwards and all the women found themselves flat on their backs. Gray liquid seemed to gush from their mouths soiling their clothes. Slowly, they attempted to stand by their own power because no one dared approach them. Triana, still holding her mug and insisting that Shirra stay where she was, smoothly glided down the steps and back to where the women lay. Everyone gave her plenty of room. Michael and Klingor were right behind her. Taking each woman by the hand, the two helped them to their feet, trembling. Triana touched no one.

All stood except Roxandra.

Triana, still holding her mug, knelt without touching her and checked for her breathing. But she was dead.

Triana looked at the four women now standing before her, liquid still oozing from their mouths. She held out her mug.

"I'm going to ask you—and I know you can hear and understand me—from this moment on, who are you going to serve, God, or Grott, as you call him, or the evil one? *[At that instant, whichever language was being spoken began to be heard and understood by whoever it was intended for.]* If God," she continued, "you must beg His forgiveness for your evil which He calls 'sins,' you must completely turn away from your past, and you must trust in the death and resurrection of His Son, Jesus — who you call the God-Son — who will be your Savior and will forgive you. Promise to give Him your whole life and follow Him with everything that you have.

"Everything."

Little did she know what this would mean.

"But if you wish to serve the evil one, drink from this cup." Michael knew that her gentle, but firm no-nonsense words were as understandable to them as well as to him. "But you must decide now, *immediately*. Today is the day of salvation."

Galandra was first to fall on her face and declare her allegiance to Grott, and that she would forever ["eyefor"] serve him. The other three fell prostrate right after her.

"Stand!" Triana declared. Surprisingly, all quickly sprang to their feet by their own power.

"Grott and His Son," declared Galandra, "Grott and His Son who you call Jesus" — she paused, a locked door seeming to open in her mind — "I, Galandra, beg forgiveness, and will turn from my evil ways, destroy my evil possessions, and ask Grott and His Son, Jesus, to be my Savior." The other three carefully but clearly articulated the same words.

"As a human child who has lived in another world," said Triana, "I have done the same thing," she continued.

"And so have I," added Michael offering his first words.

"Jesus, Jesus, Jesus, Jesus," said the women.

Then holding out her cup for all to see, Triana turned it over. Nothing spilled out. She had drunk it all without being harmed.

"Hear my words," declared Triana, though not loud enough for those far away to hear, "If you truly believe what you've said, go home and burn your karponas, bathe, put on fresh ones and return."

Forgetting their canes, they briskly moved to the back of the bewildered crowd, only to be stopped by a middle-aged man with brown hair parted in the middle just arriving, carried on a chair fastened to poles on the shoulders of two men. He wore a karpon that was carefully made. He called to Galandra, who without a moment's hesitation came, and he whispered to her. Then she nodded her head and disappeared with the other women. Michael moved quickly toward the man and motioned to those holding the poles to lower the chair to the ground so he could speak to him face to face. They did. The man in the chair looked puzzled. Michael extended his hand. The man received it.

"Rise, so I can talk to you face to face." Why had he ever said that? he wondered.

The man slowly stood.

A gasping came from the crowd.

"We are still children," Michael announced. "I come from still another world, Earth." He cupped his hands that suggested a circle like a basketball and pointed up, to a point in the ceiling of the cave. "And I come in peace. We come to tell you about the God of Heaven."

"Whom you call 'Grott,'" added Triana.

"The woman here," Michael continued—he pointed to Triana—"comes from still another world, Emryss"—and with another circle, he pointed in another direction to the ceiling—"as well as from here, Elphia." He stomped his foot. "She has visited Earth, though she is not part of that world. Together, we have just come here from Earth." Most surprising of all was that the words he needed easily came. And he easily spoke them! And the people seemed to understand!

"Cai Grott!" declared the man. "You must tell us more." He whispered some instruction to one of the two who'd carried his chair. At once they disappeared with the chair in the direction from which they'd come.

The man walked with the two of them to the front of the crowd. Everyone started whispering and talking. Two men were already pouring water over the poisonous filth the women had left behind. Someone quickly gave up his seat so the man who'd been carried in could be comfortable at the front. Triana and Michael returned to the platform.

"Speak to the people, Michael," Triana told him softly. "This special gift may end in minutes—as well as our lives! *Let the words come!* I'm praying for you."

"Uh…"

"Speak to them, Michael."

He stood. There was no podium to lean against.

Everyone fell silent.

He willed God to make his lips to shape his words in the right way.

Triana rose, stood beside him, and began first.

"Mancaren dorno mancarena, tonuda a special day." Never had Michael heard her speak so loudly and clearly. "Sometimes when the Truth comes to a new place God lets you hear things very clearly as if by magic. But it is not magic from the Evil One," she continued. "Nor is it because of us. It comes from God. You must listen carefully to every word tonight, for *tomorrow we must begin to learn your words for our-selves.* Michael"—she pointed to him—"and I speak a different tongue. I am Triana, Triana from Emryss and Elphia…Triana"—she pointed to herself—"Triana from Emryss and Elphia…Triana from Emryss and El-phia." She cupped her hands and pointed up for Emryss, then down for Elphia. She paused. She cupped her hand to her ear indicating she wanted them to respond.

"Triana from Emryss and Elphia," said the people as a group.

She looked at Michael and again pointed to him. Never had he felt more foolish.

"Michael from Earth." She pointed to another spot in the ceiling. "Michael from Earth…Michael from Earth."

"Michael from Earth," the people repeated.

"We have come here in a space bird from Earth."

"O cai Grott!" exclaimed several people.

"Can the blood of three worlds come from this?" said someone near the front. "Three worlds!" said another. "Can this be possible?" said another. "Can what we have seen tonight be possible?" added another.

How can one language be changed into another? Michael wondered. The fact of what was happening, however, was simple. Whatever words were spoken by anyone were understood by anyone willing to hear them.

"What color bird?" blurted out a child.

"White and made of metal," Triana declared. She cupped her hands and moved them up and down drawing the shape of the Space Goose in the air. "Then it fell in the water and broke apart." She scrambled together her hands and held her palms out from her side. "Then Klingor and the fishermen—and Gurdon and Shirra who sit with us—kindly brought us here." She turned to Michael.

"Tell them why we've come, Michael."

Michael swallowed hard.

"We come to tell you about God, whose Son Jesus long ago came to my planet Earth, at the same time long ago as He came to Triana's planet Emryss"—he pointed to the ceiling of the cave—"and Elphia, where we now stand. God and His Son Jesus. God and His Son Jesus, who you call 'Grott dorno Grott caino.' Then a man from Elphia, named Igneal, came to Earth. He says your world Elphia has lost all its copies of the Holy Book."

"The white ones made us burn them years ago," exclaimed someone midway back.

"Not all the white ones, which include my grandfather," said Klingor who, except for exposing the poisoned drink, had remained silent.

"Superstition. They said it was silly superstition," exclaimed a man near the back. **"Can't what we've seen tonight be some trick?"**

It was Gurdon's turn.

227

"**My sister!**" said the boy, who found himself standing beside Michael. "**My sister is no trick!**"

A bit of laughter brought needed smiles to many.

"My sister and I fell far far far many feet, many many feet down a cliff path. I died, but Triana brought me to life again." This brought some whispering and light laughter. "But my sister…stand, Shirra" — with little persuasion he drew her to her feet — "broke her leg and the bone came out" — instantly everyone was silent again — "and Triana put the bone back in, Michael wrapped it with his rope, and two hours later Shirra took it off and was healed. See the scar…" Slowly he raised the hem of her fresh, longer karpona just enough and touched her scar. "And now she is completely healed."

"**But,**" exclaimed the man in the back.

"**But NOTHING!**" exclaimed Noli who sat with his fishermen friends near the front, who stood and declared, "**It is true!**" he declared. "**It is true! We saw this ourselves!**"

"Do you have children?" asked a woman near the front.

"No," said Michael.

"Triana, are you klepta or kleptini?" she asked.

Michael turned to Triana, puzzled.

"**No klepta. No kleptini,**" Triana declared for all to hear.

Then she turned to Michael and whispered. "There's no exact words in English for these. I think it's mainly directed to a woman. A *klepta* is a woman bound to a man by a 'forever promise.' A *kleptini* is essentially a 'kept woman,' a 'temporary partner,' or a property."

"How then does a child happen?" asked the woman.

Michael was happy this was for Triana to answer.

And she quickly did.

"A mother of a child who carries the blood of three worlds loves God and does what the Bible, or the Holy Book of Earth, says," declared Triana. "She would certainly be a klepta."

"And you?" asked the woman.

"We are still young," answered Triana, "and are orphans waiting to see what God will do. And what He would have us do."

"And what must you do?" the woman asked.

"For one thing," said Triana, not even pausing for a second, "we must learn your language. *The magic of our knowing each other's words ends as we leave this gathering tonight.*"

How could she be so sure? Michael wondered.

"And where will you go?" asked the woman.

"Well said. We have no place to go," said Michael. "There's no way to return to Earth. So there is no place."

"That's one thing you've said that's *not* true," said a new voice. It was the brown-haired man who'd been carried in on a chair. "I am Lemron who, by the will of the people"—he turned to Michael and Triana—"rules the world inside the great doors that lead to the sea. You now have a place for as long as you need." He pointed to the Gate-house straight ahead, just beyond the stone stairs to the sea. *"Because of you, I've just taken my first steps in ten years.* That's where you two will stay."

"We thank you, but I did not do anything," said Michael, who hadn't fully recognized what had happened. "It was God."

Then to the entire group Michael spoke.

"Tomorrow we begin to learn. We have come to your land. We must learn your words so we can understand you and teach about God. We must live the way God wants us to." He stopped and pointed out to the crowd. "If you believe in, and trust in, the God-Son Jesus, and want to give him your life, you should be baptized in water to show others you believe."

"How much water?" asked someone.

"It can be little or much," said Michael. "The amount used has changed through time." After he said this he wondered how true that was.

"How much water was used at the 'beginning'?" the man replied.

It was at that point weariness and hunger fell upon him like a heavy weight.

"We will talk more tomorrow," Michael said.

"Carenay demanga arto enga," said the man, extending his arms in bewilderment.

Both Triana and Michael looked puzzled.

"What did you say?" asked Triana.

"Carenay demanga arto enga," the man repeated. "Manga hannen fohr lowan. Manga, gorin da…"

The time of special understanding had ended.

And Lemron as well as Triana and Michael seemed to understand that at the same time.

And now the hardest part of their lives was about to begin. They must begin at once to learn a new language as perfectly as they could, going at it night and day, the language of their new world.

Michael pointed to his mouth and Lemron understood.

It was time to stop.

Michael waved to the people and they clapped their hands, at least most of them did, in the strange up-and-down manner they'd seen earlier on the beach. Klingor, Gurdon, Shirra, and a couple of fishermen, who'd carefully looked after everyone's belongings, followed the three through the crowd, which carefully gave room for everyone to pass through, to the unusual house that somehow belonged to Lemron.

As they climbed the steps to the higher stone level where the three houses stood side by side, Michael noticed through one of the larger crevasses overhead the bright stars in the otherwise black sky overhead. Whatever star patterns captured the imaginations here? In what direction was their old solar system? And the Milky Way?

At the top of the steps they were met by two of the witches who had fallen down, accepted Jesus, quickly bathed, changed into fresh clothing, and already returned. Michael was stunned. There was even spring in their steps. He hardly recognized them.

Through the front door of the Gatehouse, the women, Lemron, and the visitors from Earth entered the living room, lit by several faint electric lights. Lemron pointed to a long, narrow table at the right. Two could easily squeeze in there, one on each side, and work or eat—if the plates weren't too large. Despite the table's length, more than two would be too many.

At the end of this small room, which Michael oddly thought of as the "alcove," was a small window. The other end faced the living room, the back side above the counter was open to the kitchen, and the front side of the small room was narrowed by accommodating a large china cabinet and some kind of closet or wardrobe. The room could be both cosy and still open to all that was going on in the front of the house. Michael sat, laying the bag he carried on the floor. One woman took Triana to a room behind the kitchen, that was entered from a hallway that ran straight to the back of the house.

The woman put some cold food on a plate. Soon there would be tea.

Michael reached into his bag and pulled out a short thick candle and put it in the middle of the narrow table. With a match he lit the wick. *She would like this,* Mrs. Crandel had said. Two plates appeared with food and two empty cups waiting for tea that soon arrived. Triana reappeared and seeing the table, smiled, but hid the rest of her surprise. He helped her get seated across from him, which was for show, rather than need. They turned in their seats, facing those in the living room.

"They're watching every detail, Triana, and one advantage now is that they *can't* understand what we're saying." She smiled.

"If only Jonas could see us now," she offered. "It would give him

231

something else to wonder about." The old Triana was back, at home in a place where she'd only seen a couple rooms and tea hadn't even been served.

"They'll be watching, Michael, always watching to see what we're made of, and Michael, I'll be watching, too. We don't want to disappoint them…or each other."

After eating and some conversation—now much more difficult—it seemed like resting, or sleeping, was what should come next. Others seemed to agree, but then came a mixed surprise. As if they were alone, he walked her to what he assumed was her bedroom door. He opened it. Immediately two hands were on his shoulder. He turned. The two former witches insisted he go no farther.

"No klepta!" said one.

"No kleptini!" said the other.

"Grott argo no, no no!" said the first.

Triana smiled, trying to hold back laughter.

"Thank God, they've saved me, Michael. How they can conclude so quickly what God expects—and act on it—is astonishing. I think they're afraid if their new 'orphan children' disobey what God obviously expects, they'll lose their blessing. And you know, maybe they're right. But"—she whispered in his ear—"I'm a little disappointed." Michael swallowed hard. Triana seemed to struggle to keep from laughing. "But aren't you relieved—just a little bit?"

The old Triana was definitely back. And so was he—and ready to stay as long as necessary for whatever came next.

Michael motioned with his hands that he was just taking her to the door and—of course—he would be going somewhere else, but just where, he hadn't a clue. Then, as if on a stage, he turned to his audience and raised one finger in the air. Spinning back on his heel, he pulled her into his arms and kissed her, but only briefly. They must accept this much as okay. Then he whispered "Hotel Crandel" into her ear and

232

pushed away. She disappeared inside the door. He returned to the table and blew out the candle. Without a pause, the two women who only a couple of hours ago had tried to poison them, led him across the living room to another hallway, parallel to the first one, that led to another bedroom, a guest room, which was the first of three he would learn.

Lemron, he would soon also learn, was a widower who lived alone in the Gatehouse. He could — and gladly would — go stay with his widowed mother who lived in a house far down the tunnel that led away from the great door that opened to the beach. Such a walk to her home would have been impossible earlier in the day.

No longer.

Once in the middle of the night, not easy to detect in a house overshadowed by a ceiling of rock in a strange world, Michael heard a sound outside his door. Tiptoeing across the room, he cracked it open. The two former witches were still there, rolled up in blankets on the floor. He realized then that even "after hours," these two along with the other two were not only totally changed, but were not to be trifled with.

*   *   *   *   *

[From this point on most of the narrative will be presented as if all were happening in English — with a little explanation now and then. However, since several memorable Elphian words such as klepta, kleptini, "karpon" and "karpona" (and soon "mareena," "marana," and "vanchi" which will then be explained) seem to work as well or better than their English equivalents, those Elphian words will be retained. Immediately, the immigrants from Earth will begin to immerse themselves night and day in Elphian history and culture and learn — learn well — the Elphian language with special help from Klingor's family.

Also "ALOE" at chapter headings will obviously stand for "after landing on Elphia," beginning a special time count for those from Earth. "Days" and "weeks" will, of course, remain the same as Earth days and weeks, though the "12 months in a year" when it appears, will be the longer 35-day Elphian months (only two of which will be named). Elphian years with their 420 days will be 55 days longer than Earth years).

Very soon the story will jump six months ahead.]

CHAPTER 22

The Holy Women

Time: Day 5 ALOE

Michael rubbed his eyes, arose, and put on and tied the karpon he was given the day before. All his belongings had been methodically laid out in a line beyond the foot of his comfortable double-sized bed. He tiptoed to the bedroom door and opened it to his new world.

The two witches who'd been so completely changed, who'd curled up to sleep on the floor, were gone. Michael wondered if his dreams had gotten the better of him. However, after a glance toward the kitchen, he found the other two converted witches busy hovering over a small stove that used electricity, as well as sometimes wood! Well, if electricity were available anywhere, it should be here. But just where was "here" exactly?

Wherever it was it included Triana, wearing the beautiful karpona she'd been given the evening before, smiling and helping and definitely real. And, of course, Gurdon and Shirra privileged by all the attention they'd been given, had not been successfully kept away.

He would start as Galen had in *The Secret of Zareba* by watching and being as agreeable as possible. After all, many now expected the two of them to do something special, but just what, he'd no idea. With his first minute outside the bedroom door, he would "start slow" — the "squiggly 11" had to apply to more than just special personal relationships — in memory of what Esther Crandel had given to his green clock. He would begin by opening his eyes and ears wide to everything around him. Conversation now, except with one person — or so he thought — was next to impossible.

But it was Shirra who announced what was going on...sort of...

"Prooohh..tek...prooohh..tek...noo...woo..men. Noo hoh..lee woomen pro..tect Triana."

"Protect?" Where did she learn that word? And "holy"? Where did that come from? If he didn't scramble to learn her language, she would learn his! He'd better get busy.

"Triana no klepta, no kleptini. Shirra no klepta, no kleptini," the girl continued.

Gurdon laughed, Triana smiled, the "holy women" — so called for better or worse — pretended they didn't hear, and Michael, dumbstruck, found himself sitting at the narrow table that ran out from the window in the alcove just in front of the kitchen.

"Can...dill?" Shirra asked, tilting her head and raising her voice at the end of the word, converting the single word into an unmistakable question.

"No," said Michael, "No candle *early*. Only *late*. Candle late with supper when you're across the table from someone you *love* — yes, klepta or no klepta." Let her try to figure that out while he approached the plate of breakfast just placed before him. It smelled delicious though he couldn't quite figure out what it was. He could sense the princess from Emryss standing just behind him. When Shirra started to speak again, Michael raised a finger in the air by which he was suggesting that he wanted to focus on the food in front of him.

"Michael 'keeess' Shirra?" she asked with perfect inflection, eyes growing large.

"No! no! no!" Michael shot back waving his arms. "I want to eat!" He pointed to the food, then his mouth. Everyone laughed. Triana gently pulled the girl away, whispered something in her ear, giving Michael a chance to down nearly a whole cup of tea, which felt good against the slight chill he still hadn't adjusted to. Such was natural, of course, inside a cave house in Elphia or anywhere else.

*   *   *   *   *

As soon as the table was cleared, one of the holy women tapped on Michael's shoulder and indicated that he should go in his room and change his karpon. He looked to Triana, who somehow had quickly changed into an ordinary karpona she'd been given. She nodded okay and whisked him to his room. But before they could get there, Gurdon raced ahead, and took Michael's hand shooing Triana away.

This brought more friendly laughter.

In the room he discovered a plain, ordinary karpon laid across his bed, that somehow had gotten made while he wasn't paying attention.

Returning to the main room in the fresh garment, it was obvious that everyone in the house was intent on going somewhere and that he was to go with them.

"Triana, wha…"

"What's going on? Well, nothing that 'Michael the Baptizer' can't solve."

"Triana, I can't…"

"Yes, Michael, you can and you will. Last night you yourself said that if people wanted to trust in Jesus, the God-Son, they needed to be baptized. There's been a big discussion about this. You know the New Testament. Did you ever wonder if the hundreds that suddenly wanted to be baptized were ready yet? Did they know enough? Once I sure wondered."

"But..."

"We were *there* last night. But we didn't cause what happened."

Just then Lemron entered the door and smiled. Michael stuck out his hand. They shook, but didn't linger over it. People whispered as he walked by. The man didn't show even a trace of a limp. He pulled away and returned outside without attempting to say anything in El-phian. Michael was glad. He had too much to think about and it was still morning.

"Where are we going?...And is there a pitcher or jug to hold the water?"

"A pitcher? Michael," said Triana, "they asked me how baptizing was done where we came from. I took a pitcher and poured some water on my hand and sprinked some on Shirra's head, and said, 'Sometimes like this'; and then I actually poured some on her head, which surprised her and I thoroughly enjoyed, and I said, 'Or sometimes like this.' Then I said, 'Or sometimes like this,' and I pinched my nose shut with my fingers, shut my eyes, and leaned back and said, 'Or go under.'

"Then two of the holy women declared, 'Go under! Go under the water for Jesus, the God-Son! Others took up the chant: 'Go under for Jesus.'

"When I explained if they did it this way they would have to keep on their clothes, they seemed to indicate that it didn't matter. 'Go under for Jesus,' they repeated. 'Baptize!' They seemed to even enjoy saying the word in English. So now Michael, it's your turn to show us how to do it. Oh...and people are waiting outside right now to do this."

"And where? Michael asked.

"The ocean, Michael." The great doors are already open. God made you strong. You can do this. I will help you, and, perhaps Klingor and Lemron will help, too. We've got ten minutes to figure this out as we walk. Michael, despite their enthusiasm, they are very serious. I know God can stop us, if we're wrong, but they've witnessed some amazing things and, for now, the momentum is going our way.

"God has brought us here, Michael." He rolled his eyes up to the ceiling.

"And me to you," he returned, pointing to her accusingly. For a couple of seconds he studied her face. Then he touched his lips and pointed to the ceiling with two fingers.

"Yes, Michael, but only later tonight. And only at the right time. I'd be very pleased."

"But there's always someone—"

"Don't worry, I'll arrange it…Now listen, Michael. Focus. She put three fingers in the air. When you say the words, it's 'In the name of "Grott a Harven" ["*God of Heaven"*], "Grott-domor" ["*God-Son"*], "ana" ["and"] "Grott-Spatro-Loomin" ["*God, the Holy Spirit' "*].

He immediately repeated:

"Grott a Harven"

"Grott-domor"

"Grott-Spatro Loomin."

Michael moved toward the door. "God help me," he prayed in a voice only God could hear. "Stop me dead before I dishonor you." If he just put one foot in front of the other, and did so again and again, this day would finally have to end, and with it would come a small, welcome, promised reward. His growing fear slowly melted away and peace from somewhere else invaded. After descending the wide stone steps to the sand, he was met by Lemron and Klingor and about a hundred others—whether seekers, or merely the curious, he'd no idea.

Triana, barefoot, took his hand and added her easy dignity to the procession. She told him to remove his shoes, which he did, and continuing without breaking stride, she reached up and cupped her hand to his ear. Tilting his head down, he heard her whisper:

"I love you."

Where did that come from! And now? But, again, it was Triana, so it was okay. He recalled her *mun ana munlo*, Galen and Fairold, from the stories of their adventures in Emryss. She came by this naturally. When unusual things had to be done, they did it one footfall at a time. He must use this time to think. If she was at his side, he could take one step after another and go around the world…or worlds if necessary.

*   *   *   *   *

On the shore, he entered the water. The tide beyond the great doors seemed much gentler than yesterday.

After a gentle drop-off of three feet, the water gradually sloped deeper and deeper, suggesting that what he must do might be easier than expected. Eleven people stepped inches into the water and stood ready to go first. Michael had Triana tell **Lemron, Klingor, Shirra, Gurdon, Noli,** the two other fishermen, **Galandra**, and the three other new holy women to turn and face the others. After a prayer that he offered in English, he told Triana to explain, as best she could what he said line by line. And she did with words and gestures, the others assisting. To his surprise, the holy women who'd been so dramatically changed physically as well as spiritually were unusually accepting. It was as if they understood without any translation at all exactly what was going on.

"We have come from a far world" — he pointed to the sky — *"to tell you Good News about the God of Heaven,"* he began.

PAUSE….. (Triana and the others exchanged some motions and words.)

"If you are sorry for the evil things which you have done wrong – big things and little things – "

PAUSE…..

"And if you will believe, and trust in the God-Son, who we call Jesus, He will change you and save you from your sins."

PAUSE…..

"You can show that you have done this by being baptized, by going under the water and rising up to a new life." He pushed his hands down and then raised them high, palms up.

PAUSE…..

"We will baptize only two children who we know well, if they so choose. Other people, as you learn more, if you choose to give your life to the God-Son, we can baptize you later, for we are staying here because God has brought us here and we have no other place to go."

A LONGER PAUSE…Michael could hardly believe the expressions of joy and and seeming understanding of his words.

Lemron was tall — and first. Michael stood in water about mid-chest deep. Triana led him by the hand till she was waist-deep, as far as she dared without slipping under some small rogue wave from the side. How had ministers done this, making it look so easy? How could Lemron, a man with such responsibility and power surrender so easily to a strange boy who'd suddenly appeared and had hardly become a man? But then, without hesitation, Lemron was for the first time in ten years confidently taking his first steps in water. And four troublesome, infirm old women, now called "holy women," had thrown away their canes,

241

and were right behind him. Hadn't Esther Crandel insisted that simple deeds are often more effective than fine words?

It was time to begin. Michael placed Lemron sideways to those watching on the beach while he himself faced him.

"In names of Grott a Harven, Grott-Domor, and Grott-Sprato Loomin, I baptize you." Putting his hand over Lemron's nose, and spreading and bracing his legs, he folded the man backwards underwater — without slipping himself — and pulled him back to the surface. His face was glowing. As the holy women were next, Lemron, obviously no stranger to public ceremony, helped each woman to the right depth so that Michael could easily baptize them as well. Each woman came up from the water joyfully, loudly seeming to praise God in words Michael wished he could decipher. Gurdon and Shirra also were thrilled, as was their father Klingor and his three fisherman friends in more measured ways.

Before the baptizing had ended, more had stepped forward, and thirty-one had gone under the water. With no one else waiting, it was time to return to where they'd come from. Everyone worked his way back to the great doors just as the bright sun began to burn down. Back inside the cave with its crevasses in the rock ceiling that admitted migrating streaks of daylight, eyes adjusted as the dimness slowly surendered to the rising sun, augmented in places with small electric lights. Lemron, on his own, directed the people to go home or to work, and to return if possible the next day to see what was next.

Michael, with Triana's help, asked Lemron to tell the holy women and fishermen to return in an hour in dry clothes for a meeting. Gurdon and Shirra also were not about to be denied, and no one forbade them.

*   *   *   *   *

It was back at the Gatehouse that Lemron made it clear to Triana—with Michael nearby as well as Shirra who hadn't followed her brother and father home for dry clothes—that for the present, his modest-sized, centrally located home, was theirs, for just the two of them, to live in as long as necessary.

Lemron had had children of his own who had grown up and left the island years earlier. And soon after, his wife had died. Servants had attended to his needs which now had radically changed. Hence, new provisions would be made that Michael and Triana must agree to at least for the time being. Most important, would be that the two of them must accept the already-set-in-motion endless interruptions by changing shifts of uninvited, but always present night and day holy women—the title had now taken root—who, under his instructions would dedicate themselves with a vengeance to cook for, clean for, and watch over the newly arrived young orphans from outer space.

Michael and Triana agreed to this at once. Any needed details would come later…

Lemron, for the time being would live with his widowed mother, a responsibility he was unable to assume only hours earlier.

The radical transformation of the women from fearful hags into lively women filled with goodness and concern could not be denied. Nor could be the unexpected dramatic healing of Lemron.

But how long would all this last? Michael had no idea. But for their mission to be effective, it had to move forward quickly and deliberately.

And Michael—to his surprise—suddenly came up with a plan. As hair-brained as it might sound, he wanted to try it out before he lost his courage. Triana sensed something was coming. She glanced down at Shirra, who wanting to miss nothing, sat on the floor so her damp

243

karpona wouldn't get the furniture wet.

Triana leaned down and whispered in her ear. Together they went into her bedroom and shut the door. In no more than two minutes Shirra was back, wearing the huge flannel shirt he'd given Triana.

"Why are you still here, Shirra?" asked Michael, in English.

"I to waaa-tch you," she said righteously.

"Because?" asked Michael.

"Holy women say. I watch."

"Michael, we've a little problem here," said Triana. "Now *you* go and change. Shirra and I need to have a little talk in my bedroom before the others come back. Hurry!"

Michael reached his bedroom none too soon. Just as he shut the door to change clothes, the front door opened. He could hear several voices. But what were the words? He didn't have a clue. And how could Triana and Shirra talk to each other?

CHAPTER 23

Gathering Facts

Time: Day 5 ALOE (midmorning)

The time of cross-lingual understanding was clearly over.

To decide what came next, 12 new church members—Lemron, Klingor, Gurdon, two of the other fishermen, all four holy women who'd brought two cots and blankets, Michael, Triana, and Shirra—assembled at the Gatehouse. The fishermen, except for Klingor, and the children sat on the living room floor while everyone else sat on the sofa or chairs.

All, including Lemron, looked to Michael and Triana to begin.

Michael stood, closed his eyes and began to pray—all in English, of course—and God seemed to impress him with certain things that should follow, as difficult as that might be.

When he finished, it was his turn to listen. Lemron and Klingor turned to the holy women and began addressing issues that only the ten Elphians could understand. But how orderly it seemed. Everyone seemed expectant and alert. Although Michael would be hard pressed to explain it, God's presence seemed not far away. An exchange of information was taking place. Michael, however, was still at ground zero.

It was on this second day in their new surroundings that God's gift, after the joyful baptism ceremony, appeared to be giving everyone an unusual ability to focus as a group on *what* would be shared, more than particular understandings.

When they seemed to be finished, Michael's hand moved to his slate and a piece of chalk. As if this were a signal, Shirra jumped up and flew to Triana's room and returned with her own slate and chalk. With no certainty about what to expect, Michael lay two sheets of paper he'd already cut from his roll, about 24 by 12 inches along with two pencils, in the center of the floor. He pointed to his chest. How should he start?

"Michael," he said. "Mi — kal," he repeated, emphasizing each syllable. He printed the word with chalk on his slate. *"Triana;* Tree — ann — ah." He pointed towards her and printed her name word under his.

Without being asked, Shirra stood and came over to Michael's side. She bent over, studied each word, and pointing at each one, pronounced it: "Mi-kal, Tree-ann-ah," she said wrinkling her nose. She looked up for approval. Quietly those around the circle whispered the words after her.

I'm being ridiculous! Michael thought. She can remember and say what she hears, but printed letters — in *English* — had to be a total mystery! But…but… Michael recalled her first karpona. On the border that ran around the edges had to be the Elphian alphabet! Somebody who could sew that should be able to write, and probably write well — in *Elphian*! And he would call the language that, regardless if other languages existed on the planet. That was hardly a concern now! On the slate he wrote "Michael." Then he pronounced it again. He handed Shirra the slate and piece of chalk.

"Write 'Michael' in Elphian," he directed. "Elphian let-ters," he emphasized.

She looked far away for a whole minute, saying "Mi-kal" over and over to herself. Then on her slate she wrote his name from left to right using — what appeared to be — four distinct Elphian block letters that

246

were mainly connected short lines that ran either vertical or horizontal with a touch of graceful curving where the lines came together. And over the first letter of a name (or for a "sentence start," he would later learn), if the letter was not written slightly larger, a horizontal line would cover the letter making it taller than the other letters that were all exactly the same height. Her writing was deliberate, reasonably quick, and beautiful to see. Also, fortunately, like English, it went from left to right across the page.

While this was happening, Triana was scribbling furiously in a small notebook she'd made and was holding on her lap.

Michael then took the chalk and copied what she'd written on his own slate. Gently, Shirra took the chalk and made a small correction. Everyone smiled.

"Thank you," he said.

She nodded her head.

Michael stood and showed Klingor, then Lemron the word. "Michael," "Michael," the others said approving of the letters.

Then Michael wrote his name only in Elphian at the top of one of his large sheets of paper.

Setting the sheet aside, he repeated the process for Triana. Her name required five block letters. He put her name—only in Elphian—at the top of his second sheet of paper.

He turned to Triana.

"Help me with this. I want the name of everyone who was baptized written here in Elphian. Let Shirra, perhaps with help, do it for the women. Check everything. Then, under my name list the men. I don't want anyone left out. No one. I want to hear each name, then say it out loud, after it's written; and I want to see it written down, men on one sheet, women on the other. I'm going to have these names learned and the alphabet nailed down cold before I go to bed tomorrow night."

Triana and Shirra looked at each other, without attempting a word in either language…

Then the two sprang into action, writing names first in chalk, then checking them, and eventually writing all 31 names in Elphian — 16 men and 15 women — on the appropriate sheets. Later, Michael would get the alphabet from Shirra. Then, after she repeatedly sounded the letters, he transliterated them into English ones so he could better remember their sounds. The next day he would drive everyone in the Gatehouse crazy endlessly sounding the names written in Elphian letters of those he baptized. By nightfall he would be able to sound out most of the names and write them correctly. Shirra and Gurdon would continually bring him tea and bread until Triana eventually made everyone stop and the children go home.

But this day was far from over.

Next came a "discussion" about their calendar using hand gestures mingled with Elphian and some English. How did Elphian days "go"? [First, Michael and Triana discovered that their number system was, like ours, based on "10s" and their numerals, though differing slightly, were so similar to our Arabic numerals that they will be represented in the "Earth way" in the pages that follow.]

He was handed a wooden "month board" and soon discovered it could represent any of the 12 months exactly as a similar board could on Emryss. He recalled the four Emryss stories where a year was 420 days divided into twelve 35-day, 5-week months. Once again, as far as they could tell, the universal 7-day week was in play. A "permanent" rectangle of wood with 5 rows of 7 pegs each, with 12 pegs at the top to identify each month, any day and any month of a given year — if the year number was attached in a slot on the top — could be identified by just two wooden rings.

It was a never-changing pattern much easier to use than Earth's confusing calendar.

The month they were in he learned was "Arvil." [But since no other months are mentioned in what follows except "Reglanth," which occurs six months later, it's not necessary to list them.]

The day was the 11th of Avril or 'Day 4' of week two.
(Numerals put here in English, said to be nearly identical
to numerals in Elphian)

That day in the living room, they learned, was [a "Wednesday" in Earth terms] the 11th of Avril, or "Day 4" of week two of Avril since Elphians, as did the ancient Jews, used only numbers for days—the Jewish one exception being naming the "Sabbath," which actually began on the previous evening at sundown. As Michael learned the new calendar, in a rash moment of daring, he boldly insisted that for the new believers he would call the last day of every week—the 7th, 14th, 21st, 28th, and 35th—in Elphia a "Sabbath," as the Bible does. This was hardly a radical social change since most Elphians were used to having some time, usually a day, off from work at the end of every week.

And as strange as it may first seem, the nature and place of a weekly

Sabbath would be an important part of his next time "publicly speaking," two days away, on the evening part of the 13th that immediately preceded the 14th, a day which would become a *true* day of rest — for them and other believers.

But new believers must decide for themselves just what this meant.

– A SABBATH CLARIFICATION –

[To further clarify, the following will become three soon-to-be introduced concepts.]

With a recognition and naming of the Sabbath — which had been forgotten, never recognized, or never ever considered important before on Elphia — Michael would "introduce" the *Sabbath* just as presented in the Bible. Hence, to Elphian believers the 7th day would actually begin at sunset on "Friday" (as Earthlings would say) on Days 6, 13, 20, 27, and 34 of each month) and end at sunset the following day, "Saturday," (on Days 7, 14, 21, 28, and 35).

Further, the term *"Sabbath Day,"* as used here, will often informally refer to "Saturday *dawn* to nightfall (as "day" as is commonly thought of on Earth) though technically a Sabbath begins at the previous sunset on "Friday." The term *"Sabbath Eve"* will become an important term Michael will come to use to identify the "last hours" of Weekday 6 before sunset. *"Sabbath After"* (a term Michael will create and use) will be that undefined time that immediately follows the actual Sabbath at sunset on Weekday 7, and technically the beginning of Weekday 1.

Since the Biblical Sabbath will become important, there are three practical realities to be considered about the day itself and the two

250

weekly meeting times, one just before it and one just after it, that will be created at the Church of Elfend:

(1) The Sabbath is a day of personal and family **rest** and reflection, not formal meetings.

(2) The "teaching time" immediately before it on Sabbath Eve and the "praise and worship time" immediately after it on Sabbath After will both be *evening gatherings that start at different times.* The first will end in "early darkness" and the second will begin in early darkness. Lanterns and other lights will often be useful in such meetings.

(3) "Regular daytime activites" — except for the 7th day Sabbath — are little affected on the other six weekdays.

And even further, "Sabbath," though transliterated into Elphian letters, is pronounced exactly the same as it is in English. *[For further discussion of the Sabbath see Appendix B.]*

Also, as said earlier: The seconds, minutes, and hours, and 24-hour day are exactly the same on Elphia as on Emryss and Earth.

Michael held the pegboard calendar board in his lap.

"Triana, help me with this schedule."

He stood and faced each person one by one, as Harwell would have done in such a situation.

"We, Michael and Triana, will begin teaching about Jesus, the God-Son and thank God for what He's done — *in two days* at *two hours before sundown* ends Day 13." He moved the wooden ring two days ahead. "Then we, the two of us, will 'talk,' preach about God, and lead worship after sundown on Peg 14. From sundown on Day 13 until sundown on Day 14 Michael and Triana will rest, rest, rest." He held up an imaginary piece of paper and pretended to read it. Then he put his palms together, placed them alongside his tilted head, closed his eyes and pretended to sleep.

Since sunset was sometimes not easy to detect through cave crevasse openings to the sky (after some initial confusion), a gong would soon announce when the Sabbath began and another gong would announce when it ended. *No one had to follow Sabbath rules,* but he and Triana would. Those baptized would be encouraged to do so, and the reasons for this would be forthcoming. But the choice was theirs. The Sabbath would be "God's Day" every week, a day of rest, reflection, family, *no progammed activities* secular or religious, and *no regular work.*

"On Day 13, after a meal has been prepared for later, if something isn't eaten earlier, our doors close. No one comes here to the Gatehouse. No one here until Day 14 evening. No one."

Triana, apparently taken by surprise by Michael's declaration, looked a bit astonished, but said nothing.

(With that, a model of the Jewish and early Christian Sabbath, slightly modified — since some early believers on Earth had developed a habit of gathering on the Sabbath, *though not Biblically commanded* to — was put into place. "Bookending a regular — Biblically established — period of rest, before God and each other, will help us keep from going crazy," he told Triana later. "That must have come directly from God!" she'd returned. "I'll accept that," he'd replied.)

Suddenly, in the living room there was a frantic whispering among the holy women. They turned to Lemron in desperation. The word "orphans" was said over and over. Triana leaned over and whispered in Michael's ear.

"Michael, I think the holy women are afraid they'll be kept away and lose their blessing if we do certain things" — only Triana would say it that way — "because I'm not your klepta. Regardless of what we've started here, you and I are both orphans who need some supervision, and they're insisting upon 'watching us.' 'God has called them,' they've said, 'to keep us from being foolish.' Isn't that amazing! Let *me* handle this, Okay?"

"Okay."

Triana stood. Her speaking was a mixture of Elphian, English, and moving her hands and head, sometimes pointing to the pegboard, sometimes to people.

The message: "Michael has agreed. We will honor what the holy women are saying." She pointed to him and then the door. She went to the door and opened and shut it twice, then pointed to the four holy women. "Holy women can come. Welcome anytime. Anytime, even on the Sabbath. But *only* holy women." She pointed again one-by-one to the four who sat on the sofa across from her. They seemed to understand. Then they cheered in a way that would have been impossible only a day ago, and said something that sounded so much like "Praise God" that Michael shivered.

"Now I feel much safer," Triana whispered to Michael behind her hand.

He forced himself to smile. They had to move on. A big piece of information was still missing, because there'd been no time for it. What was Elphia anyway? The "place" where they were was called Elphia, but what about the planet? How far did the name go? How big was the planet? And how did the part they were on fit in with what they were supposed to do? Had loss of the I-Rex Code occurred everywhere? Was it like a spiritual fog that had poisoned the whole planet?

Of course, language would be a big barrier. But not for long. Michael vowed he would learn the language faster than Triana or anyone thought possible, even master it, if he had to work at it all night and day — but not on the Sabbath, of course.

He began by cutting another large piece from his roll of paper and laying it out on the floor. In the center he drew a bow-shaped arc that had a curve about the size of an automobile tire rim. At the top of the sheet he wrote "Elphia" in English. "Elphia, Elphia, Elphia," extending his arms out in several directions.

Then he had Shirra write the word in Elphian letters underneath. He had Lemron check them. He nodded approval.

"Elphia," he said again. "How big?" He threw his arms out and pulled them back to the top of his head several times, expressing wonder with his eyes. Triana did the same. Though the drawing was obviously a crude view from above, he made a small upside down V that stood for the cave entrance that brought Triana and him underground to where they now were. He made a tiny rectangle for the house where they sat, added the two other next-door houses, and a larger more ragged rectangle for the auditorium where they'd met the night before. "Us," he said, pointing to everyone, then inside the circle little dots and tiny circles. Then he drew another small rectangle for the stage platform.

With a lot of white space left, he handed Lemron the pencil and asked him and the fishermen to fill in the rest of the drawing.

A half hour later Michael and Triana's knowledge of *ELPHIA* and *Elphia* (now entirely capitalized for the whole planet, while the island, named for the planet, will still be written as before) began to grow. ELPHIA, it seemed, was essentially a vast fearful ocean presumably covering a large "Earth-sized ball" because of the almost identical gravity and the easy breathing of air, that Michael and Triana had breathed all their lives...well, for Triana, for most of her life. According to what Lemron and Klingor drew, this "ocean planet" was peppered with circular, or roughly circular-shaped islands, some probably quite large, some quite small, with others "middle-sized."

And the island, Elphia, was probably between small-and middle-sized, maybe about 10 miles or so in diameter, with short peninsulas jutting out here and there. The sizes of the beaches surrounding it regularly varied greatly from a hundred or so yards of sand to no sand at all—with great variation in the tides because of the two moons.

And Elphia was just one island among many.

That was a start.

Six other things would become more-or-less obvious as their second day (the 11th of Avril) continued and others followed. Here's a sketchy summary to tell what's necessary:

(1) Travel between any of the islands was generally risky, and often treacherous, because of rough seas and extreme tides, most likely caused by the twin moons.

(2) The closest island to Elphia (note lower case) was Balara, three times larger in size and with many more people. But getting there by boat was still a small adventure. Nonetheless, trade occurred there as well as occasionally with several other islands.

(3) The population of the town they were in, Elfend (which got transliterated into English with an "f" rather than a "ph"), was 230, and counting the two other towns on Elphia (Island) was altogether about 900.

(4) As far as they knew, no electronic communication of any kind existed between nearby islands, as well as between people on their island — strange, considering their past sophistication in space travel and genetic engineering somewhere else on the planet.

(5) Added here, but more detailed later, is some information about Elphian medical knowledge, including that of Balara, that soon will be called for. It varied greatly between primitive and modern. There was, it seemed, some knowledge of germ theory and cause-and-effect diagnosis, the ability to effect a limited number of naturopathic remedies and even produce certain home-cultured antibiotics, other medicines, and certain vaccinations. Births were generally assisted by midwives.

(6) Puzzling, even though it was generally admitted that ELPHIA was a sphere, there was little known, or admitted, information about what the planet's surface was like beyond the vaguely drawn islands that Klingor and Lemron had scribbled in at the outside edges of Mi-

255

chael's map!

But, as Jonas once said, "Everyone is ignorant of some important information if you push back far enough. So to do anything, start with what you know, and go from there."

And Day 5 (as their days on ELPHIA will continue to be counted) wasn't over.

A thrilling discovery close at hand would open Michael's and Triana's eyes to much more.

But first, not to be ignored was a large wind-up clock in the living room that didn't look that unfamiliar, except for the twelve slightly different Elphian numerals on the clock's face, that chimed the passing of the three hours or so that the new Christians spent with their two teachers in their first "church meeting" on "Day 5."

At last, Michael finally rolled up his "map," everyone stood, and Lemron took center stage.

"Ya caifin!" he declared. If Michael was a betting man, that had to mean "Follow me!" Lemron sprang to his feet and walked briskly across the room—inspiring everyone else to do the same, and not be last—to the first hallway that went by the kitchen, past the bathroom and Triana's bedroom to the back of the house.

Lemron himself opened the door to the tunnel, something he hadn't been able to do for years.

CHAPTER 24

The Garden Of Eating

Time: Day 5 ALOE (afternoon)

The door at the end of the hallway opened to a tunnel partly cut through stone. At first it reminded Michael of the tunnel from the parsonage to the water tower. But here the rock was black and the farther they walked the wider and higher the tunnel got. Also, the distance was only a tenth as long. Daylight from somewhere ahead steadily grew brighter.

At the end came the sound of falling water from a tiny waterfall trickling from high above, though sometimes running in a stream from cracks in the rock above the left side of the opening.

As Michael moved into daylight, he noticed that most direct afternoon sunlight was cut off to the flat interior by high cliffs. He was entering something that seemed like a cross between a pro football stadium, but with a much larger oval "field" area, and the bottom of an unusually wide extinct volcano roughly similar, except for their flatness, to those that existed in their stories about Emryss.

But instead of grandstands, sheer walls ran almost straight up like the cliffs on the beach, but much taller. Unlike the centers of volcanos on Emryss, however, here the center ground was almost pancake flat, circled by a wide lava-like gravel walkway that with several exceptions, came as near the wall as possible. It had to be at least two miles

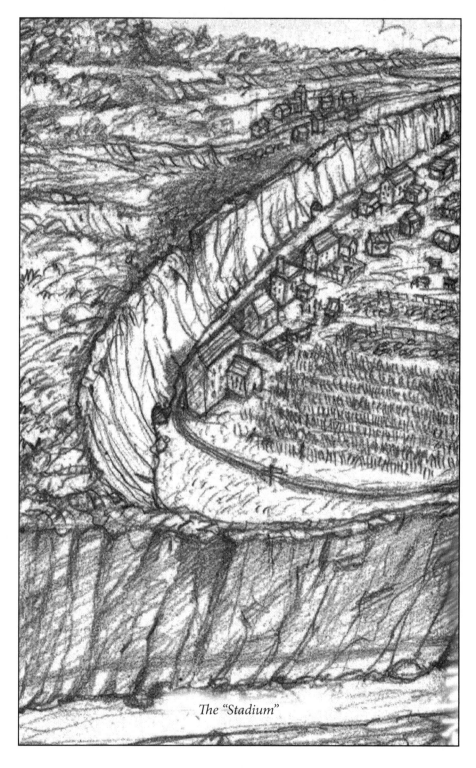

The "Stadium"

259

around. Just on the other side of the walkway, in the center were never-ending rows of plants, some attached to tall stakes, others standing two or three feet high on their own. But first came many rows of kerm, the delicious corn-like vegetable he'd eaten on the beach. Later he discovered several bean-like and pea-like plants, as well as ones covered with berries of several colors and shapes.

If he'd wondered about where Elfend, and perhaps the other two towns, got food he had his answer. Before him was a well-tended "garden for eating." By tilling the land that lay before him and harvesting fish from the sea, no one should go hungry.

In two places stood a pair of men, barechested and in their dinnies, as the fishermen had been after their day of traveling. Mostly they seemed to work in pairs, harvesting kerm by hand, pulling the abundant small cobs with sharp tugs, sometimes using a knife, to snap them from their stalks. The cobs were tossed in large baskets attached to the two long poles of a travois, so a single person could pull a large basketful between rows, or two could carry a basket on poles similar to the way Lemron had arrived in the Auditorium.

When the men saw them approaching with Triana and Shirra, they returned Lemron's wave and slipped between the stalks to another row to work out of sight. Working as they were at a *distance* seemed acceptable without explanation, but bare thighs in mixed company, as with the fishermen, seemed to be another matter. Michael was thankful his cargo shorts were much longer and hadn't seemed to be an issue earlier. Now in the karpon he'd been given that fell just below his knees, he felt more in keeping with Elphian expectations.

And Triana had shown wisdom by wearing her long tied-at-the-waist wraparound skirt—resembling the Elphian half-karpona that she'd seen a few other women wearing earlier.

As everyone neared the far end of the oval "stadium field," almost a mile away, they passed several large buildings between the walkway and the cliff. These seemed to be full of chickens and other winged fowl, as well as cages of some sort of animal resembling a rabbit, but larger and with shorter ears. On both sides at the far end were several shops with seemingly busy back rooms, special chimneys, and all sorts of add-on structures. These had to be mini-factories or workplaces of some kind, all with electrical wires on outdoor poles that somewhere had to run up the mountain wall or go underground through some tunnel that led outside to some place that provided power. Here it seemed that furniture, tableware, shoes, clothing, and who-knows-what could be made and possibly sold.

As they rounded the far end of the oval, before they returned to the sea of kerm and other vegetables, they passed several homes and a few dormitory-styled buildings that seemed barely separated by the trail from the cliff walls. He would start learning everything he could about these residences, businesses, crops and animals, and maybe do some small work — if allowed — in the dozen or so shops and factories later on.

To avoid going crazy he must often use his hands, even in helping harvest the kerm if they'd let him.

Frequently, except for the Sabbath of course.

But first came learning the language. Learning it *well*.

Not to be ignored was how the tall rock walls around this flat area provided general protection, including shadows for harvesters with sensitive skins who planned ahead.

And near the far end were two, possibly three small schools, a modest hospital clinic, and a guard station where he saw his first firearm. All these, however, were about as far from the more rural side and Lemron's entry tunnel as one could get.

But the stadium wasn't the only place people worked he would learn.

Many islanders didn't live or work in caverns or extinct volcanos.

261

"Normal," sparsely populated country land began beyond the stadium, and even farther away, were two other towns outside the stadium with their own resources, businesses, farms, mayors and regulations. Yet of the three mayors on the island, for reasons Michael didn't understand, Lemron was the "chief mayor" with greater authority despite Elfend's smaller size.

The inside of the mountain became Michael's "Stadium." He would write it in Elphian letters, capitalize it, and forever call it that to Triana. Surprisingly, others around him soon would copy this, not knowing or understanding why, but pronouncing the word just like Michael did, transliterating it, of course, into Elphian letters—with Michael's capitalization.

But first came learning the Elphian language. Mastering it.

He hadn't been a basketball point guard for nothing. He'd made himself know his teammates, how well they shot, rebounded, and played as a team, and as a player he'd make whatever adjustments that were necessary to win. He would take every word that came his way, repeat it aloud again and again and again, and if Shirra hung around she would earn her keep! Word genius Triana could help him fit the pieces together in the evenings.

One day at a time.

He would master it, or die trying.

Different languages were okay if Triana were aboard. And just being near her was a treasure in itself, with or without words. The ins and outs of a new language weren't easy. But Gurdon and Shirra, if they weren't scared off, were never far away, and since one of the children's teachers had become a believer on the first day, their frequent "absences" from school would be overlooked if they made up their work. She would declare Triana and Michael to be their "special private tutors," something Lemron immediately approved "for the time being" [which is the closest translation in English].

On the trip around the oval walkway, Lemron pointed out one thing after another that Michael could barely understand. He did, however, notice a dozen or so other openings, besides their private tunnel, that led in and out of the Stadium.

But most intriguing—and inviting—of all was the thin private waterfall where they started that dribbled and splashed from a high crevasse down into a pool just to the right of the opening that led back inside the tunnel, splashing everyone's faces with spray. Behind this falling water, rock had been chiseled out in the tunnel wall and down deep enough in the floor to form a hidden cold-water shower and pool where field workers could easily step out of sight and quickly clean up after an afternoon of sweaty work. This Lemron allowed, though entry through his house to the Auditorium or gatehouse steps he did not.

At last they were back where they'd started.

Just before reentering the tunnel, Michael had spied a cluster of beautiful daisy-like golden flowers growing against the rock wall. He picked two and carefully carried them as inconspicuously as he could inside the tunnel.

After he passed through the door to the Gatehouse, he stopped at the bathroom to add his flowers and water to a waterglass that he found there. The bathroom reminded him of a picture in a 1950s *Life* magazine that had followed him here from the Hotel Crandel, showing only a small white bathtub standing on legs. A dash into the cold-water shower they'd passed, with a little soap, might sometimes be better and quicker than the time it took filling up and and washing in a tub.

Back in the living room, Triana had them all hold hands and she said a prayer with words that everybody on Earth could perfectly understand.

But nobody else.

263

"Remember the Sabbath," she said. "In Auditorium. Auditorum. Come early." Everyone nodded as they left, suggesting said Triana, they at least understood that part.

All were respectful, and soon everyone was gone. Except for Gurdon and Shirra, who looked as ready as possible for whatever was next.

Also staying were two of the holy women who began to busy themselves in the kitchen.

Michael caught Shirra's eye, and immediately began to work on the Elphian alphabet as if his day's work had just begun. Without asking, Shirra grabbed Gurdon and whispered in his ear. He immediately ran to the door and left, returning out of breath only minutes later with Shirra's karpona from a day earlier, now dry. With a glance toward Triana, she flew to her room and changed into it. Now "wearing her Elphian alphabet," she pulled up her own chair and sat next to him in the alcove with her own chalk and slate. One by one she wrote and scrubbed out several times all 21 letters that seemed to be required.

Triana handed Michael his own slate and chalk and walked away trying not to laugh.

Gurdon brought Michael a cup of tea — giving Michael an idea as well.

Shirra began her lesson. Letter after letter after letter.

To anchor the letters would require almost two Hotel Crandel clocks that soon he could later discard. Details, details. He could do that. Never would he share with anyone his silly associations.

Finally, Triana in fresh clothing complemented by a few drops of her special perfume, sat down across the table and carefully made her own set of letters on a scrap of paper, that Shirra also inspected, suggesting small corrections, pointing to the letters that she wore. Then for Michael, Triana used English letters to indicate the sounds of the Elphian letters which immediately grabbed Shirra's attention. Then wrinkling her nose, the girl wrote everything she saw Triana write on

264

her own slate, later using paper.

This led to again going over the two sheets that listed the names of the 31 founding members of the Church of Elfend.

Gurdon, finally tiring of all this, got up to leave.

"Stop!" ordered Michael, standing and stretching his arms. "I've a job for you." Without asking, he picked up the slates and papers and pencils and chalk even though Triana was still writing, and carried them to the sofa. He took Gurdon by the hand to the kitchen. The holy women stepped back, bewildered. He opened several cabinet doors and drawers until he found plates and tableware. He took two plates and some tableware to the table in the alcove.

"Gurdon, I'm setting the table for dinner," he said. And he did. "See?" Michael pointed. "Look carefully. Carefully." Michael touched each item. Then he stacked the two plates, scooped up the tablewear he'd arranged, and piled it on the plates. "Now, Gurdon," he poked a finger in the boy's stomach. "You set the table!"

And he quickly did, with no noticeable error.

"Good!" said Michael, "but we aren't done." He took the boy by the hand to his bedroom and pointed to the flowers in the waterglass. "Put this on the table." He did. "Now table is set for dinner. Thank you!" He gave the boy a little bow. "Now you can go home."

"Can-dill?" the boy asked.

Michael provided one — leaving it unlit on a saucer Michael found — and after "arranging" it, and receiving approval, Gurdon left.

Michael stared at the sofa where Triana and Shirra sat smiling, as if they could stay there forever if they had enough words to work with. Well, so could he! Hadn't he once shot free throws for three hours straight, after missing two shots that would have won the game? But the girl…an Elphian…how long could she last? Would she burn out? Once again, he noticed that when she seemed to be deeply puzzling over something on paper she was unnaturally quiet. He must not forget this. But now she was staring back at him. He sensed something new was coming.

"Mi-kal," she asked, her large eyes pleading. "Errth letters...plu-ease."

"It's called 'English,'" he said, a bit shaken that she was already using his language better than he hers. For another hour she copied letter after letter until, this time, Michael said it was "right." Then, carefully cutting another piece of paper from Michael's roll without asking, she made her own list of letters, sounding them, her eyes searching for his reaction as she put each of them down, making notes in Elphian. When Triana saw Shirra's list was complete, she told her it was time to go home and give her father a thank-you hug which she demonstrated.

Carefully arranging her papers, as a teacher might her students' assignments to take home for grading, she put them in a bag that Triana gave her, adding her slate and chalk, and was gone.

"You'd better work hard, Michael. She's going to pass you up!"

"Thank you, Triana, for saving me."

"For what, Michael?"

"For you," he said, leaking out a thin smile.

"Michael, sometimes I still wonder about you," she returned.

Michael stood. "Time for a break," he offered.

From the corner of his eye he noticed the two holy women watching and whispering, holding bowls and a pot of soup. Michael encouraged them to bring it to the table that was already set. He lit the candle, stuck it on the saucer and set it between them. Triana smiled and the holy women seemed expressionless, but ready to bring out food. Michael turned off the small electric light overhead in the alcove. The delicious meal arrived and included several new tastes.

In the flickering shadows of the candle, the visitors from Earth relaxed for the first time.

And talked—safely in English—for two hours from where they sat.

266

The holy women cleaned up, taking away their empty plates at the right time, refilling the tiny cups with tea, but generally staying out of their way, though one always remained obviously within sight. One woman inspected the two bedrooms that were down separate hallways, of course. Returning to the sofa, the other then shamelessly finished sorting and arranging some of their personal things as if the newcomers from Earth were moving in.

Which they were.

But they wouldn't be there alone. The holy women, with books to read, and sewing waiting for their attention in large bags, settled on the large sofa with its back at the bottom of the large window in front. Through it was a view of the auditorium area across from the steps that brought them up from the sea. The stage which Triana and he had sat upon was small but clearly visible in the distance. The women had already set up two cots near his bedroom door, ready for them when they were the last ones up. They seemed to be never finished with "doing things" — until two others came to replace them.

A start had been made.

*　　*　　*　　*　　*

As promised, on **Sabbath Eve,** two hours before the new Sabbath actually began, the believers one-by-one and two-at-a-time gathered in the front of the auditorium where everything had begun.

Michael, Triana, Lemron, and Klingor sat on chairs just below the stage. All 31 baptized believers sat on benches or the ground in a semi-circle in front of them. Their names, printed in large letters appeared on a paper attached to a board facing the people that leaned up against the stage.

The holy women, sitting in pairs on stools facing the stage, two on the left and two on the right in front, began without being asked, softly

267

Auditorium viewed from Gatehouse living room

268

humming what to Michael sounded like a song of praise though except for "Grott" he couldn't understand the words. But it felt right. Otherwise, the large room with at least 50 others watching from a careful distance away, was deathly silent. The presence of the converted troublesome hags, now joyfully transformed in body and spirit, along with the presence of Lemron enjoying his third day of walking in ten years were enough of a sermon to let anyone watching know that something important was happening right before their eyes whether they could explain it or not.

Michael stood and the humming on its own seemed to die away. Closing his eyes, he raised his hands and prayed aloud in English, that the English he prayed in would soon become his second language.

After praying, with only an occasional glance down at a paper he held, he called the names of the 31 sitting before him in *Elphian*. With each called name, the person stood until all were standing. Then began the chanting and the clapping—hands up and down, of course:

"Grott a Harven, Grott-domor, Grott-Spatro Loomin, da cum for!
Grott a Harven, Grott-domor, Grott-Spatro Loomin, da cum for!
Grott a Harven, Grott-domor, Grott-Spatro Loomin, da cum for!
Grott a Harven, Grott-domor, Grott-Spatro Loomin, da cum for!"

" 'da cum for' ?" Michael whispered.

" 'I am yours,' " Triana whispered back. "It's an idiom, I think."

[In English, though it sounds awkward and doesn't rhyme: "God of Heaven, God-Son, Holy Spirit, I am yours."]

"Praise God! Praise God! Praise God!" said Michael, raising his hands. What a surprise!

"Praise God! Praise God! Praise God!" responded the people to-

269

gether, using Michael's exact words, regardless of what they meant.

Triana leaned over and whispered in his ear: "The song, Michael, it's the baptism words, and it's their own creation."

Then began a teaching about the Sabbath, Sabbath Eve, and Sabbath After—what it meant and what everyone should expect. His main point was that everyone should first of all open himself to God. The language of teaching? English, Elphian, and hand motions, all mixed together—Triana, Lemron, and Noli who became a surprising help with his graceful pantomime and a touch of humor.

Michael determined then and there that he, before God, would do everything in his power to help these people and never, never damage the new expressions of faith that God had brought to this world.

When he raised his hands to finally close the service, five people who'd been watching intently nearby, and were friends of the new Christians, wanted to trust in the "God-Son Jesus." Upon Lemron's recommendation, this was allowed. Proceeding to the beach in the growing darkness, they joyously went under the water in the name of "Grott a Harven, Grott-domor, and Grott-Spatro-Loomin." The next baptisms requested on a Sabbath Eve, or Sabbath After for that matter, Michael determined, would from then on be postponed to when morning light appeared on Sabbath After, or Day 1 of the week.

Then Gurdon and Shirra went home with their father, and Michael went home in wet clothes, but not Triana, since Klingor alone helped with the water part of the ceremony.

On the **Sabbath** itself, Michael and Triana saw no one except the rotating pairs of holy women—their number soon to add three more. When Gurdon and Shirra showed up at the door, the holy women shooed them away, and told them to go home and look after their father. Grudgingly, they obeyed. The two space travelers who'd suddenly become heads of a church collapsed into a much-needed deep sleep in their separate bedrooms. Awaking refreshed and strong, they enjoyed special cold pastries along with their ever-present hot tea. Then they sat side by side on the great sofa which the holy women not only allowed, but encouraged, moving to nearby chairs. He sat close enough to feel the warmth of her body. They both happily read without speaking or explaining. Her book? Well, he couldn't tell without looking at it. His reading? Nothing more than paging through another old magazine that had hitchhiked a ride with them from the Hotel Crandel.

"I'm going for a walk," he at last announced, "in the Stadium."

"*Alone* is okay," Triana said, anticipating the part he left out.

"And, uh—"

"If you come back, there's this." For a second only she raised a finger, but only as high as her nose.

"But the—" With his back to the holy women, he rolled his eyes in their direction.

"I'll find a way," she said, dropping her eyes back to her book.

How good it felt to be alone outside! Halfway to the end of the cinder oval in the Stadium he heard a "scraw…scraw…scraw" overhead. Glancing up, his eyes landed on a large nest near the top of the rock cliff a hundred feet above him. What glue could hold it there? What courage and tenacity of its builders! Would the two restless eagle-like hatchlings survive long enough to leave and build their own nests? How could he have missed that on his first day there?

How could the promise back at the Gatehouse—for the moment—have slipped from his mind?

*   *   *   *   *

The next day, on **Sabbath After**, all 36 came through other Stadium tunnels to the "Circle of Worship," as it was declared to be, which was no more than a hundred feet from Lemron's private entrance, on the cliff side of the cinder oval across from the kerm. About an equal number of "watchers" or visitors were also there since the place was more isolated than the Auditorium. These were especially welcomed by Lemron.

What should they do now?

Michael remembered what Jesus once told his puzzled disciples when the hungry thousands had only five loaves and two fish. After blessing them, He said in effect: "Use what you have." The disciples did.

The holy women arrived and began everything with a soft new song that began the service "decently and in order" before "order" had really been established. The humming from the holy women began as Triana stood before them, preparing herself to talk as best she could and "act out" what to say about prayer. When the humming finally faded, she pled with the new believers to pray and ask God, who was real, to help Michael and her to really learn their language, and "translate" the words of God—she held up her Bible—into language they could understand.

Michael could feel that everyone seemed to understand how important this was. And how determined they were to present them with God's message.

When, at last, Michael, Triana, Lemron, and Klingor joined hands together in a small circle and prayed, and encouraged the others to do the same, the new believers joined them. What they actually said Michael couldn't tell, but from somewhere in the vast gardens a sweet smell came and filled the air. Afterwards, on his own, one of the new believers led the others in what so soon had become a regular expression of their faith:

"Grott a Harven, Grott-domor, Grott-Spatro Loomin, da cum for!
Grott a Harven, Grott-domor, Grott-Spatro Loomin, da cum for!
Grott a Harven, Grott-domor, Grott-Spatro Loomin, da cum for!
Grott a Harven, Grott-domor, Grott-Spatro Loomin, da cum for!"

["God of Heaven, God-Son, Holy Spirit, I am yours."]

A sense of happiness and hope seemed to fall over everyone. Without a word in either language, his mind began to fill. What was really occurring? Everyone seemed so trusting, so full of joy! How long would it last? What about the many others? This was too big for him! God help me! He pled silently.

He glanced at Triana, and found her staring at him.

"It's too big for *both* of us," she said, smiling.

Michael shivered. What else did she see in his mind? Triana seemed to be holding back a laugh.

"Roll call" was made again, and six more people asked to be baptized — and they would be, but since Sabbath After also ended in darkness, this would not occur until morning light came to (this) Weekday 1. With the rising of the sun Michael and Triana found the new believers waiting expectantly on the beach to go "under the water for Jesus."

After the baptizing on Day 1 of the 3rd week (or Day 15 of Avril), and Michael changing his clothes, their language study continued with a vengeance.

CHAPTER 25

A New Foundation

— One month passes...

— Two months pass...

— Three months pass...

— Four, five, six months pass since the end of Ch. 24...

*T**he problem of two languages is over.*

Well, mostly so.

Rarely have two complete strangers to a foreign country, much less another planet, learned a new language so quickly and so well.

The day-and-night effort of Michael surprised Triana, to whom such matters came more easily. He became a machine that time after time Triana had to switch off: "Stop... Michael...now!" It was basketball all over again. "I will do everything I have to to win," he insisted. "The only thing that's changed is what I'm trying to do." He, of all people, had to teach and preach – in Elphian!

And yes, along with Triana.

It also usually pushed his mind off other things as well.

But for the 24 hours of the Sabbath he stopped, really "stopped," and God seemed to reward him for it, teaching and empowering and surprising both of them in those hours. He could not afford to detour.

Triana had spent time with Shirra, and had become more direct. "If you want to come to the Gatehouse without permission," she declared, "it's only after school and not a minute before, and all your 'work' at home is done."

Since Shirra's father was a good man, but hardly strict, Triana privately gave Shirra "assignments" for duties at her home, explaining what to many were merely ordinary things, but things that really mattered and should be done well. These included keeping an eye on Gurdon as well as her father. So Klingor, aware of Triana's behind-the-scenes teaching, gave Shirra great freedom which many thought led to the sad and bewildering event that lay ahead.

And the Elphlanders, or Elphians?

Their reactions in the last six months to the visitors from Earth varied.

Overheard in the "auditorium":

Said one, "I can now understand them better, but the 'Earth Prophet' and the 'Emryss Princess' with an Elphian grandfather have gone mad," I say. "And they say they know what we're missing! They know our language now but not each other. What's wrong with them?"

"They've done good things we cannot explain," said another in the open-air Stadium, "but why haven't they fulfilled the only prophecy we remember from our Holy Book that so suddenly disappeared?"

"Are these really the ones?" said still another. "Or have we been fooled?"

And another: "Lemron has said over and over: 'I walk and I rule, and they stay; and they live in my house as long as they desire,' and then he would emphasize: 'under the watchful eyes of holy women.' "

And still another: "But are these women casting some spell over the visitors from Earth — and us? They seem to come and go as they please, and have added several to their number, taking turns in pairs continually living alongside the two and controlling their personal lives."

"And," someone had replied, "how can that be?"

To which came the standard reply: "Because our visitors from another world have said they are children and orphans," several had chimed in.

"But haven't they come of age, or have they?" said someone else.

Also heard: "The believers in their 'Jesus' have become a tightly knit group, and though it's barely doubled in size, they are people who are good and quick to help each other. What they say and read from what they call a

'Bible' seems fascinating, but how can those so young have anything to say to those who have lived here all their lives and are twice their age? I just don't understand...?"

And: "Still they are slowly teaching parts of their Bible that speak to our needs and have translated parts of it into Elphian for us to read for ourselves. And for many of us there's a 'haunting' echo of things our parents and grandparents heard – but can't remember – from long ago."

And: "Strange...they disappear and 'rest' on the last day of the week, then reappear the next day and work twice as hard day after day, being friendly and productive without doing any noticeable harm."

And: "How do we know that?

*   *   *   *   *

The rest of the everything that follows, cuts through the language difference – usually, though not entirely. Since Triana and Michael have learned Elphian, as a rule it will be assumed that the initial language barrier has been broken.

Hence the remaining narrative will be recorded as if everything was said in English.

With some exceptions.

Certain Elphian words have been retained since they say things better and more vividly. **"Klepta"** ("woman kept by promise" – strongly implying marriage) and **"kleptini"** ("a temporary woman kept for convenience"), have been retained. **"Mareena"** ("birth mother") and **"marana"** ("gift mother" – our closest, but still inadequate, equivalent would be "adoptive mother.") In Elphian, however, these two words have equal power and force, though the second one, "marana" – if declared and recognized – often brings with it a special dignity, for while every child in Elphia will be cared for and "tolerated," by his mareena, he will not automatically be considered "worth his mareena's trouble," as harsh as that sounds. But the proclaimed child of a marana is a

276

non-birth child of special value with legal rights. Here both words, when appropriate, will be used without translation or further comment. As to **"vanchi,"** *it has no good English translation, though "pest" may come close. The word, however, does not necessarily imply negativity. Other retained Elphian words will be clearly defined in context.*

Aside from language issues, there are cultural differences that Michael and Triana have been made aware of in these long months – some Elphian be-haviors and attitudes that may seem inappropriate or harsh to people on Earth.

But what happens here is not on Earth.

Three examples of this:

(1) The manner of expected grieving.

When a person loses a child or a spouse (but not a parent), that person may grieve for six months, or 210 days, with relaxed responsibilities. On Day 211, however, the slate seems to be magically wiped clean, usually informally, with no further "allowances for loss" expected from others. The tragedy is over, the mature have dealt with it, and "time with all its responsibilities moves on equally for everyone" as if no loss occurred. The Christian call to put first things first and the command to be tender and understanding to someone still suffering is often hard to be understood here.

(2) The allowance for personal intrusion and/or loss of privacy.

Certain societal expectations can trump personal freedoms, often more than in America on Earth. While there is no "outside-of-the-church" expla-nation for what happened to the holy women, their "approved" intrusion as outsiders into private homes for the public good as directed by a public leader, such as Lemron, is not automatically considered too irregular. The same is true for their willing acceptance of a "forced," or unusual, adoption of a "dis-carded" child.

(3) The role of children.

Many children, even good ones, are surprisingly blunt and open in Elphia. If any of these, especially those on the verge of becoming young adults, seem worthy of adult responsibility, they may be taken seriously despite a young age — much more so than in America on Earth — even if such acceptance is risky. This actually helped pave the way for Michael and Triana's initial acceptance. But such children who fail to "measure up" (as Earth-human eyes may see it) may be shockingly and "justifiably scorned" for the rest of their lives without pity. This will underline a great problem that will arise.

The main thing to note here is that Michael and Triana have done significant and thorough homework as well as learn a new language.

And have done it well.

*   *   *   *   *

The Time: *The story continues at a **regular weekly Sabbath Eve teaching** late in the afternoon on the 6th day of the week (and, to be exact, on the 13th of Reglanth, which for Triana and Michael is roughly < 6 mo. ALOE >). Exact mention of times mainly concerns the Sabbath. Curled brackets ("< >") indicate time approximations, which from now on are all that's necessary.*

The Place: *"Inside" at the Stadium, where both Sabbath Eve and Sabbath After weekly meetings now take place in the open air, at the edge of a new planting of kerm, but outside of the oval walkway not far from the tunnel entrance. For Christian believers, Sabbath dinner has been already quickly eaten, or already prepared, except for a final warming, in many — but not all — of the new Christian homes after the church meeting is over. Twenty-five men are gathered in a semicircle on stools, or small benches they have brought. Michael and Lemron sit in front. A similar group of women, including the holy women and Triana, are gathered not far away just out of easy earshot. Nearly a dozen children old enough to participate sit with their parents. The group altogether represents two-thirds of the adult and young adult church members.*

But including, of course, Gurdon and Shirra.

After several songs and a prolonged discussion about some practical matters, Lemron, the leader of Elfend, stood with his back to the cliff, to pray. The men stopped talking and bowed their heads. But just as he began, the women began singing quietly in their group nearby. Lemron stopped and smiled. Michael looked up and caught sight of a small hawk of some kind coasting to a hidden nest high up in a niche under just where the sunlight ended. How wonderful the privacy up there must be. At last the women's prayer chorus ended, Lemron offered a brief prayer, and indicated that Michael should begin.

Michael stood and opened his Bible.

"As I've said before," he began, "we have entered this beautiful church without walls using the strength that the God of Heaven has given our bodies, and the air he has made for us to breathe. I'd like to begin with another minute prayer…silent prayer." He lowered his head.

He'd struggled to make his words sensible and in the right Elphian order. Even when his goal was to encourage questions, he typically began by reading aloud a short passage from his Bible. He'd planned once again to talk about the death and resurrection of the God-Son. Many times he'd wondered how the lost Elphian Bible told the story. And he'd wondered what he'd say in a situation like this if the old Elphian I-Rex Code were found and varied significantly.

An old conversation he'd had with Jonas flashed into his mind.

Jonas had been blunt: "As to the Bible, I'm convinced it says nothing at all about whether or not humans created in his image lived on other planets beyond Earth other than, possibly, the passage where Jesus said, 'Other sheep I have that are not of this fold.'" Of course, the common interpretation of that was that he was referring to gentiles, or non-Jews on Earth. To say it could have broader implication was a stretch.

Michael was now living at the end of such a stretch.

Jesus' parting words given in a world where travel to anywhere more than a dozen miles was unexpected and dangerous, was to **"go into all the world** and make disciples, baptizing them in the name of the Father, the Son, and the Holy Spirit."

"But Jonas," Michael then had replied, "given the four stories about Emryss, what if the outrageous possibility for a trip through space became possible and you had the chance to go to Elphia, a place you knew nothing about, and you arrived, learned the Elphian language, and found they seemed interested in God ...what would you say?"

"I'd preach about the God of the Bible I knew, and tell them about the need for salvation." After which he'd asked, "What Jonas, if they didn't believe?" Without hesitation he'd replied, "I'd prepare to become a martyr."

It was a memorable moment, but now everyone was waiting for him to begin. Eyes were starting to peek up at him.

Michael opened his worn Bible and began by reading from the third chapter of John. He would not be pushed. He looked up and briefly fixed his eyes on each person as Jonas had taught him and began:

"We have peace because of what Jesus the God-Son has done for us by dying for our sins and rising from the dead more than 1700 (that would be 2000 on Earth) years ago. As we are about to begin our Sabbath Day of rest, do you have any questions about this?"

Three hands went up. Michael pointed to Harmund.

"I see you have your Earth Bible open. What does it tell us about His death? I know you've said it before, but tell us again. Just the short part."

"Gladly. The God-Son, Jesus, as we call Him, did no sin. After coming to Earth to live as man, his family and tribe rejected him and nailed him to a cross of wood, where He bled to death, was buried, and rose again three days later. People who put their trust..."

280

"Excuse me, Michael, but tell us again how he could die on a cross there, and also die on a target pierced by darts here, as our tradition teaches us. Did the God-Son die many times?"

It was Michael's turn to interrupt.

"And He also died in Emryss staked by his hands and feet in an X in the hot sand," said Michael. "I'm not sure I can explain this, but here's what my teacher taught me: First, we do not believe Jesus died many times. In fact, my Scripture…" — forgetting and using the English word.

"Scrip…ture?" asked the man on Harmund's right.

"Sorry, that's another word for 'Bi-ble.' Our Bible says Jesus died 'once' for everyone's sins — everyone in the whole universe, I believe — at the same time."

"But how can a hu-man, just one person be so many places at once?" said Redant, sitting two down from Michael's left.

"Good question!" said Michael. "The God-Son, though born of a human mother, made pregnant by the Holy Spirit, was therefore both God and man. Science can't explain what I just said, but there are many things that science can't explain about itself." Michael shook his head and smiled.

"Do you want me to say more?"

"Yes! What can't science say about itself?"

"Yes!" Two more were now smiling.

"O…kay. Everything that exists came from somewhere. Do you agree?"

"Yes!"

"Yes!"

"We believe that God existed before everything. Then '**BLAM**!'" — Michael spread his arms, then stooping, picked up a tiny pebble — "everything blew out of something smaller than this in a big explosion eventually making Earth, Emryss, Elphia, the Sun, and the stars, and everything else. On Earth we have strong evidence from science that supports this, *even though science can't explain where the pebble came from.*"

"I thought you were just going to tell the 'short part,' " interrupted Gallard.

"Oh, believe me, I am!" exclaimed Michael, laughing. He looked up and saw that the women had turned his way. He shouldn't have said "BLAM" so loudly.

"I'll be quick. The Bible says one of the first things God created was light. And one thing science has explained is that light travels very fast and this speed can be measured. Now listen carefully. I'm in no way a scientist, though my adopted father was. He told me that science has also learned that the faster a person goes the shorter the distance he actually has to travel becomes. Even if you measure it with a measuring rod. Now *a set of numbers called, I think, the Lorentz Transformation, but don't worry about that name, suggests that if someone travels extremely fast the distance to anywhere can become zero. [For "Lorentz," see Appendix C3.]* Some say this is nonsense, just a set of numbers. I can't tell you more than that.

"But if God could make light, as we believe He did, He could go as fast as light or faster, and if He continually did that, God could be everywhere at once. If God the Maker, or Father, can be everywhere, so can God the Son—even if He is infinitely 'vibrating' "—since that word needed help, Michael extended his hand and rapidly moved his fingers back and forth—" 'vi-brat-ing' his 'mol-e-cules,' or tiny, tiny parts back and forth in several bodies. If so, He could be born, live, teach, die, and rise again from the dead in several places at exactly the same points in 'straight-line' time." He drew a line in the air with his finger.

Silence.

The glassy-eyed looks showed that he'd definitely overreached, but

282

no one seemed to want to challenge him to go farther. Michael recalled how scientists on Earth would often silence critics with fancy words like "quark," "qubit," and "multiverse," inviting mystery and wonder instead of providing information that could be understood.

"This is just one way to look at this, and I was told it. I don't pretend to know much about it," Michael said, smiling. "But think of it this way: Either God or 'stuff' had to come first. If stuff came first and *on its own* became everything, it probably 'started' in tiny pieces since there was no 'builder' or mind to 'put things together.' And this stuff accidentially" — he waved his hand back and forth — "became people who in turn created 'god' or god ideas. If it's the other way around and God came first and created everything including time itself, then the Bible and science go together very well to help to explain that. To me, that pattern makes much more sense.

"That second choice is still hard to understand…as are the miracles here that several have experienced, or seen, and no one can logically explain."

"Amen!" declared Lemron, responding as if he were a Christian on Earth.

"Another question?" asked Michael.

"I have one," said Dr. Robi Hartlin, a middle-aged man who lived with his family across the Stadium. Years earlier he and his family had braved their way across the sea from Balara with medical supplies and had built the modest medical clinic at the other end of the Stadium. Dr. Hartlin had been long concerned with the dark human behavior that seemed to "infect" many in his world, and at first he'd quietly witnessed the miracles that had come with Michael and Triana. He and his wife had become friends, and soon "Christians," as the new believers insisted on calling themselves (transferring the sounds of the word Michael used into Elphian letters). And they were baptized.

283

"My question," said Dr. Hartlin, "is do you ever puzzle over how humans who are flesh and bones could travel as fast as light?"

"I suspect…" suggested Michael. He stopped, pausing for the right words. "First think of the God-Son Jesus. If his Holy Spirit hereditary molecules, which on Earth we call 'DNA' are dominant over the human DNA of his mother, maybe — but maybe not — that accounts for the sinless nature of Jesus at his birth. And for His 'God-like power' to *bodily* travel wherever He needed to be at what we would consider infinite speed." Michael hoped he'd used the right Elphian words…

Silence.

"And allow 'movement' of His body to be in several places at once," Michael added, wondering how his Elphian was coming across.

"I never thought of that before!" declared Hartlin. "And, as I recall, you once mentioned that in another place in your Bible that we haven't studied, that was written by a doctor, your telling us that Jesus, in mental agony over people's sin before He was killed 'sweat great drops of blood.' I know of no physical cause that could make that happen."

"Interesting, Dr. Hartlin, and I haven't thought much about that either," declared Michael. "But I will.

"Now let me go on a different path that I have questions about. Here I am from Earth! That much is *clear*" — he noticed several in front of him, their eyes now off somewhere else, but still smiling — "clear at least to me. Now and then, small pieces from our spaceship have washed up on shore, reminding me that we are fortunate aliens to have come safely to your world from so far away. And in what seemed hardly any time at all! I can't explain this, or why pieces of our spaceship are said to have been found even in Balara." Michael noticed he had everyone's attention again.

After 10 minutes or so of more questions, Furlane raised his hand. "How can the blood of three worlds mingle in a child…here in Elphia?"

This brought kind laughter, loud enough that the women were now staring.

"Please," said Michael, extending his arms, "some questions are harder to understand than others. I need to think more about this one." Again there was laughter. "Lemron, I think the Sabbath it about to begin" — he made himself smile — "Help me! Please dismiss us in prayer."

CHAPTER 26

The Candle

Time: Immediately follows — Sunset, the beginning of Sabbath,
moments before the 14th of Reglanth (< 6 mo. ALOE >)
Place: The Gatehouse

Somehow Triana and two of the holy women arrived back at the Gatehouse before Michael, who discovered Shirra right behind him with her bag of writing materials. Without making a scene, he bent over and whispered in her ear.

"Go."

"But you haven't checked my words!"

"*Briefly* tomorrow morning, Shirra."

"Yes, Michael," she whispered curtly. With her nose high, she picked up her bag and immediately left.

Inside, Michael had already laid out the tableware as he, or sometimes Gurdon, always did before the Sabbath, ready for eating whatever treat or meal prepared earlier would appear as the seventh day began. And, to the bewilderment of the holy women, he'd stuck a handful of greenery that he'd cut off on his way back from the Stadium into an empty vase already on the table. Again he lit a candle which he pushed to the side. He invited the women to join them, and they refused as he knew they would, retreating to a small but wider table in the living room to eat — and watch.

They insisted, however, on first personally serving the previously prepared food which he and Triana welcomed. Hot tea was a perfect way to end the late evening teaching—that "closed off" the 6th, 13th, the 20th, the 27th, or the 34th days of *every* month.

The meal that began the Sabbath was special in that blazing hot food was not the focus of sitting down. Nor was the candle that accompanied the meal, for Michael did that every night, still drawing puzzling looks from the holy women. Once Galandra asked why he did this when there already was sufficient light from the lamp near the table.

Michael had pondered his answer.

"Because it makes her hair shine," he'd said. He really wanted to say "sparkle," but he hadn't found a word for that in Elphian. When he'd seen Galandra whispering to her companion as the two sat across the room, he deliberately got up, and again turned off the small lamp so the flickering flame would have an even greater effect.

On this Sabbath evening he did the same.

At the table in the dim light they sat, ate, and talked—in English—as if no one else was there until the small candle burned out.

And with her, it was the easiest thing in the world to do. The effect of EMP in their previous world in removing distractions was perfect preparation.

CHAPTER 27

The Sabbath

Time: Daylight morning, still 14th of Reglanth (< 6 mo. ALOE >)

The next morning, a Sabbath Day with no school, of course, brought Shirra, as certain as the rising sun. Michael, as he'd hastily promised, checked over her self-imposed lessons in English which unlike school lessons were not formal "work."

She was determined to learn Earth language! And since she was a gold mine of Elphian detail, Michael, in his slave-driven attempts to master Elphian, accommodated her interest as best he could. Further, when she was done with duties at her own home, some of which Triana had assigned, she was available when Triana was otherwise occupied. School for her was easy, though how she managed schoolwork with everything else seemed never a problem. When Michael once talked with her teacher, who was a Christian believer, she smiled and told him not to worry.

"You, Michael, you and Triana, are her 'first' teachers and, unless she becomes a vanchi, or if you need to get rid of her for a while, send her to me. Anytime. I can handle her. It's easy to see how important she is in helping you two translate."

As quickly as possible Michael checked the girl's words and dismissed her.

"See you tomorrow, Shirra," Michael said. "Spend Sabbath time with your father and rest."

Reluctantly she left.

It was time for a walk to the Auditorium, perfectly acceptable to most of their daily guardians, moderately so to others. The "rule" they had to follow was they had to keep themselves "in the presence of others" whatever that meant. The last thing Michael wanted was to be called out for violating this. That kind of trouble he didn't need. He shook his head picturing friends on Earth facing such circumstances.

"What really happened to 'Sunday'?" Triana asked, as if she really didn't already know, as they stepped out the door.

[The Auditorium area was generally considered "off limits" for Christians on the Sabbath only for "doing regular work" and participating in "organized, formal events." If new Christians went there on the Sabbath, they were encouraged to consider why, and how it fell into place with God's command to rest and "share" with one's family and others. And what kind of family did Michael actually have? There was only Triana. And, of course, no children. For many Christians, the Sabbath was not much more than a time "to sleep in, eat cold food, and let things happen," putting off without guilt other things until the next day. "Open yourself to God and let Him work in unexpected ways in your life," Michael frequently encouraged. "And get ready to work twice as hard the next day." At the testimony time that began worship on Sabbath After, often fascinating Sabbath Day experiences were shared, but were understood best if heard in a group.]

"Sunday comes right after the Sabbath," Michael replied, "and doesn't exist at all here."

"Michael…"

"Since Sunday means nothing here, and it's nowhere made special in the Bible, as the Sabbath is, let's go over this again. And help me with some details. As I've told you before, Jonas and I discussed this. First,

"Sunday activity" is ignored in the Bible. Totally ignored. Yes, earlier Christians at times met on the 'first day' of the week, for teaching, and sometimes collecting money for expenses. But they also did that on other days as well. And yes, our Lord rose from the dead on the first day of the week. It helps us remember that. But do we need a day every week to remind us of the core truth of our faith? " This was wonderfully distracting. "Should I go on and on about this again?"

"Yes, if I can hold your hand."

"To disrupt my thoughts?"

"If I can."

He smiled.

"The Sabbath, however, is mentioned over and over—even in the New Testament. As a day of rest. Rest. Rest. It was never a prescribed 'go-to-meeting day'—even in the Old Testament—though it's not wrong to do that. God wants us to work hard, but also to rest and 'let go,' not do usual, programmed things. In fact, it's singled out in one of the Ten Commandments. Why would God do that? And where has honoring the Sabbath ever been cancelled? Or changed to Sunday *according to the Bible*? Nowhere! In fact, according to Jonas, the Sabbath existed before the Ten Commandments and the Law. In fact, according to Jonas, it goes back to Genesis and creation. [For more see Appendix B.]

"You can help me go further with this. There are so many—good—things to think about."

"Helping you is a joy in my life, Michael."

Why was he going on and on when her mind was clearly on something else? Why did he feel something was missing? He obviously had a clue. His obsession with learning Elphian had been a God-send to help him lock the door on certain temptations. It had terrified him that he might become careless here! What would God do to him—and the church—if he was? But he still had his clocks. They were safe. He must carefully keep winding them. If he'd only had more time with his first-friend. Dare he push Triana now? No, not before she was ready. But he could tease. In fact, he'd learned that art from her.

They stood on the small porch of the Gatehouse. They had nothing to do. That was the idea. And how releasing that felt. They held hands and started down the wooden steps in the direction of the "auditorium." He suddenly stopped. She turned with a puzzled look.

"Hey, I know what we could do!"

"What, Michael?"

"We could rest. I know the ideal place." He raised her hand and kissed it.

"Where?"

"Your bedroom."

"Michael!

"Michael, how can you be so serious one minute, and be *that way* in another?"

"I had one of the best teachers."

"What?"

"You! That's one of the first things I learned about you. Except often with you it was the other way around. You would say something ordinary and then thank me out loud for 'loving you' right in front of Jonas, who almost fell out of his chair once. And then I hardly knew you! I think it almost drove him crazy. But I loved it! Don't you remember?"

"That was one of the dumbest things I ever did…because…"

"Why do you say that, Triana?"

"Why did you say 'I loved *it*,' Michael?"

"I think we're talking past each other…" he replied. "But just think, Triana, a Sabbath to walk with you—who got me into all this—and with nothing we have to do! Isn't it wonderful? I feel absolutely no guilt because it's God-ordained!"

"Until tomorrow, Michael. Then you'll get over it."

"Well, if I find it's the first work day of the week, you know what? I'll start looking ahead to the next Sabbath — to be absolutely alone and absolutely together with you!"

"Stop, Michael."

"What?"

"Nobody's looking. You get a kiss for that." And before Michael knew it, though it was nothing Earth-shaking, she'd delivered. "I think you're really on to something here."

Almost immediately, it seemed, they reached the main area of the auditorium. Picnic-type tables with seats attached were scattered here and there. The "last day of the week" was a ragged sort of thing in Elphia, a day for most people to do things leftover from the first six days...if not actually use it as a workday itself. Though the idea of a Sabbath Day of rest was foreign to everyone except maybe the eighty or so who'd encountered their new church, it actually grew as a fad when people could get away with it simply as a "day off" for many, Christian or not. And for that, many welcomed *this* new idea from the new church.

One table on the left side near the stone wall caught Triana's eye.

"Look, Michael!"

There sat Lenora and Rendon, two young people about their own age who were baptized the morning after Michael had first spoken. On the table, flickering in the dim light, was a candle. There was a basket on the seat where Lenora sat. A picnic was in progress. The couple looked embarrassed as they approached. They pulled back their chairs.

"Please, Lenora, don't stand," said Triana, walking a couple of steps ahead of Michael. "We couldn't help but see your candle."

"Oh...I hope you don't mind, Triana."

"Certainly not, Lenora, but...but I hope I'm not being rude, but I've never before seen anyone doing this here."

"Me either," said Lenora.

"What started…"

"I brought it!" volunteered Rendon. "We heard…we…well everybody knows that you, Michael, do the same thing for the Emryss Princess" — he nodded to Triana — "to show…to…to show your…"

"Love?" Michael interjected. "Well, you're absolutely correct. Burning a candle at supper — and it's a boy's, or man's, job to do this — shows first respect to the girl or woman, or even one's mother or a respected older woman, who sits across from him. And, if with a younger woman, it may show your intention to take the next step in expressing love that is proper under the eyes of the God of Heaven."

"It means all that?" exclaimed Rendon.

"It does! And remember, Rendon, I'm the expert on this! But remember, too, it doesn't come from the Bible, just from me! And don't forget the words, 'expressing love that's proper and as God intends.' And if your kind and beautiful friend here thinks you're pushing too fast, she can blow it out, or refuse to let it be lit again. And either person can politely leave. Love is important to the God of Heaven. And love for each other that leads to finding a klepta must be carefully sought. Strangely, in English we have a word that I can't find in your language. It's called *romance*."

"Ro — mance, ro- ro- romance," said Lenora.

"Love," Michael continued, "is much more than the physical uniting that animals do, because people are created in the image of the God of Heaven. It often leads a woman, or a girl years later, to become a klepta, but never a kleptini. The key is making a lasting promise, just like a Christian promises to love God forever come what may."

"Princess —"

"Please, Lenora, 'Triana' is just fine. I'm hardly a princess and am

293

about as far away from my kingdom as I can possibly get. Besides, I'm just as old as you. And I'm sorry my *friend* here is *working* so hard giving a sermon."

"And you Triana, you're in 'romance'?" asked Lenora, ignoring Triana's words.

"Yes I am." She glanced at Michael. "I guess that's one way to say it."

"Meaning?" asked Lenora.

"Since God is watching, I plan to say No more times than I first say Yes. Michael can explain this better than I." Michael felt his face burn.

"Triana, may I ask you some questions, personal ones?"

"Of course you may, but about some things I probably have more questions myself than answers."

"Triana, you and Michael live at the Gatehouse?"

"Yes."

"Triana, are you then a klepta, or secretly a klepta?"

"No."

"Are you a kleptini?" At this point Rendon accidentally pushed his cup of tea into his lap. He winced but otherwise said nothing.

"No," said Triana, smiling.

"Then how do you —"

"It's really pretty easy," said Triana. "God has sent at least two holy women who are stationed inside to watch our every movement. We are forever under their eyes until they send us off to our separate bedrooms. Then they sleep in cots in front of our doors. They're convinced that 'unmarried couples in bedrooms together are acting like kleptinis' as they put it. We haven't had the chance to test that out."

Only Triana could say something like that without making it sound terrible.

Lenora's jaw nearly hit her chest. "You've got to be kidding! You let the holy women do that?" Rendon laughed a bit louder than necessary.

"Sorry," he said.

"Lenora," said Michael. "Sorry about our honesty, but you see, we're doing the best we can. We're still working on reaching the highest level to make a good decision. We still have some questions for each other."

"Like what?" asked Lenora.

"At the top are questions like 'What kind of questions will you and your partner ask each other in 30 years as you face each other across the table?' What will you talk about? We're still working on things like that."

"What sort of questions should we ask now?" asked Lenora.

Triana took Michael's hand and gently pressed it to her lips. Michael's mind reversed backward to the old Triana in Jonas's office.

"One of the first things you should discover," said Triana, "is, when you're together like this, who does the most talking—you or him? If it's always you talking, or always him—like Michael has been doing here—it's not going to work. If you can't talk and listen about equally, it's going to be difficult later. Save receiving a lighted candle for somebody else. Of course, you can try to even things up. People can change. I think, maybe, it's something similar to imagining yourself lying in bed beside the other person."

"Uh...I think I could handle that part," Rendon interrupted.

"God made us to want things like that," said Triana jumping back in. Michael struggled to believe what he was hearing. Maybe his own feelings might not be as bad as he thought they were. Was he hearing her correctly? "If you can't stand the idea of sharing that way," she continued, "things are over before they start. But you have to be sensitive and kind, becoming truly interested in what the person across the table is thinking. Romance is wanting 'yes,' but saying 'no' far more often because that is the wise thing in the beginning.

"And Lenora, if you just try out everything you feel, you'll probably soon find you've become a kleptini, which displeases God. And you create trouble for yourself later in life."

"Wow!" interrupted Michael, "Now, Triana, who's talking too much?"

"Just trying to even things up, Michael." She squeezed his hand. "But you're right. I see...I still have much to learn." Michael was glad he wasn't holding a cup of tea.

"Hey! When will you be back here, Michael?" asked Rendon. "And could I bring a couple of friends with me?"

"Oh..."

"We can meet *informally*, of course," said Triana. She glanced at Michael. He nodded. "We'll very likely be back for a walk in a week in the daytime of the 21st," offered Triana. "If Michael asks me to pray at the Sabbath Eve service, that will be our secret sign that we'll probably be walking around here at about the same time then as we are now."

"And we can talk about this again on the Sabbath?" asked Rendon.

"Of course," said Triana. "Some details are private, of course, and can be held back, you realize. But questions can be asked. Right, Michael?"

"All kinds of questions can be honestly asked together under the eyes of God," offered Michael. "And we'll ask Him to be with us. Can you handle that?"

Lenora and Rendon looked at each other.

"We think so," offered Lenora.

*   *   *   *   *

Halfway back to the Gatehouse, Michael finally spoke.

"Triana, where did all that stuff about romance come from?"

"Obviously from a book, Michael." She glanced up and smiled. "And from you, of course." She pulled his face down to her level and touched her lips to just his cheek. Hand-in-hand they climbed the steps that led to the front door of the Gatehouse. At the door she stopped. Michael noticed that she was breathing more deeply than usual.

"Thirty years is too much, Michael."

"Then what should it be?" he asked.

"Twenty…ten…maybe five," she answered.

CHAPTER 28

Blowback!

Time: 13 days later, Sabbath Eve, 27th of Reglanth
       (< 7 mo. ALOE >)

Place: The church gathered for teaching at the Stadium. Word had
         been passed around that for this evening of teaching men
         and women and boys and girls would meet in a single
         group. Many now brought small benches or chairs as well
         blankets for sitting.

A brief lesson from the Gospel of Matthew that had been recently translated into Elphian had just ended.

Michael hoped that he could respond to some outside conversation he'd heard about by, again, asking for questions.

"Tonight and for our next few meetings," he said, "men and women will meet together, along with the older boys and girls for our weekly teaching. Now, for the rest of this Sabbath Eve I'd like to try to answer any questions."

With his back to the mountain wall and The Gatehouse tunnel farther down to his right, Michael faced at least fifty-five baptized believers along with about a dozen visitors or onlookers—including four new "candle-carrying couples," or "ccc's" as he privately came to think of them. Of all things, the candle-with-a-meal tradition had burst forth with fad-like intensity. Somehow this non-Biblical tradition must now be addressed in the presence of the several visitors who were just curious about whatever was going on.

Shirra, and two of the holy women sat on benches near the front, but Triana, who'd missed the teaching on the previous week, still hadn't arrived. Many of the new Christians, after the first two months, had started bringing pencils and tablets to write down notes, to go with their own handwritten copies of portions of Matthew that had been put into Elphian.

Only days earlier, Triana had led a group in comparing their notes and had found them surprisingly accurate and consistent. She had complimented them on their hard work, and had reminded Shirra beforehand to keep her mouth shut and to discuss her reactions, which Triana insisted she valued, *privately* later just with her.

And later, Shirra actually had volunteered to Michael that Triana had taught her a very important lesson that day: If she was to truly love God, and not just play games, she said, she must continually accept and thank Him for her special gift, which everyone knew she had. And she must accept and love new believers for their beginning understandings, no matter how ordinary and flawed they might seem, without acting like a selfish know-it-all.

Michael had been amazed that at her age she'd seen this and been able to receive it—as well as tell him about it later. Almost overnight she'd understood and accepted this advice and had become able to sit quietly without seeming to suffer, though it was a bit scary to think where her mind might be going.

But many minds now were on something else.

Tarig and Marlea were one of the new candle couples.

"Where does the Earth Bible talk about candles, and what does it mean?" Tarig asked.

"It doesn't talk about candles in the ways you are thinking," said Michael.

"Then why do some of your people use a candle with meals?"

"Can somebody help me here?" asked Michael. "I think I'm a little puzzled about this myself."

Gurdon waved his hand from the back row. Michael pointed to him.

"Because Michael and Triana do it!" he declared.

"And why, Michael, do you do it?" Tarig continued.

"I'm not sure I can explain, but I'll try." Michael laughed. "It's...it's sort of a tradition I personally have." He wished Esther Crandel could hear this... "I light a small candle when I eat a meal with a woman I especially love or value—this could be one's mareena (birth mother), one's marana (gift mother), even one's klepta, or someone you might want to become your klepta."

"How about a kleptini?" asked someone from the end of a row. "Should a person light a candle for a kleptini?"

"Well, like I said, the Bible doesn't say anything about this. But how do I feel? I wouldn't burn a candle for a woman who intended to be only a kleptini. Four months or so ago I talked about the 10 Laws of God in our Bible that I believe must have been in yours. The seventh law was 'Do not commit adultery,' which means, in part, that a man who has a desire for a woman, or a woman for a man, must express it fully only with their klepta or kleptor—those they have promised to love and serve until death parts them. Desire and marriage are both from God. Whether or not we obey God is our own choice.

"This relates to what Jesus, the God-Son, said was the second greatest commandment: 'Love your neighbor as yourself.' We are all neighbors here. The last thing we want is for people to take advantage of each other, especially those closest to us, or fall into sin."

"Is Triana really a princess from Emryss who also has an ancestor here in Elphia?" interrupted someone from the back.

300

"Yes, she is."

"Are you really from Earth?"

"I am."

"Is Triana your klepta? And, do the two of you live at The Gate-house?"

"She is not. And, yes we do."

"Are you aware that an old prophecy here says that 'when the blood of three worlds mingles in a child, that many people here will once again believe in Grott'? And is Triana aware of this?"

"I am. And yes she is."

"Where then is this child?"

"They are still young orphans," declared Galandra, standing and slowly turning, seeming to dare any challenge.

Silence.

It was Gurdon's turn.

"The holy women are their marana," he declared. "They don't leave them alone together — ever!"

The light laughter that followed was welcome. But tears formed in Michael's eyes. Though he was certain his cheeks had reddened, he refused to look ashamed.

At that moment, Triana appeared from the tunnel opening that led to the Gatehouse. As quick as a bird, Shirra stood and darted away, running to her. Seconds later they both turned and disappeared back into the tunnel.

"And are we content to let a young orphan stand before us to tell us about God and how to live with women?" one of the seekers blurted from the back.

"We are!" declared Lemron, turning and facing the newcomer. "And I *stand* before you today because of the Word of Grott that these orphans have brought us from their world."

But the young man and his partner were already several feet away shaking their heads, heading for a tunnel on the far side of the Stadium.

The beginning of the Sabbath was not that far away. Klingor, who was now an elder, along with Lemron and Dr. Hartlin, came to the front and without asking had everyone stand. The teaching was a bit shorter than usual. His concluding prayer was also specific and brief.

The people were dismissed.

*   *   *   *   *

Just after Michael got back to the Gatehouse, there was a knock at the back door that led to the tunnel. It was Klingor.

Michael walked to the door and opened it.

"I must tell you this, Michael. After you left, Marlea ran to the front and approached me. 'What can a kleptini do? Can she change, or is once a kleptini always a kleptini?' she'd asked.

" 'She can repent and tell Grott she's sorry, trust in the God-Son and ask him to forgive her and make her clean,' I'd told her.

" 'I will! I will!' she'd said.

" 'And you must never be a kleptini again,' I'd said.

" 'I will not, ever, ever, ever be a kleptini again,' she'd replied.

"Then Tarig appeared.

" 'Why are you saying this?' Tarig had asked, aghast.

" 'A candle can only be offered to a klepta, or a woman who intends to be one. And, from this second on I intend to become a klepta!' Marlea had replied.

"What's happening here, Michael?" asked Klingor. "I'm confused. Where did this candle thing come from and how important is it?"

"What else did you tell her, Klingor?"

"I said that we've been living in some ways like animals without making important promises for too long. People suffer, especially the young—young women who as they age get cast aside. But by what authority do I say that, Michael? Our I-Rex Code is lost. *We* have seen Grott's power, but many have not. Marlea was so happy to know there was a choice, and that being desired does not require her sleeping with Tarig or anyone else. Tarig was totally bewildered."

"Anything else, Klingor?"

"Well, I reminded them about the 10 Laws you've taught about, and how they are a part of something much larger in a world beyond this one. But how should those Laws really affect them? And what do candles have to do with any of this?"

"Is that it, Klingor?"

"No, I told them to see you and Triana—and someone else they trust who's a believer and a klepta."

"Then you and the holy women must pray for me—and for Triana and me. Especially now."

"God be with you, Michael—both of you." He spun on his heel and made his way back to the Stadium.

Michael recalled the almost unlimited distractions on Earth before EMP.

That was not so here.

And he'd loved and trusted the widowed Klingor. And he'd generously shared his young daughter with the newcomers from space.

The fisherman-elder-father of Shirra was probably already into a deep conversation with God while still on his way home.

CHAPTER 29

What Matters Most

Place: The Gatehouse

Time: The Sabbath begins (in darkness), 28th of Reglanth

  (< 7 mo. ALOE >)

— continues from last chapter —

Shirra pointed to the bedroom door, indicating to Michael that Triana was in there, and that the holy women had ordered Gurdon and her to stay and *watch* until they arrived. Oh, how people on Earth would have loved that!

But now Earth was only a memory.

For Michael, loneliness fell like a curtain with a broken tieback. The Bible made it clear that life sometimes was like that. He must check more passages for answers. Had he made respecting a girl across the table with a candle a foolish distraction? He paged through the New Testament epistles. At the ends of several he found Paul stressing doing "general things" to show that kindness and ordinary respect could be a witness for God. But was he reading his personal habits into these passages unfairly?

Triana strode into the room wearing her light button-up-to-the-neck blouse that she once wore at Grace Alliance Church. Her hair seemed carefully combed. She carried one of her few books and, without even a glance at Michael, she sat at the table in the alcove where they usually ate. Head down, she opened her book. Across the room Gurdon sat with his own book. Shirra was spread out on the living room floor with a large now unfolded piece of paper covered with words, her eyes aimed across the room just above the slate she held with both hands. She moved her lips silently, ready to not miss anything about to happen.

The Sabbath had quietly begun.

"Michael, we need to talk," Triana said without looking up. Though he hadn't noticed at first, tears were slowly trickling down her cheeks. She coughed and cleared her throat. Moving to the kitchen sink, she filled an enormous pitcher with icy water that had been ingeniously piped inside from a spring. She poured herself a glass and left a second glass, presumably for Michael, empty.

"Outside, Gurdon!" said Michael, firmly but not unkindly. "Take your sister and leave!"

"But…"

"But nothing. Go!"

"You promise to stay in this room?" He pointed to the floor like a suspicious adult.

"YES, but can we go to the bathroom?" queried Michael, tilting his head.

"Yes, but only one at a—"

"OUT!" said Triana, signaling something to Shirra, after which she jumped up, grabbed her brother's hand and nearly jerking him out of his sandals, pulled him through the doorway, leaving her slate and paper, and slamming the door behind her. If only doors in Elphia had locks!

Triana was not smiling. Michael picked up a napkin and gently patted her cheeks. Memories of a time in Jonas's office came racing back. Glancing back at a window by the door, Michael saw Gurdon peeking in. Suddenly, his face disappeared. Shirra must have jerked him away. Michael moved to the window and pulled the curtain over it. When he came back Triana was standing.

"What is wrong between us, Michael?"

He stood before her and examined her slowly from head to toe.

"Thank you, Michael, for starting with my face."

"No, Triana, I started with the top of your head." And so he had. Her hair fell long and naturally just as it was meant to be. He couldn't imagine a more beautiful girl in the whole world...of worlds. No one was like her. If she only knew how he felt about her and how much the holy women were needed when she talked like this, pulling out of him words and ideas that would sound ridiculous to anyone else. They could fiercely argue, then instantly become a team again when necessary. And now, because of her, he was forever "out of his world" on another planet. He studied her part by part once more. Perfect. Together they had come so impossibly far to an impossible place to do the impossible...except...for—

"Michael, whatever are you thinking about? I said we need to..."

"I think you're the most wonderful person in the world, so perfect...so—"

"Michael, you're being ridiculous! But since you said that, and I saw you looking at me, are you so distant to me right now because—please don't laugh—because I'm not somehow made the way you want?" She slowly raised her hands and covered her chest.

Michael could...not...be...lieve...his...ears.

"Hmm..." he offered, trying to keep from biting off the end of his tongue. "If you would kindly unbutton the top buttons there, then I could..."

"**Michael!** How could you—"

In spite of herself, she let him gently but firmly draw her into his arms. He hugged her as tightly as he ever had on this planet or any

306

other as their lips just touched. Then with a force within him that he didn't even realize was there, his arms automatically slowly pushed her away. Not a button had been touched.

" 'How could I?' you ask. There's more than one way to find out. I just did. You *feel* wonderful. Your size everywhere is just perfect, too. I guess that makes us even for your doctoring me when I was poisoned…and you still accepted me."

"**Michael**! I can't believe what I'm hearing!"

"Nor can I!"

The doorknob suddenly turned back and forth without the door itself opening. Michael sprang toward it and eased it open. Two holy women looked anxious, two children, awestruck.

"Gurdon," said Michael, "I didn't break my promise! Explain that to Galandra. We need more time. God is working."

"Okay," said Noleen, the younger holy woman. "We pray…but stay in living room!"

"I promise," he replied as seriously as he could without laughing, which this certainly wasn't the time for. With such ready soldiers ready to break in, Triana's safety could never be in jeopardy—if he just could keep his word.

He closed the door. Triana was back seated at the table. Once again there were tears.

"What's happening to us, Michael? Maybe you need to look at your clocks."

"Clocks! How did you know about them?" he returned.

"You…you talked about them in your sleep in the attic of the Hotel Crandel. You considered them so important though I have no idea why. Michael, I thought you were so, so…" She lay her head on her hands, now covering her book. Tears came again.

She paused.

Where was she going with this? What was he missing? What have

I...His mind whipped its way down his first clock to Number 5 and the importance of little things, then Number 6 with its discussion of the different love languages that matter differently to different people in expressing themselves. He knew English and he knew Elphian, but it wasn't about that. What was he missing? What was he doing wrong?

Suddenly, a possibility dawned.

His first-friend would be proud. He walked to where she sat with her head on her book. He lifted her head just enough to slide the precious volume far to the side. She gave no response. Perfect.

Without a sound he lifted the pitcher over her head and emptied half of it.

"EE-O-OW!"

He ran to the door and cracked it open.

"Everything's fine, don't worry, just pray harder." He closed the door without waiting for a response.

He returned to find her standing as water ran through her clothes to the floor.

"Michael, why... why did you do that?" She pulled hair out of her face and her blouse away from her skin.

"Because I love you."

For a full half minute she stood as still as a statue staring as water continued to dribble into a noticeable puddle on the floor.

"Because *what*?" she finally asked as if the word were a new discovery.

"Because I love you...I love you...I love you..."

"Michael, do you realize you've...you've never, never, never ever said that to me before! Why are you saying it now?"

"But, Triana, you *knew* I loved you. You even thanked me for loving you in front of Jonas."

"And I told you that was the dumbest thing I ever did. Michael, if you really mean you love me, *you need to TELL me! I need to be told that*

308

every day OUT LOUD! Every day!"

As she glanced down and bent over to squeeze water from the hem of her skirt, Michael quickly emptied the rest of the pitcher over her head, bringing her back up face to face. She was completely soaked.

"I love you," he said again. "I love you I love you I love you. If that really matters, I'll say it every day. Every hour! I thought you just knew it…and that if I said it over and over you'd think I was silly…or redundant."

"No, Michael! No, No, No. That's not the way it works with me. Those words — *the very words* — mean so much. And, of course I love you, and I remember, even telling you that just before the first baptizing. But I couldn't keep saying that to you if you never said it to me. That…that just wouldn't be right. Because…because maybe you didn't."

"But, Triana, doesn't even the Bible say that *deeds* matter most to most people…much more than words? Didn't I *show* you that I loved you by what I did — and didn't do, by the way?"

"Michael!" Her eyes flashed in a way he'd rarely seen. She brought her hands to the top of his shoulders, then curved them up to the sides of his neck. "Let's get this straight, I'm not 'most girls.' Got it? Michael, I could never, NEVER, marry someone who didn't tell me SINCERELY every day that he loved me. I'm a 'word girl,' remember, and I don't care if you think I'm silly. That's me, and that's part of my baggage. But now, if you're concerned about deeds, take this."

She pulled his head toward hers.

"Hey, you're getting me wet!"

"And you think I care?" Her lips touched his and her arms pulled him tightly against her, soaking the front of his clothes.

Michael's mind flipped back to Number 3 on his first clock — the girl with baggage standing on the railroad tracks with two suitcases in one hand and one in the other. If this was what her baggage was, then, oh boy, he could handle it.

"I love you. Will you marry me, Triana? I love you. I love you."

Without answering she squeezed again as hard as she could. "Yes," she whispered in his ear.

"Hey…I love you…now I'm soaked!"

"That's your problem. Yes, of course I'll marry you. But if you tell me you love me one more time, I might start unbuttoning buttons. That's *not* what needs to happen…*right now*. Consider yourself warned!"

Buttons…Michael's mind spun. He actually felt dizzy. When he began to wobble, Triana reached out and grabbed his hand.

"But…"

"But nothing, Michael. You still have a promise to keep: To save me from myself…*as long as we're together.*"

"I still have to do that?"

"Yes!"

"I…I…*like* you," he offered. "I think we'd better let the others inside now and do some explaining. Let's eat and enjoy our Sabbath rest. We've got a lot to talk about before our worship meeting tonight after the sun sets."

CHAPTER 30

"Things Decently and in Order"
– I Corinthians 14:40

Time: The Sabbath continues, 28th of Reglanth (< 7 mo. ALOE >)

When the doorknob turned again, Michael raced to it and slowly pulled it open as if nothing had happened. **"Come in!"** he announced.

Gurdon, Shirra, Galandra, and Noleen one after another cautiously entered and found Triana, with her back to the door, sitting at her usual place at the table holding her open book just above a wet surface. Water dripped from both sides to the floor, as if they were unaware that a sudden rainstorm had poured water through a hole in the roof. And, oddly, it seemed that those who'd entered had interrupted a deep conversation.

"Come on in!" Michael repeated cheerfully, as if everything were business as usual, "but watch the floor" – he pointed to the center of the room – "it might be slippery." Then, as if it were business as usual, he lit the candle that was already on the table.

"What happened Triana?" asked Shirra, her eyes growing large. "You're soaking wet!" Gently, she pushed back strands of Triana's sparkling wet hair, which contrasted sharply with her own shiny black hair.

"We had a little problem with that pitcher over there" – Triana pointed to the sink – "but we were lucky, it didn't break."

"Michael," said Gurdon, "you're wet, too!"

"Yeah, it was an unusual spill, but you, Gurdon, were the one who gave us a problem we couldn't solve. Since I'd promised we would stay in this room, we couldn't go into our rooms to change." Michael held out his hands, palms up, to express perplexity.

"We have something to tell you," Triana suddenly announced.

"Something big!" Michael added.

"But not before you two go change your clothes!" declared Galandra.

"And," Michael added, "Gurdon, while we're changing clothes, you change the table arrangement, which is *not* regular work. Listen to me, carefully. Today our Sabbath meal will be at two small tables — he pointed — that you will put together in the middle of the living room. This time we will all eat together, a holy woman on each end. Triana and I will sit together on one side, and Gurdon, you and your sister directly across from us on the other. Got it?" His glance at the holy women warned them not to interfere.

The boy nodded.

"I'll explain your lateness to your father. Now Triana and I will go change — in our *separate* rooms."

"And me?" asked Shirra, her eyes large.

"If your brother asks for help, do what he says."

"We do what you say..." said Noleen, "so go! We warm up food — not work for us today."

A second holy woman had found her voice — and assumed a measure of authority, that strangely, had never been spelled out.

"I will set the tables," said Gurdon.

"Do it right," said Michael, "and that means checking with the holy women."

"I know how," said Gurdon. Michael arched an eyebrow. "I have watch you," he said in *English*. Michael couldn't help but notice how much his secret language with Triana was melting away.

*   *   *   *   *

Michael and Triana, in dry clothes, appeared and found everything in order…and now with a lighted candle in the middle of everything. Everyone stood behind his appointed chair waiting for what would come next. Then, Shirra, glancing to the side, without any show, directed her brother to a knife she pointed to. Stealthily, Gurdon moved to the knife and rotated it so the edge pointed to the plate. Without a word, Shirra gave him a little hug which he accepted as both returned to their places.

Michael was speechless. He smiled at the boy's work. Gurdon smiled back.

"Who is candle for tonight?" asked Gurdon, pointing.

"Especially for Triana, but also for the kind holy women, and for tonight *only* we'll add Shirra," said Michael. The two holy women looked at each other dumfounded.

"Not me, too?" asked Gurdon.

"No, Gurdon, it's a boy thing for girls and women. Some day you can light a candle for a special girl who loves God."

"Nooo…not ready!" said Gurdon.

"That's fine," interjected Triana, "because she's not ready either—yet."

"But the food is," offered Michael. We have something to tell you, but we eat first with no nervous I-can't-eat appetites allowed." Gurdon groaned. Calmly, as if it were business as usual, Michael and Triana talked about ordinary things as they ate the previously prepared food, and everyone else mainly listened, waiting for the big news. Shirra didn't utter a word. "Some important things must be taken care of,"

313

said Michael, "before the gong sounds, announcing that the sun has set, the Sabbath has ended, and the evening worship service is ready to begin in the Stadium. And we want the four of you—"

"To hear about it first," interrupted Triana.

Their unplanned teamwork was back in play. They glanced at each other and smiled.

When their simple, but delicious, meal was over, Noleen served the special dessert pastries and the tea, refusing out of fear or impishness, to let either Michael or Triana get near so much water.

Michael looked puzzled.

"No more accident on floor," offered Galandra, who then covered her mouth, Michael suspected, to maintain her composure.

The time had come. Michael stood.

"It gives me great joy," he said, "to tell you that—"

"I," Triana interrupted, "have agreed to become Michael's klepta."

"Yes! Yes!"declared Gurdon. Shirra's eyes moistened and her smile broadened. The holy women, smiling, praised Grott and clapped their hands up-and-down (much easier to do at a table).

"When?" asked Shirra, offering her first words.

"In six days, before the teaching near the end of the 34th," announced Triana. This was actually news to Michael, who wondered at how such life-changing plans—that they'd yet to discuss—could be laid out so quickly. But then it was Triana at work. He began taking mental notes. Six impossibly short and impossibly long days. And, of course, the two of them taking a Sabbath Day's walk in the morning to see Lemron at his mother's house!

Like a royal from Emryss, he worked to keep his feelings under wraps. Their team was still in action, and again, the script they were following was unrehearsed.

"And," Triana pointed to the ceiling, "we, just the two of us, will celebrate a special—private—'three-day Sabbath' where no one is in the Gatehouse but the two of us. No one!"

"But what will you do without us?" asked Gurdon.

"Tell him, Michael," said Triana.

It was his turn, and he had the holy women's undivided attention.

"We'll figure that out when we get there," offered Michael, "the two of us together, because, Gurdon, boys are different from girls," his words tumbling out before he reflected on them. "First, we will pray to God, then we'll get to know each other a little better. A klepta and her husband need to do that alone, you see." Suddenly, Michael's jaw almost locked in a cramp trying to keep a straight face. For Triana it seemed easier.

"But don't you know each other already?" Gurdon continued.

This time it was Noleen who brought a hand to her face. Galandra released a small smile.

"Gurdon, Triana will explain more," said Michael. It was her turn.

"Gurdon, listen carefully," she began immediately. "The Bible says a man and his klepta must love each other. You do this with the words, 'I love you,' like Michael says."

"He does?" Gurdon wrinkled his nose. For a couple of seconds Michael stared at his plate.

"Yes, he does. You need to listen more carefully. Even more than words though, you do things for your klepta that make her life easier and make her happy. You pray with your klepta to the God of Heaven, on your knees at the sofa, or by your bed."

"Together by the bed?" interrupted Gurdon.

"Of course!" said Triana.

"Really?"

"Yes, but even more than that, you promise to sleep with your special klepta, and no one else, as long as she lives."

315

A shiver ran down Michael's spine. He forced himself not to move. "But why sleep with her?"

Noleen squeezed her eyes shut. Galandra held her smile. Shirra was all ears, not missing a word. Triana turned to Michael.

"Gurdon," said Michael, "there are several reasons. Here are just two: First, if you sleep very close to her she will keep you warm, and you will keep her warm. You never have to shiver again in bed. Or always use a blanket. And second, sometimes life is very sad and you will cry or want to cry. Then she will hold you close and dry your tears, and will understand and not tell anyone your secrets. And you will do the same for her if she wants to cry. And when she is happy, you will be happy with her, and when you're happy, she'll be happy with you. You will always be there for each other, and share secrets that you will tell no one else." Michael prayed no one could see movement while his head spun.

"Why?" asked Gurdon.

"Because you will love her with all your heart, and will do so *until one of you dies.* There's a lot more, Gurdon, but let me tell you just this: Somewhere, out there beyond the Gatehouse is a girl who loves God and is waiting to be your klepta, but she doesn't know it yet."

"Uh...I'm not ready yet!"

"Good! Because neither is she," Triana added. "Now the dishes don't need to be washed, but could you and Shirra clear the table and let the holy women rest? I think they need it. And Michael and I need to rest — in our separate bedrooms, of course — and do some talking and planning together before our Sabbath today ends and our worship service begins.

"Now, Gurdon, after you and Shirra clear the table, we want you both to immediately go home. You may tell your father all about this, but *no one...no one else.* Remember, your father is now waiting and is probably worried, so hurry!"

*   *   *   *   *

*After a good night's sleep and the busy private day that followed, sunset ended the Sabbath Day and the Christians of Elfend found themselves gathered at the Stadium. The rich darkness of **Sabbath After** beginning the 1st day of the 5th week (the 29th of Reglanth) arrived.*

About 70 believers, including children, carrying lanterns, having heard rumors that something was up, had gathered on benches and chairs and blankets. They'd finished singing their second song, one newly written by the Christians. Dr. Hartlin offered a prayer.

It was Michael's turn.

"Before I talk about God specially speaking to us on the Sabbath Day, I have to make an important announcement."

"Seven months ago," he began, determining to keep his voice strong, "Triana, a princess who'd been captured from Planet **Emryss,** who also had an ancestor from this planet, **Elphia**, and I, Michael, from Planet **Earth** came here as orphan children, landing in the ocean near the shore several miles away. Our pilot died as our spaceship fell apart.

"Triana and I survived. We are believers in the God of Heaven and his Son who made everything here and everywhere else.

"Another Elphian named Igneal who'd years earlier come to Earth, told us about an ancient prophecy from your planet: 'When the blood of three worlds flows in a child, a remnant in Elphia will once again believe in the God of Heaven and the God-Son,' who we know as God-the-Father and God-the-Son, or Jesus.

"However, as I've said before, we arrived as orphan children, or very young adults.

"Lemron, who God miraculously healed on our first day here, and who sits by me, has given us food, clothing, and a place to live. Also that day, four witches who troubled you and tried to poison us came to trust in the God of Heaven. They have since served and protected us in more ways than you know." Michael couldn't help but notice the smiles of several. "Triana and I have worked night and day to learn your language. And yes, as you can tell, we are still working on it.

"Today, however, we have 'come of age' — in Elphia. I have asked Triana to become my klepta for as long as we both shall live, and she has said yes. God has..."

"Michael, Triana, Michael, Triana, Michael, Triana," interrupted the people, rising to their feet.

Michael smiled, but raised his hands and encouraged them to stop. Slowly they sat.

"Thank you for receiving us," he continued, "being patient with us, and helping us get this far. God has led me to Triana and her to me and us to you. We hope to share with you the best we can all we know about God, who you call 'Grott a Harven' who made everything, and His Son, who you call Grott-Domor and we call 'Jesus,' and the Holy Spirit who you call 'Grott-Spatro-Loomin.'

"We pray that you believers will still recognize and repent of your sins, as we do, and will continue to believe in and worship God. Or if it's the first time you're here, we pray that you will commit yourselves to the God of Heaven who is God of Elphia, God of Earth, God of Emryss and the whole universe. And since you have lost your I-Rex Code, that probably differs in many historical details but has the same message, we will translate and share in small pieces the Bible God has given us.

"Jesus, the God-Son, has told us that we are to love Him with all our heart, and mind, and soul, and strength. We believe that as we worship Him here together and alone at home, especially on the Sabbath, that His Holy Spirit can change us and turn us around and make us clean and useful to others.

"That is the first and great commandment. The second commandment, as I've preached earlier, is for us to love our neighbors, the people around us, as ourselves."

He paused.

"There are special, important things that the Bible tells us to do. In several places it tells us to love our kleptas in a special way, and to be faithful to them as long as they both shall live.

"I will love Triana that way.

"I love you, Triana! I love you! I—"

She stood smiling and waved her hand for him to stop.

He did.

"Our wedding will occur here in the 'Stadium' in six days. You are all invited to come. Pray for us. Pray for each other.

"Our lesson today was, again, to be about God's seventh day, or Sabbath, that my klepta-to-be and I will continue to honor as God's special day of rest and openness to Him in the days ahead. I will say more about this next time."

The congregation then stood and began chanting in unison:

"Grott a Harven, Grott-domor, Grott-Spatro Loomin, da cum for!
Grott a Harven, Grott-domor, Grott-Spatro Loomin, da cum for!"

With a final prayer the service ended early. Very early. But a time of extended discussion, sharing, and planning led by the elders and women leaders began at once.

On the way back to the Gatehouse, Galandra came up to him. Rarely did she talk to him about anything outside of the house.

"Michael, I think God has given a message to me, and I think it is also from the I-Rex Code."

"And that is?"

"God-Son says, 'Anyone who wants to find me must be willing to leave family to do so, and he must take up his target and follow me.' What does that mean?"

Michael stopped dead still.

"Galandra, where did you hear that?"

"I hear, Michael, while praying."

"Galandra, that's almost exactly what our Bible says that Jesus said! And it's not an easy passage to understand. Our Bible says—and I haven't talked much about that yet—that nothing, but nothing should get in our way of serving Him. You know, like the first and great commandment. Yet it says in our Bible that a person must 'take up his cross and follow Him.' We must talk more about this later."

A cross...What did he really know about anything so gruesome?

*   *   *   *   *

Minutes later inside the Gatehouse

"Galandra, I must talk to my klepta-to-be alone," said Michael as soon as he'd closed the door behind him.

The holy woman stood before him face to face.

"What you want?" she replied.

"I want to walk with her inside the mountain."

"But it is dark."

"We will stay on the path, go around once, and come right back here for a hot cup of tea. One hour only—no, one hour and a half."

"One hour and a half only...I agree," declared Galandra.

"No!" interrupted Noleen. "Not safe for girl! Not safe for us! No! No!"

"Yes, yes," said Galandra, overruling her companion.

Immediately, Noleen untied the belt around her robe. Fortunately, buttons still held it together. In a flash she circled the heavy cord around Triana's waist and tied it with a vicious knot, jerking it tight.

"Is...is it all right to breathe," gasped Triana, who had pushed her

320

stomach out, pretending to reach for air as Noleen tied the knot.

"It is if you obey the God of Heaven!"

"Time us!" declared Michael, pointing at the clock. In seconds, they were through the back door and into the tunnel.

In the Stadium, the sky overhead was already black, and one moon was clearly visible, the second partly visible just above the rocky crest. The air was warm and calm.

"Let's run," said Michael. "We've a long way to go!" Slowly he began and she followed. When she stopped and was gasping for air, he pulled her into his arms and kissed her. Then he took off again, increasing his pace as she raced to keep up. Stopping again, she blamed it on Noleen's belt. Michael laughed and kissed her again. When they were two-thirds the way around, they slowed down to a walk when they heard the sound of a barking dog. By then there was plenty of time to walk the rest of the way without breaking their curfew.

"I don't know what to say, when no one's across the room straining to hear or see," Michael offered. How pleasant it was to be alone, alone together.

Eventually they were back to the tunnel, the sound of falling water at the waterfall beside the entrance ending their conversation. Just inside the entrance, Michael bent over to take a rock out of his shoe.

""Wow, I haven't been so hot in a long time!" he declared, standing on one leg to put on his shoe.

"Thank you, Michael, that's just what I needed!" Leaning to the side, she shifted her weight and swung back up to the other side, knocking Michael headlong under the falling water and down in the pool under it. When he was slow to rise, she reached down, "Michael!"

That was all she said as she found herself on top of him, pelted by water colder than ice.

When she gasped for breath, he kissed her again. "I love you," she said.

"I wish I could tell you the same," he replied, "but you warned me."

"I've warned you about 'unbuttoning buttons,' Michael. Well, what I have on doesn't have any."

"I love you! I love you!" he declared.

CHAPTER 31

The Ceremony

Time: 6 days later, early Sabbath Eve, 34th of Reglanth
       (< 7 mo. ALOE >)
Place: The Stadium

Three hours before the teaching time on the 34th everything began. And this time there would be no regular teaching — in words. And typical at this time of the week, as the Sabbath approached, special new outdoor lights, dim as they were, were ready to flick on as the sixth day neared its ending and people would make their way home to privately begin their Sabbath "rest."

This time, however, an informal gathering would occur around mountains of already-prepared food.

Tables of food.

Since word about the upcoming wedding spread, three-fourths the population of Elfend, along with many from the the other two towns on the island — more than 400 altogether — had arrived. And even a few from the closest island, Balara, who happened to be nearby at the time, had come to witness the marriage ceremony of the young "Earth Prophet" and "Princess from Emryss," as both were commonly called beyond the new church community.

Triana was beautifully attired, as was Shirra, her "maid of honor," a "custom from Earth," Triana said, which soon would be copied by new kleptas here, as Michael's "candle custom" had suddenly exploded from nowhere. Michael, of course, appeared in his finest, with Klingor, as his "best man."

In the flat field of crushed grass across from the fragrant kerm,
the place where they'd taught and worshiped week after week,
was pitched the small marriage tent without sides,
under which they would promise
themselves to each other.
Surrounded by
Christians,
friends,
and strangers.
The sky erasing daylight minute by minute,
letting time itself eventually shutter out the sky for the upcoming Sabbath.

Michael stood facing her. And she, him.

And the mayor of Elfend, now the head elder of the church, stood silently, facing them both.

Though the sun was blocked off by the cliffs, and darkness had hardly descended, by the two flickering candles in tall holders on either side of Lemron, Michael studied her face, remembering when he'd first done that, the day when Marvin Cample had accused them of cheating. Her steadfastness, her sense of purpose come what may, the beauty of her eyes that miraculously had healed in another world and had come to see much more.

Now these eyes were upon him. The girl he never could have let naively travel alone on *his* home planet—or away from it. The girl to whom he'd quickly promised, that he would help "save her from herself." And now look at him. At them. What had he done? If his eyes could now see just one day at a time, maybe he could shelve his moments of fear. After all, he was the luckiest man in the world.

The world of worlds.

Just how would they soon approach each other?

"Don't worry, Michael," she whispered, gazing into his face. Was she reading his thoughts—again? "I have names already picked out."

"Names?" he whispered.

"Yes, you may think one is better than the other," she whispered back.

"Oh…"

"Or you may have forgotten that I'm a twin."

"I love you," he whispered back, not knowing what else to say, but remembering the magic those three words had brought only days ago. Words—they were everything to her.

As they whispered to each other standing before Lemron, he waited patiently, seeming to wonder when it would stop and he should begin. The throng standing before them, was as silent as death, straining to hear. The whispering ended. Smiling, Lemron, briefly described in strong words he'd practiced saying over and over, the history of events that had taken place during the previous seven months.

Then both Michael and Triana pledged themselves under the eyes of the God of Heaven to be faithful to the God they both deeply loved, and to each other until *"death do us part,"* the portion of the ceremony that hardly enters anyone's mind at a wedding. Then Lemron read the love chapter, 1 Corinthians 13, that had been translated into Elphian.

The ceremony was brief.

Time came for dancing and the tables of food. Hidden talents for fixing food and entertaining from church members and the town lost their secrecy. Michael had never seen such celebrating on either planet!

Too soon came the sounding of the Stadium gong, similar to the one at the Gatehouse, and the Sabbath began, the wedding was over, and

the kleptor and klepta, as planned, left immediately with a large basket of food for the Gatehouse and three days of promised night-and-
day seclusion, interrupted only by — brief — arrivals of just more food
from the holy women, who immediately, and unnaturally it seemed,
left. Their main job at the Gatehouse was temporarily over. How much
would continue?

Though the Sabbath had arrived, people were allowed, even encouraged, to stay and mingle and eat and talk informally as long as
they wanted. All were invited to come to the worship service, this time
in the Auditorium that would begin in 24 hours as soon as the Sabbath
Day finally ended.

It was the first worship service that Michael and the third that Triana would miss. Lemron preached. The crowd was by far the largest
gathering ever since they first arrived — and perhaps before that.

CHAPTER 32

The Next Three Days

Time: The Sabbath, 35th of Reglanth (< 7 mo. ALOE >)

Since most Elphian homes had no front door lock, Michael tilted a table chair against the doorknob, effectively blocking possible entry. Triana had carefully closed, checked, and rechecked every window curtain. Since they'd returned to the Gatehouse with a basket of food at the beginning of the Sabbath, and good cold foods had already been laid out for breakfast several hours later, nothing would occur at the front door until the gong sounded the end of the Sabbath 24 hours later. All electric lights had been turned off. Somehow they found a single candle on the alcove table already lit. Triana's hair glistened in the dimness.

"Michael, may I go first into *our*…"

"Second," he interrupted. He took the candle and led her by the hand to the sofa. Together they knelt beside it. He put his arm around her. "Remember that first day on the beach? We must again thank God. Her hair fell against his cheek. I can wait one minute more. Can you?"

"I think so."

*   *   *   *   *

Many hours later, the moment after the gong finally sounded ending the Sabbath, and seconds after that the doorknob rattled as Triana said it would. She peeked sideways behind the curtain and with her hands indicated to Michael a distance a bit more than a foot.

Michael opened the door only that wide.

Slowly a tray of delicious-looking food, freshly warmed, was slid on the floor into the darkness inside. Without a word, Michael slowly closed the door and returned the chair to its former tilted position. He carried the tray to the table that was already set with a lit candle on it. He laid out the food at her place and started to seat her.

But she remained standing. She wrapped her arms around him.

"Why do I need food?" she said. "But then I know you. You're probably starving."

He held her tightly, and ran his fingers through her hair. This lasted longer than their first prayer. The candle flickered. "I've always wanted to do this here," he said.

But that was only the beginning.

Her lips found his.

"No one is watching, Michael," she said. "No one."

"Except me," he added, "and God, of course."

"And that's enough," she replied. It was the first hot meal that, together, they would eventually eat cold since coming to Elphia. Days later she would ask him about it.

"How was it, Michael?"

"Delicious…the best ever."

"Did I warm it up enough?" she asked, tilting her head and examining his face.

"I don't remember," he replied.

*　　　*　　　*　　　*　　　*

The second of their three evenings passed much as the first. In the middle of the third morning, however, Michael learned through a note from Triana that she'd passed under the door that two bags of foods she'd requested had arrived. Off and on during the rest of the day Triana guided the two of them in preparing a special meal for some invited guests.

Promptly, as the gong outside sounded the hour of sunset, eight guests arrived: Gurdon and Shirra of course, Klingor their father, Lemron whose house it was, and the four original holy women who were always available needed or not. At four small tables in a row in the center of the living room they sat, Michael and Triana at each end, sitting and serving the whole meal they'd carefully prepared.

When the holy women seemed ill at ease being waited upon instead of serving, Michael enjoyed giving them a little lecture on learning how to receive as well as give because that was part of the Christian way. This was an important lesson, he said, to pass on to future couples they probably would find themselves visiting. Even Jesus, he said, at one time had served his disciples, washing their dirty feet before sitting down to eat. Gurdon's and Shirra's eyes grew large as they watched the holy women struggle at being waited on. Triana glared at the children. Later she would explain that, because of who they were, sometimes they'd be included with adults when important things were going on and they had to keep certain feelings to themselves. And be careful about bringing up delicate issues, as well as sometimes being perfectly quiet.

329

The holy women finally relaxed, and everyone knew that Galandra would soon have her own say with Noleen and the other holy women as well.

The meal was a success, everyone entering into the conversation at some point, even Noleen. It was a beautiful time to remember, for it would never occur quite the same way again.

CHAPTER 33

The Blood of Three Worlds

10 months later (< 17 months ALOE >)
at the medical clinic

To call it a "hospital" would be stretching things. Michael smiled. The small building lacked so much that Big Bend took for granted — that is before EMP changed everything. Here were medicines that may resemble, or work like, antibiotics, and even some machines that could electrically check heartbeat and breathing.

But is was clean. And there was no shortage of able and caring staff. In the birthing room, Trivan came first, loud and strong; then a second child, Émrica, right on his heels, immediately giving her brother a run for his money.

Twins.

And the names?

Trivan — "Tri" (or Try) for 3, the very, very first child, by a minute, to carry the blood of three worlds in his veins. He was a "marker" for something. But what? Already people had come to know Jesus. How else would he distinguish himself? And **Émrica** — from **El**phi**a,** from **Em**ryss, *and* from **E**a**r**th (Am**erica**). How would she fit into all this?

This was heterosis of a unique kind, never before witnessed: the blood of three worlds mingled not in just one child, but two.

The blond-haired boy with sharp blue eyes resembled his mother and the girl with dark hair and dark eyes resembled her father, and in some way even Shirra — who Em first called her "big sister," then later "Marana" — as soon as she learned the words.

Shirra, only about ten-and-a-half (12 in Earth-years) older by more than a decade than the children, when not in school or shooed away by Triana, still seemed always nearby, playing with, changing, and dressing the babies, and later teaching them as they grew. Her frequent presence, however, sometimes gave Triana and Michael well-needed time for other things. One day, however, when Michael heard a loud "GO!" and ran to where the children were and saw them scampering to their rooms, she turned to him triumphantly: "See, Michael, how well you've taught me!"

The growing little Elfenders proved to be very intelligent, however — which fascinated Shirra. Helpers, sitters, and eventually teachers who were carefully screened by the elders and holy women, who now only came one-at-a-time, were readily available to care for the newcomers.

Michael was aware that hybrid vigor could bring surprises. Look, for example, at Triana, the only known child to carry the blood of two worlds, though neither came from Earth.

Much more was still to come. Michael, the "one-blood" from Earth, still smiled at the obvious math: Pregnancy on Elphia was eight-and-a-half months, not nine, since human gestation, along with human appearance, ability, and the need for God apparently remained the same as on Earth.

CHAPTER 34

A Clock to Summarize

Time: < 7 years ALOE >

(Arrival to twins' birth: < 17 months >

1 year since the birth, then

2 years

3 years

4 years

5 years, 7 months later)

On an end-of-the-month Sabbath (Day 35) – in early morning darkness

Michael suddenly awoke in pitch darkness and sat up in bed. It was a Sabbath morning, much earlier than he or anyone else awoke. He felt the warmth of Triana who lay beside him sound asleep. Gently, he ran his fingers through her hair. There was no sound from the five-year-olds in their rooms down the second hallway.

"Arise, go to the track and walk. Recall all that has been done," said a voice only he had heard.

"Ye…s, Lord."

Quietly he put on a light-weight karpon and heavy sandals, careful not to wake the children. He scribbled a note on his slate in the living room and tiptoed down the long hallway that passed his and Triana's bedroom that ended at the tunnel that led to the Stadium.

The outdoor Stadium was the second true hub of Elfend, the first being the Auditorium, where everything began and continued. The seven years had brought some change to the inside of the mountain. Just beyond the tunnel, to his left was the school and Tabernacle where they'd ended up regularly gathering for both evening teaching and worship. An electrical system, primitive according to modern Earth standards, now provided indoor, but little outdoor, lighting in both places.

Across the track, or pathway, was the beginning of extensive gardens. The far end of the oval was still fringed by shops, minifactories, businesses, homes, the jail, and the medical clinic. Behind these were a few cattle and some ranching that bled into the gardens. Across from the tracks were a few small houses and what appeared to be several apartment buildings. All around the huge opening were scattered public tunnels leading outside to the other two towns and the rest of the island. (Other features will be soon described.)

At Lemron's tucked-away private washing pool Michael took a thick bright blue cord from a hook and tucked it through his karpon cord. This was a Sabbath signal which he'd created years ago to show anyone that while he would greet them, he was unavailable just then for conversation. Of course, it wasn't always needed, because conversation was certainly permitted on the Sabbath if his time alone with God had been satisfied. And it shouldn't be needed now. Who else in his right mind would be wandering around in the middle of the night?

Suddenly he dropped to his knees to pray.

"Up!" said the voice he'd heard before. **"It is time to walk."** He rose, continued in the darkness, staying as close to the mountain wall as buildings, fencing, and pathway permitted.

His mind took off—not unusual for him during his morning time, usually inside.

He fixed on that place miles away where the two of them had awakened unhurt after the Elphlander crashed seven years earlier. There was the miracle, too, of how both of them—Triana, unable to swim—had made it to shore unhurt with all they'd brought.

There was their first night honorably side-by-side on the beach. How precious and positive their frustrating caution had proved!

Then came the poisoned fish.

The children falling off the cliff path. The raising, it seemed, of Gurdon from the dead. The healing of Shirra's leg.

The fishermen escorting them to Elfend, the immediate first public meeting that was so dramatic, and their ending up at Lemron's house, now married and with two exceptional children more than 5 years old (nearly 6 in "Earth years").

His feet crunched into the gravel that lined the pathway — or runway for those in a hurry. He couldn't see just where his feet fell, but he knew the way. Knew it well from many previous trips.

He had met an impossibly wonderful girl, who seemed to love him almost as much as he loved her. And their quirky courtship and the dramatic start of the church that had forced them to quickly master a new language. Then they'd married and worked together even better afterwards. He could never have imagined that.

On the second day in Elfend he had baptized more than thirty, something his mind had never touched upon earlier. But Triana, had insisted he do it. And she was right. It was done just like in the Bible.

And why did he do it? Because he'd loved her, and at her request had trapped himself into promising "to save her from herself." Because she was so brilliant, honest, and trusting. So beautiful. So shockingly naïve about so much. But not everything. And what a strange request she'd made! He couldn't have done otherwise. He would do anything, everything, to protect her as long as she lived. And so far all had gone well, perhaps too well, with Lemron, now against Michael's wishes, assigning continual private protection for both of them. And rumor had said this had paid off at least twice.

As to guns, they were on the island, but locked and hidden away by the three mayors for emergencies. Though some hunting was allowed, little was done—and none with guns. In fact, the only pistols he'd seen since coming were occasional ones carried by the tiny police force.

There was no motorized transportation.

He passed by the medical clinic with its small staff—such an odd mixture of the old and the new technology.

Finally after one year, five months, the ancient prophecy that so many whispered about finally came true.

On nearly every Sabbath—before and after the birth—Michael, like an old man alone, would briefly walk in the early hours on this path. He would ponder, and pray like a child about the bits and pieces of all that was happening, about Scripture he'd been reading, and then attaching some things God reminded him of to two new unforgettable "clocks" he'd built into his mind. His early private Sabbath time was not for precise "notes" —in fact he rarely wrote down anything because for him, that was "work." But plenty of notes would appear the next day.

God had planted so many seeds during morning walks. And smart people like Lemron, Klingor, and Dr. Hartlin—all reasonable people who should know better—seemed to depend on him for advice. And kept coming back for more. How proud Esther Crandel would be! If he had a great secret that held him together, it was his early Sabbath time. Like right now. Without it he would be lost. Totally lost.

But this morning he was up much earlier than usual.

Now he was about 26 and Triana about 24—in Earth years. Or was he? What years was he thinking in? What did they know, so young and as parents of young children, that was worth sharing, especially to those in a world they still knew so little about?

What had really happened after coming here? Before his marriage and the twins' birth? And after it? He had never been off the island. And what did this really *mean*? What evil force had caused this awful collective washing away of everyone's memory of the past as it pertained to God? And had led to such unexpected defining moments where he would share a truth from his Earth Bible and the holy women, or someone else, would exclaim, "Why that's just like what the I-Rex Code said!"

And what did this really mean to those beyond Elfend, the two other towns on Elphia Island, to Balara or farther away on this strange planet? To those who were indifferent, amused, or even hostile to what had taken place? Had he gone far enough? Or had he become too comfortable, and leaned too much on Triana, or stopped too short of what God had called them to do?

As he walked in the blackness, Michael tried to sum things up:

Their arrival to ELPHIA had been electric. Regardless of obvious religious implications, why did having such children really matter?

Their teaching that "God's purpose" in getting married with a determined promise to be faithful to a single partner until death had caused much discussion. Had they overreacted about this? Many, however, still suffered from "accepted" temporary relationships and were eventually cast aside. Kept promises of faithfulness until death were still very rare.

Lemron, mayor of Elfend, and "first" in rank among the three mayors of the island, Klingor the master fisherman, Dr. Hartlin and some of

337

his staff, several teachers, as well as others, had seen value in Michael's teaching, however.

If, he suspected, his marriage could be shown to "work," it could set a model for the young. Did the holy women sense this and did that inspire their obsession of protecting them? Like it or not, he and Triana could never avoid the spotlight of being on display.

Except for certain times on the Sabbath.

He passed a guard, one with a gun, at the police station that housed the few jail cells on the island and waved. The man, staying in place, acknowledged the gesture.

Triana had first shown a passion for the people. But he quickly grew to share that passion.

But how much?

He had preached that knowing and loving God first was the most important thing the Bible taught. Loving and caring for others came next.

Did he really practice this? Did he live it?

And what did those who listened to him really believe?

He'd observed the Christian believers—and yes, they insisted on calling themselves "Christians," the word now transliterated into Elphian and completely accepted. This also was true for "Jesus" and "Christ" which they, with the holy women agreeing, considered without hesitation to be one and the same as their "newly remembered God-Son." So many words, "sounded" from the Earth Bible had been copied over and over in Elphian script.

At last count, 97 had said they'd come to believe and had been baptized. Visible life changes seemed evident in maybe half of them. It was a happy revival, said several, of their old religion, rather than the beginning of a new one. Dirt had been scrubbed away from old hidden truth, and blind eyes had been opened. He'd pointed out again and again how Jesus had made a one-time payment that would erase the power of sins for anyone who accepted Him. And without such a commitment, one would be forever "lost" — whether on Elphia, Earth, Emryss, or elsewhere.

Had he emphasized that enough?

Michael's path was now passing several of the larger, privileged residential houses, set back dozens of feet by pale grass still blackened by the night. The faintest touch of daylight now penetrated the sky revealing the enormous opening that was completely walled in by mountains.

His mind turned to *evidence.*

The Spirit of God seemed to have worked upon many. But to what extent? What other evidence did the sensible Elphians have to support making such life-changing commitments? What "compelling visible reasons" were there to minimize the effect of so much that they couldn't explain?

He would number them as he ran and walked, and record them on a new mental clock—a light blue one:

(#1) First, for Number 1. Yes, here in ELPHIA, at least the part that he knew about, the "God of Heaven," and the story about Him somehow had been thoroughly debunked, and all copies of the I-Rex Code, their "sacred fantasy" as scoffers had called it, had been collected and destroyed. Still, one haunting prophecy from that book wouldn't go away: "When the blood of three worlds mingles in a child, a remnant from ELPHIA (the planet, he supposed) will once again believe."

Seven Elphian years ago when they'd arrived there was little reason to suggest this was anything more than a curious piece of folklore.

(#2) Second, then things had suddenly changed: Seventeen months later not one, but two children with a "mother from two planets" and "a father from a third planet" had been born here. But while the children were very intelligent, they'd done nothing extraordinary. But were they supposed to?

(#3) Third, as to the truth of their backgrounds, four fishermen and two children from Elfend had declared they had seen remains of their white spaceship and had brought Triana and him from its crash site, unhurt, back to their town.

(#4) Fourth, several pieces of white metal, said to be the color of their spaceship, had later been found on the shores of both Elphia and Balara.

(#5) Fifth, on their first day here, when two Elphian children had fallen from a great height off a mountain trail he and Triana, with God's help, had "raised one from the dead" and had "healed a broken leg" of the other. At least one of the two children was still alive, in great health and, along with the four fishermen, could testify about this. For him this was an unforgetable bedrock memory.

But, to be fair, there was a dark side to this.

One of these children, as well as a couple of older teens earlier, had recently defected and disappeared (which will be described later). But why Shirra? He realized that we don't know as much about people as we think we do, and that the baggage they carry may be dark and heavy — and unseen. He struggled to push the memory of "little Shirra," usually a delightful vanchi, one, who like Triana was brilliant with words, out of his mind. In the book of Acts, hadn't the twice-mentioned "faithful" Demas suddenly forsaken and left the Apostle Paul? And yet Paul's mission hadn't fallen apart. God had even let Luke put this in the Bible to remind Christians that seemingly reliable people can still fall away.

And this had happened.

Was he reliable? Reliable enough?

For half a lap he increased his speed.

(#6) Sixth, Lemron, the mayor who'd been paralyzed and unable to walk a single step for ten years, had been dramatically and totally healed when they first encountered him. This was witnessed by more than a hundred.

(#7) Seventh, the leader of a band of five notorious witches who tried to poison them fell over dead without either of them touching her. Their deadly poison had no effect on Triana, him, or the fishermen who had drunk it, even the young defector. This was witnessed by several dozen at close range.

(#8) Eighth, the four other witches had immediately repented of their evil and pledged allegiance to Jesus. Immediately they'd been so changed that scoffers, and then believers, began to smile and call them "holy women." The name stuck. With tired old bodies now youthfully limber, attitudes that were kind, and determination that was laser-focused, they were new believers not to be ignored or trifled with.

In particular, these women had suddenly become radically obsessed with his and Triana's purity and in their strictly following the God of Heaven. Surprisingly, even the new elders had been reluctant to challenge them. In retrospect, their continual service had made the new church ministry possible. The dramatic change of the women was witnessed by more than a hundred people who'd known, even feared, their strange behavior earlier.

Living in a house together, the women had displayed a keen sensitivity to spiritual power, and their obedience to the Spirit of God. Soon a few other women who they carefully screened had joined them. Together they often voiced strong warnings about the spirits of evil as well as providing practical service. They also gave occasional moments of insight about the continuing translation of the Bible into Elphian, that most Christians took seriously whether they welcomed what it said or not.

(#9) Ninth, he'd been informally referred to — though rarely to his face — as the "Earth Prophet," which he did not encourage. He'd openly confessed that all he could teach that was "authoritative," or from God, would have to come from his holy book, which he called the "Bible," of which he had four copies in English, one thin concordance, and a hymnal. Further, he'd said that unlike past Earth prophets, he couldn't guarantee the correctness of his translating and teaching, but he would "try hard" not to make mistakes. This left some question among Elphians, as well as to both Triana and himself, as to just how his Bible directly applied to Elphians.

Is this what had caused Shirra to eventually disappear?

Some resolution of this had to still lie ahead.

By the end of six months, they'd become fluent in Elphian and by the end of two years they had nearly mastered the language. And to Triana and his surprise, the twins had become bilingual — in Elphian and English — as well as "Shirra the defector," as some called her, who was a language savant like Triana. With Shirra's help before she disappeared, Triana and Michael had completed translations into Elphian of the **Gospel of Matthew,** the **Ten Commandments**, The **Lord's Prayer, Genesis 1 and 2**, and parts of the **epistles and Acts**. And during their second year together he and Triana had worked on **parts of the Psalms** to encourage Elphian believers to create their own music of praise, which they had done.

(#10) Tenth, at first the Elphian idea of a God-of-Heaven and a God-Son corresponded well with the God-the-Father and Jesus of Earth. The "Spirit" of both places also seemed similar. When he taught that what God wanted most was for people to love Him first and before everything, and then "love one's neighbor as oneself," the new holy women emphatically agreed, and their discovering this seemed to peel back a veil over a "forgotten memory" that *this* was *"exactly" what the I-Rex Code taught.*

The holy women also enthusiastically *affirmed that the Ten Commandments that he'd introduced were almost exactly the same, as well as the "Go into all the world and make disciples"* command at the end of the book of Matthew in the Bible. Similarly, the chief holy woman Galandra also had mentioned that when Michael encouraged believers to *"take up one's cross and follow Jesus"* that it was almost the same as the I-Rex Code's declaration of *"taking up one's target and following the God-Son"* which reflected upon the different way the God-Son was said to have died long ago on Elphia, presumably at the same time as on Earth and elsewhere.

But how far did such similarities go?

(#11) Eleventh, there was the Sabbath. He'd gone out of his way to introduce it as a day—from sundown to sundown—24 hours—("Friday evening" to "Saturday evening" as most Earthlings, especially Jews, would think of it)—of individual meditation and reflection first, of teaching and loving one's family second, of informal sharing with friends next, and of *rest* with *no formal scheduled activities* "boxed in" by an evening service of teaching and a second evening service of planned worship.

This had been well received and, according to him, seemed to be in harmony with the Ten Commandments much more than Christians had accepted it on Earth. Never in the Bible, according to Jonas's words, was the Sabbath declared to be a time of going to Temple or church, though early Christians often found themselves informally gathering on the Sabbath (or "7th day) to worship.

But real rest on the Sabbath? Modern Christians on Earth with all their time-savers had no idea about what the fourth great commandment of God meant! But now he and Triana did! It had made and saved their ministry!

And Elphians would get a chance to obey and benefit from it. For the most part, Christians could decide for themselves how to live on this day with, of course, practical exceptions for emergencies and public and private need.

Nonbelievers in no way had been compelled to follow this new pattern, though surprisingly, some welcomed the Christian way of looking at the last day of the week—especially when it suited their plans, or when they worked for Christians. Also, a stopping from all work and "resting" that was approved by God seemed refreshing to those who felt guilty when they just "stopped" for no reason at all and "did nothing." There was always the next day to begin scrambling again.

These were eleven good reasons to share with anyone asking why the Church was born, still going, and what it was trying to do.

(#12) Twelfth—of course Michael couldn't leave that number blank! The number at the top of his "clock" for remembering all this would be held open for his continual questions about just how God was working here and what should be next.

Next?

Fortunately, he had outstanding church leaders. And Dr. Hartlin, Klingor, and Lemron, had made excellent choices in selecting four more elders, all who had genuinely accepted the God of Heaven, and who also felt the great need in Elfend and its moral shift away from what his Bible pointed out was "God's way." Social problems that had been building for years. And, of course, loving God with one's all was "foreign" to their thinking.

This attitude obviously wasn't shared by everyone.

Michael continued into his second loop around the oval. One by one, he created a memorable picture for each of the 11 numbers.

But to believers who were close to what was happening it should be easier to see that a real God was truly at work. For one thing, more were getting married, as klepta and kleptor, and were having and raising children.

Some hard decisions, however, had been ignored or postponed. How far should the holy women's "sudden expressing of God's will" go? What should be taught and preached? How long could they go without a reliable *Elphian* holy text for guidance? Or was this really necessary? How could they understand the history of humanity on *Elphia* without any spiritual record? Who was the first man? What about the line of people who had produced the Mother of the God-Son long ago? And was there prophecy about his birth, life, and death? Would it be compatible with the — Earth — Bible? Would the history and theology of the "stories" from Emryss have any bearing on what God wanted and expected?

Fortunately, he had the weekly Sabbath to think over these things. If he opened his mind to God, He could continue to infect and guide his thinking.

After he'd carefully examined the book of Acts, didn't the Early Church move along and explode into being with an incomplete and a fragmentary history and only a growing set of *official* rules? Hadn't the Holy Spirit really worked then? And hadn't the Holy Spirit been working here?

Would he and Triana "run dry"? Or had they already? Did Shirra, now a young woman, finally find herself bored with what seemed an endless stack of papers, before she'd selfishly disappeared? Or had someone stolen her away? And what damage had she done? Was she still alive?

The elders were golden for the practical wisdom that he continually sought. And Scripture — their Earth Bible in English — had a lot to say about this, though the information was often general. Like it or not, he knew the church was depending on both of them for overall direction.

Really depending on them.

But how far and how long could they go, with only a high school education, and now with only a single holy woman for daytime work and responsibilities for active young children?

Then there was the sudden diversion of Earthball.

Earthball

He could hardly believe how this had suddenly happened.

By the third loop, he was sweating heavily and breathing deeply. Looking up, he found himself passing the first Earthball court that had been built beside the pathway as they approached the first of the four factories. Smoke from a previous day's small fire was barely visible from one of the chimneys.

Earthball.

It had happened suddenly in his Year 2, the fourth month after his children were born. It was during a Sabbath Eve teaching just before the darkening that began the Sabbath. The Bible passage — he'd forgotten which one — was about determination, cooperation, planning, and patience.

Offhandedly, he'd mentioned his experience on Earth playing basketball. "The purpose of basketball on Earth," he'd said, "is for a team to pass and bounce a ball a bit larger around than a dinner plate up and down a rectangular court" — he drew a shape in the air with his hands — "and throw it up in the air and through a metal hoop — think of a basket with the bottom ripped out with a net with a hole in it — more times than the other team did at the other end of the court where a similar basket was attached up high. And all this happened within a certain time limit." His allusion, as he remembered it, was to life itself and its real limits, duties, the need to be patient, and the differing responsibilities everyone had. "In basketball a person must…" Then Michael had stopped. Every male eye and even some young female eyes were staring his way. The instructive words he'd planned to say after that were totally ignored, and even he forgot what they were a week later.

At the end of his teaching a dozen men and boys as well as a few girls raced to where he stood. Patience and planning were forgotten.

"Tell us about Earthball," said Brevand. Everyone nodded. The real teaching then began up and into the Sabbath, which Michael soon cut off.

"It can't work here," he'd declared. "You need metal hoops welded to other pieces and boards nailed to posts to attach the hoops to. And besides, I haven't seen here a single ball this big"—he extended his cupped palms in front of him—"that's strong enough, could hold air, and would bounce right."

"We will find balls that will work!" declared Feymore.

"We can make hoops!" said Blandor. He'd recalled seeing a primitive welding torch during a recent visit at the blacksmith shop at the end of the Stadium. "Tell us what you need. Draw it!" He was handed a piece of paper and a pencil just as the newly erected overhead electric lights, dim as they were, flicked on.

He'd been astonished by what followed. Quickly, he'd scribbled a quick drawing and handed it back. He remembered that of the two dozen or so paper photographs he'd brought from Earth, one was of his shooting a short jump shot several feet from a free-standing outdoor basketball goal that clearly showed all parts of the rim, net, backboard and post holding it up. A couple of girls asked questions about the net. When worship on Sabbath After, that began 24 hours later was finished, an unasked-for "altar call" brought a dozen young men and women rushing to his podium that was covered with notes. Their encounter had nothing to do with matters of faith.

Before he was even asked, he'd handed them his basketball photograph. Within ten days he'd been presented with seven different balls, one of which to his surprise seemed to have a good bounce and could hold air quite well—and discovered more balls exactly like it could be readily obtained from, of all places, Balara—if one could manage safe trips to and from there!

Which, of course, safe or not, quickly took place.

Within six weeks a half-dozen almost perfectly formed leather balls, and later even rubber ones, that could hold air were obtained, actually "exchanged" from Balar City, Balara's main town, for another pair of welded rims that could be attached by bolts or screws to wooden back-boards, and a set of drawings, measurements and rules. A new Elphian business had begun.

Now in his office-bedroom hung an enlarged picture made from his small photograph, painted and framed, that was presented to him for his help after a teaching service.

For better or worse, Earthball—the name "basketball" was smiled at and dismissed—had arrived. An outdoor court more than a hundred feet away across the trail and into the first two rows of kerm—all ap-proved by Lemron—of hard-packed soil and cinders from the factories was marked off and edged by wood. He, of course, from then on was continually sought for approval, clarification, and recommendations that he offered—spending much time at first, but slowly backing away as other responsibilities called.

Four things had come from this: (1) He made it clear he would in no way play or watch others play on the Sabbath. (2) He would however teach, assist, and play two mornings a week from 6:30 to 8:00. Groans followed his first announcement of this. Nonetheless, to the surprise of many, a number of Elfend boys, especially the Christian ones, de-veloped new early rising habits. (3) Practice and games soon became popular. (4) Church attendance of young men—and young women— grew.

That was five years ago. Interest in Earthball after an explosive start, continued to slowly grow. As of now, there were three Earthball courts in the Stadium, several more elsewhere and sets of rules had been printed in Elphian and were passed around.

But was that what God had called *him* to do?

His legs were tired from walking. He had run a bit before. He started running again. It felt good, but he'd wished he'd at least worn his cargo shorts. He came to the end of his fourth circuit of the oval near where the new Christians had first sat in open air to worship.

The Tabernacle

But now much of the open-air area outside the walkway oval on the near side was covered by crushed lava gravel. Far from Lemron's private tunnel, but still in the grassy area, had been built the "Tabernacle" — and yes, they called it that, spelling it in Elphian to sound the way it sounds in English — two years ago during his fifth year. (The term "church" would usually refer to the people, rather than a building.)

How it contrasted from similar structures that had been built long ago in Pennsylvania! The climate in Elphia outside the mountain, seemed nearly subtropical, not unlike Florida, varying slightly by season though a bit less extreme in both hot and cooler seasons. It was naturally still a bit cooler inside the mountain and in the Gatehouse. Rain, however, could be a problem, and a long period of rain had actually led to constructing the large house of worship. Hence the building was essentially a large peaked roof held up by poles covering rough-cut benches with backs that could be moved, when needed, away from facing the wooden stage in front. To make room, Lemron pushed the trail into the field of kerm a couple of dozen feet from where the building stood, but only there.

More than 250 people could be crowded in for special events which might include the entire church membership, interested attenders, and others, though usually for worship and preaching only no more than one-third of that number would be attending. If, however, the canvas sides were rolled up, even more could see and hear from the outside. All teaching services from inside the cave-like Auditorium had already long ago been moved to the open-air Stadium, so by their fifth year the Tabernacle had been built, quickly becoming the central gathering place for Christians.

Next to the Tabernacle was a hard-walled one-story building, called "The School" that was just that. Built more than two years earlier, just after the Tabernacle, its six large rooms were continually being added to, since as a new "school of choice," demand to use the building had seemed to fill any open space that presented itself. So the near end of the oval had lost much of its rural flavor.

But at the moment, both the School and the Tabernacle were empty. And would be — that is for any religious services — until the sun set and the Sabbath was over. Michael resisted stopping and sitting. He would be there soon enough…

On he jogged, stopping occasionally to walk.

Michael's mind went blank until halfway around the fifth time.

Then several problems came to mind.

One of the holy women had suddenly died without explanation. Of course, they weren't immortal. But since they'd been so dramatically changed, the death had caught many by surprise. Perhaps this was a good reminder that everyone was human even those who God had especially blessed. The Earth Bible told about times when even strong believers suffered and, of course, Jesus had been crucified. John the Baptist had been suddenly locked up away from the action wondering if his mission had ended. Then he was shamefully beheaded. The Apostle James the elder had been suddenly seized and killed with no reason given why he should be singled out. It all seemed so unfair.

In Elfend, a few believers had walked away and made themselves scarce so to speak, erasing any connection with their new faith. And it wasn't easy to totally disappear on an island, as some had, if they were still alive, or hadn't been captured, and perhaps enslaved by outsiders. Some fickleness among the young could be expected, and piracy was not unknown. But with Shirra this was especially troubling.

Shirra

Once again Michael went over her disappearance.

Two years earlier, just after the school was built, Triana was busy in the new building working with some women, as Try and Em, who'd gone with her, played in an empty schoolroom across the hallway. Back at the Gatehouse, a holy woman, thinking that Shirra was the only one there, left for several minutes on a personal errand. Shirra, who earlier had seemed upset about something, was working away at several pieces of paper on the table in the living room alcove. Then apparently, she'd gone to the kitchen to get something to eat or drink. Michael, however, been working alone with the door shut in the bedroom, just before the children's two bedrooms, that had become his office. Suddenly, he'd heard a scream from the kitchen. Racing to the sound, he'd found Shirra holding a glass and sucking her thumb and fingers while a small plastic plate was melting to flatness on the stove.

With a towel, he picked up the plate and quickly dropped it in the kitchen trash basket.

"Sorry, Michael, I ruined it," she'd said, emptying the rest of her water over the plate.

"Nothing to worry about, Shirra," he'd said. "It's from the Outpost and it's made of plastic though it doesn't look like it. It's not going to set anything on fire." He couldn't help but notice how perfect her English words sounded. Back in Big Bend they would never suspect she was from another country, much less another planet.

"I just had my mind on something, Michael. I didn't mean to spoil it." Again, perfect English. He looked at her injured hand, examined it, and turning it over, he pressed it to his lips and kissed it. Then, seeing some butter on the counter, he stuck his finger in it, and turning her hand back over, he rubbed the butter over the redness on her palm to take away the sting.

"There, you'll be fine." In less than a minute, his mind still on the problem he was working on, everything was over, and he was back in his office with the door closed, and finally an answer to his own puzzle. When he left his office an hour later she was gone.

He never saw her again.

After being missed for a day—everyone at first just thinking she was somewhere else—a frantic search had begun. When Klingor, who was away for a couple of days with his fishermen returned, he was devastated. Gurdon, with his father and skipping school, was also crushed and had no explanation. He knew that some older boys had broken away from their parents, but all those had safely returned or been found. Then Klingor had a big disagreement with one of the new holy women, perhaps one that was supposed to look out for her—no small job now at the girl's present age!—but whether this was connected to her disappearance, Michael had never learned.

In tears, he and Triana wept over her absence.

After Klingor missed worship and teaching class for two weeks, Michael had sent Dr. Hartlin to make a "house call." Klingor returned the following week, and after Triana and he had confessed their total bewilderment to him, and a thorough search by many was made inside and outside the mountain even to the two other towns, things returned to as normal as possible after a young woman, especially a pretty daughter still in her teens, goes missing without a trace.

Michael remembered learning that in Elphia, traditionally a child, especially a teen, could quickly earn great respect and assume more responsibility, more so than on Earth—that is, before EMP. It certainly had been helpful to Triana and him when they'd first arrived. But sadly, the downside was that if extra privilege to the young was ever abused, the road back to acceptance was nearly impossible. Even a repentant person was usually ignored.

And this was Elphia, not Earth.

Two weeks later when he and Triana, with the twins' help, did a thorough cleaning of the Gatehouse, several scraps of Shirra's endless writing and translating showed up, but nothing that gave any clues about what had happened. However, one truly odd thing, which wasn't an object but an oversight, Michael did discover. But if it had any connection with Shirra's disappearance, he couldn't see it. So he kept knowledge of it to himself.

Finally, he approached the end of his fifth lap.

The Tabernacle stood no more than 200 feet from the small waterfall next to the tunnel that led to the Gatehouse. He had been walking, jogging, or running 10 miles. He collapsed on a bench in the back.

As soon as he sat, the voice came to him again. **"Do YOU love Me more than all these things?"**

He sat up erect. Then it dawned on him. One thing he hadn't done at all was confess his growing fear. But why should he be afraid? Could Lemron and Klingor shake their heads and walk away, too?

353

"Do you LOVE me more than all these things?" came the voice again. The words were the same but the emphasis was different.

His mind raced. So many played religious games. People spent their time on what they loved. He was exhausted. People loved what they spent time on. What did he spend time on? The rich young ruler in the Bible was a good man who had so many good things that he walked away from Jesus sad because he couldn't — or wouldn't — give them up. He should take warning.

He had come safely to a new planet.

He had a good...a wife more wonderful than he deserved.

He had two adoring children.

He had respect, power, a home.

Yet it was because of her, all these things had come...

"You are not ready to die and glorify ME. Do you love ME more than all these things?"

He sensed he would not be asked again.

Deep down, as imperfect as he knew he was, he knew how he felt. He confessed his sin.

"Yes, Lord, I do...I now do."

"Then feed my sheep."

*   *   *   *   *

When he awoke, two of the boys he knew from Earthball stood over where he was lying on the bench.

"You okay, Mr. Michael?" asked one.

Uhh...ohh...just fine. Wha...what time is it?"

"About one o'clock," said the other.

"One o'clock! Thanks...thanks."

He stood and forced his aching legs toward the tunnel opening. He ducked behind the waterfall and noticing the large towel hanging there and that no one else was around, he took off his karpon and stood under the icy water. Later, toweling off, he wrapped the towel around his waist, and carrying his karpon and sandals he entered the tunnel. Moving from sharp light into darkness, he was momentarily blinded. Arriving at the door, he knocked.

"Daddy, is that you?" asked Try.

"Yes, Try, please open the door."

"Say something more. Mommy says I have to be sure it's you," said the five-year-old.

"Your mommy's right. This is your wonderful, handsome, loving father. How's that?"

"Daddy's doing it again," came a second voice in the background.

The door slowly opened.

Michael entered.

"Mommy, Daddy's wearing a towel! Mommy, can I wear a towel in the tunnel, too?"

"Me, too!" said a second voice.

Triana tried to use her "you're all ridiculous look" but failed.

*   *   *   *   *

Later at the Tabernacle
Time: Hours later. Day 1 of the next (unnamed) month arrives,
            ending the Sabbath Day and beginning Sabbath After.

The sky had begun to lose its light, and the inside overhead lights flicked on including the one at the podium. The music had ended. The time had arrived for him to speak. The Sabbath was finally over, and a soft, warm breeze pushed through the open walls.. About 60 people sat in scattered groups on the front benches with only a few empty spaces between them. With so many

benches available, this had been encouraged to keep everyone from scattering,
clustering in the back. On the stage, sat Triana, Michael (behind a simple lec-
tern), and Dr. Hartlin (the current head elder).

Michael stepped up and lay his open Bible and notes on the lectern. His morning adventure and the rest afterwards was just what he'd needed. He prayed he would say the right words that he'd prepared the day before the Sabbath had begun. As he glanced out to the people, something unusual caught his eye. Two young men about his age sat 23 rows back on opposite sides of the audience. One wore a karpon much too bulky for the weather. The ushers, the fisherman Noli and his brother Sarmon — with their canes — were the only ones sitting behind them.

Canes. He'd taught them what could be done with canes, and that in a time of trouble what they might have to do with them. First, the code: "29," one more chapter than the Gospel of Matthew has, then the number of the row as "verse," and place in the row would be "a" for center aisle, "m," for middle of the row, and "s" for the end of a row at the side [letters expressed in appropriate Elphian]. Whichever hand held the Bible would indicate the half of the audience where trouble was suspected.

"This evening I want to read from" — he held up his Bible not with one hand but *both* hands — "the Gospel of Matthew, chapter 29, verse 23, parts s and s."

The ushers, alert, sprang into action. Rising, they raced forward to Row 23. When Sarmon saw the rifle pulled out of the man's karpon, he sprinted ahead. He would be too late for the first shot.

BLAM

Noli, at the opposite side of the Tabernacle, knew he had to act fast and hard to help his brother. With a mighty horizontal swing, his hardwood cane caught the second man, now holding a pistol aimed at Michael, squarely in the side of the head, crumpling him to the ground, and later as they would discover, he was stone-cold dead. Noli flew towards his brother. The man who'd fired, was cocked for a second shot.

Sarmon's cane had found the gunman's shoulder, but with lesser impact. The man ignored the blow and was still aiming at the stage. Noli, threw himself forward as far as he could, and with his cane straight ahead of him, came down on the rifle sending it to the ground. The man was immediately punched in the face and wrestled down by four worshipers and pulled from the Tabernacle by his feet, his right arm limp, his broken nose bleeding profusely.

But there was blood also up on the stage.

Triana had been hit somewhere in her side, and was slipping into unconsciousness. Dr. Hartlin was immediately shouting instructions to two of his staff members nearby.

Michael knelt by her side, cradling her head, holding her hand, his tears mixing with all the blood.

CHAPTER 35

The Chapters End

Day 1 of the next month, 8 AM (< 7 yrs. ALOE >)

••Her eyes are opening!" Michael exclaimed. A nurse standing at the door flew to the bed, turned and raced back outside. Dr. Hartlin appeared and in his shadow darted Trivan. When the nurse reached for his hand, he pulled away, slid under the bed, and came up on the other side.

"My mareena!" he declared defiantly. Tears stained his dirty face. A nurse was waiting for him. "Little boy, you aren't supposed…"

"He stays!" ordered Hartlin, still measuring Triana's pulse and not even looking Trivan's way. The accusing nurse immediately found something that needed to be done in the room and started doing it.

"Where's your sister?" asked Hartlin, his and Michael's eyes still on Triana.

"I'm just behind you, Dr. Hartlin," announced Émrica. How'd she managed to sneak down the long aisle to her mother's room, or even get into the clinic, or even where she'd spent the night, was anybody's guess.

"Listen to me," said the doctor, "because I'm saying this only once. Try, take your sister down to the bathroom and, both of you, wash your faces and hands until they're pink. Then come back. Em, you and your brother will always stand, sit, and walk, *without running at all* while you're in here. Is that clear?" In all this time he still hadn't even looked at them once.

"Yes."

"Yes."

"Then go. *Now*. If anyone complains, tell them I need you."

The hardest part was *walking* to the bathroom Trivan later told his father, and not being able to even speak to or touch his mother. "How did he know about my face?" whispered Em as she left the room. "Because he knows you," said her brother. Em told her father about this later and declared that from that day forward her face would never, never stay dirty again. Never. Together they disappeared.

"Michael…Michael…I…love you. Looove you…" Finally her lips were moving.

"I love you, too!" he returned.

Her eyes closed.

Dr. Hartlin motioned to Michael to move to the door.

"The bullet passed through her body and she's lost a lot of blood, Michael. Fortunately, we got her here pretty fast on the gurney kept at the schoolhouse for emergencies. We had to run, however. Our first step was to stop the bleeding, so we still don't know how much internal damage was done. She's receiving saline solution and a general antigerm fighter, and we're carefully watching her blood pressure, which is pretty low. We're assuming—as we have all along—that humans everywhere are pretty much the same. But there are environmental factors here."

"And?" asked Michael.

"It doesn't look good, Michael."

They returned to her bed.

The children returned, each carrying a blanket. When Michael looked puzzled, Émrica informed him that they were their "beds" because they weren't supposed to lie on the bare floor. Michael nodded, and Em put them against the wall by the window. They came and stood at the far side of the bed.

Again, Triana's eyes opened.

"The children, where are the children?"

Try grabbed Em's hand and held it, keeping her from running around the foot of the bed to the other side. Triana turned and looked into their eyes. Michael gave them their mareena's hand that he held.

"Émrica, Trivan, you must obey your father," said their mareena.

"Mommy, Mommy, we will, we will. You'll make us, we know."

"And Shirra will be your marana. You must — "

"Mommy, Shirra isn't here anymore."

"Oh...oh...I for...forgot." She twisted her head and stared at the ceiling.

"You must love God always. And be quick to forgive."

"We will, we will, you will always make us."

"I love you both so much, so much."

"Doctor," said Triana, "could you take the children down the hall for a couple of minutes? And send me a nurse?" Hartlin stepped forward and took a child with each hand. A nurse quickly appeared.

Michael learned later that the doctor walked only as far as the next room where they stopped and knelt at a bench. Hartlin put his arms around the children, and together they prayed.

For a minute Triana's voice was strong.

"Michael, I want the nurse to hear what I'm going to say. Michael, Michael, I beg of you a favor. Tell him I forgive him. Do not kill him. Let him rest in jail for a time, but send him back to Balara where I was told he's from. Let him go free."

"NO!"

"Michael, I forgive him, just as God has forgiven me. Remember, I killed a man in Big Bend. It's only fair that..."

"No, Triana, that's nonsense! You're not thinking straight! You hit him in self-defense. Someone else shot him!"

"But Michael, I was *there*…If I hadn't been…"

"I disagree with your whole argument. Get well and we'll discuss it!"

"Michael, I want God to deal with him. Please…"

"You're…you're out of your mind!"

"Michael, thank you for loving me…"

Michael shivered and broke into a sweat. His mind shot back to their encounter with Cample at Big Bend. That was one of the first things she ever said to him when they were together, catching Jonas and their teacher off guard.

And starting their adventure together.

He touched his lips to hers.

The nurse glanced up at the one machine that was monitoring her heartbeat. She ran to the door and screamed, "Get Dr. Hartlin at once!"

"Michael"—she smiled—"kiss me again."

He did. Then she handed him her ring.

"I'm remembering my great-grandmother's words: 'I won't be buried with this.' You will need it. You are the most wonderful, wonderful person in the whole world. I love you, Michael! We made it here! We're in Elphia, Michael! You…you kept your promise!"

"The one from the attic of Hotel Crandel?"

"Yes."

"And?"

"I…I…I…re…release you from it."

Their goal together had been reached.

She closed her eyes.

It was over.

Epilogue

Day 2, the next morning (< 7 years ALOE >)

Death to burial occurred in quick succession in Elphia, so at noon on Day 2 the mother of the only children that carried
the blood of three worlds, was put to rest.

Even at short notice, 800 or so had gathered inside and far beyond
the benches under the rolled-up canvas sides of the Tabernacle. This
was surprising since word of mouth was the only means of communication. Balara would get the news too late. The primitive sound system,
which they'd been experimenting with, was finally rushed into service
to help those outside the canvas walls to hear. Lemron and Klingor con-
ducted the service, and they, Michael and the 5-year-7-month-old twins
(6 ½ in Earth years), and the other elders stood by the open casket and
shook hands with everyone who passed by.

Some, by their looks, seemed to actually expect the Emryss Princess to rise up from where she lay. But finally the lid of a special casket
was closed forever ending that hope. Michael quietly wept, his children buried their faces into his soft karpon, as his beloved klepta was
lowered into the ground behind the Tabernacle.

Lemron made it clear that everyone was welcome to come to the
teaching on the upcoming Sabbath Eve on Day 6, two hours before the
sun set, and then again to the Christian worship service on the follow-

ing evening after the Sabbath ended.

After the burial service, there was the sharing of food and conversation. Michael, however, with his children and two of the holy women retreated to his office in the Gatehouse and locked the new locks that had recently been put on the outside doors. The women insisted upon putting the children to bed. He retreated to his office, which was his old bedroom before he was married.

The bed was still there.

He fell upon it.

He would sleep in that room every night, next to the children's two rooms beyond his. Soon he drifted off into a deep sleep.

*   *   *   *   *

The late night darkness beginning Day 3 (after the funeral on Day 2)

Michael tossed and turned. Finally he awoke. It was many hours after the night darkness of Day 2 changed into the darkess beginning Day 3.

It was hours past midnight.

He put on the shorts and shoes he played Earthball in, and tiptoed to the doors of the two kids' bedrooms behind his and, hearing nothing, went to the living room. From the kitchen he could tell his children had been fed the night before. Only one holy woman was still there, asleep on the sofa. He scribbled a note on the slate on the table, and tiptoed down the other hallway to the tunnel that led to the stadium.

On the dark gravel walkway he began to run. It was completely black overhead, but he knew the way. On his first lap it was "WHY?" with every other step. WHY?... WHY?... WHY?... WHY?... WHY?... WHY? He found his way back to where he started. Then it was "Tri-an-a," "Tri-an-a," "Tri-an-a" for lap 2. He would never forget her. Never.

Halfway around he was startled to see a small boy about Trivan's size standing with his back to the wall near a tunnel opening about as far away as possible from the tunnel where he began. He was wearing a frayed child's karpon. Why was he there? Especially then? He ignored him. But as he passed him, the boy moved and began running, following two yards behind him but coming no closer even when Michael slowed down. Michael sped up but the boy kept pace longer than Michael thought possible. Then the boy, gasping for air stopped. Michael continued running without looking back.

On lap 3 it was "Try," "Try," "Try," "Try." To his surprise, he met the same boy a bit farther from where he had first stopped. Though he'd stopped running, he'd continued walking. As Michael passed this time, the boy began running just behind him as before. Again Michael speeded up. Again, the boy held his own for longer than before. Then he stopped as before.

On lap 4 it was the same. Michael held his "Em," "Em," "Ems" to a whisper and the boy continued as before. This would take the two of them back to the place where they'd first met. With a burst of speed that burned his lungs, he could leave him there.

However, on lap 5 the boy had walked much farther ahead. Then he came closer as the sky slowly began to lighten and Michael approached his own tunnel.

But that wasn't all.

There was another boy standing at the entrance.

"Daddy! Daddy!" Tears were in his eyes.

Michael knelt, still panting. The other boy behind him, also panting, stopped several feet away. Suddenly, he crumpled to the ground.

Michael and Trivan turned to the fallen boy.

"Your name, boy?"

"Ravel," he gasped.

"Your mareena?" said Michael.

"I have no mareena," said Ravel. "She is dead."

"Your father?" asked Michael.

"I have no father," said the boy.

"Because?" asked Michael, wondering why he asked such a bad question.

"He is dead, too. Both of my parents are dead."

Trivan could hold back no longer. "Daddy," he said in English, "please don't di…" Looking at Ravel, he couldn't finish.

"When did you last eat?" asked Michael.

"Uh…uh…"

"Tell me the truth, Boy. We tell the truth here."

"Two…t…t…two days ago, but I'm…I'm…"

"Daddy," interrupted Trivan, still speaking in English, "the holy woman is fixing breakfast."

"Try," said Michael in English, "run and bring Rav a pair of your play shorts and a pullover shirt."

"But what would…Mom…" He stopped. Tears filled his eyes.

"Go! Rav is a mess! I've got to get him cleaned up before I bring him inside for breakfast. Tell the holy woman and Em—and say it nicely—that one more is coming. And we're hungry." Before Rav could respond, Michael pushed him, clothes and all under the waterfall and, pulling him out coughing and sputtering, began scrubbing him with soap. It was then he saw the marks on his back. Some were fresh.

"Hurry, Try! And bring *me* some dinnies and a karpon—an old one."

*   *   *   *   *

Daylight on Day 3

Though ever too briefly, breakfast took minds off the sorrow of the previous day. Em, startled, but curious at the intrusion of the newcomer, took the first opportunity she had to pull him aside out of hearing range and thoroughly instruct him about how to behave around her father and the holy woman. This could be said and done but this and that could not, and he'd better not forget it! Then, for a moment forgetting the day before, she ran to her parents' bedroom and not finding her mother there, ran crying to her own bedroom, the second one in the second hallway.

After breakfast, and offering the proper thank-you that Em had prescribed for Rav to say to both her father and the holy woman, Rav disappeared through the tunnel, wearing a fresh shirt and a pair of Try's shorts. Under his arm were his still damp karpon and dinnies that Michael had scrubbed at the waterfall.

When Galandra came to replace the holy woman who'd spent the night, Michael sent the departing woman to fetch Noli, and told her he wished to see him immediately. He would be in his office-bedroom. If he came, she was to wake him if he was asleep. Em and Try, who would stay home from school, of course, could come in and wake him any time, but no one else.

Noli arrived sooner than he expected.

"Anything, Michael, ask me anything and I'll do it."

"There's a boy who lives in and about Tunnel 8 who calls himself 'Ravel' and claims he's an orphan. Find out if that's true and learn all you can about him. All. And talk to him if you can. You can tell him you're my friend, but don't tell anyone else anything, no one—and tell him to say nothing to anyone—or that I've sent you. By the way, he likes to run."

Noli smiled.

"I'm on my way!" Noli was a man of few words, but there was none more faithful.

"Galandra, I still want to be left alone, except for Try and Em—and

Noli. I don't want to be disturbed."

Exhausted, but chilled back to life by his own quick shower, Michael disappeared into his office and collapsed on his bed. Tears returned, and by winding the clocks in his mind, he finally fell into a deep sleep. When he was awakened by a knock on the door, he discovered Try and Em were asleep in bed beside him.

"Why are you two *here*?" he whispered, feeling foolish as soon as he spoke.

"To…to help…help you, Daddy," said Em groggily. "Dr. Hartlin said we had to carefully look after you."

Galandra eased open the door and motioned for him to come.

"Noli is back, and I've fixed a full pot of tea."

*   *   *   *   *

Day 4 (again, beginning at the darkness ending Day 3)

The following night, he again awoke, but not quite so early. As before, he made it past a sleeping holy woman, not the same one, and through the tunnel without being detected. This time the sky wasn't quite so dark. His anger returned. "Why? Why? Why? Why, God, did You bring us so far and then *this*?" He began to run.

When Michael approached the entrance of "Tunnel 8," as Michael had referred to it for Noli, he noticed the boy, sitting this time with his back against the wall. How thin he looked in the early morning light! He hadn't really noticed the extent of this before.

"Up, Rav!"

He stood and hung his head. Michael extended his hand. The boy took it.

"Look at me, Rav."

The boy obeyed, his eyes full of sorrow.

"Listen to me. Today we're going to walk and talk—just the two of us, understand?" He nodded. "You know what—people who like to run can talk to each other. And when they do talk they tell the truth and can keep secrets. Now we're going to walk and talk all the way around back to here." As soon as he said these words, he shuddered at how horrible they might sound on Earth. But he was not on Earth. He must go on. "And, if I think we haven't talked enough, we're going to walk around again. Understand? And one more thing: When I think we're done, there's a big breakfast at the end. Got it?"

Ravel broke into a smile.

Altogether it took Michael two laps, though for Rav it was just a lap and a half, but not because he didn't talk. He couldn't stop talking! God had to be in this somewhere, Michael realized. But when they'd reached his tunnel opening a second time, Michael told him to go get and bring everything he owned. After disappearing for no more than three minutes Rav was back. In his arms were the clean karpon and dinnies Michael had washed, a single shirt, and a dirty blanket. He hung his head.

"Ravel, raise your head!" He jerked his head up. "Ravel, we've all had bad experiences and have done bad things in our lives. Even me. Are you sorry for the bad things you've done?" Though perhaps he was afraid not to agree, he nodded. "Well, so am I. Do you feel bad about what you don't have?" Again, he nodded. "How about the bad things you've done that nobody knows about?"

The boy paused for about a minute without moving.

Then he nodded his head.

"Well, so do I! And you know what else?" He shook his head. "God knows all about this. All about everything. About you and everything that's happened to you! And about what you're thinking now! And God knows about me. And everything that's happened to me. As for

368

me, my klepta has just been killed!" He pointed to himself. He felt his eyes moisten. "We all have sorrow. Do you know what you can do about yours?" Michael pointed toward Rav, who had dropped his eyes again. The boy shook his head.

"Look at me!" Michael pointed to the lightening sky overhead. "Grott, or the God of Heaven loves me and He *loves you* just as you are." Michael dropped to his knees. "You can ask God to forgive you for everything — EVERYTHING!" He found himself shouting. "He will forgive you and He will take away your sorrow…"

Michael paused. Whatever was he saying! Why did he sound so harsh?

Immediately, the boy melted and fell to his knees. He would never get over his own sorrow.

"God forgive me for everything I've done wrong," said Rav, perhaps because he was afraid to do otherwise. Then he burst into tears and cried until his shirt was wet. Michael also wept. He put his arms around the boy. He flinched at the first touch and his back went rigid. Then he softened and let go, welcoming Michael's embrace.

"And you can ask God to come live inside you."

"God, please come inside me," he said almost automatically.

At last the tears ended. Ravel forced his eyes up before Michael could bark at him again.

"You know what?" said Michael.

Ravel shook his head.

"I'm hungry!"

"Me, too!"

Michael took the boy's possessions and watched him start off. He never dreamed Rav could run so fast.

*　　*　　*　　*　　*

Day 4 Daylight arrives.

Since no long running had really been attempted, it was still early when Michael and his new companion reached the tunnel opening to the Gatehouse. Nonetheless, he found two young runners in shorts and proper shoes waiting for him.

"Okay, what are you two doing here?" Michael asked.

"The holy woman didn't even see us," Em offered in English, smiling.

"Well, we'll see about that!" said Michael.

At that moment the holy woman, who was the youngest of the present seven of them, appeared in the tunnel opening, obviously distraught. And embarrassed. Michael thought quickly. He handed her the clothes he was carrying.

"Mola, don't worry. All's well. I'm taking the kids, all three, for just a short run. Oh…and we'll be back real soon. Breakfast won't be cold by then, will it?"

"Daddy, she hasn't even started breakfast," said Try in English.

After Mola disappeared, Michael looked at his children and spoke to them in Elphian so Rav could overhear.

"Try, look at me. Em, you too. Think! I was pretty sure she hadn't started breakfast. But listen to me. She's feeling bad because you two slipped out here with her knowing it. This can't happen again. Understand?"

Both hung their heads but said nothing.

"Now, that's enough head-hanging. I'll bet a nice big breakfast is going to happen…No complaining, you hear?"

"Will Rav be coming for breakfast?" asked Em in English.

"Yes, and he'll be staying for a few days."

"Yes!" said Try.

"Now, you two, two more things," said Michael in English. "First,

370

when our visitor is with us, like now," not saying "Rav" because it sounds the same in both languages, and he was standing nearby, "we will speak Elphian—not like we're doing right now. We don't want to hurt his feelings. Do you understand?"

"Yes," said both twins in Elphian.

"What's the other thing you were going to tell us?" said Em in Elphian.

"You came out here to run?"

"Yes!"

"Yes!"

"Then let's go!"

Off they headed. They would go half way to the other end and then all the way back—one mile. That would give them something to think about. On the way Rav and Em ran ahead. Michael motioned for Try to hold back. Before Michael could say anything, the twin spoke:

"Daddy, Rav doesn't have anyone, does he?"

"No, he doesn't."

"Is he an orphan?"

"He is."

"Didn't you say God loves orphans?"

"Yes, he wants us to look after them, too."

"Daddy, can he stay in my room?"

Michael stopped. Again, he couldn't hold back his tears.

"Daddy, don't cry. I'll look after Rav. You look after Em. She cries all the time when you're not looking." Michael gave him a big hug.

"Let's catch up!" said Michael.

*   *   *   *   *

What happened that afternoon Michael was told later.

When Dr. Hartlin arrived late in the afternoon, Mola, the holy woman, had simply pointed him to the second hallway that led to the three bedrooms. All was quiet. He tiptoed to the first one, Michael's office, whose door was ajar, and found it empty. Skipping the second and moving to the last one, easing its door open, he was startled to find a strange boy asleep in the bed. But the doctor actually jumped back when a familiar voice whispered loudly in the darkness from a blanket on the floor.

"It's okay, Dr. Hartlin," whispered Try. Like an adult, he motioned for the doctor to step outside, which he did, following him. "Rav doesn't have a bed. He's learning how to use mine. Daddy's in there." He pointed to the middle bedroom door.

"Try," whispered the doctor. "I want to talk to you first."

Mola brought the ever-simmering pot of tea to the sofa in the living room and poured a small half cup for Try, which he was proud to have offered to him, and a large one for Dr. Hartlin. Try had the doctor's full attention and even took small sips between the doctor's questions, to which he provided good answers.

Michael appeared from Em's middle bedroom.

"She's finally asleep," he announced.

"It looks like that's what you need," said Hartlin. "Now what can I do for you?"

"Really?" Michael stared back into the doctor's eyes. Hartlin returned the gaze without repeating himself. "I want Try and Em back in school tomorrow," he said, "or at best, the next day, and I want you to get Rav enrolled in their class."

"The boy? Where does he live?"

"For the time being he lives here."

"Michael, are you C-R-A-Z-Y?"

"My father is not crazy, Dr. Hartlin. Just sad," said Try.

"And," said Michael, "don't try I-N-S-A-N-E or even D-E-E-P-L-Y …T-R-O-U-B-L-E-D either, because Try is 5 [more than 6 in Earth years] but he reads and can spell very well."

" 'Insane,' no Daddy is not," said Try. "'Deeply Trou…trou…troubled.' " He turned and looked at his father, not sure what to say.

"Yes, I am deeply troubled. But I love God, I love my children and yes, Dr. Hartlin, I love this orphan boy. Please…talk to Noli about him."

"Don't worry, I will!" Hartlin emphasized.

The doctor stared across the table and met Try's eyes straight on. The boy returned the doctor's cold gaze, breaking into a smile that Hartlin couldn't refuse. He smiled back.

"I want to shake your hand, young man. You also speak well. I'll be here at the back door in time to take the three of you to school tomorrow morning. Be ready!" Without waiting for a response he turned to Michael. "But Michael, I have to tell you, the elders are restive about what's going on. You've cut yourself off from everybody but your family. Expect a visit from Lemron and Klingor very soon. You've preached about how to live and about praying. We are praying for you. In spite of this horror that's taken place, you've got to rise above it. The church needs you! God forgive me for saying this, but several in your church have had tragic lives. Lemron has lost a wife, and so has Klingor, as well as a daughter. *This is an important time to practice what you preach.* We need you, Michael. Please, forgive me."

The words burned. Michael made himself into an empty shell of steel, refusing to show any emotion. He clenched his teeth to hold his words in. He would not give Hartlin the satisfaction of seeing any anger or pain. It was the hardest thing he'd done so far on Elphia. Let the man wonder where he was.

Try, watching intently, imitated his father. He walked Dr. Hartlin to the hallway that led to the tunnel.

"Try, if you need me at any time let me know," said the doctor, just loud enough for Michael to overhear. "Be ready by…?" — Try mentioned the time — "tomorrow morning. I'll be here to go with you. Tell Ravel what to expect."

After Hartlin was gone, Try ran to his father and the two burst into tears together. The next one to join them was Em.

Then Em put her finger to her lips exactly the way Triana did.

"Shhh. I think Rav needs his sleep," she said.

"Yeah, he's not used to a bed," said Try.

*　　*　　*　　*　　*

Day 5

The next day before Hartlin arrived, the four of them somehow got up early enough to run part way down the track and back. And for the next day (Day 6), Rav reported that Noli said it was all the way around if they got up early enough.

Which they did.

On the second afternoon, the last school day of the week, just as the kids arrived back through the tunnel loudly discussing something Michael couldn't follow, Lemron and Klingor arrived at the front door, with Noli, breathing a little heavily, which was unusual, right behind them.

"Try, introduce your friend who's staying with us," said Michael.

"Mr. Lemron and Mr. Klingor, this is Ravel, my new brother."

374

"*Our* new brother," corrected Em.

Noli smiled, Klingor less so, Lemron not at all. Together, they nodded to the children.

"Okay, kids," said Michael, "that school assignment you've been working on—take it to your bedrooms for now. *Right now!*"

Those were the code words—"school assignment." It took just seconds for the kids to disappear. The three men looked at each other surprised. The holy woman, who knew of this arrangement, soon followed them with a plate of cookies before losing herself in the back of the kitchen.

It was then that Dr. Hartlin appeared at the back door and entered.

Without announcement, or even asking, the holy woman returned with five cups and a pot of tea on a tray.

"Michael, we're so, so sorry," said Lemron.

There was a minute of silence except for the clinking of cups.

"Are you doing okay with the children?" asked Lemron, nodding toward the hallway and the unusually quiet bedroom.

"The holy women, as usual, have been wonderful," said Michael. "We've had only a couple of real arguments and only one fight."

"Fight!?"

"Nothing that's worth talking about." Michael offered his first smile.

"It was something about clothes," said Noli. "But it's all worked out."

"So you know what's going on, Noli?" asked Klingor.

"A little bit." Noli smiled.

Michael, twisting to set down his cup, glanced down the hallway. A door was cracked open and he spied a small head peeking out. He ignored it.

"Do you have something to say?" Michael focused on Lemron and Klingor.

"Michael, you've shut yourself up in here four...five days now. People feel very sorry, I mean very very sorry for what's happened, but you're their... you're *our* leader. Michael, Klingor and I have also lost our wives, and Klingor has lost his daughter as well. These things have been awful for both of us. Yet God is working in our church. Most of the island came to the funeral. You and Triana made this happen. We don't mean to sound cruel, but we can't afford to let anything...*anything* get in the way of this. Jesus, the God-Son, is very real to both of us. You have to come out and talk to us. And this child...do you have any idea what you're doing? Michael, this child must leave. Someone else can take him."

"Is that all, Lemron?" Michael interrupted.

"One more thing," said Lemron, pointing his finger. "Don't worry. We'll handle the teaching scheduled for tonight in just a couple of hours as well as the preaching at the end of the Sabbath the next day. Let me be blunt. God's work is at stake. Remember what you've preached, finish your grieving enough to preach on the second Sabbath After in nine days."

"I will never finish my grieving," said Michael. "But let me say two more things: First, I will preach at the first Sabbath After *in two days*. Is that understood?"

"But..."

"But..."

"But nothing! Try to stop me and I'll preach on the cinder pathway outside. Do I make myself clear?"

Silence.

"Since there's no objection, that's settled. Now second, the boy Ravel has accepted Jesus, has prayed to be forgiven, and is now one of us. He stays here — in this house — until I say so! Is that understood?"

"No...I say No," declared Lemron.

"No!" said Klingor.

They turned to Noli.

"I say Yes! He stays."

They turned to Dr. Hartlin.

"Yes, he stays," said the doctor.

"Yes," added Michael. "That settles it. As a group we agree! Now let's pray."

Like a magnet they all seemed pulled to the center of the room. They got down on their knees and put their arms around each other. But there was more.

Pad, pad, pad, skippidy, pad, pad, pad. Three more from the hallway joined those in the center. The adults spread a bit so the children could squeeze in. Everyone prayed aloud to the God of Heaven, even the children offering a few words.

Later outside, Michael cornered Lemron and the two had some heated words, though they were hardly above a loud whisper. "I hate this as much as you do, Lemron, but do it! Do it for me! I don't even want to know his name. You can probably get away with it sooner rather than later, but make sure he's suffered a bit first, and don't tell me more about it until it's done." That said, Michael turned on his heel and almost stepped headlong into Noli who was on his way out.

Noli had been both the first visitor to come and last to leave. But almost as soon as he was outside he was back in, carrying something he'd left near the door when he arrived — a medium-sized chest with an arched cover that was hinged to the back. He had carried it to the boys' bedroom. Inside were some shoes to work or run in, two karpons the right size, some play shorts, some shirts and dinnies, and three or four other items of boy's clothing. Rav's jaw had fallen open.

"Rav, here's a place to put your things," he said. "And there's still plenty of space." When the boy finally turned to thank him, Noli had already left.

Day 8, The Sabbath After (beginning in the early evening darkness)
[Day 7, the Sabbath, had come and gone.]

"Daddy," whispered Try, "you said to look up when you're around people. Your eyes are on the ground."

As they entered the Tabernacle from the side near the front, the four continued to front row places that had been saved on the first bench on the left side. Across the middle aisle on the front row sat seven of the elders; the eighth one, Lemron, was on the stage making his final announcement behind the lectern. Several songs had been sung and the believers, by prearrangement were scattered throughout the packed worship center.

"I will raise my head when I get up there and see them all at once. Right now I am praying," whispered Michael.

"But Daddy, your eyes are open," whispered Em.

"There are sooo many people!" whispered Rav.

"That's why I'm glad you're with me to make me feel better," whispered Michael. "But if you all keep this up, the elders will carry you off to the babies room and three less people will be here. Remember everything I've told you."

"Daddy, why are your hands shaking?" whispered Em. "And why are your eyes wet again?"

Michael turned and glared. A tear squeezed out. Em wiped it off his cheek with her hand. Try handed him a page of notes that he'd dropped.

"And a word…several words…from Preacher Michael," added Lemron. That was it. The man didn't waste words on what everybody knew.

Michael walked up the two steps to the stage. Only then did he look up for the first time. The lights overhead were already lit as well as lights on the poles outside. People were everywhere as far as he could see. The new sound equipment was in place. Still he must be loud, slow, and clear. There was no place for fear—except fear before God.

And God had brought many to hear about Him.

"First a prayer," he declared as loud as he dared. He scanned his eyes over the whole crowd to see how the sound was received. He couldn't see where the people ended beyond the rolled up canvas in the back, but Elphians were used to quietly listening in dim light. Slowly his eyes detected many at the sides who spilled outside.

"A public prayer," he began, "is first to the God of Heaven, second, it comes back as a reminder to the one praying, that it's a serious matter to speak on behalf of the God who made the universe and created people in His image."

He bowed his head.

"O God, may everything said here that's true and important be remembered.

"May anything that's false or trivial be forgotten or do no harm.

"May your Spirit touch everyone here by what is read and what is said.

"In the name of Jesus, the God-Son,

"Amen.

"For those who are here for the first time, I am Michael Hammond from Planet Earth."

At this point everyone who was not seated was on his feet, clapping—with their hands going up and down, which is easier to do in a large group. It continued a whole minute.

Then, as a single person it seemed, those who had seats sat.

"I, Michael and the woman Triana arrived on your planet about 7 years ago, about 8 years as we count them on Earth.

"Triana's mother and father were from Planet Emryss. Her great-great grandfather is from here, Planet Elphia.

"I am a poor boy from only one planet...Earth."

To this there was polite laughter.

"We have worked hard to learn your language. Of course there's a much longer story about this."

More polite laughter.

"There is one more thing I must tell you about myself. It is serious and there is no way I can soften it."

Pause.

The audience became deathly quiet. Michael gripped the lectern so tightly that his knuckles got white. He pulled one hand off and pointed to an empty chair on the stage five feet away.

"Last week, my klepta Triana sat there at that very spot. At about this time she was fatally shot. She died the next morning. I've learned that an old marriage tradition here allows a klepta or 'kleptor,' that's your old word for the married man that's almost been forgotten, six months of extra time to privately grieve—though I will grieve forever. There are many things we still must do, and I will do, and I ask you to help me do that."

Once again he gripped the lectern and leaned on it so hard it made a cracking sound. Try, Em, and Rav raced to the platform and grabbed his legs.

"We'll hold you up, Daddy," said Try.

Michael reached down and kissed each of them on top of their heads. He felt a surge of strength fill his body. A wave of peace enveloped him. He took Rav by the hand.

"Rav and I each have only the blood of one world in our bodies. I am his 'parana.' "

Michael noted the sudden look of wonder from several in front of him. Just who was this child? And what had been said? "Parana"—a new word—had just been born into the Elphian vocabulary. He'd invented it. If a "marana" was a special "mother by promise," rather than by birth, then "parana" would be a "father by promise."

Next he took Try and Em each by the hand.

"These two children are ordinary, very ordinary, children just like your children — except for one thing: As the children of Triana and me, Michael, they are the only children in this world whose bodies contain the **blood of three worlds."**

Pause.

Then, again, there was applause.

"And they are *your* children."

Again, everyone stood and applauded.

Michael sent the children to their seats.

Those who had benches at last sat, Michael asked them to squeeze closer, and they did. And he asked them to move closer in at the sides and down the aisle and they did. And so a few others found seats. Some found seats on the ground in front, others in the center aisle. There was a sea of silent people everywhere.

Michael began.

"I know you believe you have a 'phuma,' what we from Earth call a 'soul.' Forgive me if I use that word that's so familiar to me. The phuma or soul is that part of you that loves, desires, rejoices, sorrows, knows when you've done wrong, feels guilty and scared sometimes, and hopes as well as being afraid. It is that part of you that asks questions and remembers and wants to learn, and is a part of you that you know is real and something science can't explain.

"It's a part of you specially created by God, and that still lives after your body dies.

"Now let me read from Earth's holy book, the Bible, from the Gospel of Matthew chapter 11 verses 28 through 30. Many of you in this church now have copies of Matthew in your own language, as is the copy I have here that lies on top of my Earth Bible.

"Jesus, the God-Son is speaking: *Come to Me, all who are weary and*

381

heavy-laden, and I will give you rest. Take My yoke upon you, and learn from Me, for I am gentle and humble in heart; and YOU SHALL FIND REST FOR YOUR SOULS. For My yoke is easy, and My load is light.

"In the past few days I have found this difficult. My klepta, the love of my life, has been cruelly taken from me and I miss her more than you can imagine. I've had to examine what all this means. Let me say just two things: First, I am convinced that time spent on any planet is just a small part of a person's existence. Much more comes afterwards. Perhaps our time now is to prepare us for 'then.' One part of the Earth Bible in Second Corinthians 2:9 that I've not shared with most of you says, *'No eye has seen, no ear has heard, no mind has conceived what God has prepared for those who love him.'* "

Suddenly, a woman on the left side in the third row stood.

"Yes! Yes! That's exactly what the I-Rex Code said! I remember it now!"

Then on the other side, in the middle a little farther back another woman stood. "Yes! She's exactly right!"

Then both women sat and melted back into the audience. Michael continued.

"My Triana, I believe, now knows something about what that means. The last thing I want to say about her today is that Triana is the reason I am here, and the reason I am talking to you. She had the passion to come after she was told about your prophecy by another Elphian who'd come to Earth. And she had the opportunity to come. I loved her so much I could not let her go alone—alone to anywhere. Yes, I was a Christian. No, I did not have her passion for Elphia. Not at first. What does this mean? And mean for me now? I am here to give you that answer.

"Part of that answer.

"First, I have come to Jesus 'weary and heavy-laden' and he has given me 'rest.'

"Rest for my soul. My body still screams for rest, but my soul is at rest. The soul of Triana is already in God's hands."

Michael paused, fearing that sudden tears would end his words. He glanced at his notes. He must not let this moment slip away. The children were already on the edge of their seats ready to explode onto the stage again.

"The verses here talk about a 'yoke' like the ox wears, the kind of thing that the owner can use to make the creature go the right way to do what the owner wants done. I believe that every human wears a yoke of some kind—a yoke to something outside themselves that is bigger and stronger than the person is.

"I declare before you, I choose to wear the yoke of the God of Heaven, whatever that means. And right now I can't honestly say this yoke is 'easy,' but I can say it is "easier" than it was yesterday, and yesterday it was easier than the day before that.

"Now, as I asked, What does all this mean to me? Mean to me now?

"It means this: While I live, I...am...an...Elphian!"

Again, everyone stood and clapped. Then quickly sat to see what would come next.

"I am not an Elphian by birth, but by adoption, an adoption that God has brought about. I am now a parana, or "father by promise" to a pure Elphian by birth." He pointed to Rav.

"And father of two ordinary children that carry the blood of Elphia, the blood of Emryss, and the blood of Earth. But don't expect more from them than you do your own children!"

"And I have buried the *body* of a wife that carried the blood of this world and another world. Her soul now is with God.

"Now as an Elphian, I am also the leader of the church that meets under this roof.

383

"Let me say what being a Christian means.

"On Earth, Jesus, the God-Son, was tortured and died, nailed on a cross of wood paying the penalty for sins that everyone commits, and then rising again from the dead. Here on Elphia we have learned that the God-Son did the same thing though he was strapped to a target and shot to death by arrows. We believe that this happened at exactly the same time as he died on Earth, and at exactly the same time he was killed on Planet Emryss when he was staked to the desert sand.

"In other words, **the God-Son died exactly at the same time** as a penalty for the sin of people everywhere — even people on planets beyond these three, if such exist — people who were created in his image. Further, we believe he arose exactly three days later, and will return in the last days at the same time to rule for a time and take all who believe in him to Heaven no matter how far away their planets are.

"This is a lot to say at one time. I do that because of what I will say next: How do I feel? And how does a person become a Christian?

A cross and a target are objects associated with suffering and death. A Christian wears the yoke of Jesus. A person who becomes a Christian may be expected to suffer, but he will be cared for now and in the life that follows by the one who owns the yoke.

"Here we have studied the Gospel of Matthew in some detail. In Mt. 16:24 Jesus says, *If anyone would come after Me, he must deny himself and take up his cross and follow Me.* For an Elphian, think of 'taking up your target.'

"What we study at our church is 'What does this mean?' How does one decide to take up one's 'target' and be open to suffering, and how does one go about doing it?

"I don't have the whole answer.

"But I know a lot more about suffering now.

"Let me mention three of several goals I want us to follow in our church.

"**First,** in Mt. 22, Jesus is asked which of all the commandments God has given, is the greatest commandment. Jesus answers: 'Love the Lord your God with all your heart, and with all your soul, and with all your mind.' That's the most important thing. And the second thing: 'Love your neighbor as yourself.' We're trying to understand what this means and how to make it happen.

"For example, is Balara our neighbor? How far should we take the message of the God of Heaven to the other peoples of ELPHIA?

"**Second,** in the Earth Bible there are 10 special Commandments that God has given, but I'll only talk about one of them here. We are making a special effort to honor the Sabbath, or the seventh day of the week. God gave it to humans as a day of, not ordinary work or even services, but rest. I and my elders continually practice this. First, here we have no formal church services of any kind on the Sabbath, and while it's not wrong on the Sabbath to come to the Tabernacle informally, or to read or pray together, or to touch an Earthball or even put it through a hoop, or to walk or even run around the track, we neither sponsor, participate in, nor attend any formal sports activities from sundown on the sixth day until after sundown on the seventh day.

"Hence we have even built and set up outdoor lights on a couple of sports courts that we can turn on after the Sabbath — and *after the worship service* that follows it."

There was a moment of polite laughter. Michael paused.

"Let me speak for myself about that.

"The Sabbath is a time to privately rest — something that many of us need more than we realize, a time first to privately worship God, then to enjoy one's family, one's klepta or sweetheart, and think about what God wants us to do. And, as some say, to sleep in and learn to enjoy cold food." — more polite laughter — "But beware, God can speak to you in your dreams!" — more laughter — "My greatest experiences on this day have come, not from preparing sermons or teachings, which I do not formally do on the Sabbath, but by simply opening myself up to God. If you make time for God, He is ready to teach you things you've never dreamed of, without your feeling guilty about not racing off to do something else that you think 'has to be done.'

"And after opening yourself to God, there are people around you that welcome your opening yourself to them.

"**Third.** This relates back to #1 just as #2 did. In the book of James in the Earth Bible (1:27) we find this: *Religion that God our Father accepts as pure and faultless is this: to look after orphans and widows in their distress and keep from being polluted by the world.* We call this our 'widows and orphans obligation.' It means much more, however. Many, many parts of the Bible tell of how God is concerned about the poor, the injured, and the troubled. Since God cares about this, as his children we hope to actively and continually do the same.

"For example, Triana and I came here as orphans. We know what that means all too well.

"I will end today with a practical announcement and a prayer that Jesus taught us to use from the Gospel of Matthew.

"You may ask, How do I become a Christian? If so, ask people who are members of our church and they will be happy to tell you. Elders, will you please stand, and baptized church members, will you stand as well?" He paused, and from all over those in front of him people stood without shame. "We of the Church at Elfend will be happy to try to answer any of your questions.

"If you want to learn more, we will have special question sessions and studies *every night this week,* but remember, on the sixth day we cut off early and just after the seventh day we start a little late. In addition, if you want copies of parts of our Bible, bring paper and pencils to make copies of what our adults and young people have written down." Let the elders wonder about that unexpected announcement! They wouldn't dare deny him this!

"Most important, if you want to accept Jesus, the God-Son, and make him your Lord, the best time to do that is tonight. Any of our church members will be glad to help you do that.

"Bow your heads, please. Church members pray along with me:

"Our Father in Heaven
   hallowed be your name.
   your kingdom come,
   your will be done
      wherever you've created people
      as it is in Heaven.
   Give us today our daily bread.
   Forgive us our sins,
      as we also have forgiven
      those who have sinned
      against us.
   and lead us not into temptation,
   but deliver us from the evil one.
      — Amen

"You are dismissed. Thank you for coming."

With his message delivered, Michael felt a wave of peace come over him. In spite of his willingness to stay and talk, an extreme weariness followed, so much so that he found it difficult to walk. He had done all he could. And more than what was expected. He was grateful his three children, on their own initiative, took his hands and insisted he go back to his office-bedroom. He did. Em brought him a cup of tea and kissed his forehead.

"I will take care of the boys, Daddy," she said.

Soon after he fell into a welcome deep sleep.

Postscript: *And the Children?*

— 8 months later —
< approx. 7 years, 8 months ALOE >

Place: The Gatehouse
Time: 5:00 AM on a Sabbath Day

Everything in the Postscript happens within 32 hours.

[1] Behind the Shadowing

His unplanned Sabbath reading fell open to the epistle of James. "*...Consider it all joy...when you encounter various trials...let endurance have its perfect result...*"

Why, of all times that passage!

" 'Joy' ? God, I'm crumbling without sleep. Your Church...Your Church! I'm Yours, I know...but I doubt...take me away before I destroy it! *If* You hear me, keep me from sin. My children...Protect my children...I throw myself upon Your mercy. I know you exist...somewhere...but I...I can't do this anymore..." He lay his head down on the open pages, careful not to tear them.

A ringing in his ears was drowned out by a knock on the door.

A knock? So early?

The light was dim at the narrow table in the alcove.

From where he sat, he faced the front entry. His back was to the kitchen. He hadn't slept more than an hour at a time for two days. The single holy woman on duty, not for regular work, of course, quickly rose from the sofa and answered it. A young woman with long silky black hair, her eyes and eyelashes skillfully but lightly darkened stepped through the doorway. She wore a beautiful karpona that seemed exactly cut for her slender body. She was carrying a middle-sized tote bag.

Shirra!

"God, help me," Michael mumbled to himself.

Except for the holy woman, he was alone, the children sound asleep. The content of the Epistle of James floated away. How could the Devil do this now? But wait, the holy woman seemed undisturbed. She'd returned to her reading. Didn't she understand who this was? He stood, beckoned to the young woman as if he were meeting her for the first time. She came, and he found himself seating her on the other side of the table where he usually sat when he ate alone. He would read and write there, almost cramped in, but with open space that extended out into the living room. It wasn't his daily working station, however. He was now across from her, not quite two feet away, the narrow table occupying that space. He slid his chair back.

"O my God!" he exclaimed.

"O He's my God, too," she exclaimed, smiling.

"It's...it's little Shirra!"

"Yes, Michael, it's still really 'Little Shirra' much of the time, though Little Shirra is now a bit older than the woman we both loved when you first met her. And you're *much* older." She pointed her forefinger towards him. "Uh...could you excuse me for just a minute?"

Without waiting for an answer and leaving her bag, she bounced up and briskly, without running, headed for the first hallway. She was gone for twenty minutes. Had he imagined all this? Puzzled, he approached the bathroom. Certainly, she had gone to check her face. She wasn't there. Nor in the large bedroom that hadn't been used for more than eight months.

At last he heard movement coming from the end of the hallway that led to the tunnel. He felt a slight breeze from the door at the end opening and closing. Both reclaimed their seats. Hot tea was waiting as if preordered. How did that happen? A beautiful, haunting smell, tickled his nose, but not from the tea. He first thought of Triana, but it wasn't quite the same.

"Can you…"

"It's from the garden, Michael, that is, what's left of her and my garden. But enough of that. The rest is my secret, okay?"

"You know there are four kinds of secrets, don't you, Shirra?" Why he'd said that he'd no idea. Was he out of his mind? But now he had to follow it.

"Four kinds?" He had her full attention.

"Yes, according to the number four on one of my clocks. And one kind of those secrets is quite personal, the kind of secret kept between a man and his klepta — or klepta-type," he quickly added.

"Clocks, Michael?"

"That's one of *my* secrets, Shirra." Now he was even. Their old sparring and bantering had sprung back into play. He'd almost forgotten.

"The kind that one might tell a klepta?" She cocked her head slightly and Michael's knee bumped the bottom of the table jiggling the cups. His dreadful tiredness was melting, but not fast enough. God be with me, he prayed silently.

"Usually, but it can refer to that type of private secret. I probably should say 'klepta-type secret.'"

"Michael, I've just come from Triana's grave," she returned, changing the subject. At last she'd mentioned her name. "I couldn't go there until nightfall. Noli watched out for me." Her eyes started to moisten. "Remember when we used to talk for hours about things?"

Noli! How did he fit into this? he wondered.

"Yes," he answered.

"Can you still do that? And since it's the Sabbath, would you possibly like to do that now? Or have you now become 'old' Michael?" She smiled.

"First, yes…sometimes, second, I think so, and third, I'm not sure," he answered taking the three questions in order. So went their old give and take, as they did when translating. If either made a mistake or went in a wrong direction, each could back up and mend things without apology.

"I see." Raising her cup, she took a sip, the cup covering her face except for her eyes.

"Your eyes…"

"It's just a little make-up, something like Triana used to wear. She told me a good man starts with the eyes, and the holy women advised me." Michael almost teared up at hearing such perfect English. It had been eight months since he'd had an adult conversation in English!

"You're staying with the holy women!"

"Yes, but I'll explain later. First, the holy women insist that 'men are sallow.'"

"Sallow?"

"They mean 'shallow,'" she whispered, "but they can't pronounce it right. And they're not talking about color — you know, like your eyes are looking."

Where did that come from! How did she know that word? Michael was now fully awake. It had to have been from Triana.

"Men are *sallow*? This came from the holy women?"

"Yes, Michael, don't be naïve. If you're going to run a church, you have to know these things," she said, moving her hands for emphasis, "and besides, I know that had to first come from you anyway. To get off on the 'right foot,' as you say it in *our* English: You can't afford to be 'sallow.'"

"But maybe I really am," said Michael. He raised a finger to indicate she'd scored a point. Shirra let her eyes grow big as if she were shocked.

"Does this…mean you're going to try to kiss me?"

"Do I know you well enough to?" He struggled to look neutral. *She still remembers that silly routine!*

"I think so," she replied, trying to look as innocent as possible.

Michael recalled their first evening in this very room seven or was it eight years earlier? *What was she up to now?* Yes. A Christian kiss on the cheek he could manage. But how would she take that? As he scraped his chair back to stand, there was a sound from the second hallway. Trying at first to be secretive, Em poked her face around the corner.

"SHE'S BACK!" she screamed at the top of her lungs. The holy woman dropped her book.

"Sorry, Michael, you weren't quick enough."

She turned just as all three children burst into the room.

"MARANA! MARANA! MARANA!" All three hugged her at once. And she kissed them all. When she came to Rav she gave him an extra hug and then held him back.

"And just who am I kissing here?"

"It's Ravel, Ma'am."

"And why am I your marana?"

"This is my brother and sister," he said, pointing to them.

"I see."

"Do you know what a marana is, Ravel?"

He hung his head.

393

"Don't hang your head in front of your marana!" ordered Em, "unless you've done something really bad."

He raised his eyes.

"I don't know," he said.

It was Shirra's turn.

"I'll tell you what a marana is, and listen, all three of you. Listen well! When a marana says 'go' you go, and when she says 'come' you come, and when she says 'do this' or 'do that,' you do this or that. Understand?"

All three nodded their heads.

"Does it mean that when teachers send papers about us home from school that we give them to you?"

"What papers?"

Em ran to the table and picked up three papers that were tucked under the lamp and almost hidden. She brought them to Shirra. Receiving them, she read them silently, letting her eyes grow large. She drew in a deep breath.

"How can I be marana to children like this?"

"It's Rav's fault!" said Try. "He gets us in trouble!"

"Do not!" declared Rav. "I try to keep them from riding horses high."

"Will you really throw us to the wild dogs?" said Em.

Michael bent over and covered his face. Shirra kept her composure without flinching.

"Look, all of you...and I want to see all six eyes. This is serious business that must be attended to! Do you understand?" All three nodded. "If I am to stay for even a day, or *ever* come again, I have to have a long talk with your father. And some of that has to be *alone* with him. Do you understand that?" All three nodded again.

"Now before you go back and get properly dressed for breakfast, which I see you haven't done" — she nodded to the holy woman who scrambled to the kitchen to serve the cereal and cold breakfast treats that waited there. "It's time for another hug." She knelt on the center of the rug. "Down on your knees, everyone."

This hug took all of five minutes.

"Maybe we should pray," said Em.

"Good idea," said Shirra. So they did.

Then they stood. Rav was first to speak.

"Marana, did you really once threaten to throw Try and Em to the wild dogs? They say you did."

"Once, when I was much younger, I did, Rav."

His eyes grew large.

"It was not my best moment"—she paused—"but then sometimes wild dogs do get hungry, but I think they've now been taken care of." She glanced at the window, speculating. "But you don't have to worry about that. Remember, Rav, in this family, we always look out for each other and tell the truth so I'll have to be careful about what I say. Can you do that?"

"Yes, Marana," they all said together.

"Now let's see if you've been listening...All of you, GO!" She pointed to their hallway.

Immediately, they disappeared to their rooms.

Shirra returned to her place at the table as if nothing had just happened. Michael found his own seat.

"Michael, remember where I learned that? You were a good teacher." She cocked her head as she used to do when together they'd successfully translated a difficult passage, and smiled.

"About the 'dog thing': you said you did that when you were *much* younger?"

"Not too much younger, Michael."

They paused as Galandra and Noleen entered, replacing the holy woman who'd spent the night.

Why two holy women? Michael wondered.

"Remember, Michael, I've been gone for more than two years and I've gotten older."

"Yes, and so have I."

"Well, as I said, I'm older now than Triana was when you married her. And you're *much* too old for me, so nobody should be worried."

Michael wondered if she knew how silly that sounded — or would have sounded on Earth.

"Yes. Triana was quite young...and so was I. And now look at you. You're so different! You're...you're beautiful!" She started to roll her eyes but caught herself. He stared, smiling. "How can I be sure you're really not some imposter?"

"There's one sure way to find out if I can still trust you."

"And that's okay?"

"Just use your head and don't get caught." She glanced at the sofa.

She dug into her tote for a handkerchief and inched her chair a bit further under the table. Michael dropped a pencil and reached down to pick it up. With his other hand he touched her ankle and slid his hand upward just under the hem of her long karpona. Yes, it was still there, the thin short smooth scar just midway up to her knee. He traced his finger up to where the short scar ended.

"Mi-chael!" she whispered. Her eyes grew larger.

"Uh...sorry."

"I think you were a bit over the top!"

"No...no...Did I...I hurt you?"

"No."

"I mean in a...a..."

"No, Michael, not in any kind of way."

"Uh...can this be our secret then?"

"Of course, I'm a God's girl. So would this be a klepta-type secret on your Number 4?" she asked.

"You're catching on, but you don't quite understand my clocks. But I'll find a way somehow to slip it in at Number 4, okay?"

"Of course, Michael. You can always trust me."

"This is silly. What am I saying? But you're still something of a mystery," he added. "But we…we haven't done anything wrong, have we?"

"No, Michael, of course not, but it was memorable, and I'll never forget it."

*   *   *   *   *

7:30 AM

[2] The Package

The tables were quickly moved next to each other in the middle of the room, and stools and chairs were put into place, so everyone could sit together. Tables were covered with bowls of cereal and plates of special breakfast pastries and other things that were good cold — except the tea, which was always served hot every day, even on the Sabbath. The children sat around Shirra hovering for information. And the school reports, they would definitely be dealt with — but not on the Sabbath. As to the story of where she had been for more than two years, that must wait for the time being.

And she clarified (in Ephian, of course) that "high horse" was a better "met-a-phor" than saying his "horse was high" and that's why adults, of which she was one, had been smiling earlier. The original

397

expression that one's "horse was high," however, was not about to disappear from the Gatehouse anytime soon.

Other serious conversation would have to wait.

After breakfast, the small tables and stools were returned to where they belonged, not considered work in such circumstances, as both Michael and Triana, with Shirra often nearby, knew. After breakfast the five of them had some playtime together—inside, of course. At midmorning Shirra glanced at Michael whose sleepless nights seemed to be finally catching up with him.

"Go, Michael. Rest for a couple of hours," she offered. "You've got to speak at Sabbath After. I won't leave—yet. I promise."

She was right. Shirra never lied. And after all this, how could the holy women let her? He took a couple of steps toward his office-bedroom and almost fell. What was happening to him?

Shirra, with a holy woman carefully watching, gently pushed him into his office-bedroom and closed the door after him. This was good. A couple of hours of rest would do him good. Besides, Rav could get to know Shirra, and Try and Em could have some uninterrupted time with their old caretaker.

But why would that matter?

Then, as she told him later, she demanded a tour of the six-year-olds' bedrooms, making a careful list of overlooked chores that had to be done—not then but the next day. Also, she'd requested and gotten some private time with Em. When the boys had complained about being left out, she'd explained, "Girl things. You wouldn't be interested." They agreed.

Whatever was going on? And why had he ever greeted her the way he had without waiting for any explanation? He'd never touched her like that before. Where was his guilt?

Some things made no sense.

But a couple of hours of rest and reflection made perfect sense.

Just two hours. He'd been running on empty. He was smart enough to know that. But to keep from making a fool of himself? From sin? People would be waiting in the Tabernacle. That was another matter.

Why had she run away and disappeared so long? And not told her father or even acknowledged Triana's death? And who knew she was now back and who didn't? Strangest of all, why did the ever-present holy women seem to be more accepting than concerned. This acting on their own. He and the elders must start dealing with this. He stared at the ceiling. Why *now* did she suddenly appear and seem to care? And why did he? What had happened to her during her last two years?

And there was the "package" that had arrived at the Gatehouse a month earlier. It was about the size of a loaf of bread, tightly wrapped, but without any writing on the outside to even say who it was for, nor was there a single word inside. He was going to ask the holy women about it, for they had to know something, and probably had even delivered it, but when he finally opened and carefully examined the contents, he changed his mind, tucked it away, and almost forgot about it. Was he losing his mind?

Almost.

Shirra *had* to be involved somehow, but how? And how old was the package before it arrived?

He'd had his second restless, sleepless night in a row, and not his first bout of such nights recently. Soon he was overcome by a deep sleep.

*   *   *   *   *

5:30 PM (7 hours later)

[3] *The Replacement Preacher*

There was a knock at the door.

"Come in," he called, rubbing his eyes. It was Lemron.

"Michael, listen carefully because I'm not going to repeat myself. You're in no condition to go to the Sabbath After worship service that's just an hour away. After your sleepless nights I've been told about, I'm glad to see you've finally got rest and have had time to think some things out.

"But you're in no condition to speak, and since I know the elders will agree, I'm taking your place. With all that's been happening lately, it's likely many will be at the Tabernacle. And we can certainly worship without you. Your children are taken care of. They've been fed. They'll be at the service and they've been sufficiently threatened not to breathe a single word about Shirra's sudden reappearance. Soon after they return, they'll be tucked away in bed. And in no uncertain terms, they'll be warned to stay there.

"There's more. As far as I know, Klingor knows nothing about Shirra's return, and she can't afford to be seen — now — at the Tabernacle. She will stay here and, don't worry, at least two holy women will be here to protect you — and the rest of us! But the world outside will soon be watching." Veins stood out on his neck.

"You two can talk longer together at one time than anybody I've ever seen. She'd drive me crazy. But, God knows, we now have translations and copies that, even with Triana, wouldn't have been possible without her.

"I'm pretty sure you two have some serious things to talk about. So do it, Michael. Quickly! I don't know what's going to happen when

400

Klingor finds out she's here, and I think he has a problem with one of the holy women as well as some family issue.

"Do you understand me, Michael?"

"I do. Any advice? You are my parana, you know."

"Act fast! There's a lot at stake! Do you have any questions? Anything to say?"

"Pray."

"Shirra's now in the kitchen. The children are already on their way to Sabbath After. Talk to God. Then strap on your armor and come out. And don't be a fool. Good-bye." The door closed behind him.

What a blessing to have true elders—elders in every way—like Lemron. There was no question why he was mayor of Elfend. In minutes, Michael rose and put on his karpon, but his legs were rubbery and he sank to the floor.

*   *   *   *   *

[4] The Wise Virgin

(The sun has set and Day 8 is about to begin.)
Seconds later…

Michael tried to rise, but fell back on his face. In his mind, he was far, far away, and for several seconds his head spun.

"O God, may I never disgrace your name! Never, nev-"

"Stay on the road," came echoing words that he instantly knew were heard by his ears only.

Was this a vision? Or just a dream? A tall wall of thick forest rose on either side of him as far as he could see.

"Ignore the trees and the faces behind them," continued the voice. **"Keep moving on the road. You are safe on the road."** One glance to the side was enough to see why.

He heard the rising, then falling sound of a train passing by behind him. He dared not look back, but he was sure he'd passed over those same tracks earlier — on foot on Earth, but not here. Tall trees elbowed in, their trunks touching the side of the pavement, which itself grew narrower. He walked further. Now thick foggy clouds filled in the gaps and edges of the pavement like endless two-foot spirals of cotton. His memory of clocks and railroad tracks from the Hotel Crandel flashed back: "RR," it was RR, RR... "Real, Right." Being real and right...both mattered to God...

"The clouds have no bottom. They are thousands of feet high," came the voice. What then did the trees stand for here? he wondered.

The road then began to narrow, squeezing the clouds up so high that the trees seemed to lean over his walkway and cut off most of the light. When he stuck his arms out to the side, he lost sight of his hands in the fog.

"Help! Help! I can't see the road," he cried. He dropped to his knees.

"I have others ahead of you on the road," came the voice. A hooded figure shorter than he approached and stopped just on the other side of a drainage grating in front of him. The road was now the size of a narrow sidewalk. The figure held out a welcoming hand.

He took it, suspecting who it might be. As he pushed up to stand, the wedding band on his other hand slipped off and fell into the drain and disappeared.

"MY RING!" he cried out.

The hood of his companion fell back. It was Shirra.

He reached down and pulled up the drain cover and started to enter the hole, but he was too big.

"Michael," said Shirra in the dream, "This is small enough for me. I can get it." She started to enter the hole. The sky above suddenly turned black. He reached to pull her back, but she was gone.

"SHIRRA! SHIRRA! SHIRRA!" he screamed. **"SHIRRA! SHIR—"**

He felt someone gently slapping his cheek. He found himself being pulled to his feet.

"Michael, Michael, I'm right here! Wake up, Wake up."

He stood in the light…light coming from his own doorway. Shirra had her hands on his shoulders eyeing him carefully, but keeping him at a distance. In the doorway was Noleen, standing ahead of Galandra who seemed to be holding her back. Then Shirra, standing on her tip-toes, closed her eyes and kissed Michael on his forehead.

"My forehead?" Michael declared.

"You were *screaming,* Michael, but not nearly as loud as I did years ago on the beach. That's all you get. And…and you mentioned your ring."

"I lost it in the—" he caught himself. The dream could wait, but when he looked at his hand, his ring was gone.

"Well, you wore it in here, so it will turn up." She nimbly dropped down to her knees and looked under the bed, but nothing was there. Then she pulled back the blanket and behold, there it was. She handed it to Michael. He laid it on the bureau for safekeeping.

Shirra ushered the holy women out and to the sofa, again serving them tea as she was doing before Michael's interruption. When Michael emerged from his room wide awake, Galandra was knitting, and Noleen, beside her, was reading a book as if nothing had happened.

"It was my turn," Shirra said to Michael, seeing him coming as she put the pot back on the stove. She lay her spoon on a small salad plate.

A memory flashed back. The plate was the companion to the destroyed one that was bought at the Outpost years ago.

She returned to her seat as if the prologue to her special story was over and Chapter 1 was about to begin. Reaching down she fiddled with her tote that was exactly where she'd left it that morning. Michael, of course, again sat across from her. Of everyone he ever knew, they were the only ones who would be comfortable in such circumstances. And in spite of everything he was comfortable. He returned her smile. But still, wanting more space, he slid his chair back several inches.

"I am one of the five wise virgins," said Shirra, offering her first words.

Michael arched his eyebrows.

"That's because I have brought my oil with me."

"You're waiting for a bridegroom?"

"Michael...but I think I'd better stop because we're taking this verse from Matthew out of its...neigh...neighborhood."

"Neighborhood? Oh, I think you mean 'context,' don't you?"

"Yes, Michael. Thank you, really. 'Con-text,' "she said as if to paste the English word in her memory. Michael sensed she was playing with him. This word was hardly a new discovery for her.

"*One*, notice how that doesn't bother me," she continued. "Notice *too*, that I speak English almost perfect."

"Perfect**LY**," he offered.

"Perfectly — Yes, Michael, and notice *'three,'* since you're a little slow about some things, I'm not in the least offended when you do that. I have to get my English right...rightly?...no, right. And notice *'four,'* that we can speak openly, normally, and honestly, even in the presence of the holy women because we are speaking in English."

"Yes, I welcome that. In fact, you speak beau-ti-ful-**LY**."

"I got that!" She smiled and raised her finger as if he'd scored a point.

"I got *that!*" said Michael, beaming. "Does that mean *you* are going to give me a Christian kiss now?"

"Oh, sorry…" She stood as if bound to obey. Then hearing some unexpected commotion from the end of the other hallway, she glanced at two of the children emerging, a holy woman trying to scoot them back. It was to pick up a handwritten copy of Matthew that had been accidentally forgotten.

"A few more seconds, Michael." Shirra greeted and hugged each one, whispered into their ears, and shooed them down the tunnel, the holy woman following, pushing them ahead.

"You know, Michael, your children are wonderful."

"As are the holy women," added Michael, "as nobody on my planet would ever understand."

Shirra raised what turned out to be an empty cup to her lips and stared over it again into Michael's eyes.

As soon as the children disappeared, Shirra and Michael stood and leaned across the narrow table, careful not to fall into it. What a silly picture this would be! She smelled wonderful. A strand of her long hair fell against his cheek and he resisted sneezing. She closed her eyes and started to kiss his forehead.

"I think *you* are moving up 'too high' this time," Michael offered.

Puzzled, her eyes popped open which delighted him. He softly pushed her shoulders down, her eyes again closed, and he gently touched his lips to hers. With every muscle in his body he pushed back. He felt sweat bead his forehead.

Then they both quickly sat, refusing to even glance at the holy women. They heard the sound of shuffling feet.

"I think more tea is coming," he whispered.

"You don't have to whisper, Michael. They don't understand our words."

"Okay," he whispered back. "But kisses don't require translation."

In seconds, more cups of hot tea were steaming on the table.

"Michael, you know how we've always been honest and open with each other?"

"Yes."

"Is it still that way?" She cocked her head and smiled. Michael nodded. "I mean for something very personal?"

"Go ahead."

"But first, I don't want to hurt your feelings."

"Don't worry. Go on."

"Two things, Michael. First...and I know God is hearing my words...I did not come here because of *you*. Oh, at first, that was my reason. It really was. But, Michael, then God opened my eyes. You are not number one!"

She studied his face.

"So much has happened to me because of Jesus! If I go against promises I've made to Him, I'll feel all alone.

"But still I remember very clearly the promise I made to you years ago. I said, 'I was yours—'"

" 'Forever,' " Michael interrupted.

"No"—it was her turn to interrupt—"it was 'forever, forever, forever.' " Her forefinger danced with each word.

"It was a little-girl promise," he returned.

Suddenly, her eyes moistened.

"Doesn't my promise matter to you any more, Michael?"

"Uh..."

He was speechless.

"Didn't Jesus take little children seriously?" she continued. "Here, you need something to drink." She reached across the table and raised Michael's cup to his lips. He allowed himself a long drink. She lowered the cup.

"Michael, do you want me to 'undo'... or unmake my promise?" Her hands softly circled in front of her as she seemed to be ironing out wrinkles of her second language.

"It's your turn for some tea," he said, changing direction—something he'd learned from her. Unwittingly, he raised his own nearly empty cup to her lips and she took a couple of sips until he realized his mistake and pulled it back. Without any show, she slid her own cup across the table so it would be easy for him to try again. He did and she drank.

Tears from nowhere were now running down both of their faces. She reached in her tote for a hankerchief and, ignoring her own face, she reached across the table patted his cheeks dry.

"Now, while I wait for your answer, Michael, may I ask you a very, very personal question?"

How soft and sweet she sounded. Should he prepare for an ambush?

"The holy women say a person has to be very careful about things like this, and that sometimes I say too much."

"Shirra, I've listened to you in almost every kind of situation over the years, and I've always respected you." Michael tightened his armor. Could he still breathe? "And I believed you—even when you were a little girl."

"That's because I never lied to you, Michael. Can this be a klepta-type secret?" With her finger she underlined "type" in the air.

"Perhaps." He'd hooked her with his clocks. He reached for his empty teacup.

"Michael...when you touched my scar"—she paused—"did you think about wanting to untie my karpona cord?" Her last words were almost a whisper. What was he hearing! Yes, he was on a different planet! Two real kinds of information were in play: First, her actual words; and second, the language with her eyes, tears not withstanding, that clearly indicated she would kill him if he tried to do it.

It was a struggle, but he carefully relanded the empty cup.

"Michael, Michael, I was thinking me-ta-phor...meta-phor"—she repeated, now obviously embarrassed and trying to make it sound better in English—"Sorry...Sorry if I stepped-over."

"Uh...no...no, you didn't 'overstep.' You know...you know it's been so long since I've had to think about hearing and speaking English. Thank you for bringing it back to me. Never have I seen anyone work so hard at a language." He racked his brain to see how her use of "metaphor" worked into what she was saying.

Elphians had their own ways of working words, often startling to Earth-ears. And Shirra knew all the nuances of Elphian idioms and how and where Elphian words went. She'd been a treasure when trying to select the best way to express the right words in a difficult translation.

By this time his mind had relanded safely. Facing her question, he'd risk a "step-over" of his own.

"Shirra, Shirra, Shirra, I will only answer if you ask me a second important question that should go along with what you just asked."

"You mean...like, Would you want me to untie it for you myself—if you thought I would, that is?"

How could she say that so innocently? He wondered.

"No, no, no. You're going the wrong way. Let me help you."

"Please do."

"The second question should be this: 'Would I do this to you?'"

"Oh."

"So here's your answer: 'Yes, I would be kind of *tempted* to do something like that"—he paused—"because you're so beautiful...so beautiful and you know I love you." She started to roll her eyes, but caught herself. This habit extended beyond Earth. "But, *would* I do that? No! No! No! Why? Again, because I love you."

"Michael, tell me about 'tempted.' How is tempt...tempt-ta-tion

408

different from sin?"

"Well, let me say it this way: Jesus was tempted in many ways but didn't sin. Also, my father Jonas once said: 'You can't keep a bird from flying over your head, but you can keep it from building a nest in your hair.'

"Shirra, after all we've been through, and I've been through, I would never, ever want to hurt you. But there's a bigger reason here: And this goes past Triana, who I deeply loved, who's now with God. It's because it would go against everything that brought both Triana and me here. It would go against the church and all God has done over the last seven years. Jesus is my God. And God is watching and listening. And that's another kind of secret, by the way. There's never a totally private secret because God always knows. He's watching right now and hearing our words. He made me so I *could* want you, but I pray to Him, in front of you, that I won't take advantage of you and we end up hurting and hating each other.

"And besides that, the holy women would catch me."

Sweat beaded his forehead.

Shirra studied him as if he were a marble statue.

"But Michael, isn't there a time for a bird to build a nest? Or, am I taking this met-a-phor *out of your neighborhood?*" He noticed she'd said that deliberately, "Please skip that," she added. "You talk about 'love' in sort of confusing ways." She stirred the air with her hand as if wiping a delicate plate. "Michael, let *me* be more specific: Is it okay *now* for me to say, 'I love you'? You know, as a woman?"

"I think so.

"But," Michael continued, "let me be very specific about love that no one else on this planet would understand."

"I'm listening."

"You have no idea how good it is for me to be able to talk to somebody in *English."*

"Well…you see," she replied, "I want to say certain things in language you can understand … perfect**ly**."

"Well said!" Michael smiled.

Absently, he pointed up as if she'd made a point. She started to stand.

"No, no, not this time! Only this."

He quickly touched his fingers to his lips and then reached out with his hand and touched her lips.

"That's just for your lips…and your brain."

"My brain? Does that mean you've forgiven me?"

"For what?"

"For that ridiculous package. I feel so…so hu-mil-i-ated," she said, emphasizing each syllable of the last word to get it right.

Michael smiled.

"So you really sent that…recently! "Shirra, I could never forgive you for that."

"Why not?"

"I just can't. It was so different!" He noticed his eyes begin to water again. Why now of all times? "Shirra, so much is missing here that we've got to talk about. What happened to you? Why did 'God's girl' run away? Why, as you said, does Jesus mean so much to you now? You were gone for two years! Did anyone hurt you? You don't know the effect your disappearance had. I want the truth which I know you're capable of giving me, and I want all of it."

"Another klepta-type secret?"

"Shirra, I can't promise that. People have been asking, and will ask, many questions. And they have a right to know."

"I mean about certain personal parts? I mean we do sort of love each other, don't we?"

"We really love each other, Shirra." What was he saying! "Certain parts we don't have to tell. Trust me, will you?"

"I will, Michael. I always have."

A burning smell suddenly came from the kitchen. Noleen sprinted to the stove. Somehow, a plate had gotten too close to the heat. It had already melted to near flatness. Noleen poured water on it and threw it in the trash. Suddenly, an old memory flashed back. When no one was looking, Michael pulled the plate out, wiped it off, and slipped it into a large inside pocket in his karpon.

There was a noise in the tunnel. The children, escorted by a third holy woman were back early. They flung themselves into Shirra's arms, not even noticing their father.

It was time for the children to get ready for bed. When the holy women offered to help, the children would have none of it, and insisted that Shirra tuck them away, even the boys.

*   *   *   *   *

9 PM

[5] Bad Plates

Once again they were across the table from each other. How long could this go on? Since the sun had long ago set beginning Day 8, some eggs and toast appeared. Michael thanked God for the protecting table as well as the food. Shirra was a wise virgin to park there with "her oil." The time had come for her story — safely told "per-fect*ly*" in English.

"Michael, I'm not sure how to start."

"Try at the beginning," he said.

"Well, Michael, you've known me since I was 8-and-half, or almost

411

half of my life. It all began at the beach almost seven years ago. I had fallen, my leg bone was broken and sticking out in the air, and you and Triana put the bone back inside me, and God quickly healed me and saved my life. I can only talk about my love for you and for Jesus because of what she, and you of course, did.

"When I first met you, Michael, I was screaming, louder than you were earlier, by the way, thinking I was going to die, but you kissed me —"

"On the forehead," interrupted Michael.

"And you said I was going to be okay, and in an hour I was all healed. And then I jumped on you and said 'I was yours —' but we've been over all that.

"It was little-girl love and it was wonderful. And I loved Triana, too. I loved your language, I loved your Bible, I loved teaching you Elphian words, showing you Elphian things, and I learned I was good at it. Later I loved Try and Em. And Michael, I learned one lesson very quickly. When I sensed you thought I was becoming a vanchi, and you said 'Go!' I peacefully went."

"Well," Michael interrupted, "there was one time when —"

"Only once, Michael!" For a second what was left of her new eyes flashed, and Michael actually shivered before smiling. Then she pointed at his face, only to quickly soften.

"Careful, you almost pointed at the ceiling!" he said.

Her eyes flashed again.

"Michael, don't be impossible!"

"You were *invaluable*, Shirra. We would never have had Matthew translated so quickly if..."

" 'Invaluable' means *'not valuable,'* Michael? Or am I missing something here?"

Only Shirra, traveling at full speed, could pivot to a new path like this when her interest was piqued, pondering, and holding tight without losing her next words before whipsawing back.

"Think of 'invaluable' as *'very* valuable,' Shirra. It's one of those funny English words."

"Hmm." Pause…He braced for her whipsawing back. "Then there was that time much, much later… I burned my fingers…and you gently kissed them and put butter on them to make them stop hurting, and I realized…"

She stopped, and for the first time looked away.

Noleen took this as a moment to bring two small bowls of hot soup and a plate with several slices of bread.

"I realized my love for you had changed. I…I felt…I felt…not bad… I felt all…all…I don't know a word for it…all 'melty'?" —she paused, extending her hands—"Am I crazy, Michael. Do boys feel…feel melty, too?"

"Well, let me check those fingers again."

She held out her hand. He took it in his and examined her palm thoroughly as if looking for flecks of gold. Turning it, he held it so it caught more light and examined further. Then he raised it to his lips and kissed the back of her hand once again. Her eyes filled to the tipping point with tears.

Suddenly, she had no words. He must remember this.

At last…a missing puzzle piece appeared. Michael reached into his karpon pocket and pulled out his flat, but wrinkled, newly melted plate. On it he placed a slice of bread as gently as if it were an egg. Barely glancing he noticed her eyes grow large. He put the plate in front of him and broke the bread in two. He lifted a piece to her lips. She opened her mouth and received it.

"Shirra…I'm wondering now…do you possibly have—"

The waiting tears again suddenly rushed down her cheeks. She reached down into her tote and pulled out her own matching melted plate. Michael smiled. She put another slice of bread on her plate, broke it, and raised a piece to his lips. He took it. And since a napkin arrived with the soup, this time he patted her eyes dry.

She finally swallowed her piece.

"I've carried this with me everywhere. Michael, I'm so embarrassed! You knew I had this?"

"I suspected it, but wasn't sure. And I didn't know why. We did a thorough cleaning soon after you disappeared and the trash in the kitchen that we hadn't emptied didn't have your plate that I knew had been thrown there. I knew you were full of surprises—and still are. And you know what?"

"What?"

"Please realize I'm a little bit embarrassed, too. This would be hard for me to explain to anyone else. But when I'm across the table talking with you about anything, that doesn't bother me at all. All that matters to me is that you're here."

She reached across the table and gently brushed crumbs from his lips. Then she did the same to her own.

With the earlier appearance of tears, the holy women had sprung to life. Cautiously they approached the table.

"Bad plates!" said Noleen in Elphian, of course, starting to pull them away.

"No! the plates stay!" said Michael, pulling them back. Noleen jumped and slowly retreated.

Galandra examined Shirra's face.

"Your eyes are running away," she declared. "We must correct. Come!" Unceremoniously she led Shirra to the bathroom, which after all the tea, Shirra later declared was a welcome break. In minutes she was back, her eyes neatly repaired with just the right trace of make-up restored, her silky hair combed, looking as if she'd just come through the door. How could she do that so fast? Michael's break was much faster. He sat staring. Was he really that sallow? Galandra handed Michael a small towel.

"Wipe face if tears run away again," said Galandra, before returning to the sofa. "Gently," she added.

"Michael? Why are you looking at me like that?" Again Shirra tilted her head slightly.

"Shirra, you're beautiful."

"Michael..."

"I'm sorry, Shirra, but you are. I can't help it. We always promised to be honest with each other as you just reminded me."

"The holy women, Michael, as I've told you, have said that I talk too much, though you're doing your part...your fair share... and that a wise person doesn't carelessly give away secrets — whether or not they involve clocks. Michael, you are God's man here, sallow or not. It just annoys me sometimes that the holy women are so right. Men are sallow. You should talk to the holy women. They'll tell you I'm just little Shirra under all this."

"Shirra, since you said that, let me ask you a funny question."

"Okay."

"Listen. Listen carefully. If...if...for unexplained reasons of my own before you leave me, will you do me a favor?" She cautiously nodded. "This is it: If I sense a need to have you leave the room for a few minutes, and say, 'GO,' but say it kindly, will you quickly leave the room without offence or argument, and not leave the house, but just the room?"

"For the *bedroom*, Michael?" She pointed without looking at the door.

"Uh...Yes, here that's the best place...Oh, and shut the door behind you."

"You're not going to come in *alone*, are you?"

"Well, maybe…but I'll first knock on the door."

Pause.

Michael couldn't believe how calmly she agreed without clarification. Memories of playing games that seemed so natural when he and Triana were defending themselves against their teacher and Jonas flashed back. Well, perhaps Shirra could play games to guard secrets, too. She wasn't Triana, nor would he want her to be. But she was no fool either. She was taking her measure of something, but what? Should he be concerned? *And what should he be taking measure of?*

"Shirra, not even a 'thank you'?" asked Michael.

"About what?" she replied.

"About my saying you're so beautiful. I'm a *word-person*, you know."

She rolled her eyes and seemed to file away the expression for later. She pulled back a smile that started to escape.

"Thank you…but Michael, let me go back to where we were. You were married to Triana which was definitely God's will. But I knew I just couldn't work beside you anymore like I did, even though I was still yours forever. Am I making any sense?" She paused and Michael weakly nodded to see what would come next. "So what could I do?

"As God would have it, a week before I burned my fingers you had told several of us an Earth-story. There were new 'ra – di - cal,' I think you called them, Christians in villages in a place called "China" who found Jesus and loved him so much, that since their lives had been so changed, they voluntar-i-ly sent their Christian daughters as young as I am out as missionaries alone on one-way trips to villages where no one had ever heard about Jesus.

"Then that very morning before I left I'd been reading St. Matthew and thinking about the young man who Jesus asked to follow Him. But since he was so good and rich that he couldn't bear to give away things to follow Jesus, he became sad and turned away. Then it 'morninged,' no, dawned on me, I could do that. I could follow Jesus.

"That was something I could do! Even in Matthew Jesus says that if someone doesn't love Jesus more than father, mother, or any family member, or even you, Michael, that that person couldn't be his disciple. Back here, I could never say my melty feeling for you was bad, because I think God made me that way. But if I stayed here, I might do something I shouldn't, because I loved you in my heart like a woman does. And you really loved Triana as your klepta. Something I should never interfere with and I could never be. And…I could never hurt her."

She paused.

Though she seemed sure Michael was listening, she sensed that in this pouring out of her heart it seemed he was smiling about something trivial. "Michael, this is serious! Pay attention to my *words*, not my hands while I talk!"

"I'm sorry, Shirra, very sorry, but I'm hearing every word, every single word, though I can't help watching you."

"Watching? Michael, sometimes I wonder…"

"Keep going, Shirra. You were saying something important."

She shook her head and continued.

"I knew Triana loved you, Michael, and I know God brought you two together and here are the twins, and yes, Rav who along with Try, by the way, could use a wee bit of work." She held out her hand and curled her forefinger down to within a half-inch of her thumb.

Pause. It was her turn to stare.

"Michael, nobody else listens to me when I talk so long."

"Well, probably not in English," said Michael with a half-smile.

She rolled her eyes to the ceiling, then closed them completely.

"Shirra. I could listen to you until outside light—though not much of it—comes through the window there." This time it was his hand in motion and his turn to point. His finger aimed at the small window in the wall beyond the end of the table. "I'm listening to every word. But

417

sorry, I love to watch...your hands...just out of the corner of my eye."

She opened her eyes and drilled them straight ahead.

"And to think you're the head of a church of — is it almost two hundred counting the children?" She clasped her hands together tightly to control them, which lasted no more than thirty seconds.

"It's 187," he declared, "with twenty-five or so who come and go."

"The other thing that's important here, Michael, is that you must never forget that I also deeply loved Triana. Michael, I am *alive* and I sit here talking to you while you stare at me because God used you and Triana to heal me, while all Noli could do was turn his head and throw up. I'll never forget that day. And Michael" — he sensed a change coming — "you should never forget that now *little Shirra is older than her marana, Triana, was when you married her.* And" — she pointed straight at him — "you, in spite of how young you act, are getting old."

"I see," Michael said. "And I heard this the other two times you mentioned it." He'd been called a lot of things at odd times, but was he at 26 — or was it 27 or more in Earth years? — this was a first. No question about it, he was on Elphia, not Earth.

"It was time for me to become a missionary," Shirra continued.

"And let me tell you what happened to me. Looking back, I think I went about it badly. But I was scared, Michael, that you or my father wouldn't let me go, and I couldn't tell either one of you what was *first* behind my wanting to do this.

"Since I'd worked so hard on my English which I speak well now, thank you, *so you, Michael, can understand me*, a little better than you know and speak Elphian, though you're not bad" — her hands were back in motion — "and since I helped you with all that translation work, Triana had already given me one of her English Bibles. I packed it, also my translation of Matthew into Elphian, and some other things and sneaked on a boat at night. It's not that hard, by the way, for a girl to get on a boat.

"And by God's grace I made it safely to Balara, and by His grace He let me throw up so much on the way there that when the sailors discovered me at sea they left me alone. Then by God's grace one family traveling on my boat pitied me and—yes—protected me on my fool-hearted, but very sincere, adventure. When they saw how well I got along with their children, they hired me on the spot to look after their two older ones while they attended to their two babies.

"When we landed in Balara and they discovered I had no place to go, they insisted that I could not stay around the docks alone, so they took me into their home, until through their connection to Braygan, the Lord Mayor of Balar, the port city and largest city on the island, I went to live with him and his family on their estate.

"Oh Michael, I'm sorry! Too many details!"

"Not yet, Shirra. Keep going."

"But Michael…"

He put the second half of the piece of bread still on her melty plate to her lips, and when she opened her mouth to speak, he pushed it further in. To get even, she did the same thing to him with his bread. Then he rose, went to the kitchen, and this time he returned with the tea.

"Continue."

"My more than two years at The Lord Mayor's had a startling first day. As my protector delivered me to the man's estate, I met the Lord Mayor and his wife at the doorway as they were in a hurry on their way out. Some details here I can't avoid. Immediately, the man greeted me gruffly, though his wife later held back a bit and took me aside and whispered, 'Don't worry, my dear, he's not as bad as he sounds.' Lord Braygan said they'd be back soon, but emphasized that the rooms off the hallway upstairs were totally off-limits. Then without explanation they were gone.

"In their parlor, I sat. Two servants came and went, keeping an eye on me, and bringing me delicious things to eat and drink.

419

"As I sat alone I took out my Bible to read. That's when God spoke to me in a way like He never had before, or since.

"'GO UPSTAIRS,' He said. I protested mildly but who was I to argue with God? Up a beautiful winding staircase I went. As quietly as I could, I proceeded down a long hallway. There were four doors. On the fourth door there was a lock that needed a key on the outside but, as I soon found out, it could be opened from the inside.

"'KNOCK ON THE DOOR IN MY NAME,' came the voice again.

"So I did.

"I knock on this door in the name of the God-Son who I know as Jesus," I announced.

"What do you want?" came the sound of a child's voice.

"Open the door and come out," I said without thinking.

"Five minutes later, out came a barefoot boy about 10-years-old wearing a karpon that seemed two sizes too small.

"'Who are you?' he asked.

"'I am Shirra, from Elphia and a believer in the God-Son who I call Jesus. I am here for a visit.

"He stood, turned, and walked to a window…seeming to be very confused.

"There, Michael, I'm giving too many details."

"No," said Michael, riveted to his seat. He could hear light snoring coming from the sofa.

"More details are for another night—if I'm still here, Michael. But let me put things together. His name was Payton. The minute Payton's parents came home, their lives were changed forever. The boy had been upstairs in a coma for two years, which explains his initial confusion. Physically, like with my leg, he was totally and completely healed. After I explained to his parents what had happened, and Lord Braygan saw I knew things, and I had a passion for this God that he unknow-

420

ingly hungered for, they couldn't do enough for me. Lord Braygan and his wife quickly followed their son and became believers in the God of Heaven.

"The next day I even privately baptized them in his pond in the side yard. When they saw I had almost nothing to put on after that, Beth Braygan, his wife, began outfitting me with beautiful and work-able clothes—a project we both enjoyed. And soon I got to know her very well. In turn, Beth Braygan, Payton, and I made copies of my translation of St. Matthew into Elphian. Quietly at first, I led Bible stud-ies in their home and I did the best I could to teach about the Bible and Jesus, as well as immediately becoming Payton's and his brothers' and sisters' tutor until the day I left. Their house was big enough for a small church and one slowly began, and I actually did the teaching there.

"After a quiet beginning there came an explosion of interest in the God of Heaven that, because of certain detractors, had to be carefully managed.

"Then seven months ago I learned that Triana had been murdered. It tore me apart, Michael. I slipped away to my room in tears. I pulled out my clothing bag from the closet and began to fill it with clothes.

" 'Whatever are you doing, Shirra?' came a voice from behind me. It was Beth Braygan.

" 'My marana has been killed and I must go see Michael!' I de-clared.

" 'Yes, you must go and see him'—she paused and stared deep-ly into my eyes—'but not now. Others now can help him grieve, but you…you must wait.'

" 'Wait?' I said.

" 'Shirra, look at me. I am now your marana, whether or not you think you're too old for it. Sometimes, God can speak fast, and He just told me. And my husband will make it official whether you like it or not! Your mother died when you were a young girl—and I'…' "

421

Michael reached across the table and took her hand.

" 'And I…' —Can this be a klepta-*type* secret Michael?"

"Yes."

" 'And I know your heart,' Beth told me.

" 'Yes, Marana,' I said.

" 'Shirra, you are our only Bible teacher and Sabbath After worship leader. We still have so much to learn about God. And, my dear girl, *I* have much more to share with you. Noli' —yes, Michael, we had occasional contact with him —'can keep us informed about what's happening in Elfend.'

" 'Yes, Marana,' I said."

Shirra paused.

"Is there more?" Michael asked.

"Yes, Michael. Twice after Triana's death I saw Noli and we prayed together. He understands things. 'If someone wants to be Jesus' disciple, he must leave all behind for Him,' he told me. Balar badly needed me then, he said. Though it really disturbed him, he would still say nothing to my father, or you, about where I was, but he would tell me if and when Elfend needed me. And here I am."

"And?" said Michael.

"And there's much more for *numbers on one of MY clocks.* Just think about that, Michael!" He loved seeing her curiosity at work on things she was dying to find out about.

"There's one thing more I'll share just a piece of, but I need to keep it secret for a while. Do you mind?"

"Do I have a choice?"

"Not really. It's sort of like a klepta-type secret."

"I see." Michael tried not to smile.

"And this 'thing'?"

"It's partly horrible and partly good but it can wait." He shook his head and smiled in defeat. If he waited long enough, he knew he'd learn everything he needed to know. He may be "old" but the night was still young, God had given him seven hours of deep sleep, and if he knew any Elphian at all, he knew her. Michael thanked God for her return and prayed for help in staying on the long paved road regardless of how narrow it became.

"It's time for a walk," he told Shirra.

*   *   *   *   *

2 minutes later (10 PM)

[6] *Genesis 25*

When Michael stood and his chair scraped the floor, the two holy women came to life.

"We're going for a walk in the Stadium," Michael declared, daring contradiction. "Just for an hour—or two at most." Galandra seemed surprisingly accepting while Noleen argued against it. After Noleen lost, she removed her own karpona cord and tied it around Shirra's waist, underlining her concern. She glared at Michael. How sallow she must think he was!

He promised her and Shirra that he wouldn't do something dumb like push her under the waterfall and get her good clothes wet like crazy boys sometimes do when walking girls at night.

They proceeded down the hallway to the door that led to the tunnel. Soon they were walking on the graveled pathway. Shells and cinders crunched under their feet.

423

Though he lightly held her hand, in her other hand she carried a small bag that she'd plucked from her tote. Neither spoke until they came to the first Earthball court, where someone had forgotten to put away a ball. Shirra picked it up and eyed it strangely.

"It's just an Earthball, like when you were here two years ago," Michael said, with a touch of superiority. She threw the ball up and it bounced off the backboard far to the left. He smiled.

"A contest, Shirra? Okay? The best out of 10. If I don't get more than you, I'll stand under the waterfall." See, I can distract you just as easily as you do me, he thought, smiling.

"That's not fair, Michael. And it's stupid. Besides, how can I really play a game if I'm not at risk?"

"It's plenty fair. Besides you're a —"

"The holy women would kill you if you lose."

"Me lose? Ha. Here goes. Watch carefully." He stepped to the free throw line.

He shot 10 times making 7, just barely missing 2 other shots.

Then Shirra stepped to the line. Something about how she began made Michael feel uneasy. Her first shot hit the rim then bounced away. Without a glance in his direction, the second ball dropped cleanly through, as did shots 3, 4, 5, 6, and 7. The 8th shot rolled around the rim before dropping through the net. Then the 9th shot went cleanly through without touching the rim. With only a glance his way, she tossed the Earthball to Michael who wasn't expecting it, hitting him in the stomach.

"I stop," she announced. "You're safe, Michael, I'm dropping out of the contest. No one wins."

"Wwwhaaatt…in…the…wooorld…"

He stared at the girl he thought he knew so well, and had spent so much time with for so many years. Triana could never have done this.

Nor would she have tried, and if she had, she wouldn't have backed out. Who was this girl anyway?

"I practiced every day, Michael, except, of course, on the Sabbath. Lord Braygan had his own private Earthball court. I loved it. Many love Earthball in Balar. I shot free throws alone in the evening when I wanted to think.

"Now, Michael, I want to go back with you to where Triana is buried."

Without a word—what could he say?—they turned around and went back the way they'd come, passing the tunnel opening and proceeding to the Tabernacle more than a couple of hundred feet further, where Triana had been buried. They sat on a special bench a half dozen feet from her stone marker.

Engraved on the stone were the words [in Elphian]:

TRIANA HAMMOND
daughter of Elphia
Princess of Emryss
klepta of Michael
child of God

"Michael, I'm just 'Little Shirra' now. Is that okay?"

"It's okay, Shirra."

She got up, walked up to the marker, knelt, and hugged it like a pillow and still a few more tears quietly came. Came to both of them. Finally, he gently pulled, lifted, and carried little Shirra away in his arms and sat on the bench. He raised her feet to the bench so she sat sideways on his lap. She looped her arms gently around his neck and interlocked her fingers as if letting go would cause her to fall away. Neck to neck, she held herself there limply, resting her chin first against his, then on

...letting go would cause her to fall away.

his shoulder. He'd never held her like this before, or seen her so vulnerable. After he permitted himself one special kiss on her forehead, the last of her special eyes finished washing themselves away. Her bravado disappeared.

A quarter hour later he started to help her stand.

"Five more minutes," she whispered. He sank back. He rubbed her back and could feel her strength slowly return. He sensed she was opening a new door that would ask him to enter.

He set her on her feet and he stood.

"Michael?"

"You're so beautiful, Shirra!" he found himself repeating.

She pulled hair out of her face.

"Michael, how can I take you seriously?"

"Easy. Just ignore silly comments and ask some serious questions."

For ten seconds she was silent. She stared as if seeing him for the first time.

"Okay…Michael, are Elphians 'gentiles'?"

Again, how did she switch like this? But this certainly wasn't the first time. He'd better be careful.

"Michael, I mean really is there a special people on ELPHIA (the planet) that are descended from a special people like descendants of 'Jacob' son of 'Isaac' son of 'Abraham' who had seven other sons. Would the—"

"Stop, Shirra, Abraham had one other son, Ishmael. Everybody who goes to church—on Earth—knows that. It's a small mistake, but we have to be careful about things like that if we're going to translate and teach. Shirra, on Earth we're adopted into God's family through Abraham. That way there are millions of children of Abraham!"

"Michael, I'm talking about the eight sons of Abraham that are named in your Bible."

"Shirra, there's Isaac and Ishmael, just two, that's all. And there's important stories about both of them."

"Michael, you're not going to be mad at me if I'm right and you're wrong, are you?" Her voice sounded so sweet and kind that Michael shivered. But he wouldn't be patronized.

"I will stand under the waterfall if I'm wrong on this. Shirra, you're making a silly mistake! We can't make silly mistakes like this — or with each other!"

"Please take that back, Michael."

"Never!"

She reached into the small bag she was carrying. Had he somehow set himself up? She pulled out her Bible. Fortunately, there was a full moon overhead; it was the larger of the two.

"Okay, Michael" — carefully she found the page she was looking for — "Here they are: Of course, there are Isaac and Ishmael, but here in Genesis 25:1-2. "Abraham took another wife, named Keturah. She bore him, 'Zimran, Jokshan, Medan, Midian, Ishbak, and Shuah,' and Midian, if you recall became quite a trouble-maker."

*   *   *   *   *

One hour later (11:45 PM)

[7] Getting Dry

Galandra was first to greet them when they came through the door from the tunnel. Michael carried his shoes and left wet footprints in the hallway.

"And how is everyone?" she asked.

"We are still carefully wrapped up," said Michael.

"And?" asked Galandra, noticing the wet footprints.

"Let me handle this, Michael," said Shirra. "Among other things, Michael showed me Triana's grave. We both knelt and cried there. On the way back Michael decided to wash his hands." *Which was really true.* "He got too close to the edge of the pool and with the water spray from the falls, and because he was so tired—he is older, you know—he slipped in." *Also true. He did actually slip as he stood on the edge.* "Then he had trouble getting out, slipping on the bottom." *Also true. But the larger reason was that he wanted to see how close he could come to drowning himself.*

"Since you see I am also wet," Shirra continued, "but just in the front, I helped him climb out." *Also true to a small extent.* "And since there was no towel there, I had to help dry him off, and my soft karpona helped with that. Of course, since I was tied up with Noleen's cord, the only way I could do that was to hold him close to me. And now the cord is impossible to untie."

He could still feel Shirra's willing embrace. "Come closer, Michael," she had said. Those three words he would never forget. And he obeyed. He could have stood there forever, humiliated, wet, freezing, still very much alive.

Noleen stepped forward and picked at the knot without success.

"Let me do this," said Galandra, producing one of the knitting needles. The cord finally loosened. Galandra, with eyes daring Michael to object, sent Shirra to find something to wear from the bedroom he never visited anymore, while he got a fresh karpon from his office-bedroom.

Those things done, they returned to their regular places at the small table. Michael found and lit a candle. Tea and bread and jam appeared as if out of nowhere. Also the wrinkled, flattened plastic plates returned, perhaps because Michael had made such a fuss about their importance.

"I suspect you still haven't finished," said Galandra, one not to mince words, offering one of her longer sentences.

*   *   *   *   *

12:00 AM (still Day 8 until sunset)

[8] Back to Business

The hot tea this time was really welcome. Back at their regular seats Michael noticed by the candlelight that her eyes had again quickly been repaired.

"Shirra, you didn't tell on me."

"Michael, I told all that was necessary. The rest of our time in the Stadium was special. At least it was for me. I wouldn't trade it for anything. It's my treasure even if I have to carry it alone. There's no one besides you I need to share it with."

"I'm so, so sorry. Can you forgive me?" asked Michael.

"For what?"

"The earthball part when I was riding my horse too high."

"That part?" she laughed. "I'd almost forgotten. I was thinking of the last part."

"Will you forgive me for both parts?" Michael repeated.

Quickly, she pointed to the ceiling. Michael stood. He could smell her delightful perfume which had also been refreshed. If being sallow was part of his baggage, it didn't seem to bother her.

"Remember now, Michael, go easy, the hawks are watching!" Leaning over the table, she presented the longest kiss the Gatehouse had recently seen. Since it was *her* kiss, she extended her hands across the ta-

430

ble palm to palm against Michael's. Too soon she pushed herself away, and stood up straight ending it. "That's all the 'yes' you get. Now, let's get back to business so they can get back to sleep." She glanced at the holy women.

Michael reached deep for control. His head stopped spinning as an idea emerged.

"Let's do the 'IF game,' " he suggested.

"Okay, Michael, but this is a game I haven't *practiced*." How could she answer so quickly? Michael ignored the implication.

"To start, remember it's '*IF*.' When Christian young people, like many I have to talk to, want to become klepta and kleptor, this is helpful." Quickly, he found and handed her several sheets of paper and a couple of pencils. "Are you ready?"

In a flash she pulled two more pencils from her tote and a knife to sharpen them if necessary.

"I think so."

He knew she could never say No to something like this.

He watched as she put her name and a date and title at the top of her first page as she'd done for years working with letters and words in Elphian or English, with occasional strands of long black hair drifting down until she would stop, whisk them back and tie them down without seeming to interrupt whatever she was working on. Again she was at work on something before they'd even started. He watched, knowing that he could never look at her again in the same old way.

And why was this so brand-new? What had come over him?

Now, obviously, there were other things to explore.

What of their past?

Their love for the same woman who'd suddenly been killed?

The children Triana had given birth to and they had raised — with Shirra never far away?

And the church here, and now a new one in Balar? Esther Crandel's railroad crossing picture flashed into his mind: RR. He must be real—he couldn't deny what he felt—and right, of course.

He might be a fool, but he felt sure he'd done nothing wrong with Shirra *so far*. But if everything wasn't quickly put in its "proper place," things could fall apart and many could be hurt. Shirra seemed to care for Triana as much as he did. What did this mean? And he and Triana had deeply loved each other. But now Triana was with God. And Shirra was not Triana and only slightly older than Triana was when he first met her, and she knew all this better than anyone. But what would she think later? Later, if *what?*

And what would his own feelings be?

A decision had to be quickly made.

So much was at stake.

*   *   *   *   *

Immediately follows (12:15 AM, still Day 8 until sunset…)

[9] The "IF Test"

Here's what you're to do…And I'll be doing the same thing. If…and let me emphasize 'if.' If you were looking for a kleptor, and I of course a klepta, what would be the *three most important things* you would want from that person in your marriage. And I'll assume you want a Christian who loves and serves God so you don't have to say that. We'll both write for several minutes, and when I sense we're done, we'll stop and share what we've written. Is that okay?"

432

She nodded without hesitation. That was so much like her!

"Let's start," he said.

She'd laid out her pencils and a knife as if she were preparing instruments for surgery — or for war. She paused deathly still, and stared out the window into nothing but darkness for at least ten seconds before frantically starting to write. The holy women, sensing a change in pace, despite the hour, refilled the teacups.

Now just what should *he* write? Strangely, while the idea looked good, and he'd used it with others, he'd never seriously considered this for himself. With Triana, great things had just happened. They'd risked their lives together. And had survived. Life hadn't been perfect but oh my! And now he was supposed to be older and wiser. But how tangled life had become with Triana's absence. And the sleepless nights. Ten minutes passed. Shirra had written what looked like a full page and she was still going strong — just like she talked. Michael had yet to write his first word.

"Faithfulness," he mumbled to himself. That's it!

#1 Faithfulness he would value most. Faithfulness in marriage. Faithfulness in keeping private things private. Faithfulness in family responsibilities, keeping records, loving her kleptor and children through thick and thin, in sickness and in health, all that.

Now #2. Hmm. He looked across the table. Shirra was nearly finished with her second sheet of paper. Whatever was she saying? What could he ever put down for Number 2?

*   *   *   *   *

[10] *The Dinner Candle*

"**T**ime's up."

Michael covered the few words he'd written. He asked Shirra to go first.

"I beg permission," she began, "to let my comments be put in a specific con-text" — underlining the word in the air as she let slip a quick smile — "referring to Elfend, and in a few cases Balar, though they may fit in many other places. I can only make sense about places I know."

"Permission granted," said Michael.

"For my Number 1: I would want my kleptor to provide a dinner candle every night for dinner with a different holder for each of the four seasons which vary, though ever so slightly in the mountain, as the days pass.

"Further I would like my kleptor to allow me to move this candle to the desk in front of the window of my own office, which has a door that closes, bookshelves and worktables for all that I and my children have to do: reading, writing, and playing. This candle which will eventually burn out during the day he must replace each evening with a new one and as long as it is lit it must be available to me at all times when I might need, or want, it regardless of daylight or electric light used around it.

"My hope is that this candle will be used, eventually in a house in the Stadium, near a tunnel with a waterfall nearby, for my children and me who prefer, if at all possible, not to live forever in a rock cave, even with large cracks that only allow some sunlight, but no open sky.

"And this candle is one that can be lit by my bedside when…when I desire. There's more, but this is the kind of new candle I want on my table for every evening meal. That's Number 1 for me: I want a special candle that can remind me of, and lead me to things I think about.

"Your turn, Michael."

Pause.

"Hmm. That's quite a candle! Number 1 for me is faithfulness. A klepta should…"

Michael was interrupted by a head peeking around the corner.

It was Try.

"My turn," Michael announced before the holy women could interfere. Quickly he walked the boy back to his bedroom.

Later, he learned, while he was gone, Galandra handed Shirra a letter with the seal on it. He tucked his own sparse "If" notes away out of sight.

*   *   *   *   *

1:00 AM

[11] In the Last Bedroom

"**D**addy, I had a bad dream," said Try as the two of them entered the third and last bedroom, now with twin beds. Rav was also awake. He lay there with a sad look. "In my dream, Shirra waved goodbye and moved away, away so far that as I watched, she just disappeared. Rav also says she's leaving."

The door opened and Em entered. "Is she going to where Mommy is?" she asked. "I miss Mommy. I have no mareena now, just my marana. And is she going to leave us, Daddy?"

435

"I don't know," said Michael.

"Is it time for the huddle thing?" asked Rav.

"That's a good idea," said Michael.

So they huddled in the center of the room and prayed.

"Now," said Em, "tell us a story about Shirra. Tell us about how you and Mommy met her."

"Don't forget the part about the bone sticking out," said Rav.

*   *   *   *   *

1:40 AM

[12] *The Sealed Letter*

When Michael returned, Shirra was standing beside the table. She handed him the letter. It was addressed to her.

"Galandra said it was time to give me this. She also said I should probably read it before sharing it with you…if I ever did. It is from Triana."

"When did she give it to her? And what did it say?" asked Michael.

"Don't you see it? It's *sealed.* Galandra said Triana handed it to her more than two years ago before I had left and Triana, of course, was very much alive."

"Have the holy women read it?"

"Michael, look, it's sealed. Even more, judging from the outside, it's written in English."

"Why haven't you opened it?"

"Regardless of what it says, Michael, I want you with me, so we can

436

read it together—even the first time. We both loved her."

She slipped her arm around his waist, not caring if the whole world beyond the holy women saw. Michael broke the seal, opened the letter without looking at it, and handed it back to her. Shirra without even scanning it, began to read:

"Dear Shirra, We live in dangerous times, more so than I think Michael realizes. Last night I had a strange dream, and in it I was traveling upward faster and faster toward a marvelous golden light. Still the thought that controlled me was that I was leaving behind my beloved Michael, my two children, and my Elphian home. I don't think my dream was necessarily about Heaven, because to be in God's presence will be joyful and without worry."

She paused.

"I can't read the next part." She handed the letter to Michael.

"And in my dream," continued Michael, *"I was worried and concerned, so I have written to you as your marana, and my third wonderful child. You are on the verge of being a desirable woman who can make some man very happy.*

"Lately I have had the premonition – "

"What's 'pre-mo-ni-tion' Michael?" Shirra interrupted.

"It's a...a feeling that something bad will happen," he replied.

"Oh."

Michael continued.

"Lately I have had the premonition that I may not have long to live. Shirra, if something happens to me, and you are willing, and he is willing, nothing would make me happier than for you to become – "

"Your turn." He handed the paper back to Shirra.

"....to become Michael's klepta. If so, and if you're willing, you may wear my ring, which has a story behind it because I was not first to wear it. I've told Michael several times that if I die first, I do not want to be buried with it. Shirra, Michael needs someone day and night to keep him on the right track,

and to continue the work God has called us to do. I can't tell you what Heaven is like, but Jesus said there is no marriage there. But if somehow – "

The paper went back to Michael.

"But if somehow the three of us were standing there in the world to come, even though you might marry young, you would never stand behind me in Michael's presence, but you would stand beside me, if not ahead of me. Shirra, not are you only going to be a beautiful woman, but you are a very gifted one who, in the absence of the lost I-Rex Code – which I believe so important – can put God's Word into your people's hands.

"And as to the beauty I mentioned, here is a secret about Michael which I profoundly respect – "

"Hand me that!" Shirra pulled the letter away.

"Okay, but you have to read that out loud!" said Michael.

"…here is a secret about Michael that I profoundly respect. Michael finds a woman most interesting when, yes, she takes care of herself, is confident enough to be carefully wrapped, or perhaps the better way to say it is 'attired' in beautiful clothes that make a man first seek her eyes. You have wonderful eyes and are perfect for that. And, of course, with Michael, there is much more."

To catch her breath, she stopped, and held up the page between them so that it covered her face, all but her eyes that had been refixed. Michael offered a small smile and his finger made a small check mark in the air.

Immediately, she continued.

"There is the matter of my children, my special joy, Trivan and Émrica. Though their bodies contain the blood of three worlds, a marker for revival in Elphia, they are ordinary children, though remarkably smart. They need careful training. They can fool their father, but I know you are too clever for them.

"Of course, assuming I die first, God may lead each of you to others to marry. If so, follow what God wants. The holy women, who I've long trusted,

438

have instructions to destroy this letter if that occurs. Of course, while I'm alive, he's all mine. Michael is a treasure. I have plans." – She paused – "But God has plans that are bigger than mine or Michael's. My prayer is always that I may fit into those plans, or else go to join my Heavenly Father. I hope you will always do the same. With all my love, Triana."

*   *   *   *   *

2:15 AM

[13] The Sofa

Passing a letter back and forth between two readers taking turns in the middle of the night to a listening audience of two who didn't even understand the language of what was being said, had to be strange.

While Shirra headed for the bathroom, Michael sat at the table and stared at the wall. No more food, no more tea.

Shirra returned and headed for the sofa. Where else could she go? The sofa was unusually large. The holy women had awakened and spread apart, offering, so to speak, a space to sit between them so it had to be safe. It was too good to resist. It had been offered, she would accept. So she sat, filling the empty space, leaned back and closed her eyes. Michael stood at the table and pondered. Before his first thought began, however, Galandra motioned for him to come over. His legs obeyed. She set the bag with her knitting on the floor and scooted to the very end to make room. Michael, pressing his arms down to his sides, sat down between Galandra and Shirra, careful not to touch either.

"Rest tongues," said Galandra, touching the tip of hers. "Both

439

tongues need rest."

Galandra then dramatically shifted her weight more to the center pushing him squarely into Shirra, her eyes never opening. His arm was pinched in. This wasn't his doing! What was the holy woman thinking!

"Arm more comfortable over girl's shoulder," suggested Galandra. It took him less than a second to discover that was true. And though both were fully clothed it took only seconds more to feel her warmth from the scar on her leg up to her cheek. Her head, with eyes closed, slowly tucked itself under his chin. Her eyes were already closed. He ran his fingers through her long silky hair suddenly exposing an ear. Automatically his face leaned down for a quick kiss, and while her eyes remained locked, her arm drifted up across his chest. He pulled her even closer. He had never held her this way before. What was he thinking? He was doomed. Let the holy women think what they would...or object.

They didn't.

*   *   *   *   *

7 AM

[14] *The Awakening*

Michael dreamed. In Pennsylvania he'd heard of "bundling," the old practice of men and women sleeping together with their clothes on, but it was always smiled at and never discussed. Long ago, the famous preacher Jonathan Edwards, in spite of the perpetual shortage of beds in wintery Colonial America, had from the pulpit put a dagger to the strange practice observed here and there, even by Christians, in New England and Wales. But, despite half-sitting up for

440

the rest of the night, Michael felt a peace that he'd almost forgotten. It had to be from God. And Shirra? Still sound asleep next to the one she'd claimed she belonged to—safely walled-in by holy women with long pointed knitting needles within arm's reach.

*   *   *   *   *

The time eventually came to wake up. Someone was moving on the sofa. He would hold his eyes shut a few seconds more. Then a warm body slowly twisted to his left, then came a light kiss on his left ear. Followed by an imperceptible nibble. Then on his right ear came another kiss. A wet slobbery one.

WHOA! Something's wrong here!

Slowly, he slightly opened his eyes, then immediately sat up. Em, smiling, tumbled backwards against Galandra who was trying not to laugh.

"Daddy, I didn't know your eyes could get as big as Shirra's!" Em declared.

Michael struggled to stand but his legs weren't ready.

"Uhh"

Shirra covered his mouth. "Stay put, Michael," she whispered into the nibbled ear. "I'll handle this."

"Em, you're just not being fair!" said Shirra. "It's my turn! Nobody will kiss my ears!" Shirra said. She pointed to her own ear and Em bounced over Michael, doubling him up, and planted a slobbery kiss on Shirra's ear that was closest to Noleen, who couldn't help but laugh. All the while, Try and Rav sat on the floor across the room their backs against the wall staring like zombies, their eyes large and their mouths hanging open.

Shirra whispered in Em's ear, and suddenly Noleen was receiving

441

an ear kiss, and laughing louder than Michael thought she was possible of. Noleen, then whispered in Em's ear and pointed to the boys. Em flew towards them.

"NOOOOO!" They fled down the second hallway, Em right behind them.

"Michael, I have some urgent business down that hallway. I'll tell you what happens later," said Shirra. "The bathroom is yours if your legs can wake up." In seconds she was at the end of the hall outside the boys' room. They were inside, holding the door shut. She pointed Em to her own room next to her father's and told her to go there and wait.

"Boys, it's just me, so open up," said Shirra.

Immediately the knob turned.

"I promise you you're safe," she declared. "Now is there a possibility that I don't have to leave after breakfast today? Remember my list? Are you doing your part?"

"We're working on it, Marana," said Try through the door that was just cracked open, welcoming a change in direction. "We'll get it all done," added Rav.

"Do I have to check?"

"No...no, not now..."

Shirra proceeded to Em's room, closing the door behind her. Everything was perfect. "I have an ear-kiss just for you," said Shirra, "and notice it's almost totally dry." And Shirra gave her one. That and what happened next Shirra told Michael later.

"Since you were together," Em had said, "does that mean I'll have a sister? I need a sister, Shirra."

"No, Em. There's more to it than that. Last night we talked so long, and thank you for letting us, that we got very tired. So the holy women asked us to sit by them to rest. And we fell asleep there just like you saw us." Shirra glanced to the floor.

"Em, that's plenty for now. That is, except for one very important thing: God only wants kleptas and kleptors who belong to each other to have babies. And certainly not men who sleep with kleptinis who come and go and make no real promises to the men or the babies they make.

"And I am not your daddy's klepta."

"Why not? Mommy's gone to God. I know Daddy loves you. Then are you his kleptini?"

"NO, Em, I am not, and I will never be!"

"Why?"

"Because God doesn't want girls to be kleptinis. I am a 'God's girl.'"

"Then I'm a 'God's girl,' too."

"Good for you! And Em, even if I end up somewhere else and not here, you can come to me for girl talk anytime. You will always be special to me."

"I love you, Shirra."

There was a knock at the door. Em opened it. It was Michael.

"What's going on in here? Breakfast is ready."

"Girl talk," said Em, without looking up.

*   *   *   *   *

8:00 AM

[15] The Gatehouse Council

Michael had gotten only the briefest warning.

Lemron arrived early to explain and make sure that the eight who would come had reasonably comfortable places to sit. The sofa belonged to **Galandra** and **Noleen**, the holy women. **Michael** specially requested a dinner-table chair for himself just behind the center of the room, and another for a "companion" who would soon appear.

Dr. Hartlin had taken aside **Klingor,** who was the last man to arrive, which was unusual for him, but then he was barely on speaking terms with Lemron, who'd begged him to stay calm. He told him that **Shirra,** who her father still hadn't seen, but who'd arrived in good health only hours earlier would be here, and would make an exciting and full explanation to everyone about her absence. Further, she'd put Michael into a complicated situation that still needed to be worked out. *God and the church had to come first,* said Hartlin, and if Klingor were looking for someone to blame, it should be Lemron or him. He ignored, however, mentioning the role his fisherman friend **Noli** who was also coming, had played in Shirra's disappearance, as well as the small part Galandra had played.

The children were ordered to stay home from school. If important things happened so Shirra wasn't immediately made to leave, they must do their part. They must politely greet each person who arrived, and then promptly disappear into their rooms when told to. If they disobeyed, Shirra may have to leave forever.

As to the previous chores list that Shirra had made, Em had personally inspected it, and after some small changes Em had ordered, she reported to Shirra that everything had been completed.

The men one by one had arrived.

By 8:10 all were seated except for the three women.

Michael knocked on the "unused" bedroom door.

It opened and Galandra and Noleen, with Shirra between them, entered. Michael was stunned when he saw the girl that he'd had spent the night with. The luxurious karpona, had been dried and freshened, her eyes and lashes and cheeks delicately redone, and her characteristic perfume reapplied. She had taught in Balara, but from the Lord

Mayor's wife she'd learned important lessons as well, adding to those from Triana earlier. Michael resisted touching her, or staring at her long, silky hair. Klingor suddenly stood, nearly knocking his chair over, tears filling his eyes. Lemron, who'd delicately prepared him for this, helped Klingor steady himself. After gliding to the center of the room, Shirra ran to her father and fell into his arms.

Finally, she pulled herself away, and bypassing the empty chair beside Michael, which he pretended not to notice, she carefully descended onto the sofa between the holy women who made room and smiled. What had these women done to her? Let everyone wonder about that! Michael stood. He recalled from the Emryss stories how royalty addressed the people around them when things mattered. As also did Jonas. It was a time to be honest, humble, firm, and open just enough, not embarrassed by what one didn't know.

"I will assume," he began, "that private, personal matters that arise will not leave this room unless we all agree that such things should be shared. The elders understand this already. If any of you cannot do this, then say so now, and we will be less candid."

No one challenged this.

"Let's all of us pray on our knees in the center of the room, as we often do, before we begin."

Without hesitation, everyone got up, gathered, and knelt. Then came the unexpected pitter-patter of smaller feet as the children suddenly appeared from nowhere and knelt between the adults in the cracks that seemed to open up. Several prayed aloud including one of the children. When they were finished, as the adults found their seats, the children cautiously eyed Shirra waiting for a signal.

"Go!" She pointed back to their rooms. In seconds they'd disappeared as if they'd never come except for a door that slammed behind them a little too loudly.

"The children matter," declared Michael, who remained standing.

445

"All the children of our church, and in particular the three who just left. "Shirra is good with them. She has come back and we have had a long talk under careful supervision, I assure you.

"And I love her," he declared.

"And I love Michael, too," declared Shirra without even glancing at him or offering further comment from several feet away between the holy women.

"And," said Michael, "I consider this meeting to be happening because of what she's going to say next. And"—he turned to catch Shirra's eye—"I want the children to return and hear this." Shirra, nodding agreement, stood and moved to the center of the room.

He hurried to the bedroom where they were pressed up against the door, and after a slight knock and nothing happened, he pushed and it sprang open, bumping Try sharply on the forehead.

"Go just around the corner and sit on the floor against the wall like stuffed animals. Quietly! Go quickly." And like the spies they sometimes were, they silently slunk into the indicated space just behind the adults on one side but where Shirra could still see them from the center. They arranged themselves side-by-side against the wall. But Try's face was red and it looked like he was forcing back tears.

"Excuse me," said Shirra. She glided over, knelt down, and inspected the bumped forehead. Then she bent over and kissed it. "Me, too," said Rav. "No, you just need a pat on top," she answered, which she delivered. And so not to seem partial, she did the same with Em. With his eyes Dr. Hartlin asked if he was needed, but Shirra smiled, waved him off, and stood in the center where she could easily see everyone. She began (her words, of course, in Elphian):

"The hardest thing for me to say to my father and all of you will be my first sentences after this one." She glanced at Galandra who was studying her, and forced her hands together, gently clenching her fingers.

446

"More than two years ago, for personal reasons, I believe God let me slip away quietly to Balara on my own, without telling anyone here, to tell people there about the God I so deeply love.

"I deeply apologize, deeply apologize, to my father who I love, my brother who I love, to Michael who I love and especially for not being at his side when Triana—my marana who I deeply loved—died, and others in the church that I love. I apologize for the worry and hurt I caused you. The only thing I can say in my defense is that in certain times and situations in the Bible and times later on, Christians on Earth have done similar things.

"In the Bible book of Matthew it says that if someone doesn't love Jesus—on Earth, anyway—more than anyone in his family, that person cannot be his disciple. I took that very seriously and I have asked God to forgive me for any sin in how I went about doing this. And I believe He has."

She paused. Her hands were still together. The effect was spell-binding. Michael was astonished.

"A second thing," she continued, "I can say is that God has taken care of poor little Shirra and blessed her in unbelievable, miraculous ways that if you let me tell you about, you will never forget them.

"God is at work in Balara."

For more than an hour Shirra recounted her Balarian adventure—the boat trip, the healing of Payton, and her close connection with Lord Mayor Braygan of the city of Balar and his family who had become Christian believers, and that she herself had baptized—the story still so fresh in Michael's memory.

Why she'd told no one about where she was, Shirra cited several reasons—though not all. At first, Braygan wanted a measure of secrecy as he learned about the God that so many around him knew nothing about, or considered silly superstition. He insisted they must be introduced to God but slowly. Besides, she was their only missionary. Then there was the delicate issue that maybe her father or Michael would interfere and force her to leave God's work and return too soon.

She didn't mention, however, that when she learned of Triana's death, as she'd told Michael, she'd delayed her return because she didn't want the new turn in her love to confuse him so soon in his expected six months of grieving to honor her memory. She said nothing about Noli's part in this. That could come later. And she said nothing about the strange package she'd sent by way of the holy women a month after the mourning period. That, she would insist, would remain secret forever.

Even more, she'd learned that the shocking, unexplainable, collective amnesia about the God of Heaven in Balara was even darker than on Elphia Island. She also realized she was the only Bible teacher, had the only Bible, and at first was the only baptizer. In her favor, she now had good connections in Balar, the major city, and the church was slowly growing.

And now Lord Bragan, who'd been astonished about what had happened to Lemron, had even encouraged her to make a return visit.

Eight months had passed since Triana's death. If her soul was in Heaven, how would Michael continue their ministry? Could she help, or would her presence just complicate things?

As she finished her presentation in Elphian, of course, the holy women who'd known only few details, were excited. Shirra offered a closing comment.

"If you forgive me and accept me back, I want you elders to tell me now, if you can, so I can continue work on our translations, spend time with our youth and other church members, and, perhaps, reach out in a larger way to others again in Balara."

At this point Michael saw her lips continue to move, but his ears went stone-cold deaf. Then came clear words he was sure were just for him: **Remember my Sabbaths and take the hand that is extended to you.** *Then his hearing suddenly returned as if nothing had happened. Shirra was still speaking.*

"Noli, who helped me get me back to Elphia" — Klingor's jaw dropped as he turned toward his friend — "has my permission here, or privately, to tell you more about me if you like. Unlike Triana, I am not anyone's special klepta. Or even an ordinary one.

"Thank you for listening to me." She returned to her seat between the holy women.

At once it was the seven listeners turn to stand. All did, and began applauding. *"Praise God! Praise God!"* began the holy women. But Michael's mind was elsewhere. "Balara" she'd just said. Would Lord Braygan "extend his hand to their church?" Or did this mean something else? What was going on? Everything was happening too fast. He must stay calm.

"Why are you not a klepta?" Lemron asked. Michael's mind braked to a stop.

"First," said Shirra, "I'm pretty choosy." Several laughed. "And second, I've not been asked."

All eyes except those of Shirra, who remained sitting, turned to Michael.

"Uh…This is quite sudden," he said.

"Has the Earth Prophet run out of words?" laughed Noli.

"Shirra is free to stay in the big bedroom," Michael offered, extending his hand. "That way she and I — "

"MICHAEL! Look at me!" interrupted Shirra, springing to her feet. Michael spun around. "I will under no circumstances live here!"

"But they kiss when they sit at the table over there," came a small voice from against the wall. Rav stood and pointed to the narrow table behind Michael.

There was a titter of laughter.

"And," said Try, "when they sleep between the holy women on the sofa over there Shirra kisses and bites Daddy's ear…but not hard." Klingor covered his face. Noli guffawed.

Galandra, however, saved the day: "But as boy Trivan say, it wasn't hard bite. I understand."

"But, Try," said Em, loud enough for everyone to hear, "when they're between the holy women it can't be bad. Shirra is a God's girl, and so am I!"

"Thank you, children!" said Shirra. "You have spoken the truth to the church leaders. But I have not been a KLEPTINI, I am not a KLEPTI-NI, and I will not be a KLEPTINI! Or *risk* becoming one. I'm leaving!"

"I will not be a kleptini, either," declared Em, righteously.

"But," said Shirra, pointing, "you will stay HERE, Émrica!"

"Yes, Marana."

"How can she be Marana if she leaves?" asked Rav.

Moving to the table, Shirra picked up her tote bag which somehow had returned to the handy place she first put it the day before.

"Where will you go, Shirra?" asked Klingor.

She turned to Michael.

"Michael, the promise I made to you long ago hasn't changed. But I'm NOT living here or working here anymore. I'll become a holy woman" — she paused and offered a little bow in their direction — "and live with them."

"NO!" pleaded Noleen, wringing her hands. "Michael, please, No…"

"Like Em has made it clear," said Shirra, "I'm a 'God's girl.' I will never be a kleptini. Michael, I can't ever be close to you again. Good-bye!"

In a flash, she was through the door and gone.

In a flash, too, before anyone could stop them, Try, Em, and Rav ran

450

out behind her.

"Galandra, what can I do?" Michael asked.

"Quite simple. You make choice. Girl make choice," answered Galandra.

Without shame, Michael walked over to the table where Shirra and he had spent so much time. He knelt alone and prayed. Then he stood and faced everyone.

"Help me. I'll do anything…anything…anything *right*!"

"Well then, you've just made it easier," said Lemron.

Just then the door burst open. In returned Shirra, Try and Rav who were each attached to an arm pulling, and Em who was pushing from behind. Shirra, not strongly resisting, looked uncharacteristically bewildered.

"Why did she come back?" Noli asked Galandra.

"Simple. Girl and boy make bad choices. Choices now change," said Galandra.

"What brought you back?" Klingor asked his daughter.

"People, Father! People waiting out there! They know I'm back. And…and even Lord Braygan from Balar was standing with them. At his feet was a large trunk—a trunk of my things! Help me, Father!"

It was Klingor's turn to surprise everyone.

"Shirra, all the help you need will come from the God of Heaven and the one who stands beside you. Now you must help me!" Everyone turned. The room became deathly silent. "To get here," said Klingor, "at my front door I had to step over a kleptini whose lover had just died and was not truly a widow. The young boy who was with her turned out to be an orphan but not her son. Never have I heard two so eager and ready to accept the God of Heaven."

"God has room for people like that," Galandra volunteered. She and Noleen seemed to make mental notes. Everyone now was smiling, perhaps not knowing what else to do.

Shirra whispered in Michael's ear. Michael pulled Try aside. "Try, quietly sneak away immediately to Noli and tell him to find out what I need to know about the boy. Talk to no one else. Someone in church must help them." Similarly, Shirra sent Em to Galandra. "Don't worry," said Michael to both of them. "Rav will look after me. We won't let Shirra go away again."

Attention flashed back to the two of them as they stood whispering.

"I have something — new — to say," Michael declared, "but before I can do that, Shirra and I must talk *privately* for a few minutes, so we're going in there." He pointed to the big unused bedroom. "Go, Shirra," he said gently.

Michael followed her to the bedroom door and through it, closing it tightly behind him.

Safely inside, Michael spoke first.

"Shirra, you've been so interested in klepta secrets. Let me show you one." He put his arms around her and kissed her.

Then they sat side by side on the edge of the bed.

"Uh...yes!" said Shirra. Her hands were shaking. Michael loved it on those rare times she didn't seem on top of everything, or thinking she was.

"The kiss isn't the secret," he said, gently pushing inches away. "I want to show you something." He untied the cord around his karpon.

"Michael, do you have your cargo shorts on under there?"

"No, I don't."

"Michael, you're scaring me." Her eyes grew large.

"And you're making me fall more deeply in love with you!" said Michael.

"Why?"

"Because you stand rock solid for what you believe, and yet you still trust me. But don't worry, at least just now. *Thanks to you* — remember your package? — I'm completely covered underneath." He pulled open the karpon. Here. He gently led her fingers to the right leg hem of his dinays.

Her face turned scarlet.

"Oh Michael, you didn't!"

"Oh yes I did. In fact, I was wearing them even *before* you came through the door yesterday morning and I've kept them on ever since. They even stayed on after the waterfall. That's why they're still a little damp."

"Why didn't you take them off when you changed your karpon?"

"You were here. These are special. You made these for me. And you're still here. Can't you see the tiny letters you sewed on at the bottom of the hem? Now I understand what they really mean."

"FFF...Michael, why did you keep these? I'm so embarrassed. I've never been more embarrassed in my life! My whole life...It's so *forward* — "forward" as Earth people would say. It was such a silly, foolish, thing to give you. I knew it the minute after I sent the package to the holy women to give you after the grieving time was over. Didn't you think it was weird?"

"Weird? Maybe, but mainly puzzled. You'd disappeared. I eventually thought you were probably dead. Then this package showed up.

"FFF," she announced. "Forever, Forever, Forever — in English. Eyefor, Eyefor, Eyefor in Elphian. I'll never forget that day God healed me!" She touched the letters again with her fingertips. Michael bit his lip.

"Nor I. The day I opened your package and wondered if somehow it just celebrated a memory. And, how did this ever get to me? I questioned what God thought about this. I couldn't understand why you left. Or bear to think about what became of you. I couldn't ruin what's happened here. So I tried to push your gift out of my mind." Quickly, he stood, pulled his karpon around him and retied the cord.

"All this sounds like a klepta secret, Michael."

"It *definitely* is. One right at the top of our list!"

"Can I add something of my own to this list?" She asked. "I did hear you say *our* list, by the way."

"Like what?"

How quickly she'd found another great moment to bargain. He cautiously nodded.

"Well, when you say 'Go,' I really don't mind, because I usually deserve it, and—this may sound strange—I love the sound of your voice when you say 'Go,' but I would like to add a part."

"Like what?"

"When *I* say 'Come,' will you do that for me without being ob-jec-tion-able?"

Michael marveled at her knowing and using such a word.

"I will on one condition."

"Which is?"

"Coming is different from going. A person can go far and in many directions, but one can only come so close—and in one direction. Now I love your eyes, and you know how to use them. If you wonder about how close I should come when you ask, will you tell me by talking with your eyes? That is, without rolling them like you are now?"

"Okay…okay, but can I also beckon with my finger, since you like to watch my hands so much!"

"If you don't make a big show of it."

"It's a deal!"

Deal? How Earthlike it sounded! His handshake turned into another kiss.

"This is *really private* klepta stuff, you understand!" said Michael.

454

"So?" whispered Shirra, letting her eyes grow large. She stepped back. "I noticed"—she started to point but dropped her finger—"you did say, 'our klepta list.' Does this mean anything else?"

"Of course...Will you be my klepta?" he asked, trying to sound matter-of-factly.

"When?"

"As soon as those outside let us."

"YES!"

They embraced.

"One more little thing. Try's terrified that Em's going to bite his ear. Could you talk with her?"

"I will immediately, Michael!"

*   *   *   *   *

10 minutes later

[16] Calendar Issues

Regardless of how they felt at the moment, both Michael and Shirra had the steel to stand before a crowd. Stand and speak their minds. The crowd inside numbered nine—Lemron, Klingor, Dr. Hartlin, Noli, Galandra, Noleen, Try, Em, and Rav—and sounds from outside indicated soon facing many more.

Such an opportunity had arrived.

"On Earth," announced Michael, "we often begin some important things this way." Standing beside Shirra, he dropped down on one knee. The children, taken off guard, suddenly thinking he might tip over, bent over and put their hands on his shoulders. "I love you so very, very much," he said just loud enough for all to hear, "even when you were a little girl and sometimes a vanchi." With that she delivered a little eye kiss—that is, a kiss *with* her eyes—that no one but Michael and the children, down at his level, saw. "You have brought Triana and me hours of joy and happiness as you worked diligently at our sides. You have taught me so much.

"And above all, you love the God of Heaven more than me or anything else.

"I forgot to say something important before you ran out a few minutes ago:

"Will you be my klepta?

"I will burn a special candle every night, in a special holder, not just for every season, but every month we are together on Elphia...or wherever else God might put us."

Then came the quietest five seconds of the day as she looked down and studied his face.

"Yes, Michael, I will be your klepta," she said so matter-of-factly it sent shivers down his spine. "I will love you with all my heart and will love the three children you and Triana have brought to us, and any others that God may bring. And more than that, I will remember and cherish the times the three of us—the two of us and Triana—were together over the years. I am alive in my body and my soul because of you both."

Em's eyes got large.

Kissing her hand, Michael stood.

"And when can we do this?" Michael asked aloud to no one in particular.

"Dr. Hartlin," asked Lemron, "Are they ready? Ready *now*?"

"Yes, they are ready now," answered Hartlin, "if she can give him time to breathe."

456

"Are you willing?" Lemron asked Klingor.

"I am," he answered.

"And *right now!*" underlined Noli, now standing by Try.

This caused a stir among the holy women. They stood and side-by-side approached Lemron.

"No! We must have the girl two full days *first*! We are not done with her. She still has much to learn," said Galandra.

"Agreed," declared Lemron and Klingor at the same time, hoping to avoid a confrontation.

"And afterwards the two of them must have two days, in addition to the Sabbath, totally alone together," insisted Hartlin.

"And he has to preach immediately on the Sabbath After," declared Lemron. "We can cover the teaching on Sabbath Eve, but he's not going to weasel out of the preaching on Sabbath After for only a wedding!"

"And we will take care of the children for two days after the wedding," declared Galandra. Rav closed his eyes and grimaced.

"You may have the children *one day*, Galandra," declared Dr. Harlin. "My wife will get them the second day. Understand?"

"You will teach them right?" said Galandra.

"Absolutely!" said Hartlin.

"Then we agree," said the holy woman.

The wedding itself would occur in three days, on the fourth day of the week. And on the rest of the 4th Day and 5th and 6th Days, as well as the Sabbath, they would be totally alone whether the children liked it or not. And just after the Sabbath ended, Michael would preach. After that, they would live together happily "eyefor" after.

*   *   *   *   *

[17] *Two Faces, Two Languages*

Michael and Shirra walked outside and briefly announced what lay ahead to a cheering throng that grew by the minute. The wedding would be at midday on Day 4 at the Tabernacle. Shirra spent a few minutes outside with Lord Braygan who promised to stay for the wedding as well as the Sabbath After. Michael said that the elders would be available to say more. Further, he and his new wife would be available after he preached on Sabbath After.

The Council being over, the church leaders left, and joined the buzz just beyond the front door about what would happen next and who would do what.

As Michael closed the door on a nearly empty house, except for the holy women of course, he turned and found Rav standing in front of him. The boy, however, failed to notice that Shirra had slipped up behind him.

"Parana, I beg you—" He stopped and made several half-circles with his hands.

"Rav, is this is about your having to stay with the holy women for a day?"

Slowly, he nodded. Then, without a word, Rav made his eyes as large as he could, added a small smile in the corner of his mouth, and tilted his head.

"Rav, what is wrong with you?" asked Michael.

The boy dropped his eyes, reminding Michael of how he'd first seen him.

"Em said that when you really want something from 'Daddy,' you must let your eyes grow big"—he extended his arms—"make lovey face, and make head go like this with little smile"—which he demon-

458

strated — "because when Shirra does that to you, you do anything she wants."

Shirra stood as still as a statue.

"Rav, listen to me. Listen carefully. Only girls can do that to boys and get away with it, and it doesn't work with boys doing it to girls" — Michael noticed Shirra tiptoeing away, running the last several feet to Em's door and entering it without even knocking — "…and it certainly doesn't work with boys to boys! Got it?"

"Yes, Parana."

"Now, as to the holy women, you have to go stay with them. That's the way it is. And you have to be nice — or pretend to be. And it's smart to keep your eyes open and be helpful. You can learn a lot if you try. And remember, whether you like it or not, Em will tell me everything that happens. Now, you'd better go to your room for a while."

As soon as Rav disappeared, Try left the room for the bathroom and Shirra reappeared, walking mechanically, almost regally. She kept her beautiful eyes small and her hands at her sides. Michael shivered and struggled to look serious. How much did his being sallow have to do with how she looked at him?

"Pu…lease, don't change the way" — he coughed, fighting a smile — "you look at me! I love you just — "

She stood directly in front of him and both stared at each other eye to eye. And that they both could do, daring the other to look away first. Then she raised her hand and gave him a soft, measured pat on the cheek.

"Close your eyes," she whispered.

He could do that, too. So he did.

The next thing he felt was the gentle press of her lips against his, nothing more.

"Would you please take out the trash?" she cooed keeping her eyes small.

"If I can find where it is," he whispered back. He drew a couple of small circles in the air with finger. "I'm still a little dizzy." Slowly, he circled her with his arms and slowly squeezed. Though her back was iron, he felt her soften and melt so she could fit perfectly against him.

"You know, Shirra, your voice and your face were perfect before the Church Council earlier."

"And my hands?"

"Perfect, Shirra."

"You know, Michael, the holy women made me walk back and forth carrying a heavy book while they asked me question after question, and they made me answer slowly. It's amazing what they know that you can't see."

"And, Shirra, it's amazing what you tell me."

"Oh, don't worry, I can keep klepta secrets, even very personal ones. I tell you so much, I guess, because I've always trusted you so completely. And you've never hurt me. Never really hurt me. And I need you to help me help you with your English—and, of course, your Elphian." He wondered just what she meant. Sensing this, she smiled, but forced her eyes to stay the same size.

"Let's see how Rav's surviving," offered Michael. "It'll be good for him to see the two of us together—and help him recover."

They knocked on the boys' door.

"Come in," said Rav, casually.

Rav was sitting crosslegged on the floor, surrounded by papers. He held in his lap Michael's slate and a piece of chalk. Who is this kid? Michael wondered.

"Rav, whatever are you doing *this* time?" he asked.

The boy looked up.

"Wri...ting Eeen...glish," he said with a practiced tone.

"English? Rav, you don't have to do that! Who told you to—"

460

"Em said" — he checked a sheet of paper beside him, picking it up — "Hammond Rav...no, Rav Hammond...Rav Earth boy...Earth boy now" — he checked another sheet on the floor — "tran...slay...shun" — He smiled at Michael — "I Eeen...glish lern."

"Where did all that come from?" said Michael to no one in particular.

"From me, Daddy," said Em who was suddenly there. "And he'll learn to say and read it right, too!" she continued. "We need to make more Bibles."

"Yes!" agreed Rav, not sure of what he was agreeing to.

Michael fought tears. Shirra held his hand.

"Rav," said Michael, "what does Try call me?"

"Dad-dy," he replied, "just like Em."

"Then you must call me that, too."

"Yes, Dad-dy," said Rav.

"Em, you're doing a good job with your brother," said Shirra. "But you still need a little work." When she looked puzzled, Shirra slipped her arm around her. "Partly because you and Try carry the blood of three worlds, but mostly because I say so and I know."

" 'A little work'? Are you still mad at me, Marana?" Em asked.

"We'll talk about that later, okay?"

"At girl-talk time?"

"Yes."

*   *   *   *   *

461

One hour later (about 11 AM)

[18] The Last Secret

The children were sent very late to school, strongly, very strongly warned to keep certain details to themselves, and to avoid any discussion of what had happened that morning. They were family, there was such a thing as family secrets, and now was the time to prove they could keep them and prove who they belonged to. Rav declared that his mouth wouldn't open for anything, even food. And late in the afternoon he returned, starving.

When the two replacement holy women arrived, Shirra declared to Galandra that before she'd let them take her away, she needed two more hours because of a very personal obligation she had to take care of.

Galandra agreed, but warned her to be careful — and patient.

The time had come to see Michael alone. Really alone. This time it would be in his office-bedroom, soon to be completely rearranged.

Shirra was up to something, but Michael was glad they could be together regardless of why.

She appeared at his door, her hair carefully combed, her perfume at work, her eyelashes fixed, her eyes slightly shadowed. A klepta or klepta-to-be shouldn't be careless about herself, and yes, she'd thoroughly learned that because of the way men were. She could accept that. And so could he.

Michael knew, too, he had to accept other things about her; yes, Shirra was young and had baggage like everyone else. But hers was manageable — it had to be. And, except for the klepta part, of all the people in his two worlds that he'd ever encountered, none he knew more about than Shirra. Triana had been a surprising gift from God, but he'd only known her for a few unforgetable months before they married. For Shirra, however, he and Triana had watched her grow over the years in the world they now shared, and the three of them together had done endless complicated translation work that had changed people's lives.

And, yes, now he loved her in a new way — and it seemed with Triana's blessing.

And God's.

But the day was far from over.

Shirra had her tote, but held no notes; nonetheless, he sensed business was coming so he would stick to her eyes until his brain insisted on going elsewhere.

"Did you —" he asked.

"Yes, Michael, Em's fine. Don't worry. Details about that are near the bottom of my list if we make it that far."

Another mind reader.

"You must realize now that your wise virgin is about to disappear again…this time forever."

"Uh…what?" *But mind reading here was still a one-way street.*

"Words, Michael, we have to think about words, just like we used to." She seemed to be forcing herself to look serious.

"Uh…and?"

"The virgin's about to become your wise klepta. Michael, I'm embarrassed to say anything more."

"I…I'm never going to forget that."

"Michael do you really *love* me?"

"Shirra, I need you. You're a very smart girl. I need your brains to help me think."

" 'Brains'? 'Think'? *Me*?" — she pointed to her chest — "a runaway 'teenager,' as Earth people probably say it, who talks too much…?" Her eyes moistened.

"Yes, but realize Shirra, I've known you about half your life. Big,

big things lie ahead. And I'm...I'm lonely, too."

"For someone like *me*?"

"Exactly like you."

"What big things lie ahead?" Tears now began again to leak out.

"For one thing, the Sabbath, Shirra. It's been such a surprise to me. As I've given God time to just be open to Him, He's overwhelmed me with His presence. I can't really explain this, but I could never, never have spoken week after week without God opening up His Truth to me on the Sabbath. But Shirra, I need someone to help me think through what God shows me, and help me tell others about it."

"Me?"

"Yes, you, your purity, your honesty, and your passion. It raises a standard, yes, but it must make some girls, as well as boys, feel terrible who've learned important things too late. You must help me teach about openness to God, choices and forgiveness.

"And there's the kids..."

"Your kids are wonderful, Michael."

"They need you, Shirra."

"Yes they do, Michael. But do *you* love me, really *love* me — for more than my brains?"

"Yes...I love the 'whole Shirra,' " Michael held out his arms, smiling.

"*All* of me? Oh...sorry..." Her face reddened, something Michael rarely saw even in her unexpected moments of Elphian openness.

For several seconds they silently stared at each other.

"Then you do need my 'brains,' " she said. "Will you help me...you know in certain personal ways?"

"Yes, of course. Remember God begins His Sabbath with a period of growing darkness. All you have to do is say 'Come' in the candlelight by the table and guide me with your eyes."

"Enough of that! Now you're scaring me." She tried to keep herself

464

from smiling but failed.

Michael pretended not to hear.

"And all our klepta-type secrets are really safe?" she asked. "*All* of them?"

"Yes, but then they will be just 'klepta secrets'—and yes, they will be safe."

"Michael, let me explore one." Michael braced himself. "You never lied to Gurdon, did you?"

"Uh…no, but what are you getting at?"

"Do you remember when Gurdon asked you right before you married Triana, what you and Triana would do alone without us around? Do you remember what you said?"

"I do. I said we would never be cold in bed again because a man and his klepta would keep each other warm every night."

"Will you keep *me* warm? Do you want to? All night?"

"Yes, from nighttime together on our knees at our bedside thanking God until morningtime again thanking God on our knees."

"And in-between?"

"Of course."

"Every night?"

"Well—sometimes not. Sometimes we will pray just before going into bedroom, and other times just after leaving it."

"Michael, is 'morningtime' a word?"

"Shirra, I love you!"

"You also said, Michael, that a klepta and kleptor can cry together. You can cry with me, Michael. Can I cry with you?"

"Yes…In fact," Michael offered, "without even asking, you may sit very close to me whenever you want."

"But won't that make me a vanchi?"

"If it does, I'll say 'Go.'"

"And then what?"

"You'll have to move away—this much." He raised his hand, and with a Shirra-like flourish made a circle with his thumb and forefinger, opening it just a tiny bit to make a 'C.'

"Michael, I'm a bit young, you know—but old enough, mind you!—and you're making fun of me." It was her turn to make a C with her thumb and forefinger, obviously imitating his imitation of her.

"Shirra, let me tell you something that's on one of my clocks. You are a 'touch girl' and that's good." He pressed his finger lightly against the tip of her nose.

"A 'touch girl' ?"

"Yes. Nothing to worry about! Of all the kinds of good love that kleptas and kleptors value, each values one or two kinds more than others. You're first a 'word girl' and I'm a 'word boy.' It matters greatly the words we use and say to each other. We've already discovered that about each other. Oh, and by the way, I'm a 'touch boy, also.'" He raised her hand to his own nose, then suddenly bit the tip of her forefinger. Surprised, she danced back a step.

"But Michael, what if I'm an ice block?"

"A...uh...an 'ice block'?"

"Michael before I came to Lord Braygan's house I'd never seen water stand up by itself..."

"You mean ice *cube!*"

"Yes, that's it! And you should have seen what Beth Braygan had in her kitchen! Before coming here I'd never seen hard water float."

"And you're using that as a met-a-phor for a woman that's...that's cold?"

"Yes, Michael, I've heard it used that way and, it's not the time to make fun about how I say certain words. It's..."

"It's time for a test. Shirra, you don't know how much you've made me come alive."

"A test?"

"Yes, a 'touch test.' Are you ready?"

"Yes."

Of course she would agree. That was who she was. Her trust in him knew no bounds. Never could he ever let her go. Without a moment's hesitation about what mystery lay ahead, she opened herself to trusting... trusting him so completely it scared him. Still, whatever he did, he knew she'd somehow — without a hint of cruelty — she'd do all she could to angle things to her advantage.

But how would she do it this time?

He hadn't a clue.

"If you're ready, it goes like this. Follow my directions exactly."

"Okay, go ahead."

"Stand in front of me." She did. "No more talking!" He reached up and with his forefinger gently touched the tip of her nose. "Softly count off 10 seconds." She did and he lowered his arm. "Now do the same to me."

She touched his nose. And he softly counted off 10 seconds.

"Your left elbow, please." Without the slightest hesitation, she raised it almost to his chin. He touched the end of her elbow with his forefinger. "Count again to 10 and do the same to me." She did. He admired her not letting him get the least satisfaction in fooling her into doing something that looked so ridiculous — if she believed it could finally work her way. She would outlast him no matter what.

The next thing: He stood very close to her face so their lips — without touching — made a straight line side to side as if their faces had just missed coming together. Gently with his finger touched the space exactly between her lip and the tip of her chin.

"Count 20 this time, please."

Holding her position, she began a quiet count, her lips hardly moving. At 12 she went silent. Her eyes closed and her lips slid sideways as if pulled by a magnet until they met his. He could feel her body tremble.

And so did his.

He lightly pressed his lips against hers, then slowly drew back, keeping eye contact.

"That's not quite what I asked," he offered, "and your count disappeared."

"Are...are you sure?" she asked, opening her eyes and seeking his, finding them just above a happy smile.

"I am sure, Shirra. The test is over, you failed it, and I win. I've learned another of your secrets that will just be between us and God. Sometimes, you just can't simply follow directions, so you have to remember to pray. Oh, and by the way you're not an 'ice block' and never will be. Shirra, you're totally wonderful and I'm very happy!"

Shirra forced herself not to look too surprised. But Michael could tell that she was pleased with whatever had taken place. She eased herself away and studied his eyes. Something new was coming.

"Are you happy enough to teach me about your clocks?" she asked, gathering control second by second. Uncharacteristically, she kept her hands to her sides which scared him a little. She'd sensed a tiny opening that asked to be explored. "I want to know what Triana knew about them."

"Actually, Triana hardly knew anything about them. And she never knew about my first-friend teaching me.

"Knew nothing about him?!"

"It was a her."

Pause.

Shirra's eyes grew large. Her cover was blowing away. Michael loved watching her struggle to stay calm.

"She was...hmm" — he stared at the window, smiling — "maybe 70 or 75 years old — in Earth years, you understand," pointing, careful to aim out and not up.

"But, but…"

"I've told others about the clocks, and have given examples about how they work. But no one else knows the whole system, how to wind the clocks and such. And now you remind me of #4 on my first clock, and if you insist, I'll tell you much more, but it will have to be later."

"But why me?"

"Because you've brought this up so many times, and seemed so interested. There's no good reason I shouldn't do it, so I've just decided to. And, of course, I would do it for you because I love you.

"You realize don't you, Michael, that I loved Triana, in a different way, of course, just as much as you. And I'm alive today because of her and you.

"And Triana is now with God," said Michael, "and she has left you a beautiful letter." Finally a tear of his own sneaked out and ran down his cheek. He glanced away to the bureau top.

"And there's that ring." He pointed to where his wedding ring lay untouched since he put there earlier. "I…I just don't know what I should do with it…"

Shirra put her arms around him.

"Can I give you an idea?"

"Please."

"That ring… Triana once said that a widow from Earth gave it to her. Her first husband once wore it, but now that he was gone, the woman wanted to give it to her to give, if she wanted to, to the man she married, right?"

"Yes."

"So it has 'history meaning,' right?"

"Yes, but it 'has a history' is a better way to say it."

"Yes, Michael, I'll remember that, thank you. Here's my idea: Let's *both* of us carefully tuck the ring away and save it for Émrica to give away when her day comes."

"I love you, Shirra." His tears finally came. Michael couldn't help himself.

"It's okay, Michael, to cry with me ahead of time. After all, *we have a history together*." He sat on the edge of the bed. She sat beside him and pressed against him. "See, we touched." She emphasized her point by giving him nothing more than a 'little Shirra kiss' on the cheek.

For the moment she knew she had the upper hand, and she wasn't about to waste it.

But first Michael was ready with details of his own.

"Our new bedroom, that is, my old big one that I haven't used in months, Shirra, is yours to make your own. Rearrange it any way you want, but remember leave me a space to hang a few clothes. Any of Triana's things there that you want are now yours, even my old flannel shirt which she loaned you so often that it became yours anyway. You may wear it and anything else there without bothering me. They are just things. You can discard them or take them as your own. It won't bother me. And I, Michael, give you *all* of myself." He noticed how she caught his last words. He extended his arms. "And we are God's. He made us what we are and He is *watching your eyes* along with me, and is listening."

"Thank you for saying all that, Michael, and in spite of your moments of being sallow, I'll never forget this time.

"Now, Michael, it's my turn. There's something I must give you, something you know nothing about. But, before that, I must first tell you a story, a story I've told no one else. Parts of it are horrible, but most of it is not."

"A story?"

"It's the story of Graven."

"Graven?"

"Graven, the man who killed Triana. I've heard, Michael, you were emphatic in saying you wanted to avoid knowing anything about him, not even his name, but there's something here you must know, so please hear me out without interrupting."

"Go ahead."

"Graven was startled when he wasn't brutally treated here. He fully expected to die on Elphia Island for what he'd done. He was so angry at how intruders like you and Triana could come to our world and change it all around, infecting people on primitive parts of the planet with ridiculous superstition that eventually would work its way to advanced regions of the planet that we don't even know about. Michael, you've no idea how far the news of the God of Heaven is spreading. And neither do I, really, but it is.

"In fact, Michael, our church needs a school to train people about the Bible so they can 'go out into all the world' — in ELPHIA.

"But let me get back to my story:

"Graven was even more startled when he was released at night and taken under careful guard — Noli was even there — to Balara and when no one was looking, he was released on the dock and told that by orders of the Emryss Princess before she died, that she forgave him, and he was to be set free. But the first thing he did when he was free, *he told me,* was to sneer and curse the God of Heaven for his stupidity in allowing his stupid followers to let him go.

"Immediately after he said this, he was struck down nearly blind with his legs and one arm paralyzed. Helpless where he lay, he knew that the first sailors who came by would simply roll him into the sea at the Balara shore, and the rising tide would bury him forever, and that would be it. Instead, in a moment of pity the guard who released him dragged him from the dock, and put him down in the filthy sand underneath the wooden planks. 'You will feel more comfortable here,' he was told. He could stay there and die, or he could beg the God of Heaven for forgiveness over and over and when the tide came in, if he drank deeply of the filthy water around him he might — possibly — be

471

cured. Why he said that and how it might happen, I have no idea.

"Finally, at the very end of himself, lying in his own waste, he did exactly that and was suddenly totally restored as if he'd experienced a dream. He knew, however, that what had happened was no dream. Further, there were four silver coins in his pocket.

"That's the end of it, Michael."

"But—"

"Michael, I'm not finished. It is the end of the story about Graven, but not the end of *my* story."

"Go on."

"How do I know about this? And is it true? I'm not sure. I know none of the details for certain except that a young man—who never gave me his name—suddenly sat down at my table in a tea shop in Balar, next to where I was shopping. I had my Bible open at a table, reading. He just sat without asking or saying a word but not seeming to want to leave. After silently praying, I told him about the Bible and how Jesus, the God-Son, died for my sins and gave me peace, and if people in Balara had not destroyed their holy book here years ago, they might know more about this God.

" 'What book?' he asked me.

" 'The I-Rex Code,' I told him.

"It was then that he quietly shared the story that I've just told you. Then before I could question him, he suddenly got up and left. That was the last I ever saw of him. Somehow, he found out that I worked at the Lord Mayor's estate and that I had come from Elphia Island and was connected with the new religion there.

"Three weeks later, a package arrived at the Lord Mayor's door with 'Black-haired teacher' on it, since I'd never given him my name. And why do I tell you this *now*, a story I can't provide one shred of evidence for? I do it for one reason only.

"So kiss me, Michael. Your klepta-to-be is about to privately give you her dowry before the holy women take me away."

He did.

Then she reached into her tote and handed him a package.

He opened it.

In his hands he held a thick leather-bound copy of The I-Rex Code. Michael picked up the book and turned it over and over. He carefully leafed through the perfectly printed pages. There were even some notes written in the margins.

"Michael, I have read several things, especially the first part. And, for one thing, the Sabbath described is exactly the way the Bible does it! And there is a specially chosen people. And a person very similar to Abraham. That's how I knew about Abraham and his eight sons. I compared it with the Bible." She smiled. "Michael, you're going to love this. I bet I know what your first sermon will be about."

Quietly, his eyes down, he thumbed through several pages.

"I bet you don't."

"Really?"

"This is going take some serious praying about, and looking at before we even mention it, Shirra, and that will be first with the elders. But now I need a wise and warm klepta at my side night and day more than ever!"—Shirra interrupted by reaching out with her finger and touching his nose—"And God has brought you to me, and given us another klepta secret! My next sermon will be something about the importance of kleptas. I'm counting on you for details."

" 'Sallow,'" said Shirra, controlling her eyes. "The holy women are so right!"

"And sewing 'FFF' on my special clothing...?" Michael countered. She lightly slapped him on his cheek and smiled, pushing away any embarrassment. "You'd better listen carefully to the holy women over the next two days!" he added.

"Shirra, your getting this is wonderful!"

There was knocking at the door. Michael quickly tucked the I-Rex Code out of sight.

"Come in," he called. The door opened just before Shirra got there to face two holy women, Lemron, Lord Braygan, and Klingor. The visitors took several steps inside but stopped abruptly a half dozen feet away.

Shirra turned to Michael and smiled. She was every bit a princess if such was needed. She smiled and glanced back to the "newcomers."

"Michael, come," she said in Elphian, just loud enough to be overheard. Affecting a businesslike bearing of his own, Michael walked to where she stood, never taking his eyes off hers, the beacon that he followed.

As he reached her, she held out her hand, palm up.

"I again extend you my hand." Michael stopped stone still. "It's the one you put butter on when I burned it on the plate." Michael received it, turned it over and touched it with his lips. He drew her into his arms and whispered, "They're wondering and that's good for them." Then he kissed her just long enough.

Then, very lightly he touched the end of her nose with his finger. Let those watching their every move wonder about that.

"Go," he said in a voice just loud enough to be overheard. Then softer so only she could hear: "You have a promise to keep: You are mine forever, forever, forever." She gave a slight but unmistakable bow before her last words.

"I love you," she whispered. "Now go, change your clothes, and wind your clocks."

—The End—

The Epistle To Big Bend

The following document, typed on a manual, nonelectric typewriter and crudely printed on a hastily restored hand-cranked mimeograph machine – both at least 60 years old – was handed out at the Grace Missionary Alliance Church of Big Bend, Pennsylvania, on a Sunday in May on Day 12, AEMP 01.

The Rev. Dr. Jonas Harwell, pastor by the will of God at the Grace Missionary Alliance Church at Big Bend, to all Christians and Other Fellow Citizens and Refugees of the newly formed Susquehanna Territory:

Grace and peace to you from God our Father through our Lord Jesus Christ during these difficult and disturbing times. Praise be to God who has blessed us in the heavenly realms with every spiritual blessing in Christ.

In view of such blessing which is commonly recognized and accepted by believers who have received the Holy Spirit through salvation in Jesus Christ, I hope you won't consider me presumptuous to share my counsel, opinion, and feelings in the same manner as our spiritual father St. Paul. Not that I am an Apostle, certainly not! Nor do I claim any special inspiration for these words. But they do reflect a wisdom that

God has let me gain that I believe is relevant for these troubled days.

Having studied science in my university days at Cornell University, I have some understanding about what I think has befallen us, and as a Christian, chosen by the Lord Jesus Christ, I care deeply about how we should think and act. Above all, we must remain calm, faithful, and Christ-like in these difficult times.

It is now the 12th day since our global catastrophe.

I say "global" deliberately, though I cannot prove it. After days of continually scanning shortwave bands on the 1930 vacuum-tube Philco radio we've placed in the narthex of our church, we have picked up only two signals in addition to the intermittent broadcasting through vacuum-tube technology of Radio USA from Maryland.

On Day 4 we received an unintelligible, garbled broadcast from Radio Jerusalem. And on Days 4, 5, and 7, we clearly heard news of unprecedented horror and tragedy from one of the most powerful stations in the world, HCJB in Ecuador. But all we learned was that, like here, all electrical power had failed and Quito, with its teeming hundreds of thousands, was in chaos. We have detected nothing whatever from the BBC, Radio Moscow, Radio Persia, or Radio Beijing. And nothing from anywhere beyond Day 10, except from our own American emergency station in Maryland.

While death has also touched our rural towns and townships, our suffering must be nothing compared to what has happened in our great cities.

476

We, and much — if not all — of the world, have been
drained of our invisible life blood, regularly transmitted electricity, for 12 days, and I am convinced any transfusion to
restore life as we knew it is very far off.

What has caused this? The culprit, I believe, is EMP or
electromagnetic pulse.

Let me tell you what I think has happened: Scientists have
known about the effects of electromagnetic pulse for more
than a half century. It wasn't until 1962, however, that we knew
the strength of this electromagnetic surge, or "push," could be
so powerful and crippling from nuclear explosions detonated
high in the atmosphere. And as research from the 1990s
showed, EMP was not only dangerous with nuclear blasts, but
with nonnuclear ones as well.

And just what is the effect of EMP on delicate electrical
connections? It may be compared to an invisible foot step-
ping into a shoe filled with grasshoppers. The marvelous,
high jumping creatures are instantly crushed, destroyed, even
though after the foot is removed, insect parts are still recogniz-
able and some grasshoppers may still look intact.

The discovering of the devastating force of EMP immediately led to decades of frantic, highly classified research in
every civilized first world country to find ways to shield and
protect extremely tiny microcircuitry, which is sensitive to sudden electronic pulses. This was one major — but little publi-
cized — objective of the Star Wars Defense initiative long ago
in the Reagan Bush years. Ironically, as research progressed
a bewildering array of newer, faster, smaller, and even more

delicate electronic systems became available. There seemed to be no end to human ingenuity.

These electronic wonders spurred an economic war which, to our embarrassment, Asia began slowly to win. There was no time to wait, to properly design adequate protection. Caution was thrown to the winds. The strange new marvels of science invaded all technology like a virus. Everything became infected. In short, research at the Pentagon was always at least one step behind—if indeed it was on the right path. And large-scale realistic testing was out of the question. America couldn't keep up. But no country could.

At first, some thought that any effects from a surge of EMP would be temporary, but this was proved wrong.
What then could be done? There was the promise of "shielding." And the promise of materials like fiber optics which were said to be immune to EMP. But the digital electronics which joined nonmetal parts together was not. The long glass chain was riddled with weak links. Circuit breaking devices were also developed, but many wondered if they would work since EMP was faster than lightning, the age-old conqueror of nearly every conventional device.

For years we as everyday citizens have routinely handed the mysterious wizardry that controls our lives "across a counter" to be repaired, or more likely discarded and replaced by something from shelves of parts or whole devices that are newer, better, and faster. Now the magic has gone. The "fix-it shop" is out of business and the shelves of replacement materials are useless.

So what do we have left? We have ourselves and the God who made us. May you who read this never forget that God has saved us, and provided salvation from far greater tragedy.

When will everything be restored? I have no idea, except it will be a long, long time. The machines which made the machines which made our machines have also probably died. And so has most of the discarded materials of our older, pre-electronic technology. Science has routinely pushed away history like an ignorant, pesky child. Now the hands of technology have lost the present; to regain it we will have to relearn the past. And when our lost things once again start to reappear, if they do, lines will be long to claim them.

As to what or who is behind this— I have no idea. I think we can rule out sunspots, comets, or anything natural, because there was no astrophysical warning.

And because of what seems like a huge global effect, a simple "accident" doesn't seem likely. The effect of EMP lessens with distance, so there must have been many explosions strategically spaced, or some chain reaction, so that just the way we live has been stripped away and not our lives themselves.

Then who's to blame? A foreign country? If so, things backfired and they hurt themselves—unless they consider their lives cheap and are counting on superior numbers to offset our superior weaponry.

Are we facing a terrorist threat? If so, no demands have been made—at least that we know about.

Was it the work of a madman? I doubt this could have been the work of a single person. The destruction was too vast and selective.

Have we been visited, or attacked, from another world? This can't be ruled out, though we've no direct reason to believe it. If such proves to be true, I urge you to remember that our Almighty God and Savior is author and ruler of all worlds and not just our own.

Is this the work of Satan and his demons? First, has not our great enemy already been at work among us? If he were directly behind this, at least we can say that he employed no device beyond our present scientific understanding.

Is this the beginning of the Great Tribulation prophesied in Scripture? Or the time of Christ's Second Coming? If so, we are not the first to ask such a question in the face of great tragedy. The apostles wondered about this two thousand years ago when they suffered.

And, more recently, the suffering of Christians in Holland, in Russia, in Ethiopia, in South Africa, in New Orleans, and recently on our western coast led to the asking of these questions. And the only answer has been silence. Christ will most definitely return a second time as He promised, but the time of His coming according to Holy Scripture was not known to St. Peter or St. Paul, or even to the heavenly host.

I am no exception.

Is what has happened a sign of the "end times" as some have suggested? If so, it is hard right now to say just why. While we live from day to day we must ask questions, search

Scripture—the whole Scripture—but I cannot, yet, go further about what may happen next, for I do not know.

As Christians we have a blessed hope, a promise, a secure future. But on earth we may be called to suffer. We have just had dramatically impressed upon us the sober reality that a measure of life, a moment of death—that's all that's certain. Now everyone says so openly. None of the ancient prophecies told exactly how certain particulars would come to pass—indeed, there were no suitable words—and none of our novels or movies ever prepared us for what we have seen, and, even more important, have come to feel.

And no movie or television screens still live to take us around the world, or even our neighborhood. There are no projection screens to paint with words for worship, and no computers able to share needs and knowledge.

For our new found silence, I ask you to make new songs for us to sing, as Scripture has always encouraged.

I ask you to look your neighbor in the eye and take his hand. When you must speak, do so slowly and loud enough to be heard.

There is much we do not know. There is much for us to discover. Much to rediscover.

I do, however, know this: Our Lord has told us that if we have two cloaks and our neighbor has none, we are to cheerfully give of our bounty, and our Father will reward us.

I ask you, brothers and sisters in Christ, to walk in the way of the One who gave Himself for us. Blessed is he who puts to death his own selfish interest on behalf of another. Be as wise as a serpent with your time and your talents, but always be generous and kind, reflecting God's love.

Pray for the President of the United States, who only four days ago gave us his "Five Guiding Principles for the New Age." Pray that he and our other leaders will seek only the God of Holy Scripture.

Pray for your Governor General and mayor-colonels, who rule because of God's sovereign will.

Pray for each other continually, and cheerfully bear one another's burdens in these unusual times.

Pray especially for those beyond our walls who suffer far worse than we, and pray that kindness will—with a greater force than electromagnetism—melt away every barrier that separates us.

Above all, love God with all your heart, mind, soul, and strength, which is the first and great commandment.

Peace to you all from God the Father of all and the Lord Jesus Christ.

I and those with me here at Grace Alliance remain your servants. I trust you will circulate this letter—in the spirit in which it was written—to believers and all others living within the Susquehanna Territory.

The Sabbath: "Eve," And "After"

Observance of the Sabbath, "Sabbath Eve," and "Sabbath After" play an important background role in parts of this story. Here's how the calendar system works in Elphia. (And how it relates to the Biblical Sabbath on Earth.)

To begin, the regular Elphian calendar has rectangular blocks—for each of the months—of five 7-day weeks totaling 35 days in each month resulting in 420 days in a 12-month year. (Hours, minutes, and seconds are the same as on Earth.) Days, except those connected with the Sabbath, which is the last day of every week, are simply numbered, with no names (No Elphian "Sunday, Monday…etc." We will, however, use these Earth names to explain here.)

Every month has the same pattern.

SA					SE	S
1	2	3	4	5	6	**7**
8	9	10	11	12	13	**14**
15	16	17	18	19	20	**21**
22	23	24	25	26	27	**28**
29	30	31	32	33	34	**35**

This means that the first days of every week in every month (only two months are named in the story: "Avril" and "Reglanth") would be

Day 1, Day 8, Day 15, Day 22, and Day 29. The five Sabbaths would be on the 7th (or Day 7), the 14th (or Day 14, etc.), the 21st, the 28th , and the 35th.

Ordinary days on Elphia can be usually thought of like Earth days: "dawn to dusk," or sometimes midnight on one day to midnight on the next. No problem here. However the **Sabbath**, introduced by Michael and Triana, becomes thought of differently, as is "Sabbath Eve" and "Sabbath After" which are not used on Earth by Jews or Christians. They are special only on Elphia because they "bookend" the Sabbath as a special day of rest, individual rest, family rest and sharing, and *doing no regularly scheduled "work."* Christians are mainly, and primarily, at home, but they may gather with others. *But there is no scheduled teaching, formal public worship or preaching.*

It is a day when no Christian feels guilty about not always being busy doing regular work; rather guilt, however, may be felt by believers doing regular work! This was established in the Elphian world by Michael Hammond, with no requirement whatsoever put on nonbelievers, in accordance with his understanding of the 4th of the 10 Commandments given by God to Moses in Genesis before this law was changed, and was morphed into "Sunday," and in fact was discarded and even banned, by certain high church leaders (on Earth) in the 4th century. Michael had once discussed this on Earth with his pastor and adopted father Jonas Harwell. It is important to recognize that Elphian church members, though guided by the teaching of Michael, Triana, and the elders, were allowed to decide for themselves what was and was not "work." To some the Sabbath was humorously referred to as "a day to sleep in and learn to enjoy cold food."

Technical marking of time in Elphia on the three days connected with the Sabbath is sometimes confusing because those days technically begin in "darkness" of the "previous day" and run to the sunset, or darkness, of the numbered day.

To explain further: First, as on Earth (to religious Jews, Seventh Day Adventists, Seventh Day Baptists, and some others) the Sabbath begins at sunset "Friday evening" and ends at sunset "Saturday evening." Let's pretend that sunset (which varies somewhat with the seasons) begins at 7PM on Friday and ends at 7PM on Saturday.

If so, the first Sabbath of the month would occur at 7PM on "Friday" the 6th and end at 7PM on "Saturday" the 7th using Earth thinking. The second Sabbath would begin at 7PM on "Friday" the 13th and end at 7PM on the 14th. The fifth and final Sabbath would begin at 7PM on "Friday" the 34th and end at 7PM on "Saturday" the 35th. Technically at 7:01 PM, "Sunday" or Day 1 of the next month would begin. ("Sunday," by the way, is not mentioned in the story as, similarly, it's never mentioned in the Bible either.)

The reason for all this:

In the beginning of the Church on Earth, The Sabbath was still considered a special day because it was a part of "God's Law" that Jesus continually referred to as important to obey.

"Sabbath Eve" is also *not mentioned in the Bible,* and rarely on Earth. In Elphia it is a practical term, usually refering to the undefined hours on "Friday evening" that precede the darkness that brings in the Sabbath. In Elphia it is an approximately set time (maybe an hour or two before the Sabbath begins) that calls Christians to gather for group teaching that ends when a gong sounds to begin the true Sabbath, which, in turn begins a special time for private and family encounters with God and each other. One could think of Sabbath Eve much as one would think of "Christmas Eve": It may refer to the whole day ("Friday") or just the evening time preceding the Sabbath preparing, or even eating, food and readying other things for the arrival of the true Sabbath.

"Sabbath After" is also not mentioned in the Bible or in Christianity on Earth. In Elphia, it becomes a practical accepted time once again for Christians to come together, this time for group prayer, praise, worship, and a sermon or time of sharing. It begins at that time when the gong sounds ending the true Sabbath, and ends when such a service is over.

Four observations here: (1) The honoring of the Biblical Sabbath became Michael's, as well as Triana's, secret weapon. Young as they were, they'd assumed fearsome responsibilities. The "open window" of a true Sabbath allowed people to listen to God teaching them, as He willed, what they should know and how to live with Him, with family, and with others. Informally opening oneself to God and to each other without distraction became indescribably rich, something that many busy Christians never experience. (2) It was *not* a time for Michael to prepare sermons. That, for him, would clearly be "work." (3) Rest without being interrupted by unnecessary obligations, or the necessary obligations of regularly living that could wait, became an unbelievable blessing for Michael and Triana who quickly became inundated with hundreds of "urgent details." (4) It's interesting to note that the formal teaching and worship services both began in the evening, the first ending as light surrendered into the dark hours, the second beginning later as darkness overtook the light.

Non-Christians enjoyed the Sabbath for a variety of other reasons.

Further, it is interesting to note the Sabbath observance on Elphia in no way forbade or impeded any regular formal, planned "Sunday," (the "Lord's Day," or *revised* Sabbath Day") worship from taking place. In fact, the Sabbath After group worship already regularly occurred on the 1st day of the week in darkness that required candles, oil lamps, or other sources of light.

"Sunday" and "Sabbath Eve" and "Sabbath After" *traditions* are perfectly okay if they prove useful, even though they are not Biblical *practices* per se and are nowhere mentioned in the Bible as the Sabbath Day is.

486

As we said, to Michael and Triana the basic purpose of all this was to "bookend" and preserve the whole Sabbath Day *as a time for rest which included individual and family meetings with God and each other with no outside obligations whatsoever.* As well as to obey the 4th of the 10 commandments which God had never revoked. This kind of obedience had almost entirely been lost on Earth where they had come from.

Other Commentary

Eric Flint in his Ring of Fire series (the first book, *1632*, Baen Pub., 2012, 2nd ed.) alerted me again to the possible usefulness, rather than distraction, of certain commentary — which can be easily ignored — after a detailed story is over. Here are five further items to help clarify what's happened: *premises, science, "memory clocks," passions, and narrative.*

1. PREMISES

This story is based upon seven assumptions, propositions, or premises:

(1) The God of the Bible created the whole universe.

(2) The Bible is the Word of God and is historically reliable.

(3) The Bible neither demands or forbids the existence of humans created in the image of God, fallen or unfallen, on other planets.

(4) God specially created humans in His own image on Earth. Nothing forbids His using the same "Lego pieces" to create other humans in other places. Hence, there is the possibility of fallen humans with similar DNA, similar appearance, and similar behavior existing somewhere else on one of the tiny, tiny fraction of the now-known three thousand or more discovered exoplanets (planets beyond our solar system) that have "Goldilocks conditions" that allow planetary conditions

"just right" for human life. The assumption in this story is that this has happened. Naturalists who deny the existence of God, however, would most probably say that if evolution by a series of molecular "accidents" over long period of time on different planets occurred (as they suspect happens) it would result in a different kind of humans, if humans appeared there at all. And that would make "interbreeding" between humans on different planets impossible. Since we reject strict on-its-own naturalistic change, an assumption which denies or ignores God does not apply here.

(5) The Biblical call to "Go into *all the world* to preach the Gospel" means for Christians to do just that: sharing what they know about God and Christ, and using the Earth Bible as a source of Truth the best way they can, with anyone they encounter anywhere.

(6) Jesus Christ, the Son of God, died and rose again from the dead for everyone on each planet *only once* at one point in cosmic time. (This complex issue is dealt with in the story.)

(7) There is no known way to quickly travel on a one-way "forever" trip between planets that are "impossibly" far away from each other, at least no way—yet—that has been discovered or revealed. However, this does not absolutely forbid this happening in the future. In *The Blood of Three Worlds*, this kind of trip has become possible to at least try.

2. SCIENCE

Let me offer a few specifics before falling all over myself with generalities. "As a biologist," says Stuart Firestein of Columbia University, "I wouldn't expect to get past the first two sentences of a physics (research) paper. Even papers in immunology or cell biology mystify me—and so do some papers in my own field, neurobiology." What

489

then is the average educated person supposed to do? There are mountains of science papers published each year. Firestein ends his article (in the April 2012 *Scientific American*) by saying, and I quote him exactly, "If you meet a scientist, don't ask her [sic] what she knows, but what she wants to know."

This story welcomes such an attitude.

Add to that the words of Leonard Susskind, a respected father of black-hole physics, the multiverse, and string theory: "We may never be able to grasp [physical] reality. The universe and its ingredients may be impossible to describe unambiguously" (*Scientific American*, summer, 2013). As to how the universe may end, experts who've thought about this suggest at least six quite different scenarios that conveniently occur so far in the future they can never be proven or disproven.

As to beginnings, however, there's a lot of scientific agreement (on Earth, of course): Everything began (cause ignored) with a single tiny speck of something at a precise point in time exploding outward billions of years ago. At about "halfway" from the beginning a recently discovered "dark energy" overcame the elastic "pull-back" of gravity, and forced everything ("things") moving outward and away faster and faster away from each other. (Think of all bits of matter on the surface of a balloon that being blown up faster and faster with the passage of time.)

Such a scenario is actually quite friendly to the Biblical account of creation in Genesis (which many strict Bible-believers take seriously). This however, is disturbing to a number of naturalists. In time the idea of a "multiverse" arose from the ashes of naturalistic thinking, and more and more elbowed its way forward. One big advantage here for naturalists is that this complex theory can never be proven or disproven. And what it advocates is rather simple: With an infinite number of universes, anything…anything—like Earth with its "sudden" appearing of incredibly complex people and other lifeforms—is possible, and so here we "accidentally" are. God is not only off the hook but is completely unnecessary. This is a suggestion, not a scientifically supported fact.

In short, while science can offer splendid technology, startling health care, and unbelievable creature comforts, it can't tell us much detail about what's physically out there beyond our world. Detecting the presence of extra-terrestrial "Legos" (or "building blocks"), however, is a far cry from detecting self-building cities of "Lego castles" with parts that move about on their own. The existence of life, especially human life that accidentally assembles itself on its own, or a series of mutations that lead to the creation of "mind" or consciousness in the 100 billion neurons in a human brain accounting for the human fear, hope, love, anxiety, and wonder is still a complete mystery beyond science, or science "just around the corner."

Science can tell us about EMP, though. Electromagnetic pulse from nuclear explosions in the atmosphere, that damage no buildings and kill no people, can totally destroy microcircuitry and "kill" all commercial electrical power. In the public arena, Newt Gingrich, for one, has called EMP explosions a "mass disrupter" and one of the three greatest threats that could destroy America (*Winning the Future*, Regnery, 2006, p.1). For more see Appendix A for Harwell's take on what happened in the Susquehanna Territory, or for what others say, simply Google the three letters: "EMP."

As to the Space Goose and mention of the small X-37 space vehicles. Yes, there was development of these by Boeing at the turn of the century at their Phantom X-Works. The A, B, and C versions were hardly common knowledge, but there is no—at least public—record of anything like the revolutionary X-67 that Harwell talks about in Ch. 9. In fact, the design, structure, and propulsion system, presumably developed and installed by "outsiders," is totally different for the X-67.

This vehicle mentioned in the story is not for "short hops," as are the earlier X space vehicles, but with its advanced microgyroscopy and other bells and whistles it's been made (in the story) for the long haul. Michael gets a quick lesson in its history, though he never even gets to see it from the outside!

As to the nature and duration of the flight to Elphia, that's picked apart and discussed in the story.

As to the *Lorentz Transformation*: This exists and the way the numbers work in this equation is spell-binding. But how it could represent possibilities in actual space travel can be challenged.

However, the martial arts applications in the story all are all doable. Thanks to the Soo Bahk Do Master Frank Schermerhorn and Cane Master Mark Shuey for their excellent instruction. I offer apologies to them here for nonstandard applications of their great skills. As to information about firearms I'm endebted to Larry Proffitt, East Tennessee pharmicist and dedicated turkey hunter.

As to the mention of "biocentrism" which suggests that mind had to precede matter, this is as real as the Amazon bookstore. Further, though it's in no way presented as a Christian book, I highly recommend Robert Lanza's *Biocentrism* as a fascinating read, accessible to those with only a general science background. Lanza is a brilliant medical researcher who was discovered in the Harvard Medical School parking lot as a disadvantaged high schooler searching for those who could help him understand the cloning of chickens that he was doing across the tracks in the basement of his home. Also friendly to biocentrism as well as Christianity, but stiffer reading, is *More Than Matter* by the Oxford philosopher Keith Ward, which I also recommend. He also has fascinating lectures on the Internet.

As to "Zocentrism" there's no public record of that. You're on your own there.

3. "MEMORY CLOCKS"

A person is hardly prepared for a first encounter with what a wag may—correctly—call "Esther Crandel's Clock Catechism for Young Men." The seemingly unnecessary rabbit trail near the beginning of the story, however, weaves in and out of scene after scene right down to the last word in the story. (And, as to the Pennecooks that Esther mentions, they were a real Indian tribe that saved the lives of early colonists before the last five of them mysteriously disappeared.)

For many, many reasons Michael needs all the help he can get. He's only ("almost") 18. And as often said, "God works in mysterious ways." In this story the wife of the church elder Amos Crandel is one such way.

We're indebted to Harry Lorayne and yes, Jerry Lucas (the NBA star), for *The Memory Book* (Stein and Day, 6th printing, 1974). Their brilliant exposition of developing paperless, nonelectronic ways to memorize volumes of information that can never be taken away from a person is a treasure. Lorayne's techniques, published earlier, according to one American POW (from 1966 to 1973) literally saved the lives of several soldiers imprisoned for years with nothing to occupy their time. His system was later taught to hundreds of soldiers.

As far as I know Lorayne and Lucas didn't use "watches"—that Michael morphed into "clocks," which Esther allowed—but the idea of associating real things with "nonsensical-but-vivid pictures" is a key technique that Lorayne and Lucas used in several unbelievable ways. And it really works!

If you don't go for clocks and their systematic numbers going "clockwise," of course, take it up with Esther.

4. PASSIONS

First, I want to share an experience that happened 36 years ago where I will be specific in part, and vague in part. I was grading papers at home at 2AM when the phone rang. Four Christian college students (men) at the school where I taught begged me to come immediately to meet another fellow student who was about to be suddenly committed to a local mental health center. As it turned out, I would leave my stack of papers and not return for more than two hours. My wife, soon to give birth, was not happy about this.

But I knew, absolutely knew, I was supposed to meet them though I had no desire whatever to do so. None.

As I drove through the early-morning darkness, I felt, or imagined, a somber eeriness surrounding my car that I couldn't explain. Then I prayed. Soon I was enveloped by an unexplainable peace. Here's the best way I know to say how I felt: I absolutely knew that if I stayed in "the tunnel on route" to my destination, I was perfectly safe. But not if I moved an inch outside it. And, in the unexpected bizarre happenings that soon occurred inside the mental health center that I thought might cost me my job, I was totally assured that if I and the students "stayed in bounds" with what God allowed us minute by minute to do, we were "totally safe." I apologize for such melodrama, totally unlike me, but it helps me make an important point.

Passion of all kinds is human and real. Passion for what God puts in our path: passion to go ahead alert for caution lights and stop signs that are alongside the pathway. The steering wheel, however, remains in our hands; and out of sight, but not out of touch, our feet remember the brakes below them. The energy for moving ahead, however, comes from God.

494

Passions must be aimed right, and staying in bounds is essential. This isn't to say that missteps can't be forgiven, because they can, but ugly scars or worse can be left behind.

This story recognizes three kinds of good passions that God allows, provides, and enables for those who aim outward beyond themselves. There is passion for God Himself, passion for other people or "groups," and passion for one other person in particular, completely and "forever"—where two individuals together open private doors to discover what's on the other side: things they can share, moments to enjoy, places to mend or rebuild if something is amiss, broken, or incomplete. And there is that deep special trust in each other—a private treasure shared by just the two of them that can be foundational to whatever else they do.

As long as both shall live.

Perhaps you've noticed that the three-letter "S" word (the one with an "e" in it), and all of its derivatives, appear nowhere in this story. This, however, should in no way suggest that physical sharing is unrelated to "higher things," or to deny its important place in the "tunnel on route" to holy obedience.

To help people effectively keep moving through the tunnel, Esther Crandel has to be highly endebted to Gary Chapman's *The Five Love Languages* (Northfield Publishing, 1992) which, in places, is roughly parallel to her own take on the different love languages that men and women speak to express their deepest needs and expectations to each other. I'm sure she would be as quick to acknowledge her debts, differences, and possible misapplications of Chapman's work, just as she honestly alerted Michael to remember that sometimes she may be "wrong."

5. NARRATIVE

Extra things:

The point of view in this story is *male third-person limited-omniscient with an occasional interloping narrator* — as if anyone cared.

I will risk a few comments that may surprise some, but are easy to ignore — except for maybe a few of you.

I've broken rule after rule in writing this story, doing things that I'd never let my own writing students get away with. But the story, if I might be so bold, called for the way it went. As to *style* I'm right up there with St. Matthew and Dr. Luke in creating an editorial nightmare with extra, seemingly trivial details and several large gaps — but without their "divinely inspired stamp of approval." (For a private journey on your part, if you read this story bit by bit, I encourage you to reread Matthew and Acts — without study notes — alongside them. Christians rationalize so much away of the real Gospel. If you question this, ask the Pharisees who listened to Jesus.)

No piece of fiction (as is this story here) tells everything. A reader could care less about what every character in a story thinks, says, and does. It's the key characters that matter. *Sensitive selectivity* is a secret of good writing that's rarely discussed.

The "third-person limited-omnisicient" part above means this: The narrator, or teller of the story, lets you "see into the head of only one character" — in this case, Michael. This means the reader only gets to know Michael's thoughts! No one else's. But then, this is exactly like real life: The only "thoughts" you really know are your own. You see people doing things and hear what they say, but you never, never know their real thoughts behind everything.

You can, however, often make a good guess about their thinking by seeing what they do and hearing what they say.

And, though often not recognized, getting close to someone's real thoughts can, but not always, lead to true romance. And bring joy. I think this is one important theme in the story.

The other major narrating option is simply called "third-person omniscient." Of course, in stories you never "see thoughts" in every head, but in several heads — 2, 3, 4, or more. To be blunt, this makes for a more "godlike" or complete account — and true, because the reliable narrator, and it's his story, says so — and he can read everybody's mind. Both narrating options are used by good writers, but each author has to choose one. ("First person POV," a third choice, by the way, closely resembles 3rd lim. omnis.) The choice of POV subtly affects how the story comes across and is received. And can make the writing more interesting.

All this to underline one unusual feature in this story: The point of view of this "romance" is *male*. And from a *limited-omniscient* point of view. This is rare.

By contrast, Nicholas Sparks, who is skilled in technique, is another male writer who deals with romance issues, but his POV is always ominiscient (climbing into the thoughts of two or more heads). This choice is more common for male writers who risk dealing with romance. (And fortunately, Sparks's books are not lost on the endless shelves in the "women's romance section.")

As to the "interloping part" (mentioned in the first sentence): This occurs when a know-it-all infallible narrator jumps in unexpectedly with a comment about what lies ahead, probably to hold the reader's interest as the story he's ladling out starts to bog down a bit. For example, as Michael walked away from the Hotel Crandel, he never could have known it was his "last time" to see Esther Crandel. But the reader who's been "tipped off" knows.

The Blood of Three Worlds seemingly has a helter-skelter arrangement of content: Parts II and IV deliver cake crumbs without the promised cake, and the usually spare Postscript never seems to end. Two responses to this: (1) This is how the story developed. (2) The mountain of extraneous detail in the missing stories (written for other reasons) was pared down to its salient parts (in II and IV) and the explosive ending (in the Postscript), which is hardly a mere addendum to the Gospel reaching Elphia. It may actually be the launch pad. It had to be stretched out to make sense. Presumably, a more solid foundation has been laid to make the Gospel go farther.

My purpose then in putting all this together?

A key theme is addressing *three questions that never (to my knowledge) have been addressed in a Christian story format:* (1) What if there are fallen humans like us, created in the image of God, who live beyond our solar system? (2) What if we could go to their planet on a forever one-way trip? And (3) If so, what would we as Christians do? Could we Biblically live, love, and endure horrific tragedy under the watchcare of the God who made everything?

Who then is this story for?

Again, there's confusion.

Is it stuffy fundamentalist missiology? Does it remind a person of 19th century missionary outreach to primitive peoples on the other side of the world and the struggle to preserve transcultural values in indigenous, and differing cultures?

Or is it a theology treatise? Look at the space given to the Sabbath (important for reasons already discussed). I, by the way, am not a Messianic Jew or a Seventh Day Adventist.

Is it essentially just outer-space supposalism?

As to romance: Does too much y. a. physical passion—naïve but deliberate acceptance and denial—cloud or betray higher causes? Do such baser concerns muddle the big picture? Or do they often form a secretive "base," or foundation for God-loving people that matters so much but is often ignored or overlooked?

Is it time to end this?

Yes.

But one more note: The two unpublished Emryss stories, *The Fourth Prince* and *Inside the Hollow Spear,* said to be found on Earth in different places, already exist on paper, about 50,000 words and 100,000 words (the latter, almost as long as this account) respectively. The manner of each of their tellings varies considerably, which seems puzzling. Their purposes, or goals, are very different from what was presented here. The first mentions Queen Lurinda, and the second mentions Lurinda, her husband and five children, and gives one mention of Elphia, but only in a minor way. Both, however, have genealogies compatable with what's here.

Triana found the genealogies helpful with her decision to leave Earth. More understandable to most readers is why Michael could never let her do this alone.

Sallow, he was.

But in the end, willing to risk his life for treasure in heaven.

Both stories, and the prequel to this, *Earth Is Not Alone,* are in harmony with the Biblical presentation of the true God, the God of the entire universe that's presented here. And they do not interfere with standard end-time scenarios.

Or so I believe.

John Knapp II (PhD in sci. ed.) is former Professor of English at SUNY-Oswego and writer of science textbooks for Silver Burdett (later Scott Foresman). His volume of poetry, *A Pillar of Pepper*, (D. C. Cook, 1982), won the first C. S. Lewis Gold Medal in 1983. A former department editor for *School Science and Mathematics*, he founded and edited *The Westigan Review of Poetry*, and later created the Endless Mountains Story Club. He is a black belt in Soo Bahk Do karate and former high school Sunday school teacher. His first full-length novel, *Earth Is Not Alone* (Ephemeron, 2009), is a sci-fi thriller that considers the effects of sudden EMP explosions that destroy the electrical power grid everywhere and all things electronic, and is a prequel to *The Blood of Three Worlds*, a story in which two precocious orphaned Christian teens take a forever one-way trip with four English Bibles to an exoplanet of fallen humans also created as exactly as they are in the image of God. He and his wife Karen live halftime in the future "Susquehanna Territory" and hallftime in Viera, Florida.

Made in the USA
Middletown, DE
30 November 2019